LIFE SONG

Christine M. Knight

About the author

Christine M Knight is a published author of fiction, poetry, short stories, and blogs. A graduate of Macquarie University, Christine travelled extensively overseas and lived for three years in the United States. Married for thirty-nine years to an officer in the Royal Australian Air Force, Christine has settled in the Canberra region. A writer, public speaker, and teacher, she continues to have a varied and enriching life.

Christine M Knight's website is www.christinemknight.com.au

Other fiction by Christine M Knight
In and Out of Step

First published in Australia by Highlight Publishing
ABN: 71212072993

PO Box 187
Fyshwick ACT, AUSTRALIA 2609
www.highlightpublishing.com.au

©Christine M Knight 2013
www.christinemknight.com.au

ISBN: 978-0-9874348-5-2

pp. 336

The right of Christine M Knight to be identified as the Author of this Work is asserted in accordance with the Copyright, Design and Patents Act 1988.

Typesetting: Chameleon Print Design
Cover design: LSD designs

Acknowledgements

Special thanks to my readers: Eva Campbell, Elizabeth Graham, and my husband as well as to my editor, Sue Moran.

Appreciation is also expressed to the following people for their technical advice: Billie Wilde, Bob Rodgers, Brett O'Neil, Casey Eidentas, CJ Gosper, Alicia Heymel, Cheryl Heymel, David Munro, Ross Eggleton, Kristie Hogan, Ed Gilmore, Gordon Wood, Chris Keeble of Penrith Panthers, and Lisa Smallacombe.

I'd like to acknowledge Edgar Penzig and Ken Newton who in different ways functioned as mentors in past years.

Although this story is a work of fiction as is the township of Keimera, I have referred to historical events and well-known people in Australia from that era to enhance the sense of reality in 'Life Song'. The characters of 'Life Song' are all invented with the exception of Pam and Lloyd Shiels and Warren Kirby, winners of the *Be A Character in Life Song* competition. Their lives in 'Life Song' are fictional, but some facts from their respective lives has been included with their approval.

Note to Readers:
A glossary of Australian terms and expressions as well as Internet links to the music of 'Life Song' can be found at:
www.christinemknight.com.au

This book is dedicated to Helen Knight
1944–2012

It takes a bold woman to choose a path less travelled.

Chapter 1

Teams of boys and men weighed down and backwards in a tug-of war, straining not only to hold their ground but also to budge the other side forward. In that moment as Mavis Mills watched the battle, the struggle seemed frozen, a sculpture of intense exertion.

Around them, the many varied events of the annual Agricultural, Horticultural, and Industrial Show formed a colourful backdrop to the tug-of-war scene. To the east of the showground, the Pacific Ocean glittered, rippling sheets of silver. Closer to shore, white capped waves crashed and foamed on the rocky coastline, sounding like distant applause. To the west of the showground, the heat haze of summer shimmered over the hilly rural landscape.

In her late twenties, Mavis knew all about struggle, about feeling stationary while life, with all of its promise and possibility, happened to the people around her. Something, she didn't know what, was needed to tip the balance in her favour just as it was needed for her son's team in the tug-of-war.

"Exciting, isn't it?" Kate Denford said, appearing at Mavis' shoulder, having returned to the scene with two bottles of water, one of which she passed to Mavis. Kate's broad-brimmed, straw hat obscured her eyes and shadowed her face. Her brunette hair was pulled back into a long thick plait. That day, she wore red Capri pants and a white cropped top. She was a striking figure, athletically slender, angular, and exuding confidence.

More frustrating, Mavis thought. She had a strong face with brown eyes behind which lurked a smile. Her body was shapely though not overweight. Although Mavis found fault with her figure, men saw her as sexy. She wore a Gypsy top, a flowing floral, partially transparent skirt, and Roman styled sandals. Striding everywhere, her walk marked her as farm bred. She was fond of saying that her walk was the result of constantly stepping over cowpats throughout her teenage years.

"Here, I bought you a hat, Mavis. Sunscreen isn't enough on days like this. I'm wishing now I'd worn a T-shirt."

"Oh … That's considerate of you, Kate, but you shouldn't have bothered." Mentally, Mavis did a reckoning of what was left of the money she'd budgeted for the day. She had a small weekly income and had not had the luxury of impulse spending since she had become a single parent six years earlier. "How much do I owe you?"

"Twenty dollars, but I can shout you if …"

"No, it's fine." Wishing it really was fine, she shelved her money worries and the problem of how she would end the inertia in her life for another day. Somehow, she *would* find a way out of her current circumstance. Mavis refocused on the tug-of-war. "Oh, oh … they're givin' ground to our side. Pull!" She donned the white hat over her luxuriously black, shoulder length hair but flipped the front brim up.

"Lean *into* it, fellas," yelled the anchorman for her son's team, Gary, with emphasis on *into*. An avid surfer and lifesaver, Gary was lean and muscular. His chequered cotton shirt was unbuttoned, revealing a naturally fit, bronzed body rather than the exaggerated physique that many men achieved through gym workouts. He wore an earring in his left-ear, although that fashion trend had passed.

Feet planted wide for support in the sandy loam of the showground, muscles straining, the men in Gary Putnam's team tilted further back almost into a reclined position.

Momentary confusion flickered across the younger boys' faces; they adjusted their positions forward and, in doing so, lost balance, allowing the opposing team to take some ground.

The opponent's supporters cheered.

Laughing, Mavis and others around her yelled, "No, boys, lean backwards not forwards. Pull! Pull!" Her six-year-old son, Dan, was one in a line of confused children. Behind them, men of one shape and size or another lined up; those men with a weight advantage were scattered along the line.

In the background, the noise of the sideshow alley, common at all agricultural shows, clamoured and tinkled above the hubbub of the crowd. Occasionally, a distorted microphoned voice announced the next competitive event in the show ring.

"It's a pity our side doesn't have fatter blokes, Mavis."

"I've been thinkin' the same thing, Kate, but look at the other side's faces. The heat and strain are takin' their toll. I think brawn is goin' to win out."

Both women yelled, "Pull!"

The noise level around them rose to an unintelligible roar. With one voice, the crowd bellowed, "Pull!"

Strain showed on all of the competitors. Gradually, Gary's team won centimetres of ground in a slow slide. With an unexpected collapse, the battle ended. Gary and the few men ahead of him thumped backwards onto the ground. The rest of the team stayed afoot somehow.

Spectators and competitors merged.

After a makeshift award ceremony and the etiquette-dictated interaction of victors and good-natured losers, the crowd dispersed.

In an effortless move, Gary lifted Dan, small for his age, up onto his shoulders. "Time for a well-earned lunch, a drink for me, and an ice block for Dan afterwards! C'mon, my lovelies!" Gary left without waiting for agreement. They threaded their way through the crowd, passed the livestock sheds and horticultural exhibits, passed the industrial stands, took a shortcut through the arts and craft pavilion, and came out onto a grassed area ringed by a caravan of food and drink peddlers.

On the western side of that area, the first band for the afternoon was finishing their set. The Keimera Show Ball Committee, after a disastrous choice in entertainers for their Show Ball the month before, were auditioning bands for the 1996 Zone 2 Show Society dinner dance which they were hosting. Auditioning bands at the show was an unusual step but local reputation was at stake. Everyone agreed it was crucial to avoid a repeat of the deafening, muddy, instrumental jangle and the related drowned vocals from their own ball.

Twenty-eight societies would be represented at the dinner dance to be held the following Saturday night. It was a very big deal. Two Show Girls from the twenty-eight finalists at the Zone judging would be chosen to go on to the Royal Easter Show Girl state competition, where a trip to the United Kingdom was up for grabs as the main prize. Another musical blunder by the Show Society would be unforgiveable. Heads would roll!

The queues at the food vans moved quickly.

"You sure you're not hungry, Mavis?" Kate looked at her askance, now very aware of how little money Mavis had after witnessing her coin counting to pay for her son's meal. Mavis had rejected Gary's offer to shout them lunch.

"I'm sweet, Kate."

"What do you want, lady?" the caravan vendor asked Kate.

Passersby stopped to talk to Mavis and Gary while Kate was served. Dan held his hotdog in one hand and his mother's skirt hem in the other.

With food and drinks in Mavis' son and friends' hands, the group headed to the grassed area under the shelter of shade-cloth sails. Leading the way, Gary looked for a spot on the crowded lawn. He wanted one with a good view of both alternate stage areas. Given the personal relationship musicians have with their instruments and their unwillingness to play on hired gear, the Show Society had organized two performance spaces. As one band performed, the next band set up.

After weaving their way through the picnicking crowd, Gary claimed a space for his group. His disregard for the personal space of other picnickers was a reflection of small-town familiarity.

"Nothing danceable about this band," said Kate, a ballroom dancer since her teens.

"Don't loll over me, Dan. Mummy's hot. Sit down next to Gary while you're eating that hot dog, and *chew* slowly."

Kate winced as she listened to the band. "Pity the girl can't sing. What she lacks in voice, she's making up in attitude though."

"Don't you miss it?" Gary asked Mavis who once had dreams of making it big in the music industry before life had happened to her. A single parent now, her dreams of a very different lifestyle had disappeared when she had fallen pregnant.

"A bit, but y' know, I still make music at home. That has to be enough. I've got Dan now, and he has to come first."

"So your mother says," Kate added. "Personally, I think women nowadays can have it all if they work it right."

"Spoken like a single woman. Between Dan, work, keepin' things straight in the house, and stayin' on top of bills, I'm worn out most nights. I don't know what I'd do without you, Gary, and my parents as backup."

Nearby, inside the bands' tent where waiting musicians congregated, tempers seemed to be flaring.

"Take it outside," someone called.

"Up yours!" another voice shouted.

Gary gestured to the tent. "Maybe we should move over the other side before anything more 'colourful' develops here."

Before Mavis could reply, two young men – one longhaired and in leather and the other in denim – emerged from the tent.

"Mate," said the longhaired lead singer from the fourth band on that afternoon's bill, "the amps have got to be cranked up enough to get the balls goin'. I can't put on a good show if I'm not happy with my sound. No way do I want to sound piss-weak like them." He gestured to the band currently on stage.

"Listen Dumbo, we want this gig and the work that can come from it; that means volume is out! The other guys get it, why don't you? They're behind me on this!"

"Yeah? Where are they then?"

The sound engineer looked over his shoulder and was momentarily taken aback. *Set up again*, he thought. He gave it his best shot anyway having told them he would. He, at least, was a man of his word. "They asked me to speak for them. There aren't any screamin' fans here drownin' you out to justify the amps you're askin' for. I know you don't get the volume thing, but most people want to hear the music, not be deafened by it. I've told you before, when it's cranked up, and you hit those high notes, it's like an ice pick to the brain."

"It's my job to get people stoked. Maybe that's goin' to take more volume than some can handle. They can leave. We're here to rock!"

"Nah, we're here to get the gig, and cater for the people, not you!"

"Blokes like you are a dime a dozen. You're not part of the band. Do as you're told, or this'll be the last gig you do sound for us. While I'm the front guy, I call the shots. I've heard you out, now do as you're told. Get back in your box." The singer walked toward one of the stage areas where a band was bumping in their gear and preparing for performance.

"No amount of loud can cover up a lack of talent," the sound engineer muttered as he walked away. "We lose this gig, I'm done! Doin' live sound sucks!"

"The sound guy's right," Mavis said, "a band should never be in charge of its own sound. They get it when they're in a studio but not when it's live. I reckon that it's a male thing. Y' know, 'How big is your gear?' In a studio, the equipment outguns a band's. The other problem is that the sound on stage seems quiet whereas to people like us out here it's loud."

"Well," Gary said, "this band have the volume right yet that walkin' ego didn't see it that way."

"Could be he's going deaf," Kate said. "Big ears aren't necessarily better to hear with."

Mavis laughed. "So you disagree with the Grimm Brothers?"
Kate grinned at her.

Gary ignored this side conversation and continued, "Or maybe they are used to playin' in their garage with no audience and don't realise the point is to entertain the audience."

"And maybe you and Gary are both right, Kate."

The audience applauded half-heartedly. The opening chords of the third band's set claimed the scene.

"Thank God, that band is done!" Kate considered the remaining food before her, a sealed plastic tub of untouched chicken and salad. "I wish I could say the same about this meal. My eyes were way bigger than my stomach. That first tub finished me off. I don't suppose, Mavis, you'd consider helping me out by finishing it off. If you don't, it'll be going into the bin."

"Well, rather than waste it, yeah, I'll have it."

"Thanks."

"Look at that wolf!" Kate referred to the lead singer they'd just been talking about.

Surrounded by a group of young women, he played the role of rock star while his band set up their gear on stage as the previous band bumped out.

Taking in the wider scene, Gary said, "So far, the music's not drawin' a crowd. As soon as people finish picnickin', they're movin' off. I feel like another hot dog. What about you, Dan?"

"Y' know, I don't like him having nitrates, Gary. I gave in today because—"

"What about that ice block I promised you, matey?" Sitting on the ground, Gary was eye-to-eye with the boy. "Your mum's a wise one. Best we listen to her, eh?"

Looking at them, Kate was struck by Gary's sensual appeal: his wind-tussled blonde hair and open face, the taut trimness of his tanned torso, and his undeniable strength. She shook herself. *It's Gary!* she told herself. He was a mate as well as her chief supporter at the local surf club which she had captained six years or so since Gary had unexpectedly nominated her for the position. *I must have a touch of the sun,* she thought. She made momentary eye-contact with Gary, and quickly switched her focus. She missed his thoughtful expression as did Mavis who ate Kate's leftovers with relish.

Dan at six years old was a handsome boy. Although not Gary's son, he could have been mistaken for him. Both shared a brilliant smile, dark eyes, and the same mannerisms. The mannerisms weren't surprising given Gary had functioned as a proxy father to Dan since his birth.

Gary, with Dan beside him, left.

"He loves your kid, Mavis. If you ever marry …"

"Not much likelihood of that. Guys run the other way when they hear I've got a kid. Besides, Gary is his godfather, and in our life for keeps, as you are, unless either of you decide to move on." After a moment of reflection, she added, "His girlfriend doesn't like sharing him, y' know."

"You're not wrong there."

"I only ever saw the positives in lettin' Gary be part of Dan's and my life. Lately …" Mavis paused.

"Lately what?"

"I've begun to think that might have been a big mistake. Dan is so vulnerable."

"Gary is as true as a summer's day is long. Seriously, you're not worrying about him being a stayer!"

"If he commits to Sarah …"

"Trust me, Mavis, it's not an issue even if Sarah becomes a permanent fixture!" After a moment's quiet, Kate added, "It's a good thing she's Keimera's Show Girl. The competition has taken her out of our lives for a while at least. It's been full on with them, hasn't it?"

"That's for sure. What I don't like is that we've had an overdose of her in our lives as well. She can even quote my mother!"

"If we're really lucky, Mavis, she'll win Royal Easter Show Girl, and we'll have an even bigger break from her. If she wins and goes to London, she might not want to come back. Don't worry about Gary, and don't cross bridges until you get to them."

"But you see, I'm beginnin' to think that as a parent maybe I should consider things more so as to avoid Dan getting hurt."

"Stop worrying, Mavis. Life is to be lived. Wrapping anyone up in cotton wool is just as bad as not taking due care."

* * *

Monday, late morning, the first week of February, 1990 (six years earlier), Mavis drove through the bushfire scarred landscape into Keimera from her family's property in the hinterland where she lived in temporary accommodation, a caravan. Her parents' home had been destroyed in a recent bushfire, and she'd had a near death experience in it.

The Country Women's Association's funds for disaster relief had been used to hire two caravans so that the Mills family had somewhere to live while the government's special compensation package for people who had lost their homes was being processed. At this stage, Mavis' parents intended to rebuild on their land and continue their pastoral lifestyle.

It was seasonably hot. By eleven, Mavis' car thermometer registered thirty-three degrees Celsius. The radio news said the day would be another scorcher.

Despite this, Mavis did not feel the heat as many other pregnant women did. She was fit, a good weight, and, from the rear, did not look pregnant. The fit behind the steering wheel was snug though, something her parents had argued was good cause for them to chauffeur her in and out of town. She had resisted, clinging to the last vestige of her freedom before the arrival of her child.

Cresting the final hill before the descent into Keimera, Mavis took in the panorama. To the north, a rugged, unpopulated headland adjoined a pristine beach, suitable for surfers but not swimmers due to its dangerous rips. Next, Pipers Point where Madison House, a white two-storey colonial mansion, dominated the peninsula. Although not visible from this vantage, Mavis knew the historically significant house, representing the former pastoral glory of the region, as well as she knew her parents' property. She had boarded at Madison House for almost four years while working in town. In that time she had forged friendships that she hoped would last a lifetime, had fallen in and out of love and, after the breakup, discovered she was pregnant.

Glimpses of the picturesque town and the coastal road that twisted southward through the rural landscape marked the road's descent. The view rapidly disappeared as the car reached sea level.

Aware of a dull backache but attributing it to the suspension in her car seat and the awkwardness of her driving position, Mavis felt ravenous. She drove underneath the new expressway that bypassed Keimera.

Gone were the traffic jams of past years when the warmer months brought the onslaught of tourists travelling south. Keimera was still busy but with genuine traffic interested in spending time in the area rather than cars edging through it on the way to Bateman's Bay and beyond.

As she turned right at the main roundabout, Mavis saw Gary waiting for her on the parkland side of the road. A real estate salesman, he was dressed business-casual, a trend set by Bill Gates of Microsoft, in a crisp white shirt, dark trousers, and polished black leather shoes.

Pulling over, engine still running, Mavis considered parking; she needed to go to the toilet. Looking at her wristwatch, she decided she could hold on until she reached the doctor's surgery. It would be quicker than stopping now. After Gary climbed in, she pulled out into the light traffic.

"Thanks for standin' in for Cassie today, Gary. It was the only appointment I could get this week." Cassie Sleight was Mavis' closest female friend and had been a stalwart support throughout the pregnancy, unwanted at first. They had met and become firm friends after Cassie came to board at Madison House just over two years earlier.

"No sweat; it's a one off! Geez, mate, have you got bigger, or is it just the way you're sittin'? You should've let me pick you up or your dad drive you in. Thank God for air-conditioning. You feelin' okay?"

"I feel great now, but I had a terrible night. For some reason, I dreamt about Terry and … that last month with him." Terry had been Mavis' boyfriend. They had lived together six months or so after she'd moved out of Madison House. The emotional scars from that relationship were something that she would live with for a long time.

Gary still remembered the shock of seeing the physical abuse Mavis had suffered at Terry's hands. If it took a lifetime, Gary mentally swore to make up for his failure to protect her from such a man.

The tooting of a car horn brought Gary back to his surroundings. "What the …?"

The driver in the car ahead of them was clearly impatient for another car to complete its angle parking. The medical surgery was a block ahead of them.

Mavis rocked in the driver's seat.

"You okay?"

"I just need to go to the loo. C'mon! How hard can parkin' a car be?"

"Let's talk about something else. You know the sayin'…"

"Watched cars take forever to park."

Gary laughed. "Something like that. Decided yet where we'll go for lunch?"

"Sails, it has the best seafood in town! I am starvin'! My stomach has had an odd sort of grumblin' the whole trip. I should've had breakfast, but the pain from last night's nightmare just sat on me, and I couldn't eat then. Maybe we should phone the order in and get them to hold a table for us."

"Kate may have the medical practice runnin' on schedule, but she says there are always hiccups. Let's not jinx ourselves."

"That place runs like clockwork because she knows her doctors and plans for problems. Nothing is goin' to happen so let's order ahead. Pity Kate couldn't have lunch with us. I … Gosh, what was that?"

"What, mate?"

"I heard and felt a 'pop'. Sort've like a balloon breakin'. Oh, *no!*" Mavis was unexpectedly quiet for a moment. "I think my water has broke."

"Are you sure?"

"Well, not really, not havin' been through anything like this before." She didn't add that her underwear felt wet, really wet.

"If it has, we're in the right place." They were outside the medical practice. "At least there are lots of parkin' spaces here. Any contractions?"

"No, the doctor said it's usual for first-time mums to overshoot their due date. I should've gone to the toilet when I stopped for you. The bowel pressure is really awful."

"Way too much information, Mav'!"

Getting out of the car, Mavis was appalled at the flow of water as was Gary. He rushed ahead of her. She tried to clench shut, her legs almost crossed, but the water just kept coming and continued to come as she walked awkwardly along the footpath toward the surgery.

Torn between excitement at the possibility of birth and concern that the lunch she'd salivated over would be missed, Mavis reached the surgery's doorway. It opened on Kate who had a wheelchair, its seat covered in thick towels. Gary hovered behind her.

"Gary, can you call Sails and order lunch for me? I'd like ..."

"Hold off Gary until she's been checked." Kate whisked a protesting Mavis into the doctor's room and then returned. "Dr Tim will run a test to see if it is amniotic fluid or not. He'll also check to see if she is dilating yet. You say she's not had any labour pain so that's unlikely. When we know what's going on, you can let her parents know and phone the school to give Cassie a heads up that we might be expecting a birth in the next twenty-four hours or so."

"Given Cassie is Mavis' support person, don't you think she should come now?" Cassie Sleight was a teacher at the local high school.

"Jumping the gun there, Gary. There's plenty of time."

The practice nurse emerged from the doctor's room. After wheeling Mavis to the curtained casualty room at the back of the surgery, the nurse reappeared and beckoned to Kate, taking her out of Gary's sight. The doctor followed moments later.

Next thing Gary heard was Kate's shocked, "Surely not!"

There was a flurry of activity and, for a while, Gary was forgotten. Eventually, Kate returned to him as the local ambulance arrived to take Mavis to hospital.

"Gary, I've phoned the school to let Cassie know she needs to get to the hospital now. The receptionist up there needs to be pastured, nice old dear though she may be. She cut me off twice before I was able to leave a message. So frustrating! Mavis wants you to go with her in the ambulance so I'll phone your office and fill them in."

"I've got an appointment at three, but I'm free till then. Ask for James to take it for me if I'm late. What about Cassie?"

"I'll go up to the school to tell Cassie. After that, I'll drive out to Mavis' parents to let them know. It's at times like this that you wish the older generation were into mobile phones."

"Even if they were, it's a black hole communications-wise out there," Gary said.

As the male paramedic wheeled Mavis outside, Mavis asked Kate, "You sure Gary can't order me something from Sails? They do deliveries. Christ!" She doubled over in the wheelchair, her breathing pattern changed, and she grunted with involuntary pushing.

The practice nurse, who stood near Kate, looked at her watch. "Five minutes exactly. She's in a regular pattern now."

"Breathe though the contraction, love," said one paramedic while the other counted the duration of it. "That's it. You're doing fine. Try not to push yet. I'll tell you when you should if it gets to that."

Now in the ambulance, Mavis said, "It can't come now; I'm not ready. It's all happenin' too fast. I thought I was goin' to be overdue. I'm not psyched to go now! Do I have to have a drip? This isn't part of our birth plan."

"Babies don't know about plans. Here mate, you want to hold your wife's hand?"

About to correct the paramedic, Gary read Mavis' anguished face and remained silent. Although there had been a trend for many women to be unwed mothers, he knew Mavis felt shamed by her situation. Worse, she worried about a fatherless life for her child.

"I really need to go to the loo," Mavis said after another contraction.

"Birth's imminent, that's why you feel like that."

To Gary, the trip to the hospital seemed inordinately long, the experience surreal. He couldn't believe it was happening. He stroked Mavis' head, encouraged her to breathe through the pain, and endured having his hand crushed periodically.

At the hospital, things seemed to move in sped-up time. He looked for Cassie, but she wasn't there yet. He stayed back to leave a word with the desk nurse, but at Mavis' insistence followed her. They were rushed into a delivery room. Like a drowning woman holds onto a life raft, Mavis clung to Gary. All of his thoughts were centred on her. He found comfort in seeing the midwife, a well-upholstered woman who was clearly in command of the situation and unperturbed that the obstetrician/gynaecologist had not as yet arrived.

During the birthing process, Gary experienced an intense connection to Mavis, a divine communion that he would never forget. As the labour intensified, fear for Mavis and her child gutted him. *It was such a small passage. Surely, the child would be crushed. What if it got stuck?* In the sweat and strain of birth, as the baby's head crowned, he marvelled at the miracle of it. *It was bloody amazing!*

Euphoric, he held the baby boy first at Mavis' insistence despite the medical staff insisting she should have first contact. She said she needed some respite, some personal space. A time to breathe without pain. To recover from the shivering that had seized her.

An intense wave of emotion swept over Gary as he held the baby. *Such a small bundle of perfection!* He had never felt as close to anyone as he did to Mavis and her son at that moment.

Reluctantly relinquishing the baby to Mavis, he committed again to making amends for his past failure to her. Unlike his own childhood, this boy would not grow up without a caring man in it. Bending over to kiss Mavis on the forehead, he said, "Y' did good. I'm real proud of you."

* * *

1996 Keimera showground. "Wonder where the boys are," Mavis said to Kate who had returned from depositing their rubbish in the bins.

"I've been looking for them too, Mavis." Kate cringed. "Ice pick to the brain doesn't do justice to how that guy sounds. Let's walk toward where the boys should be coming from."

At the juncture of the food caravans and side-show alleys, the group reconnected. Gary had a thirty-something man in tow, dressed simply in black sneakers, black jeans, a white T-shirt, and a cutaway black vest.

Kate's comment, "There they are!" and Gary's, "Look who I ran into," over-lapped.

"Tony!" Mavis said, "Sorry to hear about your group breakin' up. What happened?"

"G' day, Mavis, Kate. Creative differences … You know the rest. I'm feelin' cursed at the moment."

Mavis', "Reformin' a band can be hard," overlapped Kate's, "Why?"

"No, that was easy; I only had to replace the singer. Problem today is he hasn't turned up for the gig this arvo. When Nick, our drummer, phoned his home, his mother said Matt took it into his head to go to Queensland yesterday. Bloody dope head; this is the final straw! He might be an amazin' performer when he's clean, but what good is that if he's off his head or out of it or just doesn't show?" He looked at Gary.

"I thought you might help Tony out by fillin' in as his singer."

"Gary, I haven't sung in public for years. Besides, I've never jammed with Tony or his guys. If I remember right, Tony, you sing."

"Yeah, but only backup. We need your help, Mavis. I want to avoid us gettin' a reputation as a no-show."

"Jesus, Mary, and Joseph!" Gary cringed as did people everywhere in reaction to a high-pitched note.

Dan's attempt to be helpful by echoing advice Mavis had given him about helping out friends went unacknowledged.

"C'mon, Dan," Kate said. "Let's have a ride on the Ferris wheel while your mum is sorting this out."

Mavis looked at her gratefully. To Tony, she said, "Are you guys playin' to music?"

"It can be to sheet music if that'll get you on board, if you pick songs that we've got the music to. We're good at listenin' to each other when we play, and we'll follow your lead. Why not start with a solo, something you've written, so you get into your comfort zone. You can borrow my electric acoustic."

"Geez, I can't do this cold, and there isn't time for a run through."

"Sure there is."

"I don't see how …"

"I'll get the guys." Tony was gone.

"What have you got me into, Gary?"

Gary gave her his Mickey Mouse grin and pose. "You'll be great!"

Chapter 2

"We do all the top artists' hits as well as the golden oldies," Tony began as he, Mavis and the band grouped together behind the band tent, unplugged guitars in hand, the drummer with his sticks. The sounds and life at the showground were a blurred backdrop to them.

The drummer and bass player, after a sharp reactionary side look at one another, hijacked the discussion. They listed the musicians whose material they preferred to play: "Nirvana, Pearl Jam, Radiohead, Red Hot Chilli Peppers, Men at Work, Beastie Boys, Silverchair, U2 …"

"Stop, fellas! They're all great, but … I can't do their songs with only a rushed run-through. A lot of them I couldn't pull off at all! I'm sorry, Tony, you'll have to cancel."

Denying defeat, Tony said. "But we've stacks of material. Let's work this from your end. What would you do for the gig if circumstances were different?"

"Well … your audience is a mixed bag so I'd have a cross section of entertainment and dance music. 'Love is in the Air' is still huge given the success of *Strictly Ballroom*. A lot of the Keimera Show Society are ballroom dancers so that'd work. Don't cringe like that, guys. Maybe 'Waterfalls' by TLC or Garbage's 'Only When It Rains' as we up the beat. Some country rock like Shania's 'I'm Outta Here'. What I'd pick is no good though. You're used to workin' with a guy."

"No, we know those songs. Sylvie Martin was with us until she broke up with our drummer. That's when Matt joined us. How about Mellencamp?"

"Do you know 'Wild Night', Tony?" Mavis asked.

"Yeah, we're tight on that, and our bass player loves it!"

"Cool. So, which ones will we do?" Mavis asked.

In unison, the guys said, "Not 'Love is in the Air'!"

"Fair enough."

"One thing, Mavis," Tony said, "you'll have to wing it. We haven't got sheet music here for that material."

"I suspected that. Anyway, I can sing those songs backwards. Let's run through them and see what's what. Oh, and while we're doin' that, Gary, I want you to talk to the sound guy. The band's volume has to be based on my volume. I want it balanced and at a reasonable level so lyrics are heard. Tell him the baseline is: if you need to raise your voice a bit to have a conversation then the band is at the right volume; if you need to yell in his ear, the band is too loud. No arguments about volume, guys, or I'm out."

"We're ahead of you there," Tony said. "That's been another pain in the arse with Matt."

The drummer and bass player wore an air of sullenness, their brows lowered. Later, when Mavis was out of sight and earshot, they exchanged heated words with Tony over his capitulation. The exchange built into an expletive-laden argument before an uneasy truce was reached.

*   *   *

Nervous but maintaining the appearance of calm, Mavis settled on a stool in front of a microphone, the borrowed guitar resting on her lap. She strummed the introduction to her solo, one of her own creations, and relaxed into the music. The grassed area before her was sparsely populated. She focused on her friends, her son, and on the song penned before she had given birth to Dan.

Mavis' voice, pure and strong, attracted attention immediately. Those people already seated or standing in the grassed area stopped what they were doing, absorbed in the soaring notes of her music and the beauty of the lyrics. As distinctive as a fingerprint, her voice had a textural quality, more than vocal colour or skilled intonation, which signalled its uniqueness. She sang with passion, with the joy of someone who had reconnected with her life's love. Her performance drew people from other parts of the showground to her.

As the last bars of her solo faded, the drum, wah-wah guitar, and keyboard picked up the interlude to 'Waterfalls'. As this was happening, Mavis put aside her guitar, stood, and stepped backward to the standing mike to join the band. Entering the rhythm of the song, her hands moved in synch with the drummer's. Cued by the drummer, she began the verse. There was a sultriness to her voice in this song, a siren's call. She carried the melody in counterpoint to the rhythm.

The crowd grew.

Delighted by the bass solo, Mavis focused the audience's attention on the bass player by turning toward him. He stepped forward, pleased. At the refrain, Tony joined her in harmony. Clearly, they were having a good time in the joining.

The audience before them moved in time to the music. Music spoke to them, connected them through emotion in a way other language did not. At the front of the crowd, Mavis saw Kate dancing with Dan while Gary danced with his blonde, blue-eyed girlfriend, Sarah, whose chic dress and silver sash made her a standout in this crowd.

Through a series of chord changes and pick up in drum beat 'Waterfalls' merged into 'Only When It Rains'. During this sequence, Mavis turned her back to the crowd, stepped further back into the band, took a deep breath, and visualized her transformation. She remembered the best of past times when she'd been a pub singer. Drawing energy from the music, she returned to the standing mike. Her performance was uninhibited and her voice raunchy. The crowd was hers; the band owned the stage.

It was an easy transition into 'I'm Outta Here'. Mavis took the mike off the stand, played to the crowd, encouraged them to join her in marking the rhythm through clapping. She was alive in the full sense of that word. Tony moved forward and joined her in chorus. Transported by song, she danced and sang. The drummer's tempo on the kettles cued the crowd who joined them in, "I'm Outta Here"! Mavis spun, gyrated to the interlude, and then began the next verse.

While the crowd was cheering at the end of the song, the drummer picked up the tempo again and led into a bass riff for Mellencamp's 'Wild Night'. In time with the drummer's cueing of four strong beats, Mavis literally jumped into the song, adapting some of the lyrics to suit her gender. Tony stepped up to the mike for harmony. The music built into an emotional crescendo. The crowd sang with them in the chorus. They needed little encouragement when Mavis sang the words, "C'mon out and dance!" The showground around them rocked! The song ended sharply on a final strong beat. The air resonated with the silence that was immediately broken by the cheering crowd.

"Well," Kate said to Gary, who stood with Dan beside him and his girlfriend on his other side, "we all know now where Mavis truly belongs."

"And we all know what her parents think," Sarah said, her right arm linked through Gary's. "Dan's the picture; Mavis is the frame."

*   *   *

The onyx darkness of the night sky heightened the brilliance of the stars and moon that hot summer's night, while in the darkness, ocean waves whooshed against the nearby harbour retaining wall. Passing under the arched canopy of trees that marked the wooden gates to her parents' town house in Keimera, Mavis, her son, and her two friends returned to her home. The Mills' cream, cement-rendered, circa 1857 colonial cottage stood at the forefront of the 1500 square metre housing block that overlooked Keimera harbour, while Mavis' smaller sandstone cottage stood at the rear. Instead of rebuilding on their fire devastated dairy farm as previously planned, the Mills had invested in renovating this house back to its former glory.

"Can I see Gran, Mum? I want to tell her …"

"Tomorrow, Dan. Time for a bath and then bed for you. It's been a big day." Turning her attention to her handbag, she said, "I'm goin' to have to do something about my house keys. I always lose them no matter what size my handbag. I was sure I dropped them in …"

"Know exactly what you mean," Kate said. "That's why I have my keys clipped onto a ring and chain and then hooked onto the corner of my handbag. Finding keys is simply a matter of following the trail."

"Gran has a spare set. I can get them, Mum." Dan was already on his way to his grandparents' back door.

"No!" three voices spoke in unison followed by laughter.

Dan stopped in his tracks and looked back at them, puzzled.

"No need. I've got them, Dan!"

Passing through the front door, they entered the main living area, a simply furnished room. The house throbbed with the day's heat. "Throw the lounge room windows open will you, Kate, while I work out what we'll have for supper. Dan, I've had second thoughts about you goin' to bed. You can play out back for a while."

Dan disappeared into the dark of the house.

"Dan, did you hear me?"

"I heard you, Mum!" was the boy's muffled reply.

"Gary, can you keep an eye on him? I don't want him …"

"Visitin' your mum?" Gary held her gaze for a moment.

"You've got it in one."

Reappearing with a zippered black bag that held balls, a jack, and measuring line, Dan asked, "Gary, will you give me a game of bowls?"

"I think you're gettin' too good for me these days, matey, but I'll give it a shot. Your grandpa's a champion, and I reckon you're goin' to be one as well. So how's about givin' me a handicap lead of …"

"Not a lead, but we can bowl from the same line."

They passed through the faded stained, double French doors into the backyard.

Kate sat on one of four white stools positioned under the breakfast bar. "So, how are you going to tell your mum about performing with the band for the Show Society's dinner dance?"

Mavis looked back at Kate from her small recessed pantry. "Don't know, but whatever happens, I'm not letting this opportunity pass. I had thought of not tellin' her."

"There are some secrets that can't be kept in a small town like this."

"It's at times like these I wish I lived in the city."

"You sure you won't reconsider and let Gary and me shout dinner? It'll save on the mess and heat of preparation *and* eliminate the need for washing up."

"Friendship involves give and take, Kate. Besides, it's my turn to spring for a meal. I thought for supper we'd have an antipasto plate, and Dan can have a snag sandwich."

"Perfect. I'm not that hungry, and I doubt Gary is either given what he has stowed away today."

"His body will become an Esky for his six-pack if he's not careful."

Kate laughed. "Anything I can do to help?"

"Would you mind gettin' the cold meat out of the fridge and addin' it to these ingredients while I open up the rest of the house? The onshore breeze should cool my room and Dan's pretty quick if I open that part of the house up now. It's one of many reasons I like livin' here. When I was a kid, the farm homestead seemed to get hotter and hotter each summer's night. Bein' in a valley, we didn't get the benefit of sea breezes. I am so glad Mum and Dad decided against rebuildin' after the bushfire."

"Yeah, I know what you mean about hot summer nights in the country. When we lived in the Northern Territory, during the wet season, I learnt what awful summer heat really was. Mum longed to come back home and to the coast."

"I'll be back," Mavis said, terminating the conversation. Exiting, she paused and looked back, "I just felt like ..."

"The Terminator?"

Mavis nodded.

"Yes, that catchphrase always brings Arnie and that movie to mind for me too."

Mavis disappeared into the house.

After foraging through the fridge and coming up with only sliced ham and a lone sausage, Kate returned to Mavis' small pantry in search of more ingredients. Disappointed, she returned to the fridge, having decided to add raw vegetables to the mix. She had rejected her fleeting idea of popping down the road to the nearby shops to buy more ingredients. Chiding herself for forgetting how financially tight things were for Mavis, she regretted her thoughtless extravagance earlier that day with the hat purchase.

The envisioned lavish antipasto plate reduced in reality to marinated olives, shaved ham, a few aging mushrooms, carrot sticks, and thinly sliced tomato. Kraft cheese – a cheese product publicised across the nation for its nourishing goodness and an Australian staple – had been cut into triangular slices and positioned with slices of crusty bread to bulk out the platter. Kate put the sausage under the grill, taking care to add water to the grill pan to reduce shrinkage.

Having thrown a white patterned tablecloth over the wooden outdoor table and set out plates and drinks, Kate sat down. "Fellas, five minutes till supper." She found the chilled white wine, a budget brand, surprisingly refreshing.

"Time enough to finish this game," Gary said. "Looks like I'm trounced again."

The screen doors swung open, and Mavis emerged with Dan's sausage sandwich in hand. "Sorry, it took longer than expected. I just had to change. Fellas …."

"I've already given them the five-minute call," Kate said.

"You know our routine so well."

"I do that."

"Geez, Kate, supper looks better than I thought it would."

"So, how are you going to tell your mum?"

"I'm dreadin' it and haven't a clue as to how."

"Nor do I," Kate said. "You won't let her talk you out of this, will you, Mavis?"

"No way! I really want this, Kate."

"Good! It's your chance to be who you were meant to be and escape what you've become."

Mavis looked gobsmacked.

Gary swung his long legs over the bench seat. "Blunt and honest as ever, Kate." Dan followed Gary's lead and sat next to him.

"That sounded rude, Mavis. Sorry. I was talking about how circumstances …"

"Tryin' to get the whole foot in your mouth, Kate?" Gary poured himself a glass of wine. "I'm with Kate on this one although I'd have said it differently. I haven't seen you alive like that for years, Mavis! Workin' as a receptionist at Keimera Ford just doesn't do it for you like singin' does."

"It never has, Gary, and I knew what Kate meant. No offense taken. Problem is I just don't know yet how I can manage Mum, especially given how she sees life." Curbing her son's enthusiastic agreement with Gary, Mavis spoke to Dan. "Don't talk while your mouth's full." She picked up a napkin and wiped a drop of tomato sauce from his chin before looking up at her friends. "Let's talk about other things."

Over supper, Mavis asked, "So how's your business course goin', Gary?"

"It's interestin'. George Madison has been a font of knowledge as well. He's still an astute businessman despite bein' retired. He seems to enjoy chewin' over the course material with me. It's one of the many perks of boardin' at Madison House."

"Speaking of which…" Kate said.

"Don't you start on me too. Sarah is always goin' on at me about gettin' my own flat. She doesn't get why I don't want to downsize, and she definitely doesn't get why I don't want to move out when Minna has been so ill." Minna Madison and her husband, George, were the family Gary had wished for as a child but not had. He blessed the day the Madisons' financial situation had necessitated them taking in boarders.

"I'm nothing like Sarah, and that isn't where I was going," Kate said. "I totally understand that you feel about the Madisons the way I feel about my dad. I'd move home if he ever got ill."

Gary said, "It's tough, isn't it, when parents have only one kid? I know that Mike loves his parents, but I can't see him returnin' home with Cassie, not as long as he's in the RAAF."

Mavis added, "There aren't any military bases around here for one thing, and knowin' the Madisons as well as we do, can either of you see his parents bein' prepared for Mike to give up his career for them?"

Kate said, "The older Madisons shouldn't be put into that position. It's something Mike should choose…"

Gary responded, "Well, none of that has to be an issue as long as I'm around. I'm more than happy to pick up the slack in the Madisons' time of need, especially when it's so easy for me to do it."

Mavis asked, "You catchin' up with Sarah later, Gary?"

"Sure am, but only after I've dropped Kate home."

"I've legs, Gary, there's no need."

"And I've a car!"

Kate and Gary moved to clear the table while Mavis lingered outdoors over her glass of wine. The rest of their conversation became a muffled backdrop to Mavis' thoughts. It had been a long time since she'd had a choice. Life had happened to her without plan. She had tried to make the best of it despite a yearning for something undefined and beyond her imagining.

*   *   *

1990. Within the confines of her caravan, Mavis paced what there was of the floor, with six-month-old Dan in her arms, surrounded by the trappings of babydom. Dan would not stop crying, and nothing she did made a difference.

Defeated, Mavis cried too for the hope lost that life had once held for her. Her life and its foreseeable future had been reduced to the top of a nail head, and she could not even see to its edge.

In a collapsed state, Mavis sat on the floor rocking and singing a broken-voiced lullaby with Dan cradled in her arms. Her parents were in town. Gary was away on holiday. She didn't have a phone to call Cassie, her lifebuoy when the going got tough. *Never* had she felt so forsaken.

Finally exhausted, Dan fell asleep. Rising ever so carefully, Mavis returned him to his cot and then fell onto her bed, her grief inconsolable.

That day dragged to its inevitable close and with it came an end to that part of her life. Her parents returned in the dying light with news they had sold a parcel of their considerable land holding so they could buy a house with a detached cottage in town.

"We've given everything a lot of thought, love," Marg said. "Bein' an at-home mum just isn't workin' for you. As you've said, you need to get on with your life. Goin' back to work is definitely the first step. I can take care of Dan durin' the day. Life is goin' to get better, I promise!" Marg did not reveal their decision had grown out of fear over Mavis' depression and related consultations with their family doctor. Mavis' suffering had disturbed them more than any child's bout of crying ever had.

"Oh, Mum, Dad, thank you." Crying, Mavis found comfort within her father's calming embrace.

*   *   *

1996. The clatter of her screen door brought Mavis out of her musings.

"Kate's washin' up, and Dan's gone in for his bath. Mavis, you have a right to be better than your current circumstances and to realise your potential."

"A quote from Kate?"

"Kate's dad actually. It's what he said when we talked over my doin' a degree in business studies part-time. Don't blow this chance, Mavis."

"I won't. Well, not if I can help it."

Chapter 3

Kitchen drawers and cupboard doors shut loudly in a succession of closings as Marg Mills, Mavis' mother, unstacked the day's wash from her recently acquired dishwasher. Not a word had she said after Mavis shared the previous day's events.

Seated at her mother's wooden kitchen table, sipping tea, Mavis clung to a newly resurrected hope for a different version of her life, a version she had buried long ago when her dreams of love had been smashed by her boyfriend along with her guitar. Although she relied on her parents' support now, and knew that without them her life with Dan would be considerably harder, she had decided to go it alone if necessary.

Of course, Marg already knew about Mavis' showground stopping performance before Mavis had walked into the house after work the next day. The greengrocer had surprised Marg with news of it when she called at his shop in the main street on her way up town earlier that day. The butcher had expanded on the news when she had stopped to collect that week's meat order on the return trip. Numerous acquaintances and sometimes friends had halted her return progress, all of them full of congratulations and speculations. She had nodded and maintained a tight-lipped smile, despite being cut by the fact that she was among the last to know of her daughter's altered affairs. Arriving home, she had looked for peace and time to digest the news.

Unexpectedly, Trevor, her husband, had been home, having returned from the bowling club unsettled by the news heard there. Usually a man of few words, he had loudly fumed and fretted, making Marg wish for quieter times when Trevor had been at a loss for what to say. Having revved his wife up, he left her to handle the matter while he had headed off to a downsized version of their farm to tend alpacas, his last words being, "Dan is the picture; she has to be the frame now!"

Mavis poured herself another cup of tea. Waiting for words heard repeatedly over past years whenever she had found herself at one of life's crossroads, she felt a sadness in the predictability of her parents' reactions.

Outside, Dan played with a school friend who had come home with him earlier that afternoon.

Mavis looked at her watch. Six o'clock. Mary Selton would be picking Billy up soon. *I should be thinking about dinner*, Mavis thought. Battle-ready, she remained seated.

Dishwasher unstacked, Marg felt an unusual calm. Insight had come to her somewhere between the noisy storing of the pots and the pans. Not only had her mind quieted but so too had the final stages of tidying up her kitchen. A cup of tea in hand, she crossed to the table and sat down. "It's all night work, isn't it?"

"What?"

"Performin'. It's night work, mostly weekends, and if I remember right, you started after eight."

"Mum, are you sayin' …?"

"You're my child; I'm your frame. I can help you do this *without* Dan missin' out."

Mavis felt an intense surge of emotion edged with relief.

"It's time you had a life; it's best for Dan too if you do." Then as an afterthought, Marg asked, "Exactly where would you be off to and when?"

"Don't know, Mum. I didn't think that far so I didn't ask." Mavis reclined in the chair, gobsmacked.

"And the rehearsals for the dinner dance?"

"That's goin' to be hot and heavy." Mavis' reluctance translated into her body language. "I was hopin' you might take Dan for a few of them. Gary said he'll help out with cover as well."

"No need. Your dad and I'll cover it."

"Oh, Mum, thank you!" On her way out to her cottage, Mavis silently thanked God for her father whom she adored, giving credit to him for her mother's change in stance.

*   *   *

A stylish, super-sized white event marquee dominated the peninsula parkland adjacent to Keimera showground while behind it stood two smaller tents. Caterers used one tent and the twenty-eight Zone 2 Show Girls used the other. Nearby, long rows of green and white portaloos were discretely positioned behind a line of coastal pines; heavy drinking that night meant there would be a high demand among the guests. Two oversized caravans marked SECURITY were parked in the vicinity.

As daylight faded into a crimson dusk over the western hills, a team of parking attendants – local volunteers from the State Emergency Service – took up their positions to the sound of the band tuning up from within the marquee.

The head of security briefed the attendants on their job. "Control entering traffic and strategically position them as per your designated parking map to ensure ease of exit at one of the five exit points across the car park area. We don't want any bottlenecks when the night's over. Point out the surveillance cameras as well. We definitely don't want any knob heads or jocks cutting up trouble like they did a few years back. And please, encourage the intoxicated to get taxis."

Inside the marquee, caterers worked with a focused calm. Waiting staff of both sexes, resplendent in crisp, brilliant white shirts and black trousers, put the finishing touches on the white damask-cloth covered tables. Flowers featured at intervals along those tables. The lighting was soft and romantic. The band, having bumped in and tuned up, headed off for an early meal provided in the caterer's tent. Sound checks were timed for an hour later with a final tune up set for ten minutes before they performed.

"First dinner dance I've ever been to," Mavis said to Tony O'Brien over dinner. Like the rest of the band, he was dressed in black trousers, a long-sleeved white shirt, and a black tie. The Show Committee had strict rules about dress. Mavis wore a rich purple satin, extremely low back evening gown and strappy flats. She wore her hair simply.

"Balls and dinner dances are big business as are corporate functions," Tony replied. "If you're good, and we are now with you as our singer, that's where the money is. I'm glad you're into doin' covers rather than original material although I do like the solos you've chosen for durin' the buffet tonight. Your own material?"

"Yes, and thanks. Have you seen this evening's program?" She passed it across the table to him.

"The draft … when I negotiated the length of our brackets …. Hmmm. Apart from the artwork and presentation, it's the same."

"Is it always this organized?"

"Has to be with only two Show Girls picked to go on to the Royal Easter Show. You know the Keimera Show Girl, don't you?"

"I'm acquainted with Sarah …Why?"

"Introduce me, will you?"

"Sarah is Gary's girlfriend, Tony."

"Seriously?"

"I'm afraid so."

"No, I *meant* I didn't think they had that much in common."

"He likes her *a lot* so back off."

"No intention of doing anything else. I've put my money on her and Meredith Blakely, the girl from Robertson. They're super fine women!"

Their sound engineer called time for the final sound balances, interrupting their dialogue. As the band moved to the stage, the first of the party-goers arrived, many with gaudily decorated Eskys. One of the traditions of this Show Society was a weekend dinner prize for two at Olives, a one-hat restaurant in the Keimera region, for the best-decorated Esky.

Mavis' friends were among the arrivals. Gary beamed proudly as well-wishers paused to talk to the couple. Near them, Kate chatted with her escort, a man Mavis knew but who was not part of their inner circle. His interest in Kate was obvious even to casual observers.

"What about that favour, Mavis?" Tony said after sound balances were completed.

"What?"

"Introduce me to Sarah Murphy before she and the other Show Girls go off to do whatever it is they do?"

"Okay."

With Tony in tow, Mavis crossed the constructed dance floor, manoeuvring between guests now streaming into the marquee.

"Lookin' good, Mavis," Gary said with an amused quizzical raise of his right eyebrow. "You scrub up real fine."

"I was just thinkin' the same about all of you. Sarah, this is Tony O'Brien, the lead guitarist in my band." Mavis missed Tony's reaction, a momentary distortion of his features that reflected his annoyance. "He's a *huge* admirer!"

While Tony made small talk with Sarah, who was dressed in a slinky silver gown with her hair sculpted in curls, Mavis said, "Just as well Tony is playin' most of the night, Gary. I reckon he'd cut you out on the dance floor."

"I don't know about that."

"I've seen you dance, Gary." The memory of it made Mavis laugh.

"Not lately you haven't. Sarah and I have had lessons. I'm smooth on the floor. Ask Kate. She was hired as one of the dance teachers by the Show Society."

Mavis looked at Kate, striking in a deep red, strapless, tastefully low-cut silk evening gown, for confirmation. Kate had been dancing ballroom for years; it was one of her passions, another being the Surf Life Saving Movement. "Gary can dance, and that's a serious fact!" Her escort, Stan, whispered something in Kate's ear. She blushed, laughed, and allowed him to guide her to their seats.

Sarah, noting Gary's distracted gaze in Kate's direction asked, "Something wrong?"

"I've never really liked Stan. He's only interested in one thing ..."

The MC for the evening, having taken up position on the stage, asked the drummer for a drum roll before he spoke.

Sarah, at the sight of the MC on stage, had moved to her table and called Gary to join her. Her, "Gary!" overlapped his comment, "Kate's too fine for him."

"Welcome to Zone 2 Show Societies' dinner dance. If you move to your tables, once you're all settled the waiters will direct you table by table to the buffet. You'll see from the program we're scheduled two and a half hours for dinner with dancing between courses before the Show Girl introductions. While the final interviews are in progress and judging is taking place, we'll have more dancing. By popular demand, The Slide is back once again and will occur during the 10.30 p.m. band break. Please ensure you've filled out your waiver form and returned it to a Show Ball Committee member. There will be limited numbers sliding and no! late entries. Please put your hands together for the band, Velum."

The opening number 'I'll Get By with A Little Help from My Friends' brought a handful of dancers onto the floor. Although they knew their parts, the band, due to their lack of familiarity with Mavis as their singer, listened closely to her and to one another. They weren't just a backing band that night; they were part of Mavis' performance, cued by her. Her voice gave the lyrics meaning; they were heartfelt.

As always when Mavis sang, images came to her mind. Without her friends, she'd have been lost long ago in hopeless despair. With them, although her love had turned away, she was not alone.

Gary had rescued her in more ways than one. Importantly, he had gifted her a new guitar after her dark, destructive days with Terry. In doing so, Gary had returned her to music. Music fed her spirit, lifted her to a high.

Cassie, absent but not forgotten, had seen in Mavis' relationship with Terry what Mavis had not. Cassie had refused to be turned away even when Mavis, in anger, had turned from her. Cassie had been there in the heat and fire of crisis. She was there now, only a phone call away.

Indomitable Kate helped Mavis see beyond her present. Kate had an intellectual sharpness that focused Mavis like a tuner did a television aerial. Added to that, Kate's motto, "You only fail if you quit," had kept Mavis putting one foot in front of the other when the going was tough.

Throughout the evening, the performance rapport between band members grew. Their pre-show performance nerves had disappeared; clearly, they were having fun. That fun, like electricity, jumped to the audience.

Dance brackets catered for young and old, ballroom dancers as well as the improvising movers and groovers. For a number of dancers, there was less groove and a few very odd moves. Although there appeared to be a number of spectators to the dance scene, few were actually observers; most were engrossed in their conversations. No one needed to move outside to be heard. The sound engineer was happy as were the organizers.

The night culminated in the announcement of the two Zone winners: Sarah Murphy and Meredith Blakely. Their supporters erupted into exuberant cheering, followed by a round of hugs and kisses reminiscent of the American Academy Awards. Both Mavis and Kate noted the passion with which Gary and Sarah kissed on her return to their table after the awards.

The Slide, a time-honoured tradition at many country balls and dinner dances such as this one, had been a competitive, strictly male event before the second wave of the women's movement in the 1960s. After that, women were allowed to compete. Put simply, each competitor took a long run-up to the starting line and then with something akin to a hop, skip and drop, slid across the dance floor. The winner being the person who could slide the furthest. The prize that year was an all-expenses paid weekend to a prestigious hotel on Finger Wharf just east of Sydney Harbour Bridge. How a person slid across the four hundred square metre floor was a matter of technique. Some favoured feet first, others head first, while a few preferred a side-on slide.

The crowd gathered around the dance floor in hushed expectation. Those unlucky enough to be in back rows stood on chairs – their earlier manners, the refinements of the gala event, and the cost of the evening wear forgotten. To the cringing accompaniment of "Ooh!", "Ahh!" and "Whoa!" competitors hurled themselves across the floor, some uncontrollably careering off under tables and tangling with chairs.

With the heats completed, the finals were reduced to three competitors: a lithesome young woman, a heavy man of medium height, and Gary. Rejecting the women-and-children first principle of earlier times (this particular woman called it chauvinistic), drinking straws were cut to various lengths and drawn to determine the run-up order.

Possessing a long and aggressive straight-line run-up that took him far outside the marquee, the man threw himself at the dance floor, his eyes bulging, teeth glinting. Cricket tragics in the crowd were reminded of the approach of famous fast bowlers from their day. The dance floor reverberated with the impact of his weight as his body collided with the floor. The downward force of the fall undercut the momentum of the slide. Judges marked where he stopped with an empty beer can.

The young woman with total disregard for her gown, hitched it up into Gandhi-like trousers.

Like a panther through a forest, she moved effortlessly, noiselessly, dropping gracefully into a slide without the thud of collision. Her slide ended about five metres from the edge of the stage which was trimmed with black valance.

"Impressive!" was the widespread comment.

Gary, whose ambition was to be an Iron Man some day, had been warming up with a long run outside and so had missed his competitors' performances.

Kate's partner, a fellow lifesaver, had volunteered to be Gary's lookout.

Positioned at the marquee entrance, he whistled to Gary that it was time. The crowd inside the marquee waited. A hush slowly settled over the crowd. Spectators leant forward, eyes on the starting line.

With a bounding approach, magnificent in his speed, stripped down to the essentials needed for a quality slide, Gary's run-up climaxed in a cartwheel action that took him low into the floor and across it with phenomenal speed, past the marker set for the man's slide, past the woman's slide marker, fast and furiously toward the stage.

From the cheering crowd, Gary knew he was a winner. His challenge now was to stop. Within two metres of the stage, he knew he was in trouble. There was only one option. Adjusting his position, he bulleted under the stage, the valance tickling his nose, the dust on it making him sneeze and, in doing so, lift his head, resulting in him bumping his head.

With a groan, he came to a halt on the other side of the stage against the marquee frame and tent wall.

The crowd rushed to him. Mavis, Sarah, and Kate in the lead.

Unaware of a short time lapse and with what appeared to be a mild concussion, Gary eventually focused on the anxious faces of the women in his life. "I'm okay, mate," he said to Kate who was fussing with a makeshift icepack to treat the swelling bump on his head. "Seriously, I'm okay, mate." He looked at Mavis, knowing all too well the stress in her eyes. "I won, eh?" he said to no one in particular.

"That you did," said Sarah, who sat with Gary's head cushioned in her lap. She bent forward and gently kissed him.

At Tony's insistence, Mavis returned to the stage for the next dance bracket. Kate, aware of the claim to intimacy signalled by Sarah, left Gary to her, telling herself her feelings of disgruntlement stemmed from concern and nothing more. The surgery was open Sunday mornings. She'd talk him into being checked out for everyone's peace of mind, and keep an eye on him, from a distance, for the rest of the evening.

At the close of the evening, as patrons exited the marquee, security people directed them to a number of manned tables, encouraging alcohol breath tests before going home. The Show Committee, in a bid to reduce police bookings of drunk drivers and the 'drink and drive' fatalities of past balls and other major social events, had organized sufficient breathalyzers for every departing guest.

A fleet of taxis from Keimera and the wider region lined the street leading up to and from the peninsula. The Show Society's functions were big business for taxi drivers. Inebriated patrons deposited car keys with the security team, to be picked up the next day, and hailed taxis for home.

Police, like flies at an abattoir in summer, were highly visible in the peninsula street, booking anyone foolhardy enough to drive while under the influence. The police then relocated drunks to waiting taxis after impounding their cars. The local police station did not have a holding cell for offenders.

After the band bumped out, Mavis walked home with her friends and their partners. As it turned out, Kate's escort knew a lot about Tony O'Brien and his band's history. "Tony 's never been interested in the big end of the music industry which is one reason his band keeps changing. He's hungry for the money associated with what he calls 'small arena' functions. Hope you like travelling because you'll be booked for every festival, ball, and corporate function that he can schedule." The group parted on the footpath near the gated entrance to Mavis' parents' property.

As Mavis walked down the driveway, their distant voices carried to her.

"Gary, I'm booking you into the clinic for a check-up at eleven today. I'm not taking *no* for an answer."

"I'm fine, Kate, but since you girls are so concerned …."

"I'll drive him there, Kate," Sarah said. "You can count on me."

Walking past her mother's house, Mavis heard the clock chime three times. The lights were off; no one had stayed up to hear how the night had gone. With her earlier exhilaration capped, Mavis realised she needed to think through what she wanted from her return to the public music arena and how to reconcile that with being a mother. With Dan sleeping at her mother's that night, she would not be torn between her need for a sleep-in and her son's needs.

Chapter 4

The next week was an anticlimax. Waking early Sunday afternoon and then shocked by the lateness of the day, Mavis dressed quickly and went in search of her son. She found him with her parents on their front verandah which overlooked Keimera harbour. Tall Norfolk Pines partially obstructed the harbour view. The murmur of the wind through the treetops harmonized with the gentle shush-and-hush of the incoming tide as it lapped against the harbour retaining wall. That sound combined with the gentle onshore breeze created a soothing atmosphere on that hot afternoon.

"So sorry, Mum, Dad. Why didn't you wake me earlier?" Mavis sat in the vacant squatter's chair near her father.

"You deserve a sleep in now and then," Marg said. "From all accounts, the band was a huge success."

In response to Mavis' puzzled expression, Trevor said, "Phone calls from friends, and you know what passers-by are like when they see us here."

"Chatty," Mavis and Marg said in unison.

"It's been far from peaceful, I can tell you."

"So, what happened in the Federal election?" Mavis asked.

"A landslide to John Howard and his Liberals," Marg answered when Trevor didn't. She looked at him, aware he was upset over her support of Mavis' decision to join the band and that he was worried where that return to performing would lead their daughter and them. Last time and before Dan was born, it had led to conflict and estrangement.

"So you were right, Dad."

Trevor, aware of the intensity of Marg's gaze and the meaning behind it, looked at his daughter for the first time that day. "About the change but I never expected the landslide. It shows a lot more people than me and my mates were fed up with Keating's policies. He might have been Labor, but he wasn't in touch with the ordinary man like Hawke was. Never liked Keating after he said we had to have a recession. Didn't like where he was takin' the country. We'll see now what type of Australia Howard delivers. You okay with me takin' Dan up the street for an ice cream?"

"Course I am."

Her father and Dan left. Dan's childish patter and her father's brief replies carried back to Mavis and her mum.

"Mum, any leftovers in your fridge? I'm starvin'."

"I thought you would be so I made a plate up in anticipation; it's on the third shelf. I've been waitin' for you to get up before I visited Minna Madison. She's out of hospital."

"Gary says she's doin' well but seems really tired." Gary had boarded with the Madisons for nearly a decade and was like a stand-in son for them.

"I called George to see if she was up to visitors."

"Give her my love will you?"

"I'll be back in about three hours if your Dad asks."

"You don't want me to drive you up there?"

"No, the walk will do me good. Besides, it's shaded most of the way."

True to her mother's words, a hearty cold roast beef salad had been prepared for Mavis' lunch.

Returning to the front verandah, Mavis settled in for a quiet afternoon although she held an expectation that passers-by would stop for a chat and want to talk about the dinner dance. The wind dropped. The temperature continued to climb. The parklands and streets emptied as people retreated to their homes or to the cool of the ocean. The only activity was a noisy, single engine Cessna taking sightseers on joy flights over Keimera and the adjacent south coast region.

Aware that she had a weekend's work ahead of her and not much time to get it done, Mavis returned to her cottage, glad that she had the air-conditioning running.

*   *   *

On Monday, after an initial thumbs up from her co-workers about her performance, the routine of the working week returned. At breaks early in the week, her co-workers shared their stories of the weekend and the dance. The band and her performance were just one note in the music score of their lives.

Midweek, a female customer, someone known to Mavis for years, shared a fleeting comment about the past weekend when she stopped at the reception desk. "The band were great. You were quite good. Gary's slide was impressive."

Deflated, Mavis found solace in the ritual of her clerical duties. It wasn't that she wanted to bask in the limelight, but she did want some form of affirmation that she was right to resurrect her dream and that she was not self-deluded.

That Friday, a few of the car salesmen stopped for a chat at her reception desk midday. Business had been slow.

"It's bloody hot out there," said Fred, the only corpulent salesman at Keimera Ford and the last to join the group. He mopped his brow with a stream of tissues taken from the box on Mavis' desk behind the counter before depositing them in the bin beneath her desk.

"Sure is," was the group reply. The men were dressed in shirt and tie, smart trousers, and sported the appearance of affluence. They talked of the new rugby league season, the local and state scene.

Winner of the previous year's football pool, Mavis participated in their conversation between answering outside calls.

Disinterested in such talk, the corpulent newcomer positioned himself under the air-conditioning duct to the right of Mavis' reception desk. "Ah! That's so much better! You know, Mavis, you were bloody good Saturday night. I've heard Tony's band play before, and they were nowhere as good until you joined them. How long do you think it'll be before you can ditch this job?"

Before Mavis could answer, another salesman, Stan, responded. "Mavis has as many opportunities for a different life as I do." Although thirty-something, he looked younger and carried himself with the air of a man used to women's attention. "I've got plans for a life other than this job too."

"You do?" was the unison reply.

"I'm writing a book about my erotic adventures."

"Oh," was Mavis' nonplussed reply. For the umpteenth time since her breakup with Terry, she thought, *Definitely not a good judge of men.* She pulled back.

The other men leant forward, ready for titillating revelations. Clearly, they believed this disclosure was not only a possibility but a reality.

A younger salesman known to be a person slavishly interested in the sexual pursuits of others because he had none of his own to relish, said, "You pull the most amazing looking birds, Stan. Come on, out with it."

"Not before the foreplay, Beau." Then as an afterthought, Stan added, "Maybe that's why you go home from the pub dateless so many times."

Beau flushed. "So how many of the delectables I've seen you with feature in this book?"

Stan savoured the power of the men's anticipation.

Beau spoke up, eager to share in Stan's power through association. "A chapter a bird would make it a pretty salacious book. So how many chapters have you got?"

Enjoying the intensity of their attention, Stan produced a Cheshire Cat smile before saying, "First page of a pamphlet."

The outburst of laughter that followed was a spontaneous appreciation of the self-deprecating way Stan had set them up.

"Customer on the lot," the manager of the car yard said, passing the group.

As Beau left the showroom, Fred directed his comments to the remaining men although the group had splintered. "Don't know whether to commiserate with him for having to go out into the heat or feel envious that well-heeled customer might bring him a commission." Then to Mavis, he said, "I didn't get an answer to my question, Mavis. How long before you leave us?" The salesman in his forties had a soft spot for Mavis, primarily because his life too had been capped when, in his teens, his girlfriend had fallen pregnant, and they'd married.

"I can't see that ever happenin', Fred. I've bills to pay and a kid to rear. The band will only be a part-time thing. Performin' is more about givin' me the joy that'll get me through life rather than a new job." She deliberately withheld her aspirations. To share them with anyone at work would be to jinx herself.

"Gardening does that for me," another salesman said. "What about you, Steve?"

"Cycling."

"Ah, yes, the tour de puff," Fred commented. "I saw the write up about you in the local rag. Do you think you'll make it to the European circuit?"

Stan, now leaning casually against the reception counter, said "He's got a better chance than Mavis has, especially given her bag … luggage."

"Don't talk about my son like that, not ever!"

"No offense meant, Mavis. Look, I had dreams once, gave it a shot, and then had to face the hard reality of life. I reckon you both need to get the impossible dream out of your systems and come to terms with what ninety-nine percent of the population have had to accept, being ordinary."

The men around the speaker looked at him soberly. A balding man of fifty, who had been leafing through one of the latest glossy Ford brochures on the reception counter, looked at the speaker. "That's right, Stan, open your mouth to change feet."

Fred reacted, "Clearly Stan's true career is in the UN Peace Corps."

Two other men added, "Not!"

Feeling like she'd been punched in the gut, Mavis narrowed her eyes in an effort to stop the threatening spill of tears. She leant forward so that her hair concealed her face and busied herself with the work on her desk.

The cyclist in the group stared hard at Stan before saying, "Thanks for sharing your opinion with us, but you've made a mistake thinking we put stock in what you say." He walked off.

Stan, experiencing a deficit in the witty reply department, decided on retreat and left.

The other men dispersed as Mavis answered an incoming call. "Keimera Ford, designed for living, engineered to last. How can I help you? ... Puttin' you through now."

During the afternoon as she processed the paperwork before her, Mavis realised that, although she was older, the insecure girl of her teenage years still lived within her as did that girl's needs. *It's time I stopped letting others define me.*

Later that scorching afternoon, Fred, feeling the worse for heat, took a breather at the reception desk. "Don't listen to the naysayers, love. Go for gold."

* * *

On Friday night, Gary and Sarah dropped in unexpectedly before Dan's bedtime on their way out on the town. Dan's surprised and exuberant welcome cut Gary in a way Mavis' earlier, private discussion with him a month before had not. The scale of the boy's surprised joy highlighted the scale of Dan's previous grief (grief being Mavis' description) when Gary had reneged on his longstanding Friday night routine with Dan.

Although Mavis was welcoming, Gary was very conscious that he had ground to repair. He just didn't know how to do it so he let Sarah take the conversational lead.

"It's been hard to get back on track this week. All anyone wants to do is talk about the Ball, the Royal Easter Show, and my competition there. It's so touching that everyone thinks I'll win Royal Easter Show Girl. I can't imagine going overseas to London. It's the sort of thing that happens in other people's lives, not mine."

"Same at my work," Gary said, "except they wanted to talk about their own shenanigans and The Slide." Then to Sarah, "Oh, I've booked our weekend at the W hotel. They'd had a cancellation so we actually got the weekend you wanted."

Sarah added, "I looked it up on the Internet. It's five-star luxury. I haven't ever stayed in such a hotel before. We could look it up here so you could see …"

"I can't afford a computer let alone the Internet. There isn't much need for it in our lives. I don't think there ever will be."

"There are some great educational programs that would help Dan. He's such a bright child. The band will give you the extra cash you need for …" Sarah hesitated, aware that she had unintentionally drifted into criticism of the Spartan-like lifestyle that Mavis led. "There are always luxuries that we all want that our income can't give us."

"How's the head, Gary?" Mavis asked.

"Just like the rest of me, fantastic!" Gary looked up at her from where he had squatted to talk to Dan.

"I might need to get a carpenter in to work on the doors," Mavis said, her brow crinkling. She paused. "Otherwise you're stuck here for the weekend. Can't see Gary gettin' that big head of his …"

"Okay then, let's just say I'm fine."

"And still the braggin' continues." Mavis looked at her son. "Dan, ten minutes till bedtime. You can leave what you're buildin' under the coffee table. It'll be safe there from Gary's big feet. I want the loose Lego packed up for the night though."

"Gary," Dan said, "you readin' me a story tonight? You've missed a lot of Friday nights, and Mum said things have changed, but I don't know how."

"That's why we dropped in, matey, for story time and to see my little man. Life's a bit busier now than it used to be, and there'll be some times when I can't stop by on Friday nights." He looked up at Mavis as he spoke. "Most Friday nights, I'll be here. But I promise, when I can't make it, I will always call. C'mon, Dan, I'll help you pack up."

Sarah spoke to Mavis, "I guess you got tired this week of people telling you how amazing a singer you are."

"Does anyone ever get tired of praise? When I'm in front of an audience, their reaction tells me I'm good, but afterwards ... life seems less somehow. It's something I'm goin' to have to push past though now that I've decided on my course."

"Good to see you've decided to be master of your own destiny," Gary said, standing up. "Dan, go pick the book we'll be readin'. I'll be down to your bedroom in a minute."

In sotto tones so that her voice wouldn't carry to Dan, Mavis said, "I'm goin' to have to find a way of dealin' with the post-gig flatness and my loss of interest in the here and now. I've also got to work out how I'm goin' to do it all without shortchangin' Dan. After all, I am the only person in his life truly committed to him."

"I explained ..." Gary said. "You said you understood."

"Yeah, and I did, but it made me realise something. You're not his dad, Gary, though Dan and I saw you in that role. Your life is changin' as it should. I just have to be extra careful about the choices I make."

"I'm in Dan's life for good, Mavis." Gary's tone was clearly emotional.

Sarah joined the conversation, cutting out Mavis' response, "Gary's committed to Dan, Mavis. He's in it for the long haul. He's made that clear to me, and I get it though I have to admit I was jealous before." Directing her next comment to Gary, "But you have to see Mavis' point, Gary. Like in other families when the dad figure doesn't live in the house and has a different ... someone not the kid's mother in his life, the custody parent has an added responsibility." Back to Mavis, "And that's why I think you should not only be in the band but commit to it. The money that could come from it might mean you could quit working at the Ford dealership and have more …, and this isn't a criticism so don't take it that way, more quality to your lives."

"Gary!" Dan called from his bedroom.

"Comin', Dan."

"Want a cuppa?" Mavis asked in a bid to fill the awkward silence.

"Sure."

Sarah followed Mavis into the kitchen and stood with the preparation bench between them. "Gary says you and Kate appreciate directness and honesty."

"We do, mostly, if it isn't too unpleasant."

Sarah took a deep breath. "Okay then. When I started dating Gary, I didn't understand his relationship with you and Kate; I'm still not sure I do." Sarah waited in the hope that Mavis would explain what Gary could not. Silence followed so Sarah picked up the conversation thread. "I certainly didn't understand his bond to Dan."

"What's there to get? Gary has a big heart and connects to Dan. Dan adores him."

"Yes," Sarah said thoughtfully, "adoration is hard to put aside. You're right there." Another silence. "Anyway, as Gary and I became closer, I didn't like the way he measured out his time between us. I thought if he really cares about me, I should come first and definitely before all of you. So I put him under pressure to give more time to me."

A succession of Friday night images came to Mavis: Dan's tear-stained face, his refusal to go to bed, his insistence that Gary would come, the difficulty she'd had in getting Dan settled when tiredness overtook him. "Why are you tellin' me this?"

"The week before the Keimera Show, Gary made it quite clear that any life with him involves Dan, you, and Kate and that he shouldn't have to choose. That he would not choose. I just wanted you to have confidence in what he says now. Also, I'd like to be included more rather than be on the fringe of the group. Your involvement in our lives won't work while I'm on the out."

The kettle boiled shrilly.

During the business of tea making, Mavis considered what to say. "Thanks for the background to what's been goin' on. Gary's relationship with Kate and me goes back a long way. Kate used to be an outsider and now she's not. Did you know Gary used to call Kate, Ken?"

"No."

"They met through the Surf Life Saving Association. I think he didn't like her because of her ballsiness and her feminist values, but he," Mavis put an emphasis on the next word, "*tolerated* her because one of our other friends liked her. Gary got used to her though, and they got closer through sharing lifesaving stuff. Personally, I didn't decide one day, I'll make Kate a friend. It just changed through the give-and-take of life. I think that's how someone moves from the fringe into the group, but it takes time."

"So, you're saying ….?"

"Gary cares for you and so Kate and I *accept* you. With time, things might develop into more for all of us. I warn you though, do anything that hurts my kid like he has been these past few months and … I don't know what, but it'll be ugly!"

Silence.

"Well, Dan's ready for lights out," Gary strolled into the room. "He's waitin' for his goodnight kiss, Mavis." Taking in the tension, he struck his Mickey Mouse casual pose. "Things okay in here?"

"Sarah and I are on the same page, Gary. Thanks for giving Dan back Friday nights. I'll see you out. I've a son to see to." With the perfunctory exchange of kisses, the adults parted. Mavis waved them off from her front door. "Have fun you two."

Gary felt more than uncomfortable about the uncharacteristic dismissal. He'd expected to share the rest of that evening with Mavis and Sarah in the way he and Kate had shared past evenings with Mavis after Dan went to bed. Gary's concerned conversation with Sarah carried as a muffled blur to Mavis as she watched them depart.

* * *

"I formed the band so I'm the leader," Tony O'Brien said to Mavis as she sat with the other three guys in the band around her kitchen table the next Saturday afternoon. She was home alone; Dan had gone crabbing with his grandpa while the tide was out. "Sure, I consult the guys about the music, and I negotiate where and when we're playin', but I make the final call. After costs and payment of the roadie and the soundie, we share what's left equally."

Mavis noted the silent interaction of the other members. "Is that the way it was with your other singers?"

"Well … no, it wasn't, but that didn't work out, and I don't want the troubles I had before repeated."

"Hmmm," was all Mavis said and sat in silent contemplation.

"What's wrong with what I'm offering?"

"It won't work, not for me anyway. I'm the performer, you said as much yourself. The band backs me. The singer makes the group; it's not the other way around." She waited.

"You want a bigger cut of the money?" Tony asked. The other guys looked resigned but didn't speak.

"No … *If* I become your singer, then I perform material that I want to sing, feel like singing, and that I think fits the occasion. Oh, and that includes sound levels."

"Sound?" interrupted the drummer. He had brown hair with bleached tips and was athletically thin. He wore well-worn sneakers, jeans and a black T-shirt. His right upper arm was banded in a single tattooed line paralleled by a simple, art nouveau styled line. "No way! The drums dictate the stage volume, and then it goes from there."

"Yeah, we've got to be loud," the bass guitarist added, a solid built, honey-haired young man with a close cropped full beard and a preference for everything denim. "Loud generates energy. Loud is better!"

"Neither of you know shit about sound!" Tony said. "Loud makes us like most run-of-the-mill bands, a big blur. Look at the Show Society dinner dance audition. We got the gig because we had good sound levels, and we drew the crowd. I'm with Mavis on this."

"I'm not *in* if I don't have the call over sound and the material,"

Mavis concluded. In the face of their resistance, her confidence fluctuated, but she maintained her outward poise. She was so close to a way out of her current predicament. Was who had control really worth the risk they'd walk away from the table?

The drummer knocked back his can of coke. "Would you get me another and dump this in your rubbish. Recyclin' I assume?"

Mavis studied him before answering. Was this a subtle move to exert male dominance? She had been down that track with Terry. "I don't think there's any more coke. I don't normally buy it. There's coffee though. Help yourself. And yes, I've been recyclin' ever since my son's school excursion to the rubbish tip."

The bass guitarist sat sullenly as the drummer crossed to the kitchen.

The keyboard player, Steve, laughed. "My nephew came over all environmentalist after that excursion too. He's loud about it when we forget to recycle."

From the kitchen, the drummer said, "I'm in luck. One can left. Tough luck, fellas."

"Mavis, can I have a minute with the guys?" Tony asked.

"Sure, I've a load of washing to hang out."

With the air-spring controlled shut of the screen door after Mavis had left, Tony glared at the drummer and bass guitarist. "Are you guys aimin' for mediocre or what? There are a lot of musos out there who will always be butchers, panel beaters, or brickies. Is that what you want? Can't you see that Mavis is the real thing? Do you have the memory of a goldfish? The Show Society's dance was more than a good gig; she made us look and sound amazin'. Damn, we were amazin' because our sound was about us listenin' to her and each other! With her, we have a chance of bein' something other than what we are. Without her …" Shaking his head, Tony stood. "Bottom line; you two are replaceable." He assumed their capitulation and crossed to the screen door. "Mavis, you ready?" When an answer was not immediately forthcoming, he called again. "Mavis?"

"In a tick …"

Before her return, the drummer said, "Okay, I'm in, but I want you to book more rock gigs and give away the other stuff." With grandiose hand gestures, he mimed one of his signature drum beat sequences, making it the exclamation point to his capitulation.

"Yep," was the reply of the bass player.

Tony looked questioningly at Steve, the keyboard player. "Rock bands are a dime a dozen, especially cover bands. We play what the money demands. If you want out, now's the time. There's the door."

"You know me, Tony. It's about the money. I'll go with Mavis as long as she delivers."

Backlit, Mavis re-entered her house. She put her overfull washing basket on the cane lounge and used the process of folding and sorting to conceal her concern.

"It's agreed; you have the final say over sound, and I'll give serious consideration to any music you want."

"Consideration is not enough, Tony."

"I'm open to negotiation and compromise if you are."

Drummer and bass player exchanged an expressive look missed by the others.

"Fair enough. There's one other thing, Tony, I've got a kid to be considered so I have to agree to where and when before you confirm any booking."

The bass player stood in obvious frustration. "I'm dyin' for a smoke."

"Not in my house." Mavis pushed away the growing dislike she felt for him.

"I'll be outside then."

"As I said before, Mavis, I negotiate gig bookings with the band but make the final call."

Steve, who was dabbling in the idea of facial hair and sported the unshaved look in fashion at that time, said, "We've all got constraints of one kind or another." He wore a red T-shirt, jeans and sandals.

Tony looked around his group. "It shouldn't be a problem, Mavis. Anything else?"

Mavis frowned. "Shouldn't or won't?"

"My issue," said the bass player from outside the screen door where he now stood, "is that none of us have much money. Last year when the van carryin' the gear broke down, none of us had the money to get it fixed. That cost us in more ways than one! How about we put aside ten percent from each gig for unexpected costs, then pay the roadie, soundie, and divide up the rest?"

There was general agreement with his suggestion.

Having crossed to the kitchen tidy bin, Steve dropped his coke can in it. "So, Mavis, since we're settin' a new course, what type of music do you like? What's your preferred style?"

"She's already agreed to perform music to fit the occasion," Tony said, "and you know what *that* means already."

"Play for the payin' market." The drummer put his feet up on Mavis' coffee table.

The returning bass guitarist and the keyboard player spoke as one although they took turns in the listing. "Cash in on balls, weddings, festivals, the pub and restaurant scene, and corporate events." They crossed paths before sitting.

The drummer sniffed disparagingly. "Small arena stuff."

"I don't have a definite singin' style yet, Steve. I'm versatile and still learnin' about singin' from bein' so. I'm not closed to my parents' favourites like Sinatra, Clooney, and James, but I prefer Chrissie Hynde, Shirley Manson, Alanis Morrisette, Mariah Carey ... At the moment, you could say I'm a mimic, a chameleon."

The drummer nodded slowly, his right cheek pulsed.

As the drummer was outside her line of sight, Mavis missed the expression he directed at the bass player, that of someone tasting a very sour lemon. She did see the bass player's reaction though. She diverted her gaze from him to the drummer. "And I'd prefer it if you took your feet off my table. As for material, I'm cool with your current set lists, fellas. Chart songs and past rock hits, right?"

"A lot of the time, but I follow the money trail for gigs and that means we have to be flexible. I think that's about it. Two full-on weekends of practice and then we're back into it."

"Even though I'm a quick study, that's not enough time."

"It's all we can give you. I'm *not* prepared to lose money *or* have us develop a no-show reputation."

"Later, when we've gelled, I'd like us to play some of my material. I write R&B, Country Rock, pop-like songs which mix a variety of genres—"

"*Much* later." The drummer knocked back his coke and put the empty can down on the floor beside where he sat.

"*If* we think it's good enough." The bass player had returned to the sitting area but had remained standing.

"That's a wrap for the arvo then. Thanks for hostin' this, Mavis."

Following his band members, Steve, the keyboardist, picked up the discarded empty cans and set them on the kitchen counter. "My sister and nephew have trained me pretty good." The last to leave the cottage, he added, "A word from the wise, there's not much chance we'll be doin' your music. The guys are havin' enough difficulty bein' flexible."

"Why?"

"I'm no spoiler. You'll see soon enough."

Chapter 5

Beset by monthly bills as well as those from the May quarterly cycle, Mavis sat at her kitchen table that unseasonably hot, autumn Sunday morning, tired and overwhelmed. She hated working out money. Things were always so tight. She regretted her past reliance on credit cards. She had seen them as buoys to get her through rough financial seas, but now they were a weight pulling her under.

Dan's father, Terry, did not pay child maintenance. He did not know of Mavis' pregnancy let alone Dan's existence. She had been glad when he had taken a promotion and moved to the Canberra region six years or so ago. Out of sight had meant she had felt safe.

A year after Dan's birth, Mavis had unexpectedly encountered Terry in Keimera's main street. He'd come home to see his mother, a woman Mavis had never met. Wanting reality to be what she'd always hoped for rather than what it was, Mavis had considered telling Terry about Dan as she approached. *Everyone is capable of a change for the better*, she told herself. She half expected an apology from him for past violence. She believed in happy endings then, delayed though it might be.

Standing on the curb adjacent to where his car was parked at forty-five degrees, their talk had been of inconsequential matters. Faced with the reality of his indifference and his obvious desire to get away, Mavis had remained silent about Dan.

Terry's angry outburst as they parted, when an emerging passenger's car door hit his driver's door, unearthed trauma Mavis had thought buried after their breakup. It was in that instant, she decided he would never know about Dan. *Better not to have a father than be scarred by the man's violent temper or worse.*

Walking away, her pace matched her heartbeat, the deep bass notes of a past depression drowned out what song there had been in Mavis' current life. As the following weeks passed, the melody in her life grew increasingly louder, but the bass notes continued to sound.

Pushing thoughts of Terry aside, Mavis reworked her finances. She was grateful for the welfare payment to assist single parents, pittance though it was. It was better than nothing.

Having lived from pay-to-pay for years, the prospect of a healthier financial situation lifted her spirits, tired though she was. With the income from the band, she would be able to put money aside in anticipation of bills rather than be slogged when they came in. She hoped the years of sacrifice were over.

The mathematics needed to work out her new budget confounded her, mostly because she was tired. Her immediate problem: how to cover her current bills, some of which had been unexpected because Dan had been ill with a respiratory tract infection that had led to an asthmatic attack and a host of expensive medications and medical treatment. On top of that, after Dan had recovered, he'd had a growth spurt and with that had come the pressing need for new clothes and shoes.

Regrettably, her two credit cards were maxed out. She hated always having to rob Peter to pay Paul. No way though, would she ask her parents for financial assistance. She'd rather go without herself than impose further on their goodwill.

A knock at the front door followed by Kate's entrance worked as a signal for Mavis to put aside her paperwork till later.

"Geez, Mavis, you look pale," Kate said. "How's Dan?"

"Improvin'. He's not wheezing anymore. Dr Tim says that's a good sign. We had our first unbroken night's sleep last night. Pull up a chair."

Kate watched Mavis bundle up the paperwork. "Look, I've interrupted you. I can call back later so you can get this done."

"I wasn't in the mood for it anyway. Coffee or tea?"

"Tea."

Tired, Mavis waited in silence at the bench for the kettle to boil. Kate flicked through the latest edition of *The Women's Weekly* bought on her way to Mavis', in companionable silence.

Mavis returned to the table with two unmatched mugs. "First chance we've had to talk about Sarah winning Royal Easter Show Girl."

"I expected Gary to be chuffed rather than indifferent. Do you know what's going on with him … them?"

"Not really. I've got more important things on my mind than Gary's love life."

"Anything you want to talk over?"

"Definitely not my usual struggle to make ends meet."

"The money from the band is helping, isn't it?"

"It's made a difference." Mavis ran her hands through her hair, and held her hair back at the crown. She exhaled. "Seriously, I don't want to talk about money. I am worried though. You sure you're open to serious chat?"

"Just go for it, Mavis."

"I've only recently come to understand how much Gary is a part of Dan's and my life. Sarah's influence over him … I don't want to bitch about that but … I'm worried about the future now whereas I never used to think about it."

"It's because you have options for the first time in a long time."

"Maybe … No, it's nothing to do with me having options now." Mavis struggled to control a surge of emotion. "I've begun to realise what life without Gary would be like. If I lose you too … Sorry, I'm just emotional today."

"That's not going to happen. Not with me. Not with Gary. You're just tired, and it seems you're like me, tiredness has skewed your view. Go and have a sleep."

"I can't. Dan's up. He's playin' in his bedroom."

"Can't your parents watch him?"

"They're out for the day. They help me out to a point, but Dan's not theirs to raise."

"Then I'll watch over him and have some Dan time as well. You'll feel better once you're refreshed. If you sleep most of the day that's fine. I'll take Dan over to the park to play if he's up to it, or I can read and he can play Lego here. If you don't mind, I'll take him with me to visit my dad after lunch if you're not up. We'll stop by the surf club on the way back. Don't feel that this has to be a nap rather than a decent sleep."

"I don't know … You'll need to take his Ventolin inhaler and the spacer with you. Are you comfortable with that?"

"Of course I am. You've already been over Dan's management plan with Gary and me."

"I appreciate your offer, Kate, but …"

"You're frightened to let him out of your sight?"

Mavis nodded, unable to speak.

"It's important you control your fear, Mavis, so that it doesn't stop Dan from having an active life. I promise you, he'll be safe with me."

Tiredness won out with Mavis. "I really could do with a sleep. Dr Tim said the same thing about letting Dan get back into life and for me to control my fear."

"So you'll let me take him?"

"Yes. Thank you so much for this."

"You go to bed. I'll get Dan."

* * *

Living a few kilometres out of Keimera on a five-acre block, Kate's father was a powerfully built man. He was in the yard when Kate drove through the property's open steel gates and down the blue gravel driveway. He wore work boots, work trousers, a long-sleeved, beige, heavy-duty cotton shirt, and a broad-brimmed cattleman's hat.

The hat harkened back to his days as a stockman in the Northern Territory before Kate's mother's illness when Kate was twelve, which necessitated a return to Keimera and extended family support. In the intervening years, he had traded stock work for excavation.

The picture to her parents' frame, Kate had felt keenly the death of her mother in 1992. She had relied heavily on her father during the mourning period, and he in turn on her. Now she felt the weight of her responsibility for him as he aged as well as a fear of his passing. It was with relief that she noted his continuing vigour whenever she visited which, though not daily, was regular.

Having been beckoned over by her father who was working on irrigating his extensive gardens, Kate and Dan crossed to him. As they arrived, the man stood up satisfied with a job well done.

"G'day, Princess." He kissed his daughter on the cheek and then held her in a brief hug.

"Nice to see you again, Dan. Good to see you're feeling a lot better."

Dan extended his hand in greeting, as his grandfather had taught him to do, but Robert bear-hugged him instead, much to Dan's delight.

As he was returned to his feet, Dan said, "I *so* like comin' out here, Uncle Robert."

"You've arrived just in time to see how the irrigation works on my gardens. You'll love the pop-up sprinklers, Dan." Her father turned on the water works.

Dan laughed on cue as the sprinklers miraculously appeared out of the tall stalks upon which they were positioned across the extensive gardens near them.

"And there's more! Look at how well my flush valve works." He elaborated on the function of the valve before flicking it on. Unfortunately, he had misjudged the angle of the valve and not considered the pressure of water that would come from it given the sprinklers were still working. A massive burst of water shot from the valve, hit the ground, and muddy water gushed back onto the watchers. Dan, quick in his reflexes, stepped behind Kate who, like her father, took the brunt of what was a muddy soaking. Everyone laughed.

"And that, Dan, is what is called hydraulic power. Just as well you leave clothes here, love," her father said. "It's times like these ..."

"Dan, would you like a Mintie while Dad and I change? A cuppa afterwards, Dad?"

"Have I ever said no ..."

"Done!"

Some time later, the trio sat on the southern verandah overlooking the small spring-fed dam on the property. Dan listened in fascination as Kate's father, in response to a question from Dan, waxed lyrically about hydraulic power.

The afternoon passed with Kate and Dan helping her father stop a high-pitched squeal caused by an air leak in the float valve of his bore-fed, irrigation tank. Kate loved these shared times of working with her father as he passed on practical knowledge to her. It seemed Dan too enjoyed the closeness of shared experience.

As Kate readied for their departure, a visitor arrived: a dark-haired woman unknown to her.

Her father and the woman exchanged a warm greeting, quite different from that between father and daughter. By her skin texture, the woman definitely belonged to Robert Denford's generation. Her age though had been significantly stretched, with the help of a cosmetic surgeon, beyond the literal facts of her birth date. She was dressed stylishly in white sneakers, white jeans, a figure hugging green blouse, and what looked like a matching white jacket which she had slung over her arm.

"You're early," Kate's father said.

After introductions and some small talk that revealed her father had a long standing acquaintance with the woman, Kate departed. She was unsettled that her dad had kept the woman a secret.

Perhaps not a secret, she thought later in the drive back to town, *there must be lots of people he knows that I don't. But what if the woman was more than that?*

Their kiss in greeting, awkward though it had seemed to her, suggested this might be a possibility. Kate didn't know what she felt about that.

"Next stop the surf club, Dan."

* * *

Keimera Surf Lifesaving Club was situated on the surf beach south of Keimera harbour. Upgraded due to generous donations from a few well-funded families in the region, it was the envy of other clubs down the south coast. The Surf Lifesaving Movement relied on an army of volunteers and their passion to keep the beaches patrolled and safe.

As Kate parked, she noted Gary's car further down the line. She found him in the watch-room, something similar to that of air traffic controllers'. There was a sense of urgency there.

Gary spoke to Kate. "Just had a phone call from a lady off Rocky Flats Point. She thinks one of the rubber duckies (the uninitiated to club slang knew them as the emergency inflatable rescue boats or IRBs) has engine problems. She says they've been driftin' hopelessly for a while. No … can't raise them on the radio. Either it's out of range or someone forgot to charge it up from duty yesterday … again!"

"I thought we'd fixed that issue." Kate moved to look at the tide charts.

"The tide will be on the turn soon," one of the men on duty said.

"Another duckie has been despatched to see what's what," Gary added.

They watched the distant scene as the emergency duckie bounced over the waves of the returning tide, water clearly spraying high into the air, bow pointed skyward. Tense tens of minutes passed before the team reached the stranded crew.

The radio came to life. "IRB Keimera 2 to base. Everything's okay here. We're towing them back now. Over."

"Roger that. Anyone overboard? Over."

"Their radio was flat so Birdie swam to shore and is hoofing it back to base to raise the alert. Over."

"Thanks. Base Out."

In the watch-room, one of the other men on duty, who had been in the background of the scene, said, "Speak of the devil."

The small group turned to see Ralph Bird, red faced, his clothes dried from the heat of the day, with a can of coke in his hand. "My crew's stranded off Rocky Flats Point. We got too close to the reef. The swell is big there, and the motor got swamped. We drifted hopin' we could get it started, but it's deader than Harvey's love life."

The people present chuckled appreciatively.

"It's okay, mate." Gary put down his binoculars. "A local alerted us. A rescue boat has been despatched and is already towin' them back in."

"Bloody hot walk back!" Birdie said. "I trust, Kate, that you'll sort out this problem once and for all. This could've been a lot worse than it turned out to be today."

"It will be, Birdie. C'mon, Dan, I've a bit of paperwork to complete and then we'll be off."

Following Kate, Gary said, "Unless the crews are called to front the executive and explain their actions, this problem will continue."

"My thoughts too. Systemically there are two problems. Birdie's team should've done a radio check before leaving to make sure their radio worked. The previous shift should've checked to see that the charger was working and the radio they replaced in the wall rack was positioned properly so it was recharged."

"And how come no one saw the red low power light on the radio or the lack of the green light? "

"I know, Gary, I've considered this from all angles. I'll make sure the problem is resolved once and for all even if it means giving some people fuel for more bitchin' within the club." Privately, she thought, *Dealing with so many alpha males is such a headache!*

"Lesser blokes have mishandled stuff like this, givin' rise to factional war, but you, Ken, have been adept at keepin' the lid on things and at improvin' practice. In-fighting is part of life in a club. Don't sweat it."

There had been a time when the nickname, Ken, had stung Kate because it attributed an unwarranted butchness to her in the first days of her joining the movement. She had worn the nickname with good-natured humour, understanding that the all-male surf lifesaving clubbies misunderstood her breed of liberated women.

In the intervening years, though, the nickname had become

personal, a pet name between Gary and her, an intimate expression of affection by him that signalled their mateship and the understanding that now existed between them.

Gary followed Kate to the little cubicle space that functioned as her Club Captain's area. While Kate worked through some paperwork, Gary said to Dan, "You're lookin' a lot better, Dan, than you have the last few weeks."

The boy nodded, distracted by an ice block that Kate had given him from the club fridge when they had passed it.

Gary tousled Dan's hair. "What brings Dan here with you today? Mavis okay?"

"She's fine, just really tired. She needed a break so I've got him for the day. You've had a good day, haven't you, mate?"

Dan nodded as he licked the trickle of melting ice block off his fingers before adding, "I don't get ice blocks very often and never ones like this. I always have a really good time with you, Auntie Kate."

Gary waited in silence while Kate finished her work. "You joinin' me on a run later today?"

"Do I do that anymore? What about Sarah? Doesn't she run with you nowadays?"

"Sarah … she gave it a shot once, but runnin' on sand is not her style. The surf, sweat, and the sun are all no-goes in her book. Besides, Sarah couldn't give me a real run for my money, whereas you, Ken, can."

"Sounds like you might not measure up."

"Trust me, I will."

"We'll see. Meet here at four?"

"Suits me." Gary paused before adding, "I've decided to cool it with Sarah."

"Oh … how did she take that?"

"With a lot of talk about her. The key word with Sarah is ME. I regret bucklin' to her demands now."

"Oh?" Kate waited for more insights but none were forthcoming. "C'mon, Dan, time to go," Kate said. At the doorway, she stopped and looked mischievously over her shoulder, "And I'll see what sort of stayin' power you have, Gary, tonight." She winked at him and was gone.

*   *   *

"Mummy, we're home!"

Mavis looked up from the cane lounge on which she sat with Tony O'Brien. She had been looking over Tony's proposed schedule. "Did you have a good day?" After Dan's enthusiastic reply, she said to Kate, "Thank you so much. I slept until two and got up just before Tony arrived."

"G'day, Kate, Dan."

"Hello, Mr O'Brien"

"Tony."

"I had such a good time, Mummy. I even had an ice block. Not the icy pole kind but one with swirls of colour and—" The sound of a car pulling up in the driveway interrupted Dan. "Gran and Pop are home. Can I tell them about today? Can I?"

"Go, Dan, but let them get inside the house before you start with your adventures."

"I'll catch you later in the week, Mavis. I've got to run, literally."

The women exchanged a sisterly farewell kiss. Kate left.

"Tony, I'm fine bein' booked most Friday and Saturday nights for the pub and restaurant gigs, but not all of them, and definitely not in Sydney. As for rehearsin' midweek ... forget it! I've got Dan to consider. Why not have a whole weekend off regularly and really rehearse then?"

"It's how *we* do things."

"But it wasn't handed down to you on stone tablets, was it? As you've said, *you* call the shots. Can't you-?"

"No."

Floored, Mavis leant back on the cane lounge. She considered her options, limited though they were, in search of an answer. Rising from the lounge and crossing to the kitchen bench, Mavis poured herself another mug from her drip filter coffee maker. Holding up the pot, she said, "Tony?"

"Yeah, I'll have another."

Acutely aware that she needed a band if she was going to break free of her current situation, Mavis completed the small business of coffee refills. In every scenario, she was reliant on others. She returned to the lounge.

Tony lifted his mug to his lips, considering Mavis over the rim before he drank. The band needed her if they were to become a stand-out in the small arena of music. Band front man aside, she was only one fifth of the band. She had to learn her place. "We're a better band with you, no doubt about it, but I've conceded heaps already. So much so the guys' noses are out of joint. There has to be an end to it, and we've reached it."

"Well, I can't do the Sydney gigs. Not yet. Dan and I have to get a system set up for the workload you want. Even for a reduced load. I need time to sort things out." The air seemed to have left Mavis' body. Her dream, like a hot air balloon, had been launched, begun its ascent, and soared briefly on air currents. She'd thought all she had to do was climb into the basket, hold onto the ropes, and be carried away. She'd erred, and this unexpected current threatened to shred the balloon. She stood, aware she needed to play Tony coolly, conscious she needed to act boldly. "I guess that's it then. I'll see you off." Her heart was pounding so hard she could hear it in her ears.

"Maybe not." Tony remained ensconced in the armchair. "You know we've been booked locally for six weeks – spinoff from the Show Society's dinner dance. You've got that time to get your act together but, after that, we travel. Can't you rely on your parents for this?"

Mavis sat on the edge of the lounge, facing Tony. "No, I chose to have Dan. He's my responsibility, not theirs. They're prepared to take him nights and during the day now and again." One handed, she rubbed her forehead. Neither she nor Marg had envisioned Mavis travelling far afield let alone the impact of that travel on what Marg called 'Dan's time'. The quiet despair of the last few years reached for her. Could she live the rest of her life as she had been living? She couldn't, not now she'd glimpsed another world, fleeting though that vision had been. "If you make concessions for me this year, Tony, like dropping the Sydney gigs, I'll step up to the plate next year."

After a pause, "All right. I can give a bit more although the fellas won't like it. The new year starts with the Sydney Festival and the Parkes Elvis Festival in January. We'll aim for Sydney weekend gigs after that. In addition, we'll do the Goulburn Blues Festival in February, the Kiama Jazz and Blues Festival in March and so on. Every one of those bookings is a weekend."

Mavis regretted giving Tony a carte blanche. *How can I be away every weekend?* "The Elvis Festival? Seriously? Isn't that a light year away from what we want to be as a band? Besides, Parkes is so far away."

"C'mon, four hundred or so kilometres isn't that far, not in Australia. How can you say no to celebratin' an international cultural icon like Elvis? The festival is so much more than fun, and it's a chance to indulge in the lighter side of the business, and it's easy money to boot with an uncritical audience." Sensing Mavis' hesitation Tony said, "I'm all shook up that you're rulin' that festival out." He waited. "Don't be cruel, Mavis." He saw her suppress a smile. "The festival has somethin' for everybody. Attendees can't help fallin' in love with the whole idea of an Elvis festival. C'mon, I'm runnin' out of Elvis song titles, you hard headed woman."

"Stop! Okay, okay, Dan is on holidays. It'll work if I can bring him."

"Great!" Tony's satisfaction was reflected in his smile.

"Did Elvis really sing 'Hard Headed Woman'?"

"Yes, he did. It was part of the soundtrack for his 1958 movie *King Creole*. It was also released as a single and hit number one on the Billboard charts in the USA."

"Oh, my God, Tony! You're an Elvis tragic!"

"And not ashamed to admit it ... Y' know, Mavis, the more gigs we do this year, the sooner you can chuck in the job at the Ford dealership."

"Enough! I can't do it at bullet train speed."

"I just want *you* to know where I'm comin' from. I've got the connections for a lot of work *now*. If we're not seen and heard, other performers will grab the places I've carved out. There are hundreds of musos and singers out there all competin' for a finite sized audience. You've seen the talent in the malls at Christmas and during the other holidays."

"I have. Fantastic groups of young performers, all singin' and dancin' their hearts out. All of them hopin' for a big break, but I can't change my particular circumstance with the snap of my fingers."

"And I meant what I said earlier, but I've overlooked some extraneous factors." Tony was glad the rest of his band weren't present; they'd resent being described as such. "As I said, the work is there, but it won't be for long. Are you certain about Sydney ...?" He read Mavis' expression correctly. "If we walk away from this just because the goin' gets tough, what ... what sort of role model is that for your son?"

"You're right of course, but don't try to manipulate me. This issue is dusted and shelved. If you can't let it go, there's the door, Tony ..."

"Look, Mavis, I'm a man of my word. I'll trim the schedule back to weekend bookings and cut out the Sydney scene until next year. Practice midweek is a fixture. Really, goin' out for that is no different than you datin'. Your parents babysit for you then, don't they? It's just a matter of puttin' your love life on the back burner."

Dating, Mavis thought. *Another unresolved issue with her parents.*

At that point in their discussion, Dan returned. He sat next to his mother, aware of her tension, "You okay, Mummy?" He leant into her, physical contact still an important link between them, especially when strangers were present.

"Yes, Dan. Why don't you go tidy your room. It looks like a tornado hit it."

Dan trudged to his room.

"Pick your feet up, Dan."

"Well, Mavis?"

"Okay, Tony, I'm in." Mavis walked him to the door and watched his car reverse down the driveway. She then returned to the lounge where she flopped down and slumped.

Half an hour passed in uneasy silence. She wanted a way out of her current circumstance, a different road to the one she'd been on, but feared that any deal with Tony was built on shifting sands.

Unable to throw off her jangled state, Mavis decided to walk it off. In the past, walking had helped her find a way to deal with her problems. She called Dan to her. "You feel up to a walk around the Point or would you rather stay with Gran and Pop?"

"Can I run some of the way?" Then in reaction to his mother's expression, Dan added, "I can breathe real good now, Mummy. I could even huff and puff Gran's house down."

"That good, eh?"

Dan nodded.

"What about you walking with me today? Let's leave running til another day."

Dan grimaced.

"But you *can* play on the gym equipment in the park."

Dan brightened.

Mavis chose to walk south along the peninsula bordering the showground, across the adjacent parkland, and toward Surf Beach. She stopped on the grassy rise overlooking the beach and decided to rest while Dan entertained himself on the recently upgraded exercise equipment designed for the community as well as children. The council had tired of the damage to playgrounds caused by adult sized teenagers who still liked to play on it. The entire area had been converted to an exercise space that adults interested in fitness could use as much as the local children. Kate and Mavis used it regularly too at the end of each of their weekly walk and run sessions.

Before her stretched five kilometres of sand. The waves from the incoming tide thundered onto the beach. The tonal quality of the waves breaking over the rocky ledge immediately below her contrasted to that of the waves on the sand. In the distance, Mavis could see families, couples, and a number of runners making the most of the late afternoon and the respite from the unseasonal heat of the day. Sometimes, like this day, the sight of couples made her feel her aloneness. While Mavis saw the scene, she did not focus on it. She inhaled and tried to relax.

"Mummy, look what I can do?" Dan hung upside down on the horizontal bars.

"Very good, Dan."

"What can you do, Mummy?"

"I'm a bit old for gym equipment, Dan, but I used to be able to …. What the heck …" Mavis kicked off her shoes and joined Dan on the bars. Hanging upside down, her hair showing the effects of gravity, she added, "Just like two possums, Dan."

"Why do they like hanging upside down?"

"I don't know for sure, but I guess so they can get to food that's out of their reach. The ground isn't safe for them like it is for humans. Too many faster moving predators."

Dan changed position in a sequence of lithe moves and crossed to the nearby balancing beam. Mavis considered a dismount she'd been able to do in her childhood but opted for a simple swing and drop to the ground instead. She crossed to the balancing equipment. "It's time we headed back, Dan."

"Can you do this, Mummy?" Dan walked with balanced ease along the beam.

With her palms on top of the beam and fingers gripping the sides, Mavis mounted it. As agile as her son, she walked the beam, turned, and then said, "And this is called a tuck jump dismount, Dan." She stood in the middle of the beam facing out toward the sea. Raising her arms to the side and then upward and forward, with legs together, she pulled her knees into a tuck position toward her chest as she tumbled forward, and then landed.

"Wow!"

"I know."

"Can you show me how?"

"If I do, I don't want you trying this on the beam without a supervising adult present and not until you can do it easily on the ground. We'll practice it together so I know you can do it safely. Now, hop down, and I'll start teaching you how to do it."

On the thick lawn, they played cartwheels and tumbling until they were both out of breath. They lounged on the grass against each other.

"We'll come over here tomorrow, Dan, and practice tuck tumbling some more. For now though, it's time to go home."

Holding hands, the pair returned the way they came.

On the peninsula rise and overlooking the beach, Dan said, "Mummy, look at the seagulls balancing in the air."

"They're not so much balancing as hovering … like when you fly your kite." Standing there with her hair streaming behind her, Mavis enjoyed the bracing wind. She felt alive and that life again held possibilities for her. *Somehow, I'll make it all work.*

Looking down at the beach scene, Mavis focused on two runners who were racing south to north. There was something familiar about them. The man and woman seemed evenly matched. Slowly, the woman edged ahead. Then her running action changed into a sprint. At the same time, the man powered forward. In what seemed seconds, they were abreast before he moved on ahead, leaving her behind in an effortless sprint. He came to a stop about one hundred metres from Mavis and waited for his companion to reach him. When she did, she bent over puffed.

Recognition came as Mavis watched the couple interact.

"Mummy, isn't that—?"

"Time to go home, Dan." She took hold of his hand and tugged him after her. She didn't feel like talking to either of her friends about her situation.

"But, Mummy—?"

"No buts, Dan, this time I mean it. We're goin' home."

Meanwhile down on the beach, aware of his arousal from the exertion of the race, Gary deflected from Kate, splashing himself with the cold water. "Whew! I'm hot!" He flicked water at her. She laughed and reciprocated in kind. Their water playfulness turned into a chase game of sorts that ended with a collapse into a hug.

With the water lapping around her feet, Kate repressed the surge of emotion she felt for Gary. The heat from their body contact heightened her awareness of him. She felt her nipples harden. Embarrassed, she pulled away. She chided herself for misinterpreting the affection in his hug, his expression, and the intensity of their closeness. "C'mon, race you back," she said. Without waiting for his response, she was off, getting a good head start.

Puzzled again by what he had unexpectedly felt between them, Gary watched Kate sprint away. He could still feel the imprint of her body against his. *If she thinks she can get away from me that easily, she's wrong.* He took off after her, his heel kissing the ground after his initial forefoot made contact with it. With a rotation-free posture, Gary powered forward.Misjudging the waves awash around her feet, Kate was slowed by them. She looked back. With a whoop and a holler, she was off again.

When he was close enough, Gary tackled her. Down they went in the foaming surf. Laughing, he manoeuvred them into an embrace of sorts. The water lathed around them as it swelled toward the shore. For a moment, they clung together, intensely aware of one another.

Kate knew a moment of panic when she realised Gary might realise the truth about her feelings for him. "Geez, the water's cold!"

Gary gave her a hand up. "It looked better in that movie …what was it called?"

"I don't know …"

"You don't?" Gary registered Kate's shivering. "Sarah said it was every woman's favourite love scene … that it rated just behind *Casablanca*."

"I'm not into old movies, Gary. I'm not a romantic like Sarah … at least not in that way."

There was an awkward silence between them.

"You're shivering, Kate. Look, I've got some spare clobber and a towel back in the car. You need a change."

"So do you."

"Sadly, not enough gear for both of us."

Back at the car, Kate wriggled undressed while trying to stay wrapped within a large beach towel. Gary stood with his back to her.

"Okay, I'm done." Kate handed him the towel.

Gary stripped off his shirt, drying off as best he could.

Kate was keenly aware of him, his sculpted physique and glistening skin. She hoped he couldn't hear the thump of her heart.

Gary wrapped the towel around his lower torso. With it secure, he looked at Kate, appreciating the glow to her cheeks, the sparkle in her eyes. Without thinking, he fingered a few loose hairs that had worked free of her pony tail, back behind her ear.

Kate did not resist when Gary pulled her to him. He kissed her gently, one lip-tugging kiss after another. Kate felt his arousal. She relaxed into the moment and knew bliss for a time.

Approaching male voices intruded on Gary's consciousness. He released Kate, feeling her pull away from him, lingering though for a moment on a final kiss.

As the local men passed, Kate deflected from them, bending down to shield herself from their view. She busied herself with bunching her clothing together.

"G'day, Gazza. How's it hangin'?"

Gary leant back on his car. "No complaints, Bruce. Surf is lookin' pretty good."

"That's what we thought earlier. Pity you missed joinin' us on the waves."

As the men's voices faded, Kate stood. She watched the men depart before turning back to Gary. An awkward silence now separated them.

Gary struck his Mickey Mouse pose and laughed. For want of something say, he said, "You're a good kisser."

"Thanks. Consider the compliment returned."

Again there was an awkward silence.

"So what does this mean?" Kate asked.

"I don't know … it sort've just happened."

"Hmmm."

"Does a kiss have to mean something, Kate? I like how it has been with us three and Dan. I'm not sure I want that to change."

"That's what I'm thinking as well. I've been kissed by lots of guys, Gary, and it didn't mean anything. So I'm okay with this, but I don't want it happening again. I'm not an off-and-on again kind of woman."

Watching Kate drive off, Gary realised he didn't like the idea of Kate with other blokes. He wondered what he really felt and then decided to shelve the situation. *What happens happens,* he thought. He decided to catch up with her on Tuesday after work, telling himself it was to follow up on action taken about the club radios.

*   *   *

Monday and Tuesday of the next week passed without Mavis resolving how she felt about Tony, the other band members, and the path she'd chosen. She carried her worry throughout the day and mulled over it at night. Going to sleep easily, she was awake at two. *What am I really frightened about?* She fell back into a restless sleep around five. On Wednesday morning, she woke abruptly with the realisation that mild-mannered though Tony appeared, he was possibly a bully. *Should I risk getting involved with anyone who reminds me of Terry?*

On Wednesday, Kate stopped by Mavis' cottage after work for their routine, midweek walk around the northern and southern peninsulas. Dan stayed with his grandparents during that time.

After walking four kilometres with only monosyllabic responses to Kate's attempts at conversation, Kate said, "Something's wrong. What's up?"

"Nothing's wrong."

"Yes, there is. You've hardly said a word. I didn't even get a reaction when I filled you in on my latest workplace conquest. C'mon, you love romance; usually you're like a bloodhound when game has been scented. Yet, just now, nothing. What's going on? Dan seems well. So what is it?"

"Workplace conquest?"

"See! Your mind is elsewhere."

"Who's the conquest?"

"Just one of the medical reps. I told him I wasn't interested. Now what's up?"

"I'll tell you, but you're to be a soundin' board only. Right?"

"Okay, but you know I'm Little Miss Fix-it."

"I don't think it'll work out with Tony and the band."

"Oh, Mavis, you're not throwing the towel in ..."

"No, but ... I just don't trust Tony. He's a manipulator. I've decided I'll stay with his band as long as it works for me. It's clear there is a light year difference within the band over what type of music we should play. Do you think walkin' toward trouble with eyes wide open makes it safer?"

With her lips glued together, Kate nodded slowly.

"I know now I want a career in music and not just because it'll give me more money than I can earn at Ford. I'm happy doin' covers for a while, but eventually I want to perform my own music. This band isn't goin' to want to travel that road with me."

Keeping a lid on her questions and comments, Kate nodded again.

"Is this killin' you?"

Kate nodded, faster this time.

"One more thing and then you can talk. If Mum and Dad balk at babysittin', would you do it sometimes? Would Gary?"

"How can you ask?"

"I know—"

"I didn't mean it like that. Of course I will. Geez, I'm sure Gary will too. I bet he'll sleep over when you're away. Then, there's the Madisons. They adore you and Dan. If Gary and I can't, I'm sure they would."

"I can't ask Gary to sleep over. Besides, what about Sarah? I don't want her spending the night with him ... I've a responsibility to Dan."

"Don't give that as the reason for not asking him. He'd be shocked you thought he'd put his love life ahead of Dan's wellbeing. He said last Thursday he'd lost ground with you but didn't say how." Kate paused and waited for Mavis to recount what had happened between them. In the face of Mavis' silence and her sudden increase in their walking pace, Kate said, "He'd jump at this chance to repair whatever was damaged." Silence again as they walked. "Hey, you know he's cooled it with Sarah, don't you?"

"I didn't. His choice or hers?"

"The way he tells it, it was his."

"I was wonderin' how long he would be happy to orbit her and cut back on his own interests."

"I don't think relationships work when it's like that, Mavis. Do you?"

"I haven't a clue how healthy relationships work as you well know."

The women fell back into companionable silence.

After their workout on the exercise equipment on the southern peninsula, Mavis and Kate headed home. With Mavis' cottage in their sights, they raced the last two hundred metres. Kate as usual won.

"Comin' in for a cuppa, Kate?"

"Not tonight. I've a date."

"A surf club meeting or a guy?"

"A man. Before you ask, I don't know where it's headed, and I'd rather not …"

"Jinx it?"

"I'm generally not suspicious, but this time—"

"I get it. When it's really important to you, you'd rather take it one step at a time rather than imagine the possible life ahead."

"I've been thinking …"

"Always a dangerous thing."

Kate grinned at her, but said, "I don't think your parents would see it as a big ask if Dan slept over with them once and a while. They already cover after-school childcare."

"You're right, but Mum would say I'm making me the picture and all of you my frame."

"What's your answer to that?"

"To begin with, I'd agree with her. Then I'd point out the risk of me becomin' resentful if I continued to feel trapped by my circumstances now I have a way out. Dan and music are the joys in my life. I want to keep them untainted."

"You should point out it's unrealistic to expect you to live in a cupboard, labelled Mothers, and only have a life when Dan has need of you." Kate paused, realising there was relevance in this argument for her own situation with her father as well.

* * *

Looking at the crumpled note taken from Dan's schoolbag the next morning, Mavis discovered that not only was there a parent and teacher night at Dan's school that very night but that her son had booked her in to see his teacher at six.

"Dan, my man, you need to pass this sort of thing onto me."

"Sorry, Mummy, I forgot."

"Try to remember in future, okay, and I'll help by doin' a bag check with you every evening from now on."

The workday passed without anything to note about it.

When she arrived home at five thirty-five that afternoon, Marg, Mavis' mother, had a substantial tea ready so that Mavis could be fed and sped on her way.

Sitting outside the classroom on a chair designed for six year olds, Mavis felt like a giant. In the time that she waited, she felt the weight of parental responsibility. Other children from her son's class had their parents there as couples. With a sense of weighty purpose common to many single parents, Mavis knew she had to make music work for her. Her son would not be short-changed. His life would be enriched, not impoverished anymore.

Dan's overweight, frowsy red-haired, first grade teacher stood in the doorway. "Ms Mills, if you'd care to come in?"

After sitting in yet another small chair, Mavis felt the

disempowerment that different levels give. Dan's teacher seemed to look down at her.

"Your husband not with you?"

Mavis felt like saying, Cleary not! but answered, "No, it's just me," her tone masking her discomfort. Over six years later, it was still a sore point with her although she rarely told others this.

"Dan is such a wonderful child: bright, inquisitive. He's well ahead in literacy and numeracy. We'd like to put him into an accelerated class."

"Won't that be unsettling for him? Friends are so important to children at his age."

"At any age, Ms Mills. As it happens, Dan's three closest mates are being accelerated as well. At Dan's age, the rest of his classmates are just background scenery. If you think of his level of perception as a painting, Dan and those people important to him are painted in vivid, realistic detail whereas other people outside of his immediate personal sphere are painted in broad impressionistic strokes. Have a look at his paintings."

They crossed to the art wall. Mavis studied Dan's pictures and then looked at the artwork near Dan's. There were many more people in his paintings than in other children's.

"The size of people in kids' drawings is not about artistic perspective but about how important the people in a child's world are to the child. You and your husband figure largely and I assume," she said pointing to other smaller figures in Dan's drawing, "these are his grandparents and this his aunt."

Mavis frowned. The man was clearly Gary. *Did she need to recast Gary's role in their life?*

"Now look at his paintings of life here at school. You'll see the same thing applies. As long as the important details in his school life don't change, he'll be fine."

"That's Dan's godfather."

"Oh … Dan's father is not in the picture."

"No."

"Oh … Ooh! … Can I just say what a wonderful job you and your family are doing with Dan. I was amazed by him today."

"Oh?"

"We start our first research project next week. I've been interviewing all the children to work out their topics with them. I spoke with Dan today. His was a most unusual topic: hydraulic power. When I quizzed him about it, he was able to tell me excavators use oil pressure through special hoses to create the power for digging, bulldozing, and lifting. He also said it's used in car brakes so they can stop. I actually had to look up the details to make sure he was right."

"Was he?"

"He was."

"Oh. Is there anything more I can do to help him at school?"

"You seem to be providing him with excellent opportunities to mix with a variety of people who are enriching his knowledge base. Dan is a very secure and happy little boy. He knows he is loved. He knows he is important to the people whom he loves. Some parents are so insular. They want to be everything to their child. Such children are in danger of becoming emotionally stunted and excessively dependent on their parents. With that comes insecurity and fear of the wider world. I wish some of my other children were as lucky as Dan."

With her view reframed by Dan's teacher, Mavis left the classroom, the school, and returned home. After hearing Dan read, she put him to bed, and then rang Gary, followed by Tony.

Standing in her small bathroom, she brushed her hair the obligatory one hundred strokes. One stage of her life was ending. What would the next stage hold?

Chapter 6

The meat and potatoes business of being in a band consumed the first six weeks of that 1996 winter. Mavis' performance life became a montage.

The band played in packed restaurants where the space left for them was so small the drummer had to set up backwards on the stage so that Mavis could be positioned in his space, but one step in front. The guitarists crammed into the corners and the soundie to the side, out of line with the sound system. They played in old pubs where the band was tucked away in odd spaces out of sight-line with the audience. They played in crowded, medium-sized restaurants where the expectation was that they were background to the social setting. They played in pubs with low ceilings and acoustic problems that made good sound almost impossible. They played in pubs where the business of gambling competed with them for audience. They were interrupted by raffle draws. KENO results were announced over the top of them through the pub's PA system while all the time in the background, the chaotic sounds and intermittent flashing lights of the poker machines vied with them.

Sometimes, they played in spaces that worked for them. They travelled to anywhere and everywhere that Tony had booked a gig. Increasingly, it seemed he had followed the money trail without any thought to the material they would have to play, the venue, or their audience.

In July, at their first decent venue, the pub manager spoke to the band as they packed up. "The band is good. The singer is great. But, what you're delivering is not what I thought I'd booked. I expected the place to be blasting with music. The crowds who come here want to rock. If you want to keep the booking for the next four weeks, you need to get your material right."

"Exactly what I said we should be doin' for this crowd!" said the bass player after the manager had left.

Under pressure to deliver more rock music, rehearsals ate even more into weeknights. A playlist was cobbled together from the rock hits of the past ten years. The drummer and bass player were happy. Mavis was not. She seemed to be the only one who cared about having distinctive arrangements to enhance the calibre of their performance.

When Mavis finally made it home at night, Dan was already asleep. Her mother had little to say other than, "I'm only prepared to do this for a while, not forever."

In August with a change in venue and the need to change the style of music yet again, tensions within the band came to a head during midweek rehearsals. "Why did you book us into that shit-hole of a restaurant, man, for Friday and Saturday nights?" the drummer yelled. "I don't want to play this old stuff!" He stormed off, shadowed by the bass player.

"While I like Swing and Jazz in controlled doses, this isn't what I signed up for. I don't want to be a chameleon," Mavis said. Then anticipating Tony's reply, she added, "Yeah, yeah, I know. The money's in small arena stuff."

"I like the money," Tony and the keyboard player, Steve, said, not quite in unison.

"I do too, but this isn't …."

"Music's music," Steve added. "Hey, I trained as a classical pianist, but the money's not there for 'better than good' but not brilliant pianists."

"But 'better than good' pays really well in the music arena we're targeting, Mavis."

"I can see that Tony, but the audience is listening more to their sing-along than to us. I'd get more satisfaction out of this type of gig if you let me have a hand in the arrangements or if we played some of my own material."

"That's what you signed on for, Mavis, doin' covers and what's popular. Besides, it's what I could get. We'd have had to travel heaps more to get the work you and the guys want."

"So you did this deliberately?" Mavis deflected away from Tony.

"Our reputation is shot if ...."

Mavis held up her hand in Tony's face. "Yeah, I know, but I'm not happy. In the future ..."

"Let's just get through this, then we'll discuss it."

Apart from arguments over material, tension built over another issue. Should they be the centre of attention or background entertainment within the social setting?

Even when the venue and music style changed, goodwill within the band continued to evaporate.

So it was a relief to Mavis when the early days of Spring found them booked into Keimera pub for a month. No travel. No bumping gear in and out late at night. Fewer midweek rehearsals. A diverse audience. A decent sized venue and what now seemed a generous performance space.

The interior of Keimera pub was panelled in walnut. The bar was long and u-shaped. A tiled floor connected the bar to the lounge where the band performed. Round tables and chairs surrounded a decent sized parquetry dance floor. The lights had an orange quality to them accentuated by the tobacco smoke in the room. Changing attitudes to passive smoking, anti-smoking advertising campaigns, and government moves to extend smoke-free zones had had little impact on the pub scene.

Noting the older generational mix of the early evening audience on the first Saturday of the month's booking, the drummer and bass player reacted in syncopated complaint. "Shit! Why aren't these oldies at home? Can't a guy get a break? We want to rock."

"Stow it." Steve set up his keyboard at a sixty degree angle to the drum kit. "You'll get your chance later tonight."

After discussion with Tony, Mavis began with songs from the pop icon of the audience's day: Sinatra. She had his phrasing off pat as well as his clarity in enunciating lyrics. The audience responded enthusiastically.

The band's updated arrangement of Rosemary Clooney's 'Sway' brought dancers onto the floor. 'This Ole House', an upbeat, revamped rock and roll number, kept them there. Mavis' steamy new arrangement and rendition of Peggy Lee's 'You Give Me Fever' pulled patrons from elsewhere in the pub. As a middle-aged crowd flowed into the room, the older patrons faded away.

The tempo and style of the evening's music changed with the keyboard player's favourite seventies' song, 'Taking Care of Business', opening the next set. It was with the change to Van Morrison's 'Moondance' and its walking bass line that the bass player turned up his guitar's volume, cutting off the sound engineer's overall control. The drummer followed, working in tandem with the bass player to push up the volume. The melody, key to the song, was drowned out by the thump and thud of the bass and drums.

The duty manager crossed to the soundman and said, "Dude, turn the bass player and drummer down."

The soundie replied, "I don't even have them in the mix. Look, I've turned the bass player off, and he's still loud! He must've unplugged his amp from the mixer. He's playing independently now through his amp. As for the drummer, I don't have mics on the drums!"

The audience yelled out, "Can't hear the singer!" Disgruntled patrons used drink coasters as Frisbees and targeted the bass player and drummer. The drummer and bass player pressured Mavis to sing louder which she did for the rest of that bracket. The heckling continued.

"What the hell do you guys think you are doing?" Tony asked in the break.

"I'm playin' as I feel it," was the bass player's reply.

"I need to keep balance with the bass," was the drummer's comment.

"Turn it down and leave that to the soundie."

"I'm not strainin' my voice like that anymore! Besides, my mic is picking up the drums so it's pointless."

As the evening aged, the audience became younger. The band's music evolved into rock hits of the nineties that Mavis could sell: Oasis' 'Wonderwall', Alanis Morrisette's 'Ironic', Cold Chisel's 'Khe Sanh', and so on.

Again, the bass player and drummer pushed the sound levels up.

When the duty manager returned, the room was a cacophony of sound: muddy out-of-balance instruments, drowned vocals, raised patrons' voices, thinning crowds.

"I can't hear myself," Tony said in the next break, "with those damn cymbals bashing in my ears."

"I'm not strainin' my voice so that it's shot … back off the volume! You're takin' away my energy!"

"Then have the soundie turn you up!" the drummer said. "I'm sick of playin' like pussies!"

"Music has to be blistering," the bass player added. "Playin' like this is not cool!"

"I'm fed up with not pullin' the ladies," said the drummer. "I want to rock and that means loud!"

"Yeah!"

Mid confrontation, the manager pulled Tony aside. "Dude, you're here to pull in customers, not send them outside. You can forget the rest of the month if you can't control the sound." He walked off.

Tony turned back to his band, "I've had it with your wannabe egos and your bitchin'. After tonight, you're done!"

"Mate," the drummer said, "I'm done now!"

"Me too."

They stormed off and made a big, noisy show of packing up their gear.

Adjourning outside, Mavis and the remaining guys cooled their heels and their tempers.

"We don't need them," Tony said. "A full band is overkill. It'll work better this way. You can see how much money there is to be made …"

"It hasn't been fun, Tony, until tonight … at least the first part of the night," Mavis said. "Performin' does it for me …. not bein' background. I don't want work like we've been doin'."

"That's where I am too," Steve, the keyboard player said. "Anyway, the scene is changin'. You know DJs are pickin' up more and more of that sort of work. They're cheaper, have total control over the material …"

"We're goin' to have to rethink the whole band," Mavis said, "if we're goin' to have a future."

Steve said, "That gives us a month to find replacements and work out if we want a future together."

"C'mon, let's do the last set and finish."

*   *   *

A disaster was how Mavis saw her home. Nothing had been put away for months. She had stayed on top of washing up the crockery, cutlery, pots and pans but had left things sitting in the draining rack ready for next use. She had kept abreast of the laundry washing and partially stayed on top of folding and sorting it. Sheet music, CDs, clothing, bills, unopened mail, loose coins, Dan's toys and books, magazines, and a season of daily discards and dust clogged arteries of the living areas. And a strange smell lingered.

Dan had taken to sleeping over and having breakfast at his grand-parents on weekends so that Mavis could catch up on her sleep. She wasn't sure now how she felt about that. It had happened, and she'd been too tired, too stressed to think about it beyond relief that Dan had care.

Chiding herself for being careless with her life, again, and slip-ping into old patterns, reacting as life happened to her rather than consciously deciding, Mavis set about the chore of housework. She blocked intruding memories of her past with Terry (the man she'd thought was her 'true love') by firmly focusing on the routine and worked through the clutter of the room.

Morning phased into afternoon. Aware of her hunger and the poverty of her pantry and fridge, she walked across the small yard between her place and her parents.

Dan, perched on a wooden stool and with his hands working

dough, was chatting up a storm as his grandmother baked an assortment of goodies.

The scene reminded Mavis of her own childhood. She slipped onto the stool beside Dan after dropping a kiss on the top of his head.

"What are you makin', Dan?"

Dan passed her a large section of dough. "Gingerbread men. I like Gran's story about them better than the one in the book."

Mavis laughed. "Yes, I always did too. Anythin' I can scavenge, Mum?"

"I made a plate up for you after checkin' yesterday what you had in the house." Marg passed the plate from the fridge to her along with cutlery. "You really need to get some food shoppin' done and find a way of makin' time for the everyday things of life."

"Mummy, aren't you goin' to make some men?"

"After I eat, Dan. Why don't I make some of the animals out of the story instead? Then we can eat them. Somehow, I think that's poetic."

"Poetic, Mummy?"

"A different, better end to the story."

Looking seriously at his creations, Dan pouted. "Does that mean we can't eat the gingerbread men?"

"Can you help me out here, Mum?"

"These particular gingerbread are made for eatin', Dan. None of them are like the gingerbread man in the story. He was very special."

"You make just the best salads, Mum. This roast beef is amazin'."

"Leftovers from yet another missed family meal. Dan, run and ask Pop if he wants a cuppa."

With the boy gone, Marg said, "While we like helpin' you, we're not happy about how this is all workin' out, love."

"Didn't expect you to be. It's not what I want either."

"So why are you doin' it?"

"That's what I've been wonderin'."

"And?"

"Money's the obvious answer … Can we talk about this later? … When I'm in a better space … not so tired and overwhelmed?"

Dan returned. "Pop says he's fine and to tell you he's goin' down the street. Can I go with him?"

Marg answered without deferring to Mavis. "Wash your hands first. Then change that T-shirt. I'll put your dough away until later."

About to remonstrate with her mother over what Mavis saw as the usurpation of her parental authority, Mavis realised almost immediately that this had become their practice because of her own choices. She altered her tone and comment after the first word, "Mum! … er … What's in this sauce? It's delicious."

Reading the situation correctly, Marg answered by following her daughter's cue, "I got it from the new CWA cookbook. Your dad loved it too. We assumed you'd be havin' dinner here tonight."

"We are."

*   *   *

With the late afternoon sun streaming through the door's glass panes, Mavis stood at her ironing board, the intermittent hiss of steam from the ironing process background to her meditative state. Her mother's silent disapproval of the path Mavis had chosen was obvious in Marg's thin-lipped expression every time Mavis left Dan with her parents. Dan was not only not the picture, he hadn't even been in her frame. Her problem was that she wanted to perform now. She wanted to be heard. She had stoked her hunger for …

"Anyone home?" Kate called, having rapped on the front door.

Mavis flicked a look at the wall clock; it read six on the hour.

"Come around the side!"

Ironing abandoned, Mavis led a very chatty Kate through the transformed living space into the kitchen. Mavis scavenged for something to feed her guest as Kate concluded, "And so the sweep's oar dug too deep into the surf, and he ended up overboard. It was all very funny to watch, a whole comedy of errors."

"You love it, don't you?"

"Yes."

"Why?"

Why indeed? A high achiever since her teens, Kate had been driven by her need to make her father proud. Somewhere deep within her, she feared he regretted not having a son. Not that he had ever said so. It was something she'd sensed when she saw him coaching the Lifesaver nippers when she had been a girl herself. Something she'd felt when she had tagged along with him to the surf club and watched him mentoring the young men of the club. "It was my dad's passion, and I guess I inherited it. It's not all fun in the sun and surf, y' know. Being Club Captain is a huge headache at times. There's a lot of in-fighting between the different groups within the club."

"So what keeps you at it? … I'm sorry to say my cupboards are well and truly bare. All I can offer is coffee, but I'll have to get some milk off Mum and some snacks."

"The return I get from it. Black is fine. I'm not hungry. I had a late lunch with Gary."

"How's he goin' since the breakup?"

"He seems okay. I don't think he was into her as much as we thought."

Mavis vaguely noticed the slight flush to Kate's cheeks but did not give it further thought.

"He says stuff happened that changed how he saw her."

Mavis frowned. "I can believe that."

"What?"

"Just something Sarah shared with me, Kate."

"With anyone who would listen. She was loud and clear about her resentment of the time he spent at the surf club, Mavis. The more he conceded to her the more demanding she seemed to get." She paused before adding, "And she gave him a hard time over still boarding with the Madisons. She didn't understand what it was that he valued about living there. Nor did she get that Gary saw them as the family he never had but always wanted."

"Unless you've lived there you wouldn't, Kate."

"Well, yes, you're right there. I didn't understand … not for a long time."

"Gary ever talk to you about his life before Madison House, Kate?"

"Only that he comes from an uncaring family and understands what it means to be truly alone."

"He's such a great guy, Kate. I don't know how anyone could not love him."

"Me either. I told him ages ago he should explain to Sarah why he didn't want his world reduced to just the two of them, but …"

"She isn't the type who'd understand. If you ask me, she wants to be the solitary sun in her man's universe. That's why she tried to cut us out. To be fair though, she was tryin' …"

"I'll say …"

"So how is Gary really?"

"Irritating, funny, charming sometimes, an alpha male a lot of the time …" Noting Mavis' expression, Kate blushed. "He's moving on … I heard on the grapevine that last night at the pub was …"

"Not good? That there was a walkout?"

"Yes, and that you were the only good thing about the band."

"Oh."

"So what's going to happen now?"

"Tony, Steve and me can do the pub gig for the rest of the month. Tony thinks it'll be easy to pick up replacements but wants to audition. I realised today I've got to think this through. Do I want to work with those guys? Should I? How do I find the balance between bein' a mother and a performer? How do I make time for everything?"

"The magazines say a lot of working mums feel like that and yet they manage to have it all."

"Do they though? And what does 'it all' mean anyway?"

"Everything they want from life: career, family, sexual satisfaction."

"Yeah … well. I've been doin' a bad job at all of that."

"It's early days yet, Mavis. Don't be so hard on yourself … Give it time."

Sadness overwhelmed Mavis. "Mum says I should walk away from it. I just *can't*, but I can't go on like it has been either. It's not fair to anyone."

With a comforting arm around Mavis' shoulder, Kate said, "There's always a way through any problem. You just need to look for it and then plan how to get there. My dad says when I'm low like you are now, 'Focus on the better part of your life and move on'."

* * *

Good times with Dan and a month of satisfying work at the local pub were the joy that helped Mavis get past her working-mother-with-two-jobs tiredness. Added to that, the pub manager extended their booking for another six weeks to fill a hole caused when the band scheduled to follow them cancelled their booking. Having work close to home made a huge difference to Mavis as did the increased share in the money.

After a particularly energized Saturday night performance five weeks after the band's breakup, Mavis found it hard to come down when she came home from the pub late at night. Dan had slept over at her mother's place so Mavis attacked the housework, reclaiming the cottage as her home. She had an amusing image of herself planting her 'flag' on her equivalent of the moon. She realised she needed lots of small steps if this 'moon' was to be settled. Taken by the idea, she spent some time working out lyrics to a melody that had been developing over the past month. Satisfied, she finally went to bed.

The early morning's heat, more typical of Summer than Spring, teased Mavis awake. Lying there in her darkened room, she could hear Dan outside in the yard talking to her mother. She assumed her mother was hanging out the washing as was her early morning habit in the warmer months.

After climbing out of bed, Mavis padded around the cottage getting a much needed black coffee and some vegemite on toast. Then she dressed, choosing a red, fitted T-shirt, white snug shorts, and white sandals. She flicked the radio off after listening to the weather report which followed the nine o'clock news. It predicted that temperatures would soar above thirty-five degrees Celsius that day.

As far back as Mavis could remember, Spring had always been a rollercoaster ride with intermittent days of spiked intense heat gradually increasing in number, eventually levelling out into weeks of constant scorching highs. She emerged from the cottage to find Dan readied for a swim; his kick board, floaties, and flippers were visible in a netting bag.

"I'll take him, Dad. I need some quality Dan time. I'll just need to change first."

Belatedly comprehending the adult exchange, Dan pouted. "But I want to go now with Pop. You always take forever to get ready."

Sympathetic to his protest, Mavis said, "Count to five hundred, and if I'm not out by then, you can go." With the screen door held open, Mavis said, "Not so fast, little man. Come on, count fairly."

Having changed into a bikini and a sarong, Mavis took Dan to the southern peninsula rock pool. Although early in the day, it was already packed with swimmers. Wolf whistles marked Mavis' path through the crowded concrete area that surrounded the western side of the rock pool.

The rippling water of low tide was a lot more than cool; it was cold as all ocean pools affected by the southern currents are. Nonetheless, Mavis swam a few laps while Dan made progress up and down the pool, periodically circling children he knew as he chatted to them.

With the sun still in the eastern sky, Mavis took Dan exploring along the rocky shelf south of the pool. They lingered over rock pools and the stranded sea life in them.

"Hey, Dan, come and look at this one. There's heaps of small sea life."

In that gambolling gait common among children at play, Dan crossed to her."Wow! How come this pool has more?"

"Not much can live in the shallows. On hot days, the water in a shallow pool heats up and anything in it cooks. This pool is wide and pretty deep. Do you know what this is called?"

"It's an anemone. That's a sea star, and ... Did you see that, Mummy?"

"Where?"

"There it is! It's camouflaged."

"Oh ... it's some sort of fish."

"Gary calls them sculpins."

"Really?"

"He tried to scoop one out for me once, but ..."

"Maybe I can do something he couldn't." Bending over, Mavis cupped her hands while watching for movement.

Dan's comment, "No, Mummy, don't!" overlapped Mavis', "Ah ha!"

"Gary got stung real bad."

"What? Oh!" Mavis uncupped her hands, letting the small pool of water and life she captured within it fall back into the rock pool.

"Did you get hurt, Mummy?"

"No, I'm okay. Geez, that was close. Come on, time we continued our walk."

Before they neared what was a notorious, jagged rocky shelf, Mavis led Dan back up onto the grassy slopes of the peninsula. The tide had turned and would soon engulf the rock shelf.

From the elevated levels of the grassy slope, Mavis saw the tragedy happen. Despite the warning signs that alerted English-speaking visitors to the shelf's danger, she saw what she assumed were a migrant couple treading a cautious path through the thick web of kelp that covered the rocky ledge. She saw that their footwear in particular was totally inappropriate for the path they were travelling.

With their attention committed to avoiding a fall, the couple seemed unaware of the returning tide. The waves licked the shelf, tasted it, and then receded.

With the growing swell, waves surged big, crashing over the rock ledge, eating into the shelf, unbalancing the couple. As the foam thinned, Mavis could only see the woman, struggling for a hold, clawing at the rocks. Looking beyond the woman, the water was devoid of life. Looking around her for help, Mavis saw that others had seen them as well.

Thank God for mobile phones, Mavis thought, when the man nearest to her reassured her that he'd already called the surf club.

Looking back to the rock shelf, Mavis scanned it and then the ocean for the woman. She too had been swallowed by the waves.

The rescue seemed to happen in fractured time. Mavis recognized Gary as one of the crew on the three-manned jet boat. At a safe distance from the rocky shoreline, Gary and another male lifesaver dove into the icy waters. With powerful freestyle strokes, they searched the area, disappearing deep at times to scan the water's depths. All the time the ocean swell and size of returning waves grew.

By this time, a crowd had gathered on the peninsula near Mavis and Dan. There was an intense silence among the watchers.

Finally, one of the swimmers surfaced with an unresponsive body and headed back to the jet boat. Not long afterwards, the second swimmer surfaced also with a lifeless body in tow.

Mavis, Dan, and the crowd headed toward Surf Beach where the surf club was situated. By the time they arrived, a waiting ambulance had taken away the bodies. After seeking Gary out, Mavis found both rescuers being rubbed down with an anxious Kate in command. Gary was withdrawn and bleakly silent, as was his fellow lifesaver.

As routine returned to the club, Kate found time to talk to Mavis. "Our role is to save lives, Mavis. We're not used to tragedy like this. We've got procedures in place though to help our people deal with this sort of trauma when it happens. Gary will be okay in time."

"Yeah … I remember what he went through in 1993 after that girl died when she got caught in the rip north of Surf Beach. The award for bravery held little meaning for him then. I was scared for him today, watching the scene."

"And Dan saw the whole thing?"

"He did, but I don't think he understood that they died. I fobbed him off with talk about the vital role paramedics and the ambulance service play in saving lives."

"Maybe you should book Dan into see Emma at the medical practice for a chat about it to see what he registered. Witnessing trauma can become a personal experience for kids. It's better to deal with it early than have it become an unconscious issue for him later."

"We're seein' Dr Tim next week to review Dan's asthma management plan. Do you think we could get into see Emma followin' Dr Tim?"

"I'll see what I can do."

After a word to and hug of Gary, Mavis and Dan walked home. Arriving at her parents' gates and after consideration of what she'd seen, Mavis came to a realisation. There was something between her friends that went beyond camaraderie. There was a tenderness between them that was more than friendship, more than what she shared with Gary or Kate. *Interesting*, Mavis thought. If Gary was to be partnered, she preferred that person to be Kate. They were so different though, would it work out?

The following week, Mavis took a chatty Dan up to the medical practice for his review as well as a session with Emma Stone, the practice psychologist.

After an hour session with the psychologist, Dan emerged as cheerful as ever. While Kate took Dan behind the practice scenes to learn about how stethoscopes worked with the resident nurse, Mavis had a consultative session with Emma.

"Dan was full of the rescue but focused on Gary's heroism, Mavis. Dan witnessed the danger inherent in the rescue scene like kids do violence in cartoons. He saw it but didn't comprehend it because there wasn't any grief and suffering evident to him. He'll be fine as long as that remains the case. So, how's Gary taking it? Dan seems to idolise him and says he and Kate came over the following night for dinner."

"On the surface, Gary seems okay, but he is unnaturally quiet. When I tried to speak to him about it privately, walls came up. I can feel his sadness as can Kate, but he hides it from Dan. I think their play gives him solace. Life goes on though, doesn't it?"

"Wobbly sometimes, but it does, and lifesavers know the risks when they sign up. And the loss wasn't personal; that'll help him cope as well. He'll be getting regular counselling for a while as well, paid for by the movement."

"Is there any problem, Ms Stone, do you think, with Dan's attachment to Gary?" In response to the psychologist's blank expression, Mavis added, "Gary plays the role of father to Dan, but he isn't. I'm wonderin' if I made a mistake lettin' that happen."

"Aren't Kate and Gary Dan's godparents?"

"They are."

"Feeling loved within the family circle is the best gift a child can have. Being valued by the adults in his world is important to Dan's wellbeing. A boy needs male role models as much as he needs female role models. That's how he learns about how the adult world works. We can't shield our children from hurt, only armour them so that the hurt is less."

*   *   *

The audition process proved to be a passing parade of applicants, many of whom thought musicianship was as much about how they looked as how they played. 'The look' fell into categories that reflected the dominant bands of the nineties.

On the first of two Sundays devoted to auditions, hopefuls entered the hired hall, situated in the showground, with attitude. A number of them took in the ordinariness of Mavis, Tony, and Steve and left without bothering to try out. It was as if there was a revolving door in the hall. Some of them quizzed the trio about what they played and how much work they had. They left as well without striking a note or sounding a beat.

Those who remained were dressed in street casual and did not use dress to make a statement about themselves as musicians.

It was a three-pronged interview process after each jam session.

Tony asked, "What's your background? Can you read music? Can you ad lib? Any reasons you can't travel?" and made point notes with a considered frown. The musicians who topped his list were single and claimed they played every style.

Steve investigated, "What do you want from and get out of playin'? What sort of equipment do you have? Do you have your own transport? Why do you want to join our band?" He listened intently and said little in response.

Mavis wanted to know, "How would you sum yourself up as a musician? Are you willin' to sing backup vocals? How should a song be played?" She ruled out anyone who answered, "Exactly like the recording artist does it."

Over two Sundays, the band reformed.

The trio settled on a thirty-something male, taut and terrific looking bass player, Jack Carter, with a rich resumé in musical styles. His attitude was summed up concisely in, "I'm done working with walking egos and posers. I'm not interested in bein' in a band to pick up chicks. I want to work on *original* music with musicians who want to develop their own style. I'm cool with R & B, Country Rock, and any fusion of contemporary music that gets audiences going." To Mavis he said, "I saw you perform at the Show Society's dinner dance. I want to be part of that." Widening his gaze to include Tony and Steve, he said. "As you can see, my gear fits with yours. Of course, I have transport. No, I don't sing except in the shower."

While listening to Jack, Tony's lips pulled together as if he was sucking his teeth. "We do covers, mate, crowd pleasin' hits of the day, whatever that day was for the audience."

Looking from Jack to Tony and back again, Mavis said "But original music isn't out of the question. It's where I want to go. Do you write?"

"I do."

"Me too. I'd really like to collaborate with someone."

Noting Tony's pursed lips, Steve said, "Anything that puts us head and shoulders above other bands is cool with us. Right, Tony?"

Tony nodded, but his right cheek pulsed, a signal to Steve that this bass player might be ruled out, fantastic though he was.

In the end, the vote went two in favour and one against Jack.

The drummer was a woman, in her early to mid-thirties and a

physical echo of Suzi Quatro although this drummer's hair was longer and cut in a Cleopatra style. She was also called Susie. She was slim, athletic, and highly skilled on the drums. Her winning responses were, "My goal is to serve the music and keep the beat. I'm open to any style as long as the beat is interesting. I've seen and heard what's been good about your band and what wasn't. You won't have those problems with me. I want regular work. I want to work with Mavis. With the right backing, she's going somewhere, and I want to tag along for the ride. But, and this is a big but, so I'm telling you up front, I've got a kid and that has had its own complications. No, I'm not any kind of singer."

Tony and Steve had nodded as Susie spoke.

Flattered though she was, Mavis disliked the pressure of Susie's expectations even though it was what Mavis hoped and was determined to achieve. Mavis glanced at the men. They seemed fine with what Susie had been saying. Was that their expectation too? "I don't want anyone joinin' us with unrealistic expectations. Tony's plan is to carve a niche in the small arena. It's what we're workin' toward at the moment."

Jack closed his bass guitar case, having secured his bass. "And what do *you* want?"

"I don't have the answer to that as yet."

Susie collapsed her drummer's stool and stacked it with the rest of her kit. "I'm cool as long as there isn't a ceiling on expectations."

Mavis looked at Tony and Steve.

Tony leant back in his director's chair, his guitar case at his feet. "I want to be the standout band in the scene we're in."

Steve remained silent. Small arena stuff had been good enough before Mavis had joined the band, but, like Susie, he had a sense of the possibility that working with Mavis held.

"Steve?" Mavis asked.

"It'll work out the way it'll work out. I'm cool with that."

Tony drew the trio apart for a private conference. Again the vote went against him. Aware of the need to salve Tony's ego, they left it to him to deliver the news to Susie. "You're in."

"I've a question before I accept ... Anyone using?"

"No." Tony stood, fed up. "We've seen the downside of drugs and don't want it part of our scene." He made a show of his preparations to leave. Steve and Mavis both saw his displeasure, subtly expressed, in the way he packed up his gear.

"Okay then, I'm in." Watching Tony exit, Susie asked Steve, "He always like that?"

"Not often. It's human to be out-of-tune occasionally. Okay if I pop in during the week, Mavis?"

"Make it after seven-thirty, Steve. I don't have time before that for 'chat'."

The subsequent rehearsals over the following month of Sunday afternoons gave tuneful meaning to compatibility and appeased an on-edge Tony.

During a break at the end of that time and curious about how Susie balanced parenthood and career, Mavis paired up with Susie in the kitchen. The guys had adjourned to chairs near their gear. "You said you have a kid. How old?"

"Fourteen. She's the reason I gave up touring, put my career on hold, and became a sessions player. This year though the focus returns to me."

"You couldn't find the balance between a career and bein' a mum when she was younger?"

"That's always hard to juggle, but it's even harder when you don't have family on the spot ready to be backup."

"If you don't have backup, who takes care of her when we're out and about on gigs?"

"She's fourteen and old enough to take care of herself."

A week later during a rehearsal break, Susie raised the issue of *brand* name. "I'm not just talking about the band either. Mavis Mills just doesn't cut it! I'm sorry, but no amount of talent can carry that name. What were your parents thinking?"

"Mavis means song thrush. It's supposed to be the most beautiful sounding of all the birds. My dad says the bird's song shows its contentment with the small things in life. That's what they wanted for me: joy and contentment."

"Got a middle name?"

"Nicole."

"Any nicknames?" Tony asked.

"The kids at school used to call me M&M."

"Sweet on the outside but a hard nut to crack?" Jack's smile held a flirtatious challenge.

Mavis flicked him an amused look and then ignored him. "When I was in trouble, my teacher used to say, 'Mavis Nicole Mills…' She did that to all the kids; it was part of her discipline shtick."

"Oh, I get it," Tony said, "M.N.M."

With her eyebrows knit, Mavis considered the implications of a name change. Did taking a professional name compromise her authenticity? Was she backsliding into letting others define who and what she was?

Aware of Mavis, Jack said, "Ten dollars for your thoughts?"

"You're payin' high rates. I get a stage name sets a commercial image. I'm just not sure …"

Susie said what the men were thinking. "Audiences are into a band's image as much as their music. It's important to building a following."

The men nodded. They agreed with Susie although none of them would've been bold enough to say so to a woman despite the upgrade of the times to gender equality.

The men looked to Susie. "Mavis is an old fashioned, staid sort of name. Not an image that'll sell us to audiences. It's a good enough name if you want to be … what is your day job?"

"I'm the receptionist at Keimera Ford."

"Clearly not an image job. No offence meant."

Memory chimed for Mavis resolving the issue. *A rose by any other name is still a rose.* "No offence taken. I could be Nikki Mills."

"And the band?" the others spoke in unison.

"That'll take some thought," Tony said.

"I've an idea. Why don't you be our namesake?" Susie said. "Y' know, like The Steve Miller Band. Love their music by the way. We could be The Nikki Mills Band."

"You know there was no Steve Miller in The Steve Miller Band," Tony said with authority.

Susie looked momentarily deflated. "Really? Damn, that's disappointing."

"No, he's pullin' your leg! Steve Miller was the guitarist." Steve closed up his keyboard. "Tony has the most amazing music collection and musicography. It goes way back. Susie's onto something though. Bon Jovi did it."

"So did the Ramones," Jack added. "It's a good idea."

"I think we need to give this a lot more thought," Tony said. "Mavis is part of the band …"

"Nah, mate," the bass guitarist, Jack, spoke up for the first time. "Mavis is the *key* to any success we might have. I'm with Susie and Steve."

Tony decided silence was his best response. Lacking the familiarity with Tony that his closest friends had, Mavis misunderstood his reflex nod as he digested the situation.

Taking him to be in accord with the rest of the band, Mavis said, "Nikki Mills it is!"

Chapter 7

Life for Mavis during the transition from Spring into Summer was more rhythm and blues than anything else. With regular gigs on Friday and Saturday nights further afield after the booking at Keimera pub ended, she found herself with a swelling bank account for the first time in her life. She liked that! She didn't like the increasing tiredness.

Although travel time after those gigs provided her with some down-time after the adrenaline of performance, she found it increasingly difficult to sleep despite her fatigue. While relieved that she could prowl around her cottage on her return, setting things in order without waking Dan, she felt increasingly disturbed that he now spent Friday and Saturday nights with her parents plus Wednesdays when she had rehearsals.

Sleep, when it came to her around three in the morning, was fit-ful. Mavis usually woke around midday or a bit thereafter, relieved to escape the wordless shadows in her dreams. She caught up with her son and parents in the afternoon before the next night's work.

During those afternoons, Mavis worked at maintaining her bond with her son through play, aware that there had been a shift in the family dynamic. She left any disciplining to her mother. *Better Dan resented his grandmother than me*, she thought.

During the week, her job as a receptionist at the Ford dealership seemed to her like a single sung syllable with some tonal variation in it but without the benefit of intervening lyrics. While she liked the vocal work of Mariah Carey and Stevie Wonder, it was song that made their performance memorable, not just a few warbling notes. It was song that held meaning.

And so it was with Mavis' life.

Increasingly, her workdays gained a blues signature to them. She found herself quietly humming 12-bar standard progressions and penned lyrics when business was slow. At night when she was home, and while Dan was awake, she composed the music on an old upright piano kept in the spare room where she also kept her guitar.

In the time she spent with Dan during the week, she lived life on the hop, their interactions often looping. While her dialogue with him was melody and counter melody, it increasingly became directive and very different from interaction when she had time for such things.

*   *   *

The first Saturday in November was temperate, uncharacteristically so. Having returned by ten from that morning's grocery shopping with his grandparents, Dan played on his scooter, up and down the two parallel driveway strips in the yard on the southern side of his grandparents' house. Occasionally, he'd stop at the front double iron gate when weekend walkers and their children stopped for a chat with his grandfather. Trevor was gardening. Watching the families depart, Dan envied those children.

Scooting down to his mother's cottage, he dropped the scooter near the front screen door with a loud clatter. Entering, he called out, "You up yet, Mummy?"

After pausing to look in on his mother, Dan headed off to his bedroom. A little while later, he returned to his mother's room with an old-fashioned, rectangular school case in which he kept his treasured car collection. The case was a relic of his grandfather's childhood as were a number of the cars – vintage in more than one sense.

Positioned in contact with his mother, who lay on her side, an arm winged behind her head, Dan set up his game. Enjoying the mountain range challenge of her body, Dan drove cars up the steep inclines and then let them free glide back to the bedding. He chatted away in undertones to the imaginary people in his cars.

Around noon, Marg came in search of Dan. His scooter had been the pointer to his location. Calling to him softly, Marg looked in the obvious rooms first.

Dan leant back against Mavis, recounting his school adventures to her while she slept. Cars lined up, bumper to bumper, along her body ridge.

Eventually Marg found him. "Why didn't you answer me, Dan?"

Dan hunkered close to his mother and ignored his grandmother.

From the doorway, Marg whispered, "Dan, come away and leave your mum in peace. She'll be up later. You'll have plenty of time with her then, I promise."

Matching his volume to his grandmother's, Dan whispered, "I want to stay with Mummy. We've been playin'."

Adding enough voice to sound stern, Marg stepped closer to the bed. "Dan, do as you're told. We're goin' outside, right now!"

Dan retreated behind his mother's body, unceremoniously scrambling over her.

"What the…?" Seeing her mother first, Mavis struggled to focus, "Mum?" Then realising something was wedged under her chin, she dislodged a truck. An avalanche of cars covered her bed as she changed position. "What's goin' on?"

"I wanted to play with you, Mummy, but Gran won't let me. *We* were havin' such a good time until *she* came in."

"What?" Twisting around to see Dan, Mavis realised her bed was unnaturally lumpy. "Geez, what *is* that under my back?" She pulled out a lorry truck and a few other cars. "How on earth …? Dan, be a good little chappy, and go with Gran. I'm so tired. I need just another hour or two, Mum. I was havin' such a good dream, the most unbelievable massage."

While mother and son had been interacting, Marg had positioned herself close enough to Dan that she could scoop him up, her right arm around his waist.

"No!"

"At your age, young man, you do as you're told." Carrying Dan, kicking and screaming, Marg left the cottage.

Hearing the ruckus, Trevor came around to the rear of his house. He arrived in time to see Marg ground Dan at their back door. "I will not put up with this behaviour!"

Crying, Dan attempted to return to his home. Trevor grabbed the back of Dan's shirt as he passed. It took a moment or so for Dan to realise he wasn't going anywhere.

At Dan's eye level, Marg said, "Stop this, Dan! At once!"

Unable to cap Dan's rising distress, Marg looked up to Trevor in appeal. His one-handed gesture, while he continued to hold onto Dan, added to her feelings of helplessness.

"Dan, what on earth is the matter?" Mavis stood in the doorway of her cottage, screen door held ajar.

In response to Dan's, "I want my mummy!" Trevor released him. Dan ran to her and hid his face in the folds of her patterned, cotton night dress.

"Calm down, little man. Geez, Mum! Is lettin' me sleep in that much to ask?"

"Depends on who's doin' the lookin', doesn't it. It was time you were up anyway." Pausing at her kitchen door, Marg said, "Trev', get yourself cleaned up. You and I are goin' out for lunch."

"But, Mum, I was hopin' you'd—"

"We have our lives to live too, Mavis. As you can see, Dan needs some sort of life with you too." With that, Marg entered her house followed by Trevor.

Picking up her distressed son, Mavis returned to their cottage. "It's okay, Dan, tell Mummy what's wrong."

After calming him down, Mavis listened patiently to Dan's version of how his grandmother had *wrecked* his play. Mavis realised that her view of the morning events had been skewed by her tiredness and frustration at being awakened, that she owed her mother an apology. She did not understand the root cause to Dan's distress.

* * *

On the last Saturday in November and after heated discussion with her husband, Marg again broached their concern about Mavis' life direction. Marg did so after Trevor and Dan had headed off to the local fisherman's co-operative and while she prepared the vegetables for that night's dinner. Fish was on the menu that night. "We're worried, Mavis. You're doin' too much and short-changin' yourself. These years with Dan will pass faster than you think. He should be your focus now as should Gary."

"What? How on God's *earth* does Gary come into the picture?"

"He's always been interested in you, love. Why else does he hang around so much?"

"We're friends. He's Dan's godfather."

"There's a lot more to it than that. Gary's been steadfast and loyal for over six years now, and he's had a really hard trot of it lately; not that you've had time to notice."

"I have. I just didn't know what to do about it. Kate says …"

"You'll lose him to her if you're not careful."

"I'm not in competition with Kate, and I'm not interested in Gary that way. Yuk!" Mavis shuddered off the image that had come to mind. "Besides, I don't want a man cluttering my life. It's full enough."

"Our thoughts exactly. You're doin' too much. I don't see why you are so hell bent on singin' in a pub. In my day, *nice* women didn't frequent pubs."

"And nowadays women aren't trapped by labels like that. I'm playin' in pubs and restaurants because it gives me joy as well as a bigger income. I was able to replace that old twin tub washing machine when it died this month without worry over money. I don't have to pay off the electricity bills by instalments anymore. I've been able to keep Dan in shoes. How do little boys wear them out so fast? Dan doesn't have to miss out on anything anymore. Money might not make people happy, but it sure cuts down on the stresses."

"Dan is missin' out on time with you. That's priceless. This second job hasn't cut down on your stress levels at all. You've just replaced one set of problems with another. How long is this goin' to continue for? Are you goin' to have a break at all?"

"Yeah ... the current work ends in two weeks, and we don't have any more work until New Year's Eve."

"And then?"

"I'm not goin' to lie to you. There'll be a lot more band work, gigs in Sydney, and travel to festivals. As the work increases, I plan cuttin' back on my day job. The time I'm away will be offset by the time I gain during the day. I can be a classroom helper among other things. Dan'll like that."

"And who takes care of Dan while you're away? You're makin' this commitment without even the courtesy of askin' us. We might want to travel."

"Do you?"

"Your father's been talkin' about it. Besides, he's dead set against you goin' down this path."

"I don't believe you."

"I don't care if you do or don't. It's a fact. While we're home, in addition to child care after school, we're happy to have Dan Friday and Saturday *nights* but that's it. Face reality, Mavis. Your father says you've missed the boat for this particular dream. I'm beginnin' to think he's right."

"It isn't a dream. Like Tony says, there's heaps of money in music even if I never become a star. I can make a decent livin'. Better money than at Keimera Ford that's for sure."

With a stressed gesture to her forehead, Marg said, "You might, but if you go down this path, you need to step up to your responsibilities and not palm them off, like the way you've left disciplining Dan to me, and I ..."

Habits long since forgotten from her teenage years returned. With her hands over her ears, Mavis walked off.

"Mavis!"

At her cottage door, Mavis stopped. Memories flooded her. *Am I still that girl? Do I want to be? Is this yet another example of me letting circumstance define me?*

Returning to her mother's house, Mavis found her in the kitchen, thin-lipped and grim, setting the table for dinner. Mavis stood awkwardly for some time before realising she'd have to be the first to speak. "I get what you're sayin', Mum. I'm sorry for just now. We'll have to agree to disagree about how I live my life. I really need your help though, and I'm sorry I've taken that for granted. Music is my way to a better future. There's no way I'll let this chance pass me by."

"It may be, but don't squander your present with Dan."

In the silence that followed, Mavis decided to talk to her father about her mother's attitude, but put that appeal to him on hold when she sighted the wall clock. "Geez, look at the time! I've got to run! Sorry. I'll see Dan before I go."

After hanging up her apron on the hook behind the kitchen door, Marg moved to the front verandah. Watching the afternoon light flicker and flash on the ocean, she thought about the dreams she had once held for her daughter. Marg had thought those dreams dashed when Mavis fell pregnant. In Marg's day, they would have been. Not so for her daughter's generation. *In some ways, life is better for women. A future beyond a husband and child is possible. I won't let Trevor rev me up anymore. I'll do what I can to help Mavis achieve her dream.*

* * *

The following afternoon, Mavis sought her father out. He was sitting on his front verandah in the quiet contemplation that pipe smokers enjoy.

"I thought I'd find you here, Dad."

"I never thought I'd like livin' in town as much as I do. There's nothing more pleasant than sittin' here lookin' at the ocean. It's always changin'."

"You don't miss life on the land then?"

"Somewhat, but bein' a part-time farmer and runnin' alpacas has filled that hole. They are *such* social animals, almost human. You should see how they react when they hear me comin' in the ute. It's heart-warmin'. It's hard not to think of them as family."

Mavis saw her opportunity but not the difficulty that came with it. "Dad, I need your help with Mum, she—"

"You need to listen to what your Mum is tellin' you."

"But you don't know—"

"Course I do. We talk over everything, and she agrees with me. Dan should be the picture. We've agreed that we won't repeat the mistakes made in your childhood."

Slack-jawed, Mavis looked at her father.

"Dreams are for children, Mavis. You've been a woman for quite a while now. It's time you accepted your lot."

Indignant, Mavis stood. "My life *before* the band was soul suckin'! Did you know that?" Leaning on the balustrade, Mavis stared unseeingly out to sea for some time. "And it's not dreamin'. It's called havin' ambition."

The front screen door swung open. "Either of you want a cuppa before I take the weight off my feet?" Marg absorbed their tension. "What's goin' on out here?"

"Talk to your daughter, Marg."

"About?"

"Dan."

"*Oh!*" was more a guttural release of air than a voiced exclamation. "I thought we had this settled, Mavis."

"Apparently not, Marg." Trevor stood to leave. He disliked his daughter's breach of their boundaries.

"You should've left gettin' this business squared off with your dad to me. You're not goin' anywhere, Trev'. In fact, I want you both to sit back down." She waited for them to do so. Reluctantly, they acquiesced. The heat of their anger cooled under her glare. "I was goin' to talk this over with your father in private when his mood was right. Clearly, I made yet another bad call." Marg experienced a heady sense of power, unusual in her otherwise submissive life. "Trev', Mavis is thirty. We might not be comfortable with her life choices, but they're *hers* to make. You're always goin' on about Dan bein' the picture. You forget he's *her* picture; she's *ours*. We're lucky she wants to share her life with us. You both clear on this? …Well?"

Their, "Yes," was out of rhythm. Trevor's reply sounded as the off-note.

"Now, who's for a cuppa?"

Surprised by the new insight into her parents, Mavis did not answer.

"I'm gettin' you both one. Then we're goin' to sit down here and act like three civilised adults. Understood?" Her listeners nodded.

Alpacas are so much easier to manage, Trevor thought. Resigned, he decided to leave people issues to Marg.

Chapter 8

According to the Mills' family ritual, the first Saturday after-noon in December was devoted to decorating the family Christmas tree in Mavis' parents' lounge room and in string-ing white lights around the guttering of her parents' house and her cottage. A single, triple layered star also held pride of place on the centre post of the Mills' front verandah.

When Mavis had been growing up, Australian family Christmas celebrations had been private and decoration had been confined to inside the home. Under the influence of American television shows and films about their flamboyant public displays and celebrations of Christmas, Australians were slowly adopting the American practice of decorating the outside of their homes. Tinsel, a major decoration from Mavis' youth, had been replaced by outdoor Christmas lights and animated yard decor to fit the season.

Positioned at the front of the house with good oversight of the harbour, the Mills' lounge room was generous in size. The freshly cut conifer was centred on the floor just in front of the eastern bay windows which were an unusual feature in what was other-wise a colonial house. The family had gathered there, each with a designated role. Mavis and Dan hung the decorations while Marg unpacked and handed over her seasonal treasures for the tree. Trevor took photos of the occasion as had been his habit since Mavis had been born.

"I remember when we bought this one," Mavis said to her mother. "I was ten, and we bought it from David Jones in Sydney after we'd seen their Christmas window displays. I've always loved the story of the little drummer boy. I loved those trips too."

"Mummy, when we're finished, can we go up to The Argyle?"

"Dan, let's just enjoy what we're doin' here. Do you remember the story, Dan?"

"I'm a big boy now, Mummy, course I do." Dan recounted a potted version of the tale. "I want to look at the gingerbread house at The Argyle, Mummy. All the kids at school have seen it, but I haven't."

"Ah, Dan," his grandmother said, "here is the first decoration we ever bought for you." Grandmother and mother played tag-team in the telling of that first Christmas after Dan's birth. That story led onto other family stories as well as narratives about the decorations as more and more filled the tree.

"Mummy, when can we go to The Argyle?"

"Later, Dan. We still have to help Pop hang the house lights."

"We could sing some Christmas carols, Dan," his grandmother said. "That'd be fun."

"We do that every year. It'd be more fun seein' the gingerbread house. Billy Selton says there's a whole village too and a train set and ..."

"Dan, stop," Mavis said. "Christmas is a special time. Shared family times like these are important. They'll be memories you treasure when you're all grown up and a man."

"I'd treasure seein' the gingerbread house more. I'll remember bein' the only kid who didn't ..."

"Daniel Murray Mills!" Mavis said.

"C'mon, Dan," his grandmother said. "Let's get the lights out of the shed and unstring them for Pop."

Marg took Dan out of his mother's sight but not earshot. The grandmother's dialogue to him ran rhythmically over the top of Dan's counter comments which always looped back to The Argyle.

* * *

Purveyor of Fine Foods and Ice Creamery was emblazoned across the top of the shop front windows of The Argyle. The shop was located in the main street that separated the retail Keimera strip from the adjacent harbour parkland.

With exterior and interior walls coloured in Federation pink, The Argyle's two large shop windows featured magical festive scenes. The right-hand window featured an extravagant gingerbread house placed within a northern hemisphere winter landscape that doubled as Santa's residence. It was a synchronized, animated scene with a humorous twist. The young and young-at-heart laughed with delight. The left-hand window was equally spectacular and festively unique but set within an Australian Christmas coastal landscape, a surfing Santa in gaudy shorts with a surfboard being a major player in that scene.

Queued with her mother and son in a roped off section of the footpath, Mavis had to admit the window displays rivalled the Pitt Street David Jones' store in Sydney.

"Look, Mummy, there's Gary and Kate." Dan pointed at the couple in question who were exiting The Argyle. Linked closely together, they looked like lovers.

Sighting the Mills, the couple dropped hands guiltily.

Allowing other spectators to take their place in the viewing queue outside the shop, the Mills crossed to Gary and Kate.

"How's it goin'?" Mavis asked, amused to have caught her friends in a moment of such tender intimacy.

"Mavis, Mrs Mills." Gary nodded to each woman. "Hi, Dan," Gary squatted down to the child's height. "Give your godfather a hug hello." Gary stood, embracing Dan in a bear hug before setting the boy back down on the pathway. Dan loved this ritual greeting, begun when he was a toddler.

Kate said, "Gary has decided his hiatus from the surf club has ended. His first rostered day back is next Saturday."

"You ready for that?" Mavis asked.

Gary nodded. "Want an ice cream, Dan?"

"Really, Gary? From here? Yes, please!"

Frowning, Mavis considered Dan. *Was he still missing out on what other children took for granted?*

"Better start thinkin' about which *two* flavours you'll pick, Dan."

"Two, Gary? Really and truly?"

"You're a big boy now. I think you can handle it." Misinterpreting Mavis' quizzical expression, Gary spoke in an aside to her while Dan continued talking to everyone in general about the window displays. "Sorry, Mavis, I should've asked you first."

"I'm not fussed that you offered." Mavis assumed a quizzical manner. "Anything else that you'd like to share?"

"Not really."

"Girls, if you don't mind, I've a few groceries to grab at Coles. You right to bring Dan home, Mavis?"

"Go ahead, Mum."

Marg left.

"Hey, Dan, if you liked the window scenes, wait till you see the Christmas world inside. Amazin'! C'mon, we'll have to line up but it moves fast, and it'll give us time to choose which of the one hundred and one flavours you want."

"One hundred and one!"

"Knowing Dan as I do, Kate, Gary's just made a huge mistake. Choice confounds Dan."

Laughing, Kate said. "Yes, I've experienced Dan when he over thinks a choice. As for queues in Keimera … who'd have thought it?"

"Seems like there are lots of changes that people didn't anticipate." Mavis beamed at Kate.

Linking arms with Kate, Mavis asked, "Anything to share?"

When Kate was not forthcoming, Mavis added, "Like yours and Gary's take on 'Only Wanna Be With You' by Hootie and the Blowfish?"

Kate laughed. "Okay, we're sprung. We weren't keeping it a secret, not exactly. We didn't want to say anything until we were sure that it was more than … I don't know what to say."

"It couldn't happen to a nicer couple. I've known something was up for a while. There were, of course, the telltale signs when Gary thought you looked particularly hot. There are some things a man can't hide."

"Mavis!"

"He's always been protective of us, but when you've been down at the pub and other men were buzzin' around, he seemed … possessive isn't the right word … cavalier. I just love the implications of that word. When I'm on stage, you might think people are watchin' me perform, but the same is true in reverse. You on the other hand were much more difficult to work out." Mavis spontaneously hugged Kate. "I'm so glad it's you!"

"Are you? I've sometimes wondered if—"

"Gary and I are family, and we love each other in that way. He'd be creeped out, like I am, if he thought you thought … Yuk!"

With a double scooped ice creams in their respective hands, Gary and Dan returned.

"Back with my son so soon? I didn't expect to see you until Dan's twenty-first. You'll have to give me pointers on how you got him to decide." Impulsively, Mavis hugged Gary.

"Hey, watch my ice cream!"

Mavis beamed at him and then Kate. "You two—"

"What, Mummy?"

"Gary and Kate are a couple."

"A couple of what?" Dan asked as Gary looked at Mavis and then Kate, both of whom smiled at him.

"Geez, look at the time," Mavis said. "Sorry, guys, I'll have to catch up with you later. C'mon, Dan."

"Mummy, can't I sit and eat my ice cream here?"

"No. C'mon." Mavis set off at a brisk pace only to be brought up short when she realised Dan was lagging behind. "C'mon, Dan!"

Having stopped to lick a trail of melting ice cream off his hand, Dan looked at her. "You're *goin'* too fast!"

Gary and Kate came up behind Dan. "Go ahead, Mavis," Kate said. "We'll bring him home after he's finished. He'll be there before you leave."

"Thanks. I owe you!"

Mavis walked at double her usual pace home.

* * *

The child's anticipation of Christmas Eve may have faded for Mavis but not its magic. She felt its pull-strings every time she passed the white outdoor lights on the Norfolk pines that lined the parkland separating the harbour and the main street. She heard it in the communal Christmas carolling held in the harbour parkland on the third Saturday of the festive month. It was there in the smells that emanated from her mother's kitchen in the lead up to Christmas as she made her fruitcakes, puddings, mince tarts, and seasonally shaped biscuits. Her mother cooked for family, the local pensioners reliant on the meals-on-wheels program, for Dan to gift his teachers, and for Mavis to give to her workmates.

For years, Mavis had been embarrassed by her homemade gifts to friends and co-workers. In her mind, the gifts signalled her poverty. Two years ago, she had scrimped and saved *all* year so that she could be like everyone else in the giving season. The reaction was not what she had expected. Her co-workers at the Ford dealership had been visibly disappointed before assuming a mask of appreciation. Apparently, home baked treats were rare in their world where lack of time, hectic schedules, and money made the commercial gift options necessary. Her friends had recognised her sacrifice and had been warmly appreciative.

The Mills' decision to hold their first Christmas Eve open house that year had been a contentious one. For years, Mavis had loved being part of the Madison House Christmas Eve social event just as she loved the Country Women's Association Australia Day fundraiser, a bush dance held on the terraced slopes of Madison House which was an echo of the nineteenth century pastoral glory of the region. Like Gary, she liked being part of that family – a relationship forged during the years she had boarded there.

The Mills women were in the kitchen four days before Christmas preparing lunch when Marg finally decided to speak her mind.

"We need our own traditions," Marg said, "nice though it has been to share in the Madisons' these past years since the bushfire, it's time that we celebrated in our own way and that it represents something for Dan. I don't want him wishin' he was someone he isn't ... feelin' he's less somehow because of who his family are."

"Why would he when he's so loved?"

"Children pick up on their parents' feelings whether it's said openly or just something felt. You don't value what you have, Mavis, or who you are as a person, and until you do, you won't be happy. Isn't that the reason you cling to the Madison connection? The reason you're pushin' so hard with this band? I don't want that for Dan."

"You're wrong, Mum, on all accounts! *And*, it's not what *you* want for Dan that matters! He's *my* son!"

"Haven't I said so *many* times?"

Mavis felt the impulse to walk off but ignored it. The women worked in stung silence.

"Mum, if goin' to the Madisons makes *you* feel second class, then let's just have it here."

"Good!"

"Most people will already have somewhere to go though."

"It's not the size of the crowd that matters."

Mavis held back her rejoinder that the people she cared about most had already committed to the Madison House event and that she didn't want to spend Christmas Eve with acquaintances.

The open house proved to be much better than Mavis had expected. Neighbours and their families congregated on the Mills' front verandah and lawns, enjoying the sea breeze and respite from what had been a very hot day. Marg's cooking and the fellowship of like-minded people mellowed the evening. Dan was in his element, running around with neighbours' children, playing *Spotlight in the Dark*.

Circulating through the guests with a tray of food, Mavis caught up with people she had missed seeing that year. They filled her in on their lives, and from them, she discovered how involved her parents were in charitable activities within the community including their volunteer work with the State Emergency Service. When asked about herself, she talked about the band and the place music held in her life. All the while in the background, the waves and pines joined in whispered concert.

In response to a door knock and a woman's question, "Is it all right if we come in?" Mavis looked across to the doorway.

"Of course it is! Mrs Shiels, Mr Shiels, how great to see you!" Mavis greeted a charming little woman, who looked like every Australian mum of that generation, and her husband, a bastion of strength. Mavis knew that endurance and resilience were the foundation stones to both the Shiels' essence as people.

"Mum, Dad, Mr and Mrs Shiels are here."

Mavis' parents appeared, her father from the lounge room and her mother a little later from the kitchen.

"Lloyd! Pam! Welcome!" Trevor said. "Where are your four girls and their families?"

Lloyd answered, "Caught up with Christmas stuff. They'll be over later."

"Pam," Marg said, having just arrived and not having heard the answer to Trevor's question, "you are a sight for tired eyes." Marg looked around. "Where's the rest of your family?"

"They'll be over later."

"Come and help me in the kitchen, Pam. We can catch up there."

Out in the kitchen, the older women's conversation turned to travel.

"So how was the European trip, Pam?"

"Loved it all, although I would have liked more time in Ireland. If I had to pick a favourite place, it'd be Scotland. The B&Bs were amazing! I think it is the best way to see that world and meet the people. You and Trevor need to start while you're still young enough to enjoy it."

"Trev' has talked about it, but we can't, not when Mavis needs us to help out with Dan. She's pursuin' a singin' career again. Trev' and I don't like it takin' her focus off Dan."

"In my earlier years I might have agreed with you. Don't you remember what it was like at her age? Remember how our parents imposed their values and way of life on us?"

Images from her early married days returned to Marg. She

remembered her own railing against the limits imposed by Trevor's family expectations of them, the frustration she'd felt when trapped on the land. Where had the feisty woman she'd once been gone?

"Do we really want to do that to our children, Marg? Besides, so many of my friends who made their children the picture created quite selfish adults."

"Well, yes … if that is the real reason for their selfishness. But, you know, Mavis' interest in music has come with a hefty price tag, one that includes pain and poor choices that affect us as well."

"Parents can't sidestep the pain that comes with some of their children's choices. I don't think there's a parent our age who doesn't know that. Think about the sort of woman she'd become though if she let circumstance shape her. You don't want her to see herself as a victim, do you? All I want is for my girls to remain well and healthy, free of any of the *overindulgences* that put our kids at risk in this modern life."

"I get where you're coming from, Pam. I think this tray is ready. Would you mind helping me serve our guests? I'll follow up with this one."

The evening hummed along with Marg and Mavis in harmony until Marg met the new members in the band. Mavis had tried to shepherd her mother away from them, but Marg had been determined to have a long chat.

"Nikki's lucky to have you as backup," Susie said. "I never had that support. Zoey and I have done it alone. I envy her."

"Nikki?" Marg looked at Mavis puzzled.

"It's my stage name, Mum."

Marg exchanged small talk with the other members of the band for a few minutes before saying, "Mavis, I need your help in the kitchen."

Following her mother, Mavis knew by her mother's walk that she was upset.

Alone in the kitchen, Marg looked at her daughter, her silence speaking volumes.

"There's no need to be upset, Mum. Lots of musicians change their names. It's a marketing ploy. The industry is as much about image as it is about sound. Besides, it lets me separate my personal life from my professional one."

"It took your father and I a long time to agree on your name. The *naming* was really important to us. I don't want you to lose yourself in ... There are so many stories about so-called show business successes who ..." Distressed, Marg left, seeking privacy in her bedroom which was at the back of the house, out of the thoroughfare and away from their guests.

Mavis knew better than to follow her mother at such moments. Upset herself, she restacked the aluminium salver with hors d'oeuvres. Memories swept over her again: the ways in which she had masked her intelligence at school in order to gain peer acceptance; her Blondie period in her mid-teens followed by her Madonna episode; her disastrous venture into becoming a platinum blonde; her fear of being an outsider, and her desperate need for a boyfriend.

Sobered by the realisation that the yearning awakened with her return to performance held promise but also danger, Mavis resolved to stay focused on what mattered. She was aware that she hungered for acclaim but could easily be seduced by the glamour and clamour of fame. She knew she needed to stay on course to her true north, confusing though the compass readings might be.

Elsewhere in the house, a familiar voice asked of Trevor Mills, who had just restacked his record player with a collection of his favourite singers and Christmas carols, "Where's Mavis?"

"Cassie! When did you get back in town?" Trevor asked.

"This morning." Cassie Sleight had dark curly hair, controlled with the aid of grooming products, her line of defence against bouffy hair. Slim and graceful, her every movement declared her dance background. She was dressed fashionably but casually, and clearly came from a monied background.

"Your father and sister with you?" Trevor asked, looking past her.

"Not this year. Dad's spending Christmas in Paris with Leonie.

She's working on her collection for Paris Fashion Week and couldn't afford the time away."

"That's a pity. Mavis will be thrilled to see you. She's in the kitchen. Michael not with you?" Michael was Cassie's husband and a Madison.

"No, he's getting our son to bed before helping his parents with their guests, but Kate and Gary are.

Cassie looked over her shoulder. "They seemed to have been way-laid. Ah, here they are now."

"Cassie!" Mavis had just entered the lounge room with her tray of mixed snacks: steamed prawn rolls, mini egg Florentines, and devils on horseback, dangerously sliding on the tray in her excitement. A few actually slid off the tray, but Gary and Kate caught them deftly. Mavis laughed at their coordinated rescue. Trevor took the tray from Mavis.

Gary popped the snacks he had rescued into his mouth. "And that's why Kate and I are such a good partnership."

The women embraced followed by an affectionate acknowledgement by Mavis of Gary and Kate.

Kate took the salver from Trevor and assumed Mavis' role circulating among the guests while Gary followed Trevor, a cold drink for them on Gary's mind.

"Oh, it's so good of you to come tonight, Cassie. I thought I'd have to wait until Boxin' Day to catch up."

"I couldn't wait that long. When Gary and Kate said they were coming down for an hour, I decided to come too. Minna didn't need me. I saw Dan on the way in. He's really grown this last year."

"And little Emmet?"

"At four, he's a handful. His talk is of Santa and Boxing Day. I don't know how Mike will get him settled tonight especially with the open house going on. By the way, I love the highlights in your hair. Kate said you'd had them done in Sydney a few weeks ago."

"No way would I risk having it done here again. Do you remember that hairtastrophe I had?"

"Who could forget it, Mavis. It took about two years to grow it back, didn't it?"

"Three years. Now fill me in on what's big and small in your life, Cassie."

The rest of their conversation revolved around the detail of their respective lives. Although they no longer shared daily companionship, their friendship endured because it was based on connection, shared history, and understanding without judgement.

On her return trip to the kitchen for another salver of hors d'oeuvres, Kate, in an aside to Mavis, said, "My dad bought Theresa with him tonight! He must be more serious about her than I thought."

"Is that a bad thing?"

"I don't know yet."

"Here, give me that." Mavis took the salver and headed for the kitchen.

Gary came up behind Kate, encircling her waist, pulling her against him. He dropped a kiss on her neck. "Did you know the very model of a modern woman general is here?"

Kate rested her hands on Gary's. She loved his open displays of affection. "Just bumped into her."

Cassie smiled at them. "Who?"

"It's what we call Theresa; she's my father's friend," Kate said.

Gary added, "She's an authority on facts cosmetical, from surgical to chemical."

"What?"

"Ignore him, Cassie. I took Gary to *Pirates of Penzance* a few weeks back, and he's been playing with a parody of it ever since. What happened to our drinks, Gary?"

"Drinks … right … I got sidetracked … I'll get some for you now."

"Cassie!" Pam Shiels said from where she sat in the living area. "Come sit here, and tell Lloyd and I everything you've been up to."

Kate headed for the kitchen. Meeting Mavis at the opened kitchen door, she said, "Do you want me to take that tray and circulate with it?"

"If you don't mind. I'll get another one."

A few moments later, the kitchen backdoor slammed open and

children of assorted ages, shapes, and sizes entered in search of food and drink. It was a noisy feeding frenzy of a childish kind.

A teenage girl was a standout in what was otherwise a suburban group of children. She had short brunette hair with crimson streaks through it. Her colourful cotton plaid shirt was worn loosely over fitted jeans. Reflecting the trend to Indian cultural rip-offs popular at the time, she had a henna tattoo patterned across the top of her left hand.

"Hello, Nikki. I'm Zoey."

"Zoey?"

"Susie's my mum."

"Oh … You havin' a good time?"

"I've never been to anything like this before. I feel like I stepped into a storybook."

"Really?"

Zoey nodded. "Christmas has only ever been me, Mum, and occasionally my grandparents when they're home. The oldies travel a lot now they've retired. Most of the year it's just Mum and me."

"And how do you feel now that your Mum is away with the band Friday and Saturday nights?"

"I miss her."

"And who takes care of you when Susie's away?"

"I don't need a babysitter, and I've neighbours if I ever need help."

King of the kids, Dan called, "Zoey, your turn to be in."

"Excuse me," Zoey followed the set of children out into the yard. At the door, she stopped. "Nikki, I was thinking I could help out by babysitting Dan on weekends when you're away on gigs."

"I don't—"

"No charge, Nikki."

"Zoey, come on! We're waitin'."

"I couldn't take adv—"

"I'd really *like* to, Nikki."

Taken aback by the girl's intensity, Mavis considered the underlining to her offer. "I'll need to talk it over with your mum and mine."

Seeing Zoey's crestfallen face, she capitulated. "Come to think of it, Dan *would* benefit from havin' a big sister around."

"And he won't feel so lonely."

"You're right. Neither of you will."

After the house had emptied for that night and with Dan excited about the next day but tucked away in bed, Mavis and her father adjourned to the front verandah. Marg had insisted on doing the clean-up alone.

*   *   *

Close friends and family of the Madisons gathered at Madison House from eleven on Boxing Day. Minna Madison, plump as a pigeon and with renewed vigour after her bout of illness, chatted to the older women congregated in the huge kitchen as they organized the communal meal of the day, an important part of their annual ritual.

Outside, Mavis stood on the front verandah, binoculars in hand. The onshore breeze toyed with strands of her hair. She wore strappy silver sandals, a short white skirt patterned with tiny red flowers, a fitted white top, and a denim jacket. Her recently purchased sunglasses rested on the verandah railing. Cassie sat near her with a book, reading. She wore the latest style in sneakers, low-waisted jeans, a baby-blue lace shirt, and a stretch-knit jacket. Their sons flew kites in the onshore nor'easter with the help of Michael, Cassie's husband, and Gary. Kate was absent, having opted to spend the day with her father. The older men, George Madison and his guests, played a game of darts on the northern verandah.

From her vantage point on the eastern verandah, Mavis had a clear view of the people-packed parkland around the harbour and the southern peninsula of Keimera. Crowds relaxed picnic-style in the downtime after Christmas Day. Many found enjoyment in the cool of the northern if not the southern harbour rock pools while some people explored the rocky foreshore while the tide was out. It was always hotter in the town and around the sheltered harbour foreshore than up at Madison House. The crowd was well-positioned for sighting the competing yachts in the annual Sydney to Hobart yacht race as they sailed past Keimera, usually around three-thirty in the afternoon when sailing conditions were good.

That morning, Dan and his grandparents had watched the televised prelude to the start of the race as a flotilla of pleasure craft bobbed on Sydney Harbour around manoeuvring yachts, waiting for the race to start. Unlike many other major sailing events elsewhere in the world, this race was not restricted to a single class of sailing vessel. The scoring system was complex with yachts of different sizes handicapped to determine the overall Sydney to Hobart winner.

"So good to be back here," Cassie said. "RAAF Base Amberley is so hot and dry."

"That's not the mental picture I have of southern Queensland," Mavis said. "It doesn't fit with the tourism ad – beautiful one day, perfect the next."

"The weather is great, but I miss having a genuine winter. The coastal areas are lush and green and what you'd expect from a sub-tropical region. Locals say there's been a decline in rainfall which is why the Ipswich region is such a contrast to the coast."

"Now that you're back at work, how are you findin' it? It's been what, six months?"

"My horizons have widened. Do you remember how I reacted to Emmet's birth and his first year?"

"Your whole wardrobe changed. When you came home that year, you looked … frumpy."

Cassie laughed. "I did that. When I look at pictures from Emmet's first year, it's clear I was consumed by being a mother. I saw myself as *my* mother and lost sight of me."

"It was fun shoppin' together then."

"Yes, it was. I've realised lately though *that* change in my appearance didn't go far enough. While I regained a sense of myself as a woman – a sexual being – I still saw myself as Emmet's mother and Michael's wife. That's one of the reasons I went back to teaching. I wanted to be more than a mother, more than a wife. Don't get me wrong – I love those roles but ..."

"You wanted to be a complete person?"

Cassie nodded.

"And how did Emmet handle you goin' back to work?"

"Like a drowning child for a whole month. I had to pry him from me each day. I cried all the way to work and was sick about it."

"And you didn't think you should give work up and stay home?"

Cassie frowned. "Is that what you think I should've done?"

"No, of course not. You know I went back to work when Dan was a baby. I asked because it's the attitude I've hit at work since I returned to performin'. No one gives a second thought to a woman havin' a day job nowadays – it's a given. Work that takes a mother away from her kid at night .. now that's quite another thing."

"People are always willing to give an opinion but rarely a hand."

Mavis frowned. "You said you wanted to be complete. Surely that meant a return to dancin', not teachin'?"

"How could I justify leaving Emmet home at night with a babysitter especially with Mike away so much? How could I have another man as a partner? We have all the money we need, and more. I *can* have a career, but it has to be a day one. I totally understand the pressure you've been talking about. Women are liberated as long as we conform to what everyone says we should be."

"That's really insightful, Cassie. Maybe you can help me with an idea I'm exploring through song?"

"I'll try."

"This is what I've been thinking about. In our life journey, the compass we use should point to a true north, right? How do we stay on course when there are so many magnetic pulls to false norths?"

"Wow! Not the sort of conversation I expected to have on Boxing Day."

"Do you mind?"

"No, I don't mind, but I need time to think about it."

"How long do you need?"

"A lifetime?"

"I can't wait that long, Cassie."

"Maybe you should talk to Minna and get her thoughts. She's been it all: feminist, career woman, wife, mother, grandmother. With hindsight, she knows what matters and what doesn't."

"I intend to, but I really want your thoughts as well. I want my songs to speak to lots of different types of people. I think that's the way I'll *make it* musically. My images can't be so personal that I'm the only one who gets what I'm sayin' though. Can you tell me what *you* think before I go home?"

"I get the image, but I have to think about your question. I'll let you know later today."

For Mavis, the day passed slowly although she filled the waiting hours as best she could. Volunteering to supervise the boys while others lingered over lunch, Mavis sought distraction by playing with them in the new sandpit, a Christmas gift. She built aeroplanes around Dan and Emmet and then participated in their play as they flew over an imagined landscape. Emmet's conversation clearly reflected his exposure to planes and their military role.

"You're really good at noises, Auntie Mavis," Emmet said, liking her plane sounds.

"My mum sings and writes songs for me as well. Mum, sing 'No More Wiggles for Me'."

As Mavis sang, the boys laughed in the way young children do when something amuses them and joined loudly in the chorus.

While sitting on the grass watching the boys, Mavis mentally heard lyrics. "I'll be back in a tick." In search of pen and paper, she re-entered the house. Clearly, washing up had been forgotten. Taking the found materials from a kitchen drawer, Mavis heard snatches of conversation from the dining room as people lingered over a bottle of wine. *Family*, Mavis thought, *I love it!*

Back with the boys and sitting on the grass, Mavis dimly registered their conversation without thinking much about it. Her heart lurched unexpectedly when she heard Dan say, in response to Emmet's list of Dad-in-my-life comments, "I don't know where my daddy is, but I've got a Gary. Gary and me …"

As Mavis moved away from the boys to hide her sudden tears, their chatter became background to her louder personal conflict. Seeking distraction through the ritual of household chores, she busied herself with the washing up, making significant inroads before her mother entered the kitchen with Minna Madison and Cassie.

Minna, matriarch of the Madison household, spoke first. "What a dear girl you are."

"You should've called us," Marg added.

"I'm grateful you didn't," Cassie said. "I've enjoyed not being on the treadmill of mother and housewife."

"My pleasure," Mavis replied. While helping Cassie return tableware to its stored places, Mavis had to fight the urge to press her for a premature response.

The kitchen door swung open. Gary struck his habitual pose. "Cricket on the northern lawn in ten minutes girls. Boys still in the sandpit? Good, I'll get them."

Walking toward the sandpit, Gary could see the boys weren't there. "Dan! Emmet!"

"Up here," Dan called.

Past the sandpit, Gary saw the boys had climbed an ancient Eucalypt. As he approached, they sat on a broad, sturdy limb, chatting about the billy cart that Gary and Kate's father were building for him.

"I'm goin' to race it," Dan said to Emmet, "in a derby after Easter."

"Can I race it too?"

"You're too little! I'm almost seven. That's why I can be in the race. Last year, I was only allowed to watch. It was heaps of fun! I'm goin' to win this year."

"Come on, boys, down you get. We're goin' to have a game of cricket."

Walking alongside Gary, Dan asked, "Where's my daddy, Gary?" Emmet by this stage had run ahead to his father who scooped his son up into his arms as Gary watched them.

Nonplussed, it took Gary a while before he answered. "Don't know, mate." Gary redirected Dan's attention with, "But I do know we're goin' to trounce the other side."

Cricket was anything but by the rules. When Dan, who in batting, finally hit a slow-paced ball, Gary tackled Mike Madison, the fielder, while Dan scored runs and the spectators cheered. When Emmet was in, Mike picked his son up after the ball had been hit and carried him in a furious run between the stumps. Meanwhile, Mavis pretended to have difficulty in sighting the ball, tripped over it, discovered it with exaggerated surprise, and then battled Cassie who in a mock grotesque movement obstructed Mavis' return of the ball to the keeper. When she returned the ball, it was through a relay throw to the other fielders, the older men and women also involved in the game. It was a different matter when the adults were batting. Competition became intense and fierce. Laughter and barracking rang out across the Madison's peninsula.

On the return walk to Madison House, Gary took the opportunity to tell Mavis about his conversation with Dan.

"You said the right thing, Gary. I usually fob him off with a distraction. I figure sooner or later, Dan will just stop askin'."

"I don't know, mate, kids get better at askin' questions when they're older. Sooner or later they work out they've been askin' the wrong question. Besides, Dan's goin' to keep comin' back to you on it because he's surrounded by kids with two parents."

"There are some kids like him who only have one parent. Not many I admit, but enough so our family setup seems normal. I'm hopin' it won't be an issue. Until it is, I don't want to talk about it."

"You're makin' a mistake, but it's your call, Mavis."

"You're right there."

Back at the house, Mavis followed the other women inside while the men adjourned to the verandah with binoculars, hoping to sight the passing flotilla of yachts in the Sydney to Hobart race. Cassie's long awaited answer came to Mavis as she and her parents readied themselves and Dan to leave. The women moved out of earshot of the others.

"Okay, for what's it's worth, Mavis, here's what I think. True north and false north suggest there is a clear-cut right and wrong in most of the choices we make as we go through life. Moral issues aside, I don't think there is. That said, I understand what you mean by 'magnetic pulls to false norths'. For me, that means the identity conflicts and demands that come with being a mother, a wife, and even a daughter. They take us away from who we are as a person, away from who we are capable of being because we're meeting other people's demands of us. I think your idea of false norths comes from a fear of getting it wrong, of being hurt, again, and worse, hurting the people you love. I think a lot of people would get that. As for your question about having a meaningful life – I think that's what you were asking – I only know we can't be wallflowers. I've swapped to a dance image because I can explain what I think better. When the music sounds, we have to be on the dance floor. No one is truly alive when we sit it out or let others take over the dance."

Mavis hugged Cassie. "Thank you. I knew you'd understand."

"Just one thing … it's hard to stop others changing the dance. I've let that happen more than once, and well, you know where that story led."

Chapter 9

Thursday, the second week of January, 1997. The road to Parkes twisted its way through the World Heritage listed Blue Mountains, ninety minutes or so west of Sydney.

"I feel sick, Mummy," Dan said from the back seat of his mother's car where he sat next to Susie's daughter, Zoey.

Mavis replied, "Drink some water Dan, and try not to watch the road. Look at the scenery instead."

Susie, the drummer, asked, "Can I give Dan a peppermint to suck, Nikki? That often helps Zoey and me with carsickness."

"Would you like one, Dan?" Mavis asked.

"Yes, please."

Mavis added, "We'll be descending the escarpment soon. The road through the central western plains will be straighter after that."

"What's a scarpment?" Dan asked.

Zoey answered, "Escarpment, Dan. It's the edge of the Blue Mountains and where the land area falls away to lower ground."

"Will rocks and stuff fall on us?" Dan looked anxiously out of his window.

"No, silly," Zoey answered.

"Zoey!" Susie said.

"He's so literal at times, Mum." Then after a pause, Zoey added, "Sorry, Dan. I'm not used to little kids."

"I'm not that little!"

"You're littler than me. Nothing is going to fall on us. I meant that the road would slowly go downhill until we hit the plains. And no, Dan, I don't mean hit like you would a ball! I mean where it meets the plains – not aeroplanes, flat land."

"I knew that!"

Susie added, "There'll be some hills once we're down but nothing twisting like this."

Conversation faded out as Mavis' car navigated the steep descent and tight S curves in the road that led out of the Blue Mountains and into the rolling, grazing countryside of inland New South Wales.

As they reached the bottom of the escarpment, Mavis checked the traffic behind her. "The fellas must've stopped for a break. I can't see them."

"Wish we had," Dan said.

Zoey turned around for a better view. "I think I can see the rest of our convoy a few cars back."

Susie added, "Maybe they just had to give way to local traffic and so fell behind. There are so many interesting little villages, galleries, and restaurants on this route."

Sure enough, as the cars sped through the rolling hills and into the wheat and sheep district, the other car and the van that made up The Nikki Mills Band convoy reformed behind Mavis' car.

Well into the trip across the plains, Susie said, "I'm looking forward to this being the last of this type of gig. I'm not so sure that Tony is though. I never thought when I joined the band that I'd be performing at the Parkes Elvis Festival."

"So you'd heard of it?"

"No. I've never been into Elvis, and I don't get the obsession with him."

"I don't either, and you're right, Tony isn't happy about the direction the band is takin'. He'll get over it I'm sure; money speaks. The festival is not only a concession to him, it's a goodwill gesture as we start off the new year."

"Some people are never satisfied with a concession. In my experience, they ..."

From her rear mirror view, Mavis noted that Dan was listening intently. "I'd rather not have this talk in front of Dan."

"Fair enough." Susie surveyed the gently undulating landscape, noting more cars were headed toward Parkes than away from it. "I have to admit, Nikki, that I enjoyed working out how we'd approach our tribute to Elvis. I'm so glad we're dressing as Priscilla and that we don't all have to be Elvis. I'm still having problems with her hairdo though."

"I've got it mastered. I'll do your hair if you like."

"It's so hot out here!" Dan said from the back seat where he sat with Susie's daughter.

"I know, Dan, the air con needs re-gassing. We'll be there soon, and you can have a swim in the motel pool. Maybe Zoey could read to us what the tourist brochure says about Parkes."

"Located in inland New South Wales, the city of Parkes is best known for its role in the 1969 space program when Neil Armstrong first walked on the moon. The Parkes Observatory's giant radio telescope, otherwise known as The Dish, made it possible for that milestone event to be broadcast around the world. The area also has an interesting bushranger history and a long tradition as a gold-mining centre. The Elvis Festival, an inaugural event in 1993, has been an added attraction for the region increasing the population during the festival period and providing a boost to the local economy."

"Are we there yet?" Dan asked.

Zoey's face reflected her exasperation. "Does it look like it, Dan?"

"No."

"Then stop asking," Zoey replied.

"Zoey! You were his age once and just as ... you found travel just as hard and acted just like Dan."

"Then I'm sorry, Mum, for being so irritating. No offense, Nikki." Zoey made eye contact with Mavis via the car's rear view mirror.

"None taken. Try playin' *I Spy* with Dan."

"It's such a borin' game, Nikki."

"And yet you used to love it, Zoey," Susie said.

"When will we be there, Mummy?"

With a roll of her eyes and an exaggerated sigh, Zoey said, "Dan,

Christine M. Knight | Life Song

I spy with my little eye something beginning with g. Can you guess?" Their voices for the most part were white noise for the rest of the trip.

"Here's where we turn off the Western Highway and onto the Newell Highway," Susie said. "Not hard to see it's the main arterial transport route between Melbourne and Brisbane."

"Wow! Look at the size of that truck!"

"It's called a road train, Dan," Zoey said.

An amateur photographer, Susie was impressed by how the afternoon light affected the central western landscape. She reached for her camera, a high tech Canon, as she wound down the window. "Have you ever seen such red soil? The green fields and crops add such textures in this afternoon light! It'll be a great shot. Can you pull over, Nikki?"

"I can. There's a rest area just ahead."

"Oh, Mum, it's too hot for all that!" Zoey said. She wore a T-shirt declaring her fealty to Nirvana, a pleated mini skirt, and boot-like laced sneakers.

"Can I get out too, Mummy?"

"We all can. It's a good chance to stretch our legs. Scoot over, and get out Zoey's side, Dan. It's safer."

The rest of their convoy pulled into the area a minute or so later.

"Whoo! It's hot out here!" Susie's camera clicked away, recording the scene and the human narrative. Dan exploring, picking up rocks, and marvelling at some of them, before skipping stones across the field. Zoey looking at Dan's finds from time to time, chatting with him, occasionally walking along the horizontal logs that marked out the parking area, and later standing with Jack and Steve, trying to look more adult than she was. Tony waxing enthusiastically to Mavis about the festival as she sheltered in the shade of an ancient eucalypt. Their support crew, Lyle and Tim, leaning against their van, one of them enjoying a cigarette and the other a coke. Susie looked back at Zoey, noting her obvious admiration as she looked up at Jack. Susie made a mental note to tell Jack that Zoey had only just turned fifteen.

134

Mavis dropped her empty water bottle in the suspended cylindrical rubbish bin near her parked car. "Ready to push off, Susie?"

"Yeah, I've captured everything I wanted and more."

Car doors slammed closed in random time. Tyres churned up the dust and some gravel as they pulled out of the rest area and back onto the road.

On the outskirts of the rural city of Parkes but still on the highway, Mavis and her entourage were surprised to see rectangular Elvis banners lining the median strip.

Turning into Clarinda Street, Mavis noted the community support of the festival. Elvis decorations of one sort or another featured in the windows of the town's diverse businesses: the bakery, cafes, clothing retailers, intriguing generalist stores, motor cycle businesses, the mower shop, the Post Office, the supermarket, and even the town's older buildings which were both architecturally significant and beautiful. Both Mavis and Susie were impressed by the artistry of the stained glass windows in the older buildings and the way Elvis trappings sat oddly at ease on them.

"Susie, Tony and I agreed that our group would find Bushman's Dam in Kelly Reserve now to give us more time before the Saturday afternoon gig. While we're doin' that, they'll look for Gracelands and unload the gear there so we have more time before the gig tonight. We're meetin' them at the motel."

"Okay. This is a very long main street for an inland town," Susie said. "We're looking for a road intersection between the Leagues Club and a statue of Sir Henry Parkes."

"Not hard, Mum, if you look ahead."

"Your input is always so helpful, Zoey. A little less sarcasm thanks."

"Geez, I wonder who I inherited that from."

"What's inherited mean, Zoey?" Dan asked.

Mavis answered, "It's the ways that you are like me or like Gran and Pop, Dan. Like you inherited my hair colour and eye colour. You look like Pop was when he was a boy. You've seen the pictures of him."

"So what else did I inherit?"

"So many things it'd take the whole weekend to tell you … Well, would you look at that!" Mavis pointed at the oncoming traffic.

With their focus redirected to the road, Dan and Zoey laughed at the sight of an Elvis decorated car. It was the first one they'd seen that day.

"Look, Dan, there's another one!" Zoey called out, "and another!"

"That last one is my favourite," Dan said. "I never thought a car could have hair."

Later, the pair laughed spontaneously when a puffing Elvis looka-like rode past them, adorned in outlandish Elvis memorabilia – he was clearly the worse for his ride.

"Kelly Reserve straight ahead," Susie said. "I'm glad it's so clearly signposted. Makes navigating easy. Okay, everyone, let's play *First to Spot the Dam*."

"So who do you look like, Zoey?" Dan asked.

"Not like Mum that's for sure. I sometimes wonder if I look like …"

"Don't go there again, Zoey," Susie said. "You are your own unique person and that's what counts."

"I'm fifteen, Mum, I'd like to know about …"

"And Dan is almost seven so let's shelve this discussion until we're in private, Zoey."

"I see the dam! I see the dam! I win!" Dan said to Zoey. "What do I win?"

Zoey replied matching her actions to her words. "A tickle in the ribs and a twist of your nose."

Clearly visible from the road, Bushman's Dam at that time in the afternoon was not only impressive but breathtaking in the seasonal light.

Having parked near the Tourist Centre, the group disembarked. The heat that afternoon was well above the regional average of thirty two-degrees Celsius for that time of year.

"Your air con is working better than I thought," Susie said to Mavis who was distracted by Dan. "This feels like we've stepped into an oven."

"No, Dan," Mavis said, "you can't feed the ducks now … No, you can't explore the old train either … Don't drag your feet. Come here and hold my hand."

"Smell that, Nikki!" Susie said, "The distinctive fragrance of the Australian bush."

The area in which they stood, near the Tourist Centre, was well grassed, flat, and with a few shade trees here and there.

"There's a sense of water here like just before a storm breaks," Mavis said.

Susie responded. "If you can smell and taste the soil and a climate that a wine was grown in, and you can, then it stands to reason the vegetation in a region may have a fragrance that does the same thing, especially when it grows near water in an otherwise dry landscape."

"Nikki, Mum! You can see it!"

Susie ignored her daughter. "About a minute's walk I should think." Excited, Susie walked ahead of the group.

Lagging behind Susie, because of Dan's unpredictable stops when he caught sight of a lizard or other small bush creature, Mavis heard her say, "Wow! Look at those reflections in the dam! What a great spot for the festival!" To Mavis, she said, "They've set up the area amazingly well, don't you think? Look at that stage! I wish we could hear bands performing here before tomorrow so that we can get a feel for the acoustics. I can't wait to perform here Saturday. I think we should mic my drums for that gig."

Returning to the car, Mavis said, "Let's check out Gracelands before we head to the motel."

"But, Mummy…"

"It won't take long, Dan."

"Do you think it will resemble its namesake?" Susie asked.

"Maybe," Mavis replied. "I never ceased to be amazed at the grandeur of some of the colonial homes built in Australia in that period. Distance and cost didn't seem to be a barrier to establishing mansions."

Driving back towards Parkes in search of that town's Gracelands,

Mavis was surprised by the number of motel NO VACANCY signs and by the stretch of tents and the number of caravans in the tourist parks.

Gracelands was a red brick and cream weatherboard convention centre and restaurant owned by the founders of the Parkes Elvis Festival and Elvis Revival Inc, Bob and Ann Steele. From the sound of it, the festival was already in full swing.

"Parking might be an issue later," Mavis said. The area was already jam-packed. Cars were parked everywhere and anywhere: in the designated parking spaces, on the grass and even on the red dirt. She was glad now Tony and the other guys had arranged to unload their gear at the venue before finding their motel.

"Okay, Dan, we're headin' for the motel now, and you can have that swim I promised you."

In the role of navigator, Susie directed Mavis to their accommodation, a non-descript bungalow motel complex. Gardens around the complex were minimal but bitumen, in the form of a parking area, was in plentiful supply. There was a fenced pool though with some greenery around it and shade sails providing partial protection from the sun.

As Mavis parked, Tony came out of his room. "Thought that might be you. I've checked in for you. Here's your keys." He knocked on the doors of the other three rooms the band shared to alert them that the women had arrived.

The other men acknowledged the women before they climbed into Jack's car. Tony remained on the pavement as their spokesman. "We're off to the local pub for a drink." He climbed into the front passenger seat, his door remaining open. "Do you want us to wait for you or what?"

Mavis laughed. "I can see how well waitin' would go down."

Jack's other car doors reopened.

"Fellas, stay put! I don't want to come. I promised Dan a swim, and it's what I intend to do too. Zoey can stay with us, Susie, if you want to go."

"I'm heading for the shower and a change of clothes, Nikki. Geez, look at the red dirt on my shoes. Zoey, are you going with the guys or staying here?"

Mavis arched an eyebrow, surprised Susie thought Zoey had a choice.

"I'll stay here, Mum."

Car doors slammed; the engine revved into life again.

"Last one in the pool, Dan, is a rotten egg. Don't forget, Mum, you said we could talk about …"

"The man I'd rather not talk about. Yes, I guess it's time we did."

Tony wound down his window. "We'll meet you at the Service-men's Club, Nikki, for a quick dinner at six. You know where it is?"

"Mummy, Zoey will beat me. Open our door!"

"Yes on both accounts." Mavis opened the door to the room she shared with Dan. "We saw it on our reconnoitre of the town. See you then."

United by thirst, Tony and the four other men drove off.

After locking her car, Mavis entered the three-star basic room. The carpet, though clean, was stained with the red dirt of the region. Mavis was grateful that the air conditioning unit worked when she switched it on.

* * *

With her hair swept up into a beehive hairdo in the style of Pris-cilla during her Elvis years, Mavis and the band waited in the stage wings of Gracelands. Their soundman, Tim, was in position and had assured her their levels were right for the room.

As the second act, they followed a talented performer who had opened that evening's tribute show after the free rock and roll classes held earlier that night. His band, more by accident than intent Mavis assumed, represented Elvis at different physical stages of his career: from taut, trim, and terrific to corpulent. The singer was costumed in Elvis' iconic white jumpsuit and cape. Without seeing the price tags, Mavis knew the men in this band had spent a lot of money on their outfits.

While huge amounts of money had *not* been spent by her band on their Presley looks, Mavis was pleased nonetheless with the effect. Both she and Susie wore hairpieces that added volume and height to their overall look. Their hair seemed to defy gravity. Both women wore sixties styled makeup with lots of heavy black eyeliner. Like the Priscilla of that period, their other makeup was pale with no blush to speak of and very pale lipstick.

Having rummaged through Marg's boxes of old clothing in search of what she could adapt into her Priscilla costume, Mavis had found a vintage blue shift that suited her purpose. Her mother had made the necessary adjustments so that the dress was a tighter fit and had added an oversized black bow at the point where the V-neck plunged revealing Mavis' cleavage. Mavis wore black, low-heeled shoes.

Susie wore a simple, sleeveless, salmon-pink T-shirt and a vintage full skirt with a salmon-pink and white floral design on it, sashed with a salmon coloured ribbon. Most of her clothing had been scrounged from her mother's forgotten clothing treasures stored in the roof of the family home. Susie had added white flats as footwear for the finishing touch.

The rest of the band wore early Elvis: black leather fitted trousers, white T-shirts, and black leather jackets. Their hair, much shorter than in Elvis' heyday, was greased to imitate Elvis' look. Physically, they were a testament to Elvis' athleticism in his early years.

It had been Mavis' idea to string Elvis' hits into a musical theatre piece based on the Elvis and Priscilla story. Despite their protests, Jack, the bass guitarist, and Tony, who played lead guitar, had succumbed to Mavis' pressure for them to sing the role of Elvis in tandem. Mavis had adapted the Elvis lyrics she sang as Priscilla to fit her gender and had arranged the medley to emphasize the drama of the Presleys' story.

Having lost the earlier battle over their singing roles, it took only a little persuasion for the men to take direction from Mavis so that their performance worked dramatically, a dialogue of action and interaction during key parts of songs.

"C'mon," Mavis had said during earlier rehearsals, "audiences love it when bands interact. They like to believe in the onstage relationships. We can capitalize on their fascination with Elvis by providing a window into a small part of his life."

The closing chords of the first act rang out, the drummer sounding his final statement. With a sweeping theatrical bow, the Elvis tribute artist finished his act in true Elvis style. The crowd roared and stomped their approval, pleased with the performer's homage to their King. The tribute artist was clearly moved by their response.

"Performance can be an addictive drug, don't you think?" Susie said to Mavis. Then to the other band members, she said, "C'mon, if we don't claim the space, he won't get off and nor will his backing band. They'll be wanting to do an encore."

As Mavis' band assumed their respective positions on stage, the MC, now in a single spotlight, announced them. The lights came up as a strong drum beat, and a striking guitar riff opened the band's medley. The men sang in unison 'Baby Let's Play House' to Mavis followed by 'Love Me Tender'. There was a playful, flirtatious energy between them. Mavis replied with 'It Feels so Right' and 'Such a Night'. The mood of the bracket changed with her rendition of 'Hound Dog', partly a Priscilla vocalized criticism of Elvis and his apologetic agreement with her, that ended in harmonized reconciliation. 'Heartbreak Hotel' followed before Mavis passed the vocals back to the men for their vocal lead in 'Suspicious Minds'. Her reply, 'Don't Be Cruel', led into the men's rendition of 'My Baby Left' to which she had added a melodic spoken dialogue. Their finale, 'Always on My Mind', ended on a poignant note with Mavis' Priscilla and the men's Elvis singing key phrases in a haunting round.

There was a hushed stillness as the final harmonized notes hung in the air. Then the audience erupted into applause, some of them visibly moved.

Mavis and her band took their bows. The MC returned to the stage faster than Mavis liked. Stage lights narrowed to a single spotlight.

"Ladies and gentlemen, it's my pleasure to introduce to you, the outstanding hip-swiveling, gyrating, dance sensation from last year's festival. Put your hands together, please, for Kenny Kiss' representation of Elvis."

With the opening bars of 'Jail House Rock', the spotlight fixed on the dance floor as Kenny Kiss slid across it into the limelight. The audience cheered appreciatively during Kiss' dance parody of Elvis.

At the end of that evening's ninety minutes of tribute performances, patrons spilled into the other facilities at Gracelands.

Standing with Jack at the bar, Tony waited for their drinks order. "Kenny Kiss sure had Elvis' moves down pat, Jack!"

"A pity he hasn't got Elvis' golden throat, Tony."

"Or anything close to it, yet the audience loved him."

"Kiss or what he represented?"

With a tray of drinks in hand, Tony and Jack returned to the series of bar tables that the band had rearranged to accommodate them.

Enjoying the intimacy that came from bonds developed in performance, Mavis reflected on the mutual respect and care that existed within the band. It was what she treasured about her relationship with Gary and Kate too. Her first experience of it had been many years ago when boarding at Madison House.

Rubbing elbows with Jack to her right and Susie to her left, Mavis laughed at the wry banter that flowed between Susie and the men. Relaxed, as much by the alcohol as laughter, Mavis enjoyed Jack's physical support without giving much thought to it.

When Susie moved to the bar with Steve to get the next round of drinks, a man, whose alcoholic consumption that night had made him worse-for-wear, stopped at the band's tables. Looking pointedly at Mavis, he said, "You know you got it wrong, don't you? Priscilla never sang!"

Jack stood down from the stool he had been sitting on and shielded Mavis from the drunk. "Shove off, mate."

The man squared off at Jack.

Jack's fists clenched as he assumed a defensive strike stance. "Just you try it, mate."At the same time, their roadie, Lyle, built bigger than most front row forwards, stepped between the men. Tim, their lanky soundman, also stood to back up Lyle.

Lyle spoke softly. "Push off, mate. Thanks for your input." He turned to Jack. "The trick is to give that sort of bloke a way out or things escalate."

"Point noted." Feeling he had established his alpha status, Jack returned to the stool. He looked at Mavis, expecting admiration and was uneasy that her face was troubled.

Later that night, another inebriated man added, as he passed him on the way to the bar, "I didn't like your act. We're here to celebrate the King's reign, not remember his marriage breakup, *and,*" the man tilted and glared at the group, "you got some of the words wrong!"

Jack lifted his half-empty glass in a toast and said loudly, "To the King!"

Everyone within hearing distance responded in kind.

This time, when Jack checked Mavis, he read approval. He relaxed on the stool, sitting comfortably tall and in command of the situation.

Lyle slipped off his tool. "Another drink, Jack?"

Jack looked over the rim of his whiskey glass. "I'm good with this one thanks."

Mavis followed Lyle. "I'll lend you a hand." At the bar, she stood next to him. "Thanks for defusing the situation."

"My pleasure. You know Jack had good intentions but didn't know how to protect you."

"I know. I'm glad you did."

"Don't listen to those drunks," the barman said to Mavis and Lyle. Lyle had a pleasant face and was built to carry half a rugby team across the try line. Service demands at the bar had slowed, allowing the man a discrete comment. "Your band was fantastic."

"You caught the act?"

"Sure did. My shift began at the end of the rock and roll lessons. You're professionals, aren't you?"

"We like to think so," Mavis responded.

"Personally, I wish there were more acts of your quality and less five-minutes-of-fame wonders. Good luck with your other gigs around town over the festival. You'll find the audiences varied in their tastes and expectations. For some of them, you'll be remembered as the hit of this year's festival. As far as I'm concerned, you are!"

As the band exited Gracelands, many passing guests threw them one-liners of praise for their act that night.

Back at the motel, Mavis and the band sat on the elevated concrete path outside the reception office. They were still high on the adrenaline of performance. The crash, when it would come, was unpredictable in its timing and always delayed. Jack, Steve, Lyle, and Tim shared a bottle of Scotch bought earlier that night. Around them, suburbia slept.

"Ever seen a sky so black and stars as brilliant as that?" Tim lay back on his elbows, stretching his lanky frame out to its full and impressive length. He had 'reaching for the sky' written in his gene pool.

"Must be why they have the observatory out here." Jack savoured the single malt Scotch. "This is bloody good whiskey." He sat in close contact with Mavis, intensely aware of her. Leaning in so that her hair brushed against his cheek, he said softly, "You were great tonight." He leant back on his elbows, his glance following the line of her body, curved and sensuous, tanned and sleek.

"Consider the compliment returned. I think we should do more with the interplay between Pricilla and Elvis in 'Hound Dog' though." Mavis stood, suddenly aware of the intent in Jack's expression and puzzled by it. She positioned herself at a triangle point between the two men as she faced them. "What'd you think, Tony?"

Having polished off the last of the bottle of Scotch, Steve also stood. "The audience certainly eat up the onstage relationship. Anyone feel like a run?"

The support crew stood, but only Lyle limbered up. "Yep."

Tony reached for his room key in the pocket of his jeans. "Whatever sells, Nikki. Count me out, fellas. It's time I slept."

"I'm with you lot." Jack loped off after the men who had jogged off into the night, streetlights occasionally illuminating them before they faded from sight.

Susie picked it up and read the label on the back. "Don't know how they can run after finishing off that bottle. It's one hundred and twenty proof!"

"Sleep already, Tony? How did you manage to come down so soon?"

"I haven't, but sleeping pills, courtesy of Dr Keyman, get me the shut-eye I need to get through the days."

"It's time I went too." In response to Mavis' unspoken question, Susie added, "You guessed right, pills. It's been the only way I can function in the day, hold down a day job, take care of Zoey, avoid pouches under my eyes, and stay fit for the long haul. I've spare if you want one."

"No, I'm fine."

"You won't be with Dan waking early as kids do. Zoey will pick him up at seven-thirty and take him off for breakfast and to that park we saw down the road. Broken sleep is not the same as deep sleep, y' know. You sure you don't want to try one?"

"I am … Susie, can I ask you something really personal?"

"That depends on what you're asking."

"That talk you were goin' to have with Zoey … Was it about her father?"

"Zoey doesn't have a father, Mavis. All she has is a biological link to a guy who I once thought I was in love with. He supported my right to abortion but just didn't get that *choice* meant I had *other* options."

"So … what did you tell her?"

"A version of that."

"A bit harsh for any teenager to hear, Susie."

"I don't sugarcoat life for her, Mavis, and I'll be damned if I'm going to mythologize Max Ryan into anything other than what he was: handsome, more interested in notching women up than being in a real relationship, a wannabe rock star … I don't like being judged especially by someone who hasn't been in my shoes."

"What?"

"Something I get touchy over. You put on a great show tonight. The ladies certainly respond to Jack. That man has charisma in bucketfuls."

"He has that practiced knack of lookin' at a woman and makin' her feel extra special. Such a waste!"

"Practiced is right, Nikki, but don't dismiss how he feels about you. He likes you a lot. That means there's a potential problem down the track if you have difficulty turning off your onstage relationship. I'm assuming that's what happened tonight and that you weren't *actually* flirting with him. There aren't many bass players of his calibre around. Is it w..?"

"He's not interested in me that way, Susie. He's gay. Don't you remember him sayin' he wasn't interested in pickin' up birds when we held auditions?"

"That man gay? No way! He *meant* he's in the band for the music and not for the groupies. He doesn't *need* any sort of gimmick to get laid. Even Zoey feels his appeal, and she's still a kid."

"Oh …Oohh!"

"Surely you've seen the way women mob him?"

"I have, but I thought his allure was that he was good lookin' and mockingly distant."

"The unobtainable fruit syndrome? Nuh! Look, he's too good a bass player to string along and then decide he's not the man for you. It'd hurt the band."

"And he's great to collaborate with too." Thinking back to some of their song writing sessions at her cottage, Mavis blushed. She was glad the night hid her rising colour. She'd been *way* too intimate with the man, treating him with the easy camaraderie she usually reserved for Gary. Jack had accepted it as his due, and she'd thought nothing more about it.

"You need to be careful how you manage the fellas, Nikki. At least two of them are attracted to you. We're duffers; we should've got one of the guys to carry Dan back to your room before they left."

"Dan's not that heavy."

After carrying her son to their room and unable to sleep herself, Mavis returned to the car park and pavement outside her room. Awake an hour later and still sitting outside, her mood lifted at the sight of the returning runners. Beyond doubt, they were intoxicated as well as exhausted. Lyle held Steve up on his feet.

Jack bent over, puffing. "Couldn't find our way back."

Mavis felt like some type of blind had been lifted as she looked at Jack. He exuded pure virility. Feeling Mavis' eyes on him, he looked up, smiled, and winked at her. It was a practiced smile and one that he knew melted women's hearts. He crossed to Mavis, becoming aware of her subtle perfume. "Waiting up for me?"

In an exaggerated, "Shush," Steve, with fingers to his lips and slightly staggering, added, "People are sleepin' here, y' know."

Her eyes sparkling with amusement, Mavis kept her smile small. "And who has tickets on himself? I was unwinding, Jack, in my own way. Go to bed you lot before you fall over."

As their doors clicked closed, Mavis took her own advice. She showered in the light of the torch she carried in her handbag. Lying in bed, wide awake, listening to the unfamiliar sounds of that night, she distracted herself from the issues confronting her by considering the effect pills and alcohol had had on Elvis' life. Slowly, she drifted off into a fitful sleep.

The next morning, Dan, who had put the television on for morning cartoons, jolted Mavis awake. For a while, she lay there with a pillow over her head. Feeling much the worse for wear, a grateful Mavis opened the door to Zoey half an hour later.

"Sorry, Nikki, I overslept. C'mon, Dan, do you feel like eggs and sausage for breakfast?" They left.

The mere thought of eggs made Mavis heave. She was not an egg person at the best of times. Crawling back into bed, she slipped into a deeper slumber with the hum of the air conditioning unit in the background.

Friday afternoon saw the band at the Serviceman's club. In the evening, they returned to Gracelands for another performance. The audiences for both these performances had markedly different characters.

"Odd," Tony said as they sat again on the concrete path outside the motel's reception area. "I thought tonight was our best performance but not so the crowd."

Tim scratched his chin. "What do you mean, Tony? You went down big, and our sound levels were the best in the house, even if I do say so myself."

"Compared to the act we followed?"

"Absolutely, Tony, but for different reasons."

"How amazin' was that guy!"

Susie poured herself a plastic cup of bottled premixed gin and tonic. "He was more than inspired, Tony! Tonight wasn't just a gig to him though, was it? It was like he was going through a sacred ritual. He's like a religious fanatic but with Elvis as his god."

"And that explains the earful you got from him, Susie, afterwards when you said, 'Good show'."

Susie laughed. "The potted version of his evangelical moment with me, Tony."

Saturday, Zoey and Dan woke Mavis just before midday with news of the spectacular Elvis Street Parade and a small Miss Priscilla competition that had taken place in Cooke Park.

"Honest, Nikki," Zoey sat at the end of Mavis' bed, "you would've won Miss Priscilla hands down if you'd entered."

"I wish you had, Mummy. Zoey took me to the bushranger museum and then the gold mining centre."

Aware from her babysitting stint with Dan that he liked to cite litanies about what he had done, Zoey excused herself.

The rest of Dan's newly acquired knowledge-sharing continued as Mavis prepared for the afternoon performance. When he had nothing left to share about bushrangers and goldmines, Dan's conversation progressed to the NASA Space program and Parkes' role in it. Dan's capacity to retain and relay information never ceased to amaze Mavis.

Saturday afternoon saw them performing at Bushman's Dam at three. A huge dome-shaped marquee covered the stage there. Before the stage and on the grassed parkland, the audience sat on white plastic chairs, about three hundred in number. Trees provided some shade. There was beauty in the landscape that added an emotional component to the performances that afternoon.

Having been warmed up by numerous Elvis tribute artists with different takes on the audience's idol, the crowd were ready for something very different. With hushed expectation, they embraced Mavis as Priscilla and Jack, in particular, as Elvis.

Waves of audience emotion lathed the band during the playful onstage interaction of 'Baby Let's Play House' and the building romance of 'Love Me Tender',' It Feels so Right', and 'Such a Night'. There was an audible release of audience tension when Priscilla harmonized in reconciliation with her Elvis at the end of their version of 'Hound Dog'. As the band's set built to its climax, the depth of the audience involvement intensified. The finale 'Always on My Mind', sung and spoken, at times in a round and at times as solo, had a striking effect. Even Zoey and Dan, seated in the stage wings, were moved.

After the final harmonized notes of 'Always on My Mind' dissolved into sustained lingering silence, the crowd exploded, cheering wildly, standing in ovation. This time, the afternoon's MC allowed the band time to enjoy the applause and to take an encore.

That night saw them at another venue with another highly appreciative crowd. The wave of excitement the band rode swelled.

Later, over drinks in the bar, Susie said, "You guys were certainly in role tonight." She did not add that the sexual tension between Jack and Mavis put a real edge to their onstage interactions. Nor did she comment on the obvious intimacy between them now, reflected as much by their mirrored body language and the closeness of their heads when they shared a private comment. Looking around the group, Susie noted Steve's tension and wondered about it.

Tim stood, ready to shout the next round of drinks. "You with me, Lyle?" Talking to the band, he added, "That flirty stuff you did with Jack, Nikki, actually punctuated the songs, *and* didn't the crowd love it!"

Lyle stood belatedly. "I'll say they did! Who was the bloke you were talkin' with, Tony?"

Steve downed his drink. "Personally, I thought Nikki and Tony sold the crowd on Elvis' love for Priscilla. Jack was too much of a hound."

"Tiemo McGuire. He's a booking agent for the Lithgow-Bathurst-Orange club circuit. I've accepted two months work for our Elvis act starting next month."

"That's a long way from Keimera for two nights work each week, Tony." Lyle looked at the other band members to gauge their reaction.

"You what?" Mavis reacted.

Tony ignored Mavis and spoke to the other musicians. "First time I've ever been approached by an agent, Tiemo McGuire is his name. The money was too good to knock back. Best pay we've ever been offered. I didn't think it would be an issue. He's express posting us the booking details. I'll sign it when we get back, and he'll have it by the return mail."

"Where do you get off doing that without getting our agreement?" Susie demanded.

"Man," Jack joined in, "the Elvis act was supposed to be a one-off. It's *not* what I signed up for! What do you think, Steve?"

Mavis cut across Steve's voiced discontent. "It's not on, Tony. I thought I had this settled with you last year."

"Why not?"

"So many reasons," Mavis replied.

"The main one," Susie added, "being we aren't *that* sort of band."

"And if I don't like us pullin' out ..?"

Mavis was silent, but the others spoke as one. "It's goodbye, Tony."

"This is *my* band!"

"Anyone here join the band because of Tony?" Jack asked.

Again the reply, with the exception of Mavis, was unanimous. "No!"

There was a tense silence before Tony stood up and walked off.

"Let's push off." Jack downed his drink. "You guys up to another run after we get back to the motel?"

"Sure thing," was the disjointed response from his running mates.

"Jack," Susie said, "remember there are kids sleeping when you get back. Keep the noise down."

"As if ..."

"Thanks."

The men left.

Breaking the silence after the men's departure and taking in Mavis' expression, Susie said, "You're not going to give in to Tony, are you?"

"No, we're of a like mind on that. I just felt that it was a bit brutal ..."

"The business can be at times. Tony is a growing liability. He only wants to be a big fish in a small pond. We might need to ditch him if he doesn't get on board with where we want to go. You need to toughen up, and be ready to cope when that day comes."

"If that day comes, it'd be a double loss. He's not only a top guitarist but our business manager as well."

"Hmmm." After a pause, Susie added, "Zoey plans on taking Dan to more Elvis events tomorrow although I'm not sure exactly what. She was immersed in the festival brochure when I left her with Dan at the motel. That all right?"

"Absolutely. Anything that lets me get sleep before the drive home is *greatly* appreciated. Dan promised not to wake me up this morning and didn't. I'm hopin' he has as much control tomorrow."

"Seriously, Nikki, you should try a pill tonight. You'll be amazed how much better you'll feel. The drive home will be safer as well."

Strung out and aware that she couldn't afford another long, slow drift into early morning sleep, Mavis accepted her offer. She did not want to put them at risk when she was behind the wheel on the long drive home the next day.

The women entered Susie's motel room. Zoey was a covered bump in her bed whereas Dan, asleep on Susie's bed, lay flat on his back with his arms thrown back onto his pillow.

Susie pulled the bedding back for Mavis.

After scooping Dan up into her arms, Mavis carried him, deep in slumber, back to her room. As quietly as she could, Mavis readied herself for bed, lingering in the shower, enjoying the ease of warm flowing water over her.

With the 'aid' of the pill, Sleep came to her like a lover, its embrace cocooned her from life's distractions allowing her to fall asleep easily.

When she woke the next morning and looked at the bedside clock, Mavis was amazed to see it was almost twelve. *Thank God for late checkouts*, she thought as she hurriedly showered and packed before rendezvousing with the rest of her entourage for lunch at one.

After a mug of strong, black coffee and a hamburger with chips, Mavis truly knew the meaning of 'refreshed'.

During the drive home and with Susie at the wheel, Dan and Zoey regaled them with recounts of the Elvis events seen earlier that day.

"Mummy, there were heaps of horses dressed up to look like Elvis too."

Laughing, Zoey added, "And some of the horses actually looked better than their human competition, didn't they, Dan?"

Eventually, Dan fell asleep, slumped against Zoey's shoulder. After a while, Mavis too nodded off. Glad of the respite from conversation, Susie had time to process Zoey's growing need to meet the biological link. *I'll make contact with Max when she's twenty-one. I should be able to put her off until then.*

When Mavis woke an hour or so later, the women switched roles. The rest of the trip was spent in companionable silence.

Chapter 10

Back at the Ford dealership the next week, Mavis found her co-workers were more interested in the details of the Parkes Elvis Festival than in her band's experience. In polite disinterest, the salesmen and other clerical staff drifted back to their respective work when her recounting became personal.

Mavis' sense of post-performance flatness increased later. When she was secluded in the ladies' toilet, she overheard the dealership's accounts clerk say, "I'm sick of hearing about the Mavis Show," and the manager's secretary reply, "Me too."

When Mavis looked at life through the filter of an artist's lens, her workdays lacked depth, a focal point. Like a first glance at a Jackson Pollack painting, not much stood out. There was a lot of activity yet there wasn't anything that aroused her interest. This added to the overall greyness of her days and dissatisfaction with that world.

Life outside Mavis' workday was of more interest to her as it was filled with micro-pictures of the lives of her friends and family. It was there that she found her emotional reaction, made contact with life's picture, and had meaningful experiences.

On the Saturday afternoon following their return from Parkes, Mavis took Dan to the beach and caught up with Kate who also had the day free. Gary was rostered on as a lifesaver.

While Dan played in the surf's shallows and within the flags, the women avoided the sun under a massive beach umbrella as they chatted.

"I don't like my dad's latest female interest," Kate said. "Theresa is so possessive of him and seems to go out of her way to block me having any one-on-one time with him."

"Sharing would be hard, given you've had him all to yourself since ninety-two."

"It's not me that is the problem."

"You sure about that?"

"You be the judge. Last weekend, Gary and I went out to dinner with them. It was Gary's idea. He's such a peacemaker. It's irritating when he is, and I sort of resent it. Theresa talked non-stop all night. Whenever I tried to talk to Dad, she'd listen for a few minutes and then distract him with something trivial." Imitating the woman, Kate spoke with over-the-top enunciation. "Oh, Robert, would you look at that. Such a cute doggy. I'd so love to own one! Pity I live in a flat. I'd just love," Kate added gesture to her imitation, "to have the space you have."

Mavis laughed.

"Yes, it seems funny now, but it wasn't then."

"I'm amazed they allowed dogs in the restaurant."

"It was in some woman's handbag and not drawing attention to itself until Theresa did. The poor woman had to tie her dog up outside while she and her partner had dinner. They made a short shift of it, I can tell you." Continuing in her imitation, Kate said, "Oh, Robert, Kate has just reminded me of the funniest thing that happened at work this week." In her own voice, Kate added, "Short version … her story was as dull as … The other thing I hate is how loud she gets. When she can't stop me talking with some paltry diversion, because I refuse to give way to her, she talks over the top. From the way she dresses to everything she does, her goal is: Look at me! Look at me!"

"And Gary's opinion?"

"He thinks I should cut her some slack because Dad likes her and seems happy. Gary says I should reciprocate Dad's gesture in accepting him. Apparently, Gary was really aware of the strength of our father-daughter bond and felt an outsider at first. Gary says Dad consciously made room and included him, so I should her."

"Is he right?"

"Maybe." In the ensuing silence, Kate added, "Yes, he was. To be frank, I found it hard trying to split myself between them."

"I hear that loud and clear. Know exactly how that feels. I think you should try to see the good in the situation. With this woman on the scene, the pressure you feel about daily contact with him is lessened, surely? I'm so aware of the weight of such responsibility myself."

"We've both got picture and frame issues, haven't we?"

"That we have."

After a pause, Kate said, "Funny how things change." She paused. "When I was a kid, my mum used to bask in what she called 'the healthy sun' to get that 'sun-kissed glow' whenever we came down to the beach. Now look at us: slip, slop, slapping with sunscreen for all it's worth to avoid skin cancer." Kate looked down the beach. "Have you ever seen so many beach umbrellas?"

"We rarely went to the beach when I was a kid. The dairy farm took up virtually all of my parents' time. I spent a lot of the time at home alone with my music."

The sharp, short blows of a whistle, a lifesaver's signal for warning, cut through the air. "Oi! Oi, there!" one of the beach lifesavers yelled at two men who were swimming well outside of the flags and drifting towards the dangerous rip that locals knew was at the northern end of the beach.

Lifting the bullhorn, he said, "Get back inside the flags where it's safe to swim!"

The swimmers gave the lifesaver the bird. Their subsequent replies were inaudible, but the aggression in their manner carried clearly. Then, in a show of defiance, they moved into deeper waters, unaware that they were moving closer toward the rip.

"You bastards! You think I'm out here for the fun of it?" The lifesaver ran back to the surf club.

From where she sat, Kate recognized the lifesaver as Gary's offsider in the tragedy in the Spring. "This type of situation has to be handled with sensitivity, or it'll get worse. Excuse me for a moment."

Kate joined up with the het-up, returning lifesaver when he stopped for a brief moment to talk to her.

"They won't listen, Kate," the lifesaver said. "There's a tragedy waiting to happen out there for sure. Damned if I'm putting my life on the line for those ..."

"It's okay, mate," Kate said. "Don't take it personally. Gary is on watchtower duty. He'll have called in reinforcements."

Kate and the lifesaver moved on as the lifesaver was saying, "Those blokes meant it to be personal!"

"Yes, they did, and they win if you react to the sting in their words."

"Spoken like a woman ..."

Back at the surf club, Gary had been watching the developing conflict through his binoculars. He called the IRB crew into action and then went downstairs. As he emerged from the clubhouse, he saw Kate and the lifesaver approaching.

"No, Dan." Mavis intercepted him as he tried to follow Kate to meet Gary. "We stay out of it!" She returned Dan to where he'd been playing. Water washed around her feet as she tried to keep him distracted from the developing beach drama.

"Kate, H-man," Gary said in greeting, having crossed to them. "I sent Birdies' crew out to handle the matter."

"You reckon they'll have any more success than me? We'll need the council lifeguards for those fools!"

"Get them, Gary," Kate said. "Precaution is better than ..."

"Had a call to them before I came down. Here they are now."

From a southern approach to the surf club, the two salaried council lifeguards on duty arrived. Like council rangers, they had the legal authority to enforce intervention whereas the lifesavers had a moral responsibility and obligation to do so. Of course, they could be sued if they failed to protect the public even if it was from themselves.

After cursory greetings, one of the lifeguards said, "Let's hope this is a storm in a teacup. Do you reckon we need to cross over to the northern end of the beach?"

"Without a doubt," the first lifesaver caught up in the drama said.

Kate said to Gary, "Birdie will need to handle the situation sensitively."

Gary considered his reply carefully. "No one needs you to tell us that, Kate."

In step with Gary, Kate moved north with him. "You know what I meant."

The first lifesaver followed, half a step behind them. "Yeah, I can imagine how that would have played out. Gentlemen, are you aware you're swimming into a rip that'll not only put your lives at risk but ours as well if a rescue is needed? It's my duty to direct you to the safer waters between the flags." The lifesaver paused. "I did the shorter version and still got the bird."

"Gary!" Another lifesaver ran after them from the club house. "The IRB crew have just called in. They've been ignored and have asked for further direction."

"Tell them to take any necessary precautionary action needed to safeguard lives. Kate, we've got this covered. Go back to Mavis."

"No, I'm coming too." Looking at the men around her, she added, "The more witnesses the better. You should've brought a radio."

"In these situations, you have to trust the man on the spot, Kate. Birdie's got the only direction from us he needs."

The group moved in easy strides to the northern end of the beach. Gary and Kate marginally apart from them.

"You have to trust my handling of this, Kate. Go back to Mavis."

"I do. I could never leave you, Gary, not if there's a risk of danger."

Turning his head, he held her gaze. "You're my talisman?"

"Something like that."

Gary picked up the group's pace.

In the meantime, offshore, the IRB crew had experienced further trouble with the two swimmers. Intimidated by the size of the inflatable rescue boat but still defiant, the men swam away into deeper water.

Using a loudhailer, Birdie said, "Return to the area between the flags. I told you before there is a dangerous rip out here."

"Fuck off! Sure there is!"

"Looks like we'll have to do this the hard way. Position the IRB," Birdie said.

The motorman manoeuvred his craft in front of the swimmers who refused to be blocked or herded.

In an attempt to end the stalemate, Birdie and one of his offsiders dove into the water while their teammate took the rubber duckie a little distance away from the conflict. The lifesavers, with a swift one-two-three manoeuvre, usually reserved for the panicked and drowning, put the swimmers into a supine position so they could be towed back to shore.

When back on wet sand, a scuffle broke out accompanied by an impressive range of expletives from the swimmers. One of the swimmers threw a punch at Gary's co-lifesaver. Gary intercepted it, his reflexes being faster than his mate's. Having restrained the man, Gary said, "When you're on our beach, mate, you swim where it's safe between the flags. It's our lives you put at risk when you flout the rules."

"It's us who have to bear the burden if you can't be rescued!" the other lifesaver added as Gary released the man.

"You cunts think you own the beach!" The bigger of the two male swimmers threw a punch at the lifesaver initially involved in the incident that day. One of the other lifeguards intercepted it with a manoeuvre that ended with the swimmer's arm being pinioned behind his back.

"It's best we escort these blokes from the beach." With the bigger swimmer threatening further violence, the lifeguard added, "I've got the legal authority to kick you off this beach, mate! If you don't pull your head in and shut up, I'll have these lifesavers call the police."

Amidst the cheers from other beachgoers, as the offenders were escorted from the beach, the lifeguards 'educated' the recalcitrants about the crucial role the Lifesaving Movement played in coastal communities and the etiquette expected of anyone who came onto Keimera beaches and into its waters.

Mavis and Dan hurried to Gary on his return. "See, Dan, Gary is perfectly okay." In an aside she said, "I was frightened for you. We haven't had that kind here before." Mavis turned to Kate, impressed. "You're such a lioness."

"What?"

"You just are, Kate. So fiercely protective. It's one of the things Gary and I love about you, isn't it, Gary?"

"One of the many things … although she can be very bossy."

"It's 'one for all and all for one' with lifesavers, isn't it?"

"As it is with us," Gary said.

Kate agreed.

"Oh, you guys …"

Gary struck his habitual Mickey Mouse pose.

Mavis hugged him. "You haven't done that in ages. Kate …"

"He's on the mend."

* * *

The Sydney Festival ran throughout January and featured live music around the city; a variety of theatre events; dance parties on the foreshore of the Opera House and Darling Harbour; street theatre including jugglers and acrobatic stunt artists as well as other masters of the physical show. It was the first opportunity The Nikki Mills Band had to perform a set of their original material and move beyond the music of others.

The band had been booked for two gigs after an intense vetting process of applications for an open-air afternoon concert at Tumbalong Park. The park was situated at the southern end of the Darling Harbour precinct and included manicured grassed lawns, native and exotic shrubs, palm trees, an extensive network of ornate water features and a raised, covered stage with full backstage facilities. It also featured a fabulous free-to-the-public children's playground with various adventure play and climbing apparatus. Further south was the expansive Chinese Garden of Friendship, a tranquil haven within the busy city.

A derelict dockside area from the 1970s, Darling Harbour had been transformed during a foreshore development in 1988 into an entertainment hub within the city of Sydney. The eastern shore of that harbour featured Cockle Bay Wharf, known for its wide range of restaurants and nightclubs. The western shore was dominated by the Harbourside Shopping Centre which had huge expanses of white walls and glass and stretches of sails that reflected the beauty of the harbour. A Convention Centre and Tumbalong Park were south of Harbourside.

Booked for two timeslots, the fourth Friday night of the month followed by the Saturday afternoon, and with the license to play her own material, Mavis found it difficult to maintain her façade of calm when surrounded by celebrated names in the industry. The festival's diverse programming provided her with exposure to the richness of the contemporary jazz and blues scene of her day: jazz, soul, hip hop, R&B, and rock.

Grateful that Gary and Kate had travelled up to Sydney with her that weekend and had Dan in their care, Mavis remained silently thrilled throughout the experience. Her excitement translated into an energized, show-stopping performance. Later, she found it hard not to giggle, schoolgirl like, when a few of the top billed artists of that day complimented her.

As the band were leaving the musicians' area Saturday afternoon, an agent for the big Sydney clubs' circuit briefly met with them. He arranged a meeting at one of the nearby restaurants in Harbourside for that evening to discuss work in the Sydney clubs.

After the agent left them, the group stood in the bands area at the back of the stage, discussing the unexpected turn in their affairs.

"How is this different from the deal I brought to the table in Parkes?" Tony asked.

"A lot of ways," Jack said, "the most important being it'll be *original* material."

Steve added, "We're *all* hearin' what's on offer before a deal is struck!"

"This is all too cool!" Susie said, fingering the agent's business card.

Mavis walked alongside Tony as the group moved into the spectators' area in front of the stage. "You were right last year, when you said we had to do the Sydney circuit."

Mollified, Tony said, "It's where the money is. In the past, I found that local work was about respite from travel whereas work in Sydney is about building a reputation. You ready to increase the number of gigs per week yet?"

"If it's on offer."

With the live bands' scene in the park ended that Saturday afternoon, Mavis and her entourage wandered over to the western shore of Darling Harbour and dined early. During their meal, they were entertained by an impressive line-up of Latin dancers who took the spotlight on a specially constructed floor at the wharf's edge. After that show, the dance floor was opened to the general public.

Fired by the Latin rhythms of the night, Kate led Gary onto the crowded dance floor.

Watching them, Mavis had to admit that Gary had learnt some pretty smooth dance moves. They no longer moved their bodies and feet on the music but to the music. They were obviously physically attuned, the heat between them like steam rising off a sizzling meal. Feeling like a voyeur and uncomfortable as a result, Mavis tuned back into her surroundings, Dan's chatter to Susie being the first thing she noticed.

"Care to Nikki?" Jack asked with an outstretched hand.

"What?" Refocusing and seeing Jack had materialised before her, Mavis felt flustered. "I'd love to, but I only know the basics." She stood, ignoring the offer of his hand. "Susie, can you watch Dan?"

Susie's, "No worries," was in unison with Dan's indignant, "I don't need watchin'."

Mavis and Jack wove their way through the crowd to the dance floor.

"I do anything to offend you, Nikki?"

"No. Why?"

"You seem different since Parkes."

"I just don't want you to get the wrong idea, Jack, and I don't want to do *anything* that'll cause tensions within the band or wreck our creative partnership. I've got a kid to consider as well."

"Fair enough."

Trembling within Jack's embrace, Mavis focused on the dance and translating its rhythm into steps and body movement. She was intensely aware of the heat of Jack's hand on her back and the brush of his body against hers when they came together.

After a song or two, Mavis stopped concentrating on her feet. Instead, she developed an appreciation for their *whole* body movement and rhythmic union. They danced on the off-beat, relaxing into the slow sensual movement of the dance.

The music was bittersweet, matching Mavis' mood. It'd been a long time since she'd been held by a man in this manner, felt the sexual heat emanating from him, recognized that a man, any man, desired her. The experience was heady, the sensation hypnotic, primal. She could feel her heart throbbing and hoped Jack could not.

With applause sounding around them, Jack pulled Mavis to him, felt the warmth of her body. He inhaled her fragrance.

Caught in the moment, Mavis wanted desperately to be kissed, to savour desire and crush it to her. It felt like a lifetime since she had surrendered to passion, been alive in that way.

As Jack released Mavis, his eyes caressed her lips. He considered tasting them before leaning forward to do just that.

It has been Dan's lifetime, a small voice whispered to her. With their lips almost brushing, Mavis pulled back. With life finally on the forward step, she did not want to jeopardize its direction. "I want to keep things platonic, Jack." *I've got too much to lose if I don't.*

"Did I say I didn't?" Nonchalantly, Jack escorted her back to the group before heading off to the crowded bar.

Mavis watched him go, her emotions held firmly in check.

When the opportunity arose for a quiet word, Susie said, "You're walking a tightrope with Jack. I hope you don't fall. I don't want to have to look for another band."

"You won't have to." Later, Mavis joined Gary and Kate on the floor with Dan as her partner.

Meanwhile, the male members of Mavis' band discovered the power of being a performer, small fish though they were, in a bigger arena. A group of twenty-somethings, in ogling delight, bunched into spaces around the men.

A glamour-packaged woman pressed between Tony and Jack, making contact with them both. "Didn't you perform earlier today?"

With a spirits glass in hand, Jack altered his body angle, to better appreciate the woman. She mirrored his movement, their bodies touching. With a not-so subtle movement, she ground her hips against him, grazing his package. His dark eyes danced. "We did."

Opposite her, Steve found it hard to maintain his mask of casual interest. "You heard us?"

Another girl, skimpily dressed and with a lot of exposed breast, draped herself over Steve. "Oh, you were *so* good!"

Steve tried to keep his eyes on the woman's face, as she gushed about their performance, but failed. "Oh!" He'd never had a woman run her hand over *his* backside before. He liked it.

The remaining girls from the foursome wedged Tony between them, Jack and the first woman giving way so they could. Tony melted under the heat of their contact.

Susie, from outside the circle, spoke to the woman clearly committed to seducing Jack. "You're wearing a beautiful dress."

The young woman turned and assessed her. "Oh, thanks." She then turned back, excluding Susie and Zoey, and perched on a bar stool offered to her by Jack.

Tony and Steve followed Jack's lead, also securing bar stools for the women.

Rather than sitting naturally, the women posed, presenting their physical assets for the men's inspection.

"Looks like she needed to be registered with the meat packers union to fit into that dress," Susie said in undertones to Zoey.

"Mum!" Zoey caught the eye of a young man at the bar. "I'm getting another soda. Want anything?"

"No, love."

It was Susie who kept track of the time and pulled the men away from their groupies and Mavis from the dance floor. It took Susie a few minutes to locate Zoey who was happily chatting up a young man perched on a stool at the bar.

"You seriously think he's the legal age?" Susie asked the barman, having crossed to him and gesturing at Zoey's young man. "I can tell you for a certainty that this girl is fifteen."

The barman removed the alcoholic concoctions from both under-age drinkers' hands. "It's hard to tell the age of girls nowadays."

"You need to look beyond their overstated makeup and be aware of the flamboyant way girls dress when denying they're minors. Women don't need to claim an age. Girls work to look older. Besides, the faces of girls are a giveaway. As for my daughter, her age is obvious so your excuse doesn't wash, and what's your excuse for this boy? I've a good mind to report …"

"Susie," Tony called from where the rest of the band waited.

"Coming!" To Zoey, she added, "We'll talk more about this later."

"Oh, Mum!"

Joining the waiting group, Susie said to Kate, "Thanks for including Zoey with Dan in your party. She hasn't been to the Sydney Aquarium before. Have a good time!"

The group separated and headed off to their respective destinations.

"This is all too cool!" Steve voiced the rest of the entourage's feelings as they moved to the appointed meeting place, a waterfront entertainment restaurant and bar located in a ritzier part of the Darling Harbourside restaurant complex. It faced east toward the city.

Julius Morrow, a clubs' agent, was thin, fashionably dressed, and well-spoken. His spiked, heavily gelled hair was reminiscent of a toothbrush. Over drinks, he said, "Top show this afternoon, guys! I also caught your act at Parkes. I'm offering eight weeks' work, rotating Friday and Saturday nights at the different venues I handle across the Sydney circuit, starting first weekend in March. Some places will want your Elvis act while others will prefer contemporary stuff. You can mix up your original numbers with hits from the day. The balance, of course, always has to be given to songs audiences know."

"Can we have a moment for a private talk?" Mavis asked Julius Morrow.

"Course you can. While you do that, I'll catch up with a friend who has just walked in."

After making sure the agent was out-of-earshot, Jack said, "Well, that's disappointing!"

In sympathy with Jack, Mavis nodded but looked inquiringly to Steve for his reaction.

"I don't think we should let this one pass through to the wicket keeper, Nikki. It's good work and better money than we make down the coast. At least we have the chance to play our own music and aren't stuck with only doin' covers."

"My feelings exactly, Steve," Tony said. "I think—"

Susie spoke over the top of Tony. "I'm with Steve and Tony. We need to develop a following. I know it isn't what we hoped for, but at least it's a foot in the door. Besides, we don't have enough original material for a show for the hours Morrow outlined so hits of the day will work. Damn pity we have to do the Elvis stuff."

Tony added, "We should take on a Thursday night gig in the south-coast pub circuit."

Susie noted the slight crease between Mavis' brows. "Zoey can stay over your place and babysit Dan Thursday nights if that's a barrier to work."

"That'll be good."

"She really likes spending time with your family. I didn't know how lonely she was last year. I'm going to send her to boarding school.

That way I know she's supervised and cared for when I'm out on the road."

Private discussion over, the band, inexperienced in such matters, accepted Julius Morrow's deal.

With pen in hand and his notebook open, Morrow looked at Tony. "Details of this agreement will be posted to …?"

Jack spoke up first. "To Nikki Mills care of …" He looked meaningfully at Mavis who supplied her address.

"As I said before, and I'll say it again," Tony spoke with a sense of vindication, "the money and work is in doin' covers of hits. There just isn't enough work out there doin' our own material."

"Then how did the big Aussie bands do it?" Steve voiced what the rest of the band thought.

Chapter 11

With February came a month break from performance. Mavis found she had time for creativity, rehearsals, and life in general. With the daylight saving hours of summer, the Tuesday and Wednesday evening practices in the hired hall on the southern peninsula did not seem to take up that much of her time. Dan was still up and about when she returned home in the slanted light of the setting sun. He seemed happy enough coming in from play with neighbourhood children when he saw her walking home. In the hour before his bedtime, she made a concerted effort to be interactive. As for the Saturday afternoon practices, they made only a small dint in the daylight hours, leaving plenty of time for life and leisure with family and close friends.

The third Saturday of the month found Mavis leading practice. "Okay, let's break into smaller groups so we can explore how this song should be presented."

"This is a recipe for conflict, Nikki," Tony said. "You wrote it. It's your call."

"No, Jack and I wrote this one, and we want to workshop it by refining your parts. We need a unique sound and for your parts to be exciting musically but not overdone."

"We thought Nikki should work with you, Tony, and Steve and Susie with me." Among other things, Jack appreciated Mavis' respect for his musicianship even though she was the primary voice in determining their material.

Their collaborative sessions had worked like a finely tuned car with parts in perfect harmony. Together, they had created music that Jack doubted he could ever have written alone. As part of their open process, their knowledge of each other had deepened as did their friendship. Jack had not hit on Mavis and appeared to have forgotten his attraction to her. A tactic that from experience he knew made women go wild for him.

Piqued that her allure had such a short shelf life, Mavis had told herself, *It's better this way. I've too much to lose.*

A developing bond had not been the case between Jack and Dan. They had competed for Mavis' attention whenever Jack had come over to collaborate while she tried to find the path to appeasement.

Steve ran his fingers over the notes of his keyboard with a flourish. "I'm in. I've credentials to do more than just play."

"Yeah, yeah, we—" Tony said.

"I've never done this before, fellas. This'll be fun."

"More likely cause for argument, Susie."

"Grab your acoustic, Tony, and stop bein' pessimistic. We'll go outside."

Settled high on the cliff overlooking the Pacific Ocean and in the shade of a magnificent Eucalypt, Mavis sang, as she accompanied herself on her guitar, while Tony listened, eyes closed, feeling the rhythm.

"Sing it again, Nikki. I think I we can make that riff sharper."

"Okay."

Mavis replayed the song.

"I can hear something … Let me just fiddle with it a sec." Tony played with the chords and rhythm pattern. "What do you think?"

"Yeah, I like the change, but what if we inverted the rhythm to this?"

With his eyes closed, Tony listened intently. "Very cool!"

"Okay, let's run through the whole thing, and we'll see how well it fits."

After the run through, Tony said, "That change in rhythm adds the zing factor, but …"

"I know. It's not quite right. What if we …?" And so the experimentation continued for about an hour.

When the band reformed to hear what had been found musically, there was a sense of intimacy in the setting. Feedback and discussion led to further reshaping of their sound. As a group, they found both pleasure and competition in developing the song and in refining the arrangement.

"That's a wrap for the afternoon," Mavis said. "We'll tweak today's material next practice and then do a complete run through. In the meantime, I'll score the charts for the work done today. Jack and I might even tweak the playlist more during the week."

"I'm *real* happy with the playlist," Tony said. "We've achieved a good balance between hits and original numbers. I think you should leave it be."

Jack picked out notes on his bass guitar, trying to pin down a sound and rhythm that had been in the back of his mind for the past week or so. "You're wrong, Tony. We need to move away from bein' a chameleon band, fit for any occasion, and do as Nikki says. Like she says, we *need* a unique sound and style. Something retro but new at the same time."

"And Jack and I will continue tweakin' our music until *we're* satisfied."

"Okay! Compose away but *don't* touch the cover songs. *Anyhow,* I'm lookin' forward to March and April even though they'll be intense months."

"Yeah," was the syncopated response as they packed up their respective gear.

"You lot might be." Lyle stopped in the doorway, their sound system in hand. "Bumpin' in and out every night plus the travel over that distance is not goin' to be a picnic."

Steve collapsed his stool. "It's the deal if we want a bigger cut of the entertainment industry's pie."

"And it saves you gym fees," Jack said, "I reckon you should pay us ..."

"In your dreams, mate ... Oh, that's right, a certain someone has them monopolised."

Jack grimaced at Lyle who laughed back at him.

"Your gear ready soon, Susie?"

"To go on your return trip, Lyle."

As their gear was loaded into cars and van, Mavis said to Steve, "Won't you even consider it? I know you don't like singin', but what if you spoke the words. We could do the song hip hop style. You've a great sense of rhythm."

"No."

"Steve, come on! You're not even givin' this a passin' thought. You've a really beaut musical speaking voice and …"

"Flattery, Nikki, isn't goin' to work on me either."

"It's the truth," Susie added, "you have. I know women who feel like swooning when you give them the time of day."

"Sure."

"Seriously, I do!"

"C'mon, I need another vocalist for those songs. It's just a few numbers … a small part within the whole playlist."

"I don't want to take anything off Tony. He does backup vocals."

From his leaning post against the hall doorjamb, Tony said, "Generous of you, mate, but I can't do what Nikki wants and play the guitar. The rhythms are counter to one another."

"And we need the guitar," Mavis added.

"No, I don't want to do it. It'd take a lot of concentration for that type of song-speak, and that'd make playin' keyboards way too difficult."

"What if you don't play for the vocal passages in those songs?"

"No."

"Help the lady out, Steve." Jack said, leaning against the car in what the others had come to recognise as his characteristic cross-legged stance. "I'd do it willingly but …"

"Sure you would. Easy to say when the bass line is indispensable in the song. What she wants is bloody hard."

"Steve, what if you had a featured keyboard spot in a few other songs?"

"Maybe."

"Done deal."

"Hey, not so fast. Let's see what's what next rehearsal before you call deal."

⋆　⋆　⋆

The last week of February, Mavis felt good about her life and its direction. Dan had settled into second grade. His home routine was stable. Her parents were on board with her plans.

Insomnia was no longer an issue. It had been defeated by her doctor's prescription of a sleeping aid, his euphemism for a month's course of Valium that *he* said would re-establish a solid sleep routine.

Resigned to the nature of her day work as well as her co-workers' attitude when it came to all things musical, Mavis kept what she shared of her life compartmentalised and her worlds segregated. Her guiding principle: a need to know basis.

With the renewed vigour gained from regular sleep, Mavis increased her fitness program to eight kilometre walks with Kate twice a week and a workout on the community gym equipment in the park toward the end of the walk.

During a strengthening session on that equipment, Kate asked, "So what's going on with you and Jack? You're seeing a lot of him."

"It's mostly work. We're developin' material for our debut CD."

"Wow! You got a record contract, and you didn't tell Gary and me?"

"No. The plan is we'll pay for it ourselves. Jack and Steve are keen to do it so we can get airplay and widen our exposure. Susie's almost there. Tony still needs to be convinced."

"Jack's a real hottie."

"He seems to affect a lot of women that way."

"Not you?"

"I'm not immune to his charms." Mavis did not say that the conflict between her rational head talk and her arousal was keeping her awake at night. It'd been a long time since she had felt that particular sustained heat or been *so* bothered.

For years, she'd kept herself turned off. It had been easy. No one had made her *feel* desirable. Now that the switch to her passion had been flicked on, she felt in danger of being flooded by the blinding light of it whenever Jack and she were alone together. She battled to sandbag her defences, aware that she did not want to fall prey to the first attractive man who showed interest in her. *I've more to lose than gain,* became her mantra.

"How's it going with Tony?"

"Stressfully. The second weekend in March is heavily booked. We're doin' afternoon gigs at the Kiama Jazz and Blues Festival and club gigs in Sydney at night. Tony has the ninety minutes or so car trip from Kiama to the city scheduled with a half hour margin for problems."

"Not enough."

"Don't we all know it, but there isn't another way."

The first March weekend in Sydney, Mavis and her band were agog at the bright, big city lights, impressed with the glitz of club interiors, and excited by the direction their careers had taken. They had a sense of having made it professionally. Therefore, the band was downhearted when they discovered they were not booked into the auditorium as they had expected, not even for their cabaret-styled Elvis tribute show. Instead, they found themselves in an open-plan complex with bistro dining, a dance floor, and a significant number of poker machines at the far end.

During that first Friday night's performance, an extended version of the Elvis tribute, they quickly discovered a disturbing similarity with some of the pubs where they had performed in 1996. The business of gambling competed with them for audience. They were interrupted by raffle draws. KENO results, with meal calls thrown into the mix, were announced over the top of them through the club's PA system. While all the time in the background, the chaotic sounds and intermittent flashing lights of the poker machines vied with them.

Saturday night at a different venue, the distractions were the same but a Jackpot on a poker machine added to the noise level. At the end of a bracket, the repetitive Jackpot alert had still not been turned off. Mavis walked off the stage, her elevated arms and hands expressing her frustration. So Tony and Jack picked up the der-der-der-der sound and imitated it until the offending noise was turned off.

On their break, the band headed for a coffee shop within the club. Having reorganised the tables so they could sit together, they were pleased when their orders arrived promptly.

Mavis stirred her mug of black coffee for no real purpose. "And here we are again," she said to the original members of the band.

Steve slumped back in his chair. "I thought we'd escaped all that."

"It's *very* much like the pub scene, isn't it?" Susie commented.

"Yep," the original band members replied.

Jack replied, "It's something workin' musicians have to cope with, guys. So to combat it, let's turn up our sound."

The band looked at Mavis. "No way, Jack!" She rubbed her right fingers together about thirty centimetres from her right ear.

Jack asked no one in particular, "What *is* she doin'?"

Tim looked at Jack, surprised. "Don't you know? She's checkin' her hearin'. If she can't hear it, the band is already too loud. I swear we're not though."

Her brow furrowed, Mavis turned to Tim. "I can't hear it."

"That's only because of the extraneous noise and the added hubbub associated with the win at the poker machine. Guys, don't amplify that awful jackpot sound by joinin' in if there's another win."

"So what *do* we do?" Jack asked.

"We just stop playing," Tony said, "so management can see it's a problem."

After some thought, Mavis said, "No, we have to be deaf to it all and do the best show we can."

"I'm with Nikki," Tim said. "Do you see management around? It's just floor and bar staff. We've got regular work and pay. We put up and shut up if we want to keep workin'."

Later that night, high on the excitement of being in Sydney, the band went out on the town. The lights and nightlife around the harbour drew them to it. They walked around the Opera House, enjoying the live music and a drink in the open-air bars on the promenade. They strolled past the buskers at Circular Quay and wound their way to The Rocks – birthplace of the nation. The pubs there were rocking with a variety of live music ranging from jazz trios to heavy rock. Around two in the morning, they caught a water taxi to Darling Harbour and danced at the upmarket nightclubs to DJ music.

On the dance floor, Mavis tasted the heady delight of being attractive to more than one man. Her casual dance partners were clearly on the prowl, moving on when she did not play 'the game'. Steve though, gentlemanly and affable, was different. When he looked at her, Mavis saw the fire in his eyes, recognised the subtlety of his courtship moves. She saw a sharp contrast between her bass and keyboard players. Jack lacked Steve's nuanced sincerity. Jack was artful in his dance floor seduction whereas Steve just enjoyed moving and kept his campaign to win her to interaction off the dance floor. She laughed a lot when she was with Steve but trembled whenever Jack held her.

In the grey of the lightening day, they returned to their accommodation, spent in more ways than one.

Lying awake that morning, Mavis realised the subtle tensions between the men in her band would become destructive if she wasn't careful. She had enjoyed their competitive interest in her while they were on the town but knew now that to favour one over the other could injure ego and ignite dissension.

* * *

The dreaded weekend of clashes and overload proved to be much better than expected. The band stayed in Sydney overnight after their Friday night gig and travelled south to Kiama in the morning after a respectable sleep in til nine. Like Keimera, Kiama is a beautiful town on the Sapphire Coast. The colour of the sky and sea that day gave meaning to the sapphire coast tag given to the region.

Family and friends from Keimera drove to Kiama for the festival and to see Mavis' band perform. It was the first time in years that her parents had seen her on stage.

Watching their daughter, the Mills knew why Mavis was so determined to pursue a career in song. There was a vitality to her that they had not seen for a very long time. Dan sat on the grass between his grandparents, his face filled with wonderment at the sight and sound of his mother on stage. Near them, Kate sat within the circle of Gary's arms. The family and friends' connections of other band members sat scattered throughout the wider crowd. At the conclusion of Mavis' last song, everyone associated with them stood in acclamation. The wider audience followed that lead.

Afterwards, when Mavis caught up with her extended family grouping, Gary said, "Your material is really good, Mavis. You write it?"

Nodding, she replied, "Most of it. That last song I wrote with Jack."

"It's seriously good," Kate added.

"My girl is a singer *and* a songwriter," Trevor said, unintentionally drawing the attention of the people around him. Then to people standing next to him, he said, "This is my daughter!"

Mavis laughed before saying, "You're proud of me, Dad?"

"Proud doesn't come near to describing how I feel."

"Oh." Emotional, Mavis hugged him.

On the sideline, Kate was visibly moved, as much to her own surprise as to Gary's.

"You okay, Ken?"

"Father and daughter moments like that always get to me. They're so rare."

"Things don't have to be said to be felt, mate."

"I know, but …"

"Your dad is real proud of you."

"You think?"

"I know."

"I envy the way he gives you time, Gary. He's always so busy nowadays. I wish …"

"We have one-on-one time because he wants to stay close to you, Ken. He knows we're serious. It's not that he has a preference for me over you."

"I've always felt ..."

Putting an arm around her shoulders, Gary pulled her to him. He kissed her gently, tenderly.

"Nikki, look at the time," Susie said from outside the intimate grouping. "We have to hop it. We don't know what the Sydney traffic will be like."

"Excuse me," a man standing nearby and unknown to Mavis said, "do you have any CDs on sale at the festival?"

"Nikki!" the male band members called.

"CDs? Not yet. If you'll excuse me everyone, I have to run." And she did, all the way to the car that Jack was driving and in which she and Susie were travelling.

Enroute to Sydney, Jack said, "You see there *is* a market for our CDs. We have to push ahead with the idea. It's a way of makin' more money and widening our reach to audiences. If we got airplay on the radio stations—"

Mavis cut Jack short. "It'd have the same impact, Susie, as touring but with less grunt involved. We know our stuff is great. I reckon it's just a matter of getting it heard. With a swelling fan base and a radio presence, we could graduate from the bar and bistro scene into club auditoriums."

"I'm leanin' that way, Nikki. It's not just me who has reservations. Tony hasn't been won over yet. I wonder if it's as simple as you think?"

Jack and Mavis made eye-contact in his rear vision mirror. She was pleased that she no longer blushed when he looked at her in *that* way.

"How hard could it be, Susie? Besides, Nikki needs a demo to send off with our festival applications."

Susie scratched a suddenly itchy ear. "There's a reason record contracts are *so* sought after, Jack."

"That's because, Susie, most bands aren't prepared to invest in

themselves. They think *inside* the box. We need to break free of bein'
a covers band. This is the way we can do it."

"I'm with Jack, Susie."

*   *   *

In Sydney, club land was comprised of diverse groups such as the
RSL, Catholic Clubs, League Clubs, other sports' clubs, and work-
ers' clubs. For many people, the clubs played a significant role in the
social networking within a community.

Clubs sourced entertainment in a few ways. For big name acts,
clubs dealt directly with agents and bought shows. At other times,
agencies booked artists, took a commission from them, and offered
entertainment deals to clubs from their stable of talent, having made
a business case to the clubs. In other instances, promoters working with touring bands and entertainers approached clubs directly.
Occasionally, clubs hired bands who approached them directly. An
increasing problem for agents and promoters in 1997 was that clubs
had created a membership culture of discounts and free entertainment. Not a good long term business model for the future as far as
agents and promoters representing talent were concerned.

By the end of the two-month stint of club performances, Mavis'
band were sick of staying in the cheapest of shared motel rooms
available, fed up with fast food, weary of each other's company, and
jaded with their Elvis tribute act. The tedium of the circuit was eased
by the enjoyment that came from playing their own material. That
enjoyment was heightened by the discovery that the musical imagination of an audience had the capacity to be developed and extended
beyond the known hits of the 'name' bands.

"Y' know that song ..?" was a developing audience request for the
band's own material, heard often during April. The scales though
still weighed in on hits of the day.

The Saturday morning before their last show in their agreement with Morrow's agency, the band sat in a street-front Burwood cafe within the Westfield Shopping Centre.

For the most part, the band were positioned equidistantly around the rearranged tables with the exception of Jack. He sat close to Mavis who rested her head on her right palm, sharing asides with her intermittently.

Tony handed out a finance balance sheet to band members. "As you can see, the associated costs when tallied up against income earned mean there's very little profit."

The group stared at the paperwork in silence. The only movement being the occasional lift of and sip from a coffee cup.

Tony continued, "I should've been more on the ball when the original deal was struck, fellas. I'm sorry."

"Not your fault, Tony." Mavis sipped her mug of black coffee. "We all had a voice in this."

"But my day job is in accounts …"

"No use crying over spilt milk." Steve put the paperwork down in understated disgust.

"So future Sydney gigs are out?" Tim asked.

"No." Jack leant forward, his elbows on the table. "We can make a better deal now that Morrow wants another agreement."

Steve slumped back in his chair. "Maybe that's because we're cheap."

Jack's manner became stronger, more assertive, rousing. "Don't sell us short, mate. We're bloody good. A standout in fact! Now's the time to deal."

Lyle tapped Mavis on her shoulder. "Nikki?"

She looked at him with a tilt of her head and a questioning arch of her eyebrow.

"I was talkin' to the roadie from RedSun. You should see their gear, not to mention their luxury sleeper tour bus. Bloody clear they're headliners in the clubs. It was so cool hearin' his stories of life on the road."

In an aside to Steve, Susie said, "Ah, life packed into a suitcase and snatches of the world seen at touring speed." She paused for her words to sink in. "I think I can wait."

Having been sidetracked by Susie's comment, Mavis looked again at Lyle. "And your point is?"

"He says his band's deal includes meals and accommodation on top of what they're paid."

"Geez!" was the collective response.

Momentarily distracted by the ogling attention of some young women near them, Steve returned to the conversation. "It would be great if we didn't have to share rooms."

Having considered the matter, Susie said, "I reckon we need an *astute* business manager who knows the ropes and how much we can charge."

"Another bite out of our income pie?" Tony looked at Susie with open hostility. "Screw that idea."

"Nikki?" Jack directed their focus to her.

"Whatever we do, I have to have a break." Having run out of sleeping pills, Mavis was back to long hours of wakefulness at night. She also needed more time with Dan. Increasingly during the weekdays, she had found her tiredness tainted her patience with him. She needed time with her family and for a life too. She said none of that though. Instead, she said, "We need to develop a lot more material. I *cannot* do Elvis anymore. I have no idea how he did it. Poor man, he was trapped by his audience's emotional ownership."

The arrival of a waitress delivering their orders stopped the discussion.

"So?" Tony initiated a return to conversation after the waitress left them.

Everyone, with the exception of Tony, looked at Mavis for the answer.

"We tell Morrow we need a break and a better deal, and wait to see what he's prepared to offer."

"If he doesn't?" Susie asked.

Tony jumped in before Mavis could reply. "There's more than

one agency in Sydney. You're right, Susie, *I* need to take care of the business side of it *better.*"

Weary, Mavis added, "But not lose sight of our end goal."

In unison, Jack and Susie said, "Break free of being a covers band."

Tony sucked his teeth, irritated. Steve looked undecided.

With an eye fixed on the waiter, Mavis unsuccessfully attempted to make eye contact with him. "Well, I'm goin' to need a lot of black coffee and a *big* dose of Vitamin B complex if I'm goin' to get through tonight." Having thought long and hard about her income in what seemed to her to be interminable hours of sleeplessness, Mavis said, "I want to ditch bein' a part-time band and make music work financially. I can't do two jobs anymore."

Susie drained her coffee cup, "It's why I teamed up with you. I've never seen us as a hobby band."

"Me either," Jack added.

With hands on his thighs, Steve said, "Well that's how I've always seen it. The money from music has always been icin' on my cake, but it's never been enough for me to throw in my day job. The work is too mercurial, way too unreliable. In the past, it has swung between feast and famine. Besides, my trade is lucrative …"

Tony reacted, "We were *never* a hobby band, Steve. Bein' professional about what we do and the music we make has always been a passion with me."

"We always played it safe, Tony, passion or not. We toured whenever we could get leave but never staked our livelihood on it."

"I've friends," Mavis continued, "whose weekend passion is the Lifesaving Movement. No money made. No financial loss to them. It doesn't impact on their work week or take away from their families' lives."

Tony said, "From the get-go, I've been the one, Mavis, sayin' we should take more work—"

"You have, and now I'm sayin' let's do a lot more than we are." Mavis thought, *I don't want my last nine years to be my next nine years.* Aware that the dregs of her energy, like the coffee in her mug, were almost gone, Mavis said, "So what's it goin' to be?"

"We go for it," was the universal answer.

Mavis nodded approvingly. "You're not goin' to like what I say next, but Jack and I write the songs so I think we need to be paid more. Tony should get extra for keepin' the books."

Silence. Susie and Steve crossed their arms, backs to their chairs.

Jack was the first to speak, "Nikki isn't suggestin' you take a cut in pay. The idea is we work backwards in settin' our fee and add on the extra percentage to that."

Steve said, "That's a lot of maths."

Susie poured herself a glass of water from the bottle provided by the waitress. "Something Tony *says* he's good at."

"Give it a rest, Susie, and give me a break. Let me get this straight. We're factorin' in another night on the Sydney circuit if we can get the work, and we move the South Coast circuit gigs to Wednesday nights?"

"Yeah," was the majority reply.

To Susie in undertones, Mavis said, "I'm goin' to have to rethink how things'll work for Dan."

Overhearing, Tony replied, "Isn't your kid asleep at that time?"

"When we're performin', but obviously I'm away from home more than that."

Understanding Mavis' concern, Jack said, "He still gets more time with you than if he'd been packed off to boarding school. Don't they say it's the quality of time with a kid not the amount that matters to them?"

Tiredness etched Mavis' face. "Adults say that. I'm not so sure kids think it. Look, fellas, I'm too tired for this. I'm crashin'." She stood. "If you'll excuse me—"

Jack stood too, taking a step into Mavis' personal space. "I'll take you back."

Mavis' hand moved to his chest, resting lightly on it. "No, stay. I'll catch a taxi."

Jack brushed a stray hair out of her eyes. "Let me get one for you at least. Come on." He linked arms with her and walked her out to Burwood Road.

Steve watched them leave, wishing he had the nerve Jack had when it came to women.

Susie frowned. While the sexual tension between Mavis and Jack produced great lyrics and their collaboration a great sound, she knew all too well the risk a sexual relationship posed to the life of a band. *Does Nikki realise this?* She considered having a 'chat' with her about the situation but decided against it. *Too many things are being raised.*

On Jack's return, the band were engaged in intense discussion. "What did I miss?"

Steve looked up at him. "I was just sayin' we need to get a foot into the auditorium door. I know Nikki wants to farewell Elvis, but it's a great musical theatre piece that'd translate well into the cabaret style of auditoriums. Jack, couldn't you and Nikki develop some other musical theatre stuff as well?"

"We could, but is that the direction we want to go? I thought the goal was to develop a fan base as a *band,* not as a show."

Steve added, "Nikki's won quite a few hearts already. I'm not talkin' those wannabe boyfriends who hit on her. I'm talkin' about the people who are actually followin' us from gig to gig."

Jack considered Steve, wondering if his comment was directed at him. The man had not struck him as the sort to make barbed comments. Besides, he didn't *think* he was hitting on her. Concerned and attentive were his new modus operandi.

Frowning, Tony said, "We need to develop the fan base as a *band.*"

Susie looked to Jack who spoke for them. "We want to go ahead with making a CD and getting it out there in shops and on the air. That'd do heaps for growing the fan base."

Tony nodded. "I can see that now. You wouldn't believe how many people asked me for one last weekend."

His listeners replied, "Yeah, we would!"

Jack pulled in his chair. "So you're ready to *invest* in us, mate?"

"I'm on that page, Jack. Now let's talk about what we want in the next agreement with Morrow."

Disturbed by Tony's take-charge manner and what Susie saw as a not-so-well-hidden agenda, she put a restraining hand on Tony's arm. "We should hold off. Nikki should be involved in this."

"She should. No doubt about it, but she chose to leave. Morrow wanted the details faxed to him by one today. Nikki knew that before she left. It's up to us. Do you want to lose this opportunity? There are heaps of other bands waitin' to fill our shoes."

With his mouth full of donut, Jack said, "Susie and I have already talked this over with Nikki anyway. We know what she wants."

"And that is?"

"Forget the small arena stuff and get into the live-music, top pub circuit in Sydney: the Annandale, The Hopetoun, and The Northern."

"And how do you expect us to break into that scene? I don't have the contacts, and we don't have the followin' for them to even consider bookin' us. Can we get back to the deal we *can* make? I need to know what we're askin' for, where we're prepared to give ground, and the absolute bottom line or no deal made."

With the details of what they wanted in the next agreement to perform, Tony went off to an office shop on Burwood Road.

* * *

That night, Shaun Doyle, entrepreneur and partner in The Harbourside Agency, critically considered The Nikki Mills Band and the audience reaction to them as he sat at the bar. The reports from his talent scouts had not been wrong. This group was not typical of bistro club bands and nor was the scene.

The place was rocking. The dance floor was packed, the people sweaty and pumped, and the room smoky. As was the case with many rising stars, the audience seemed to be in love with the singer. An amazing vocalist with undeniable charisma, Nikki Mills playfully romanced them. Her band were clearly fine musicians and, like the best of bands, projected personalities that had strong audience appeal.

A still point in a room of movement, Doyle was unaware that contrast drew Mavis' eye to him. He felt like she was looking directly at him as she sang. That experience became intensely personal and oddly private.

At the end of the bracket, the crowd reaction stunned the band members while jolting Doyle back to awareness of where he sat. The cheering was so loud that it actually hurt his ears. Women mobbed the bass player, the guitarist, and the keyboard player. The roadie held back the rush at the singer, allowing her safe exit. The drummer was not so lucky. She had to push through a crush of men, all clamouring for her attention.

Crossing to the band's soundman, Doyle handed him a business card. "Give this to Nikki, will you? I'd like a moment during this break. I'm over at the bar."

Ten minutes passed. Looking at his watch, Doyle wondered at the delay. Little known bands usually jumped at a chance to talk to management of his status. Just as Doyle was considering leaving, the soundman returned.

"Nikki will see you. Follow me." He led Doyle through a narrow corridor to a backroom where the band was seated around a chrome and vinyl table, drinks and food scattered across it.

After the etiquette of introductions, Doyle accepted Jack's offer of a chair next to Nikki. Observing the group around him, Doyle read the relationship dynamics, sensing underlying tensions. He was not surprised given there were two enticing women in the room.

Assessing Doyle, Mavis noted his quiet, understated casual look that nonetheless spoke money and success. Up close, his magnetism felt stronger than when she had watched him earlier. Unsettled by him, she masked her interest by assuming a distant manner.

"You put on a really great show tonight, Nikki! The crowd really embraced your material. Some of it was original, wasn't it? You didn't play enough of that though."

"You're right; there wasn't. The club deal is that we mostly play covers."

Doyle grimaced. "Always a problem in clubs when you're not the headliner. Where did you source the songs?"

"I wrote the last one. The song leading into it was a collaborative effort between Jack and me."

Doyle spoke thoughtfully. "That makes you an extra special commodity."

Bristling, Mavis said, "Commodity?"

"You have management yet?"

"Not yet, Mr Doyle."

"Call me Shaun." His smile was warm and his demeanour relaxed.

Doyle held Mavis' gaze. The moment was breathless.

Mavis blinked first. "We've been doin' pretty well without it."

"That said, Nikki, have a *good* look at where you're booked."

Recognizing Doyle's interest, Jack placed a proprietorial hand on Mavis' shoulder. Irritated but controlling her reaction, Mavis handed Jack her empty glass. "Would you mind getting me some water?"

With his finger on his watch, Lyle indicated the time to Mavis and held up his hand to indicate they had five minutes left.

"You wanted to see me, Mr Doyle, because…?"

"To make initial contact and to offer some free advice. The Harbourside Agency *might* consider representing your band down the track *if* you build a bigger fan base. To do that, you need to target the live music pub scene in Sydney and Melbourne, *and* give the flick to being a covers band in clubs." With an elegant pen taken from inside his black vest, Doyle wrote some names on the back of his card. "You can use my name when you make contact with these booking agents. It'll get you on their bills. The rest is up to you."

Looking at the card, Mavis said, "Thanks. Why are you doin' this?"

"To demonstrate I'm someone with your band's interests at heart. If you ask around, you'll learn my company is known for its integrity. There are a lot of sharks out there ready to take a big bite out of rising talent. By contrast, The Harbourside Agency steers its stable of musicians through the music business maze and gets the right deals for them to pursue their careers."

Tony spoke up. "So why not sign us now?"

"I only invest time and effort when talent has proven it's prepared to do the hard yards. We're not interested in a factory approach to our clients or in creating one day wonders who burn out because everything was done at a fast food rate."

At the door, Lyle caught Mavis' eye. "Nikki, it's time."

Standing, Mavis held out her hand. "Thanks for this. It's been interestin' meetin' you."

Taking her hand, Doyle was conscious of its warmth and her perfume. The air around them seemed to pulse as their immediate surroundings faded into the background. His mouth was unusually dry. Unexpectedly, a farewell handshake seemed inadequate to him. With his eyes fixed on hers, in what seemed slow motion to them both, he raised her hand to his lips in an old-world gesture, lightly brushing it, all the time holding Mavis' gaze. It was another breathless moment.

Mavis felt a curious mixture of shyness and excitement followed by a sudden heat in her cheeks. She withdrew her hand from his, flustered. The warmth of his touch lingered.

Caught up in the interaction before her, Susie realised she had been holding her breath.

Without the telltale physical signs that Mavis displayed, Doyle said, "I look forward to meeting you again." He then turned on his heel and left without a farewell word to the others. After Doyle left, Susie smiled archly at Mavis who blushed and turned away.

Back in the greater club area, Doyle felt like a callow schoolboy despite knowing he was wise in the ways of the world. Worse, he was embarrassed by his farewell gesture. *Where on earth had that come from?* Her effect on him had been unforeseen. If they met again, he knew he'd have to guard against impulse.

Mavis sought distraction and distance from the people around her. She searched her *very modern* handbag and tilted her head so that her long hair fell forward, shielding her face from view. As she felt her colour die down, she produced a lipstick and hairbrush and crossed to the mirror in the ladies' toilet adjacent to the break room.

Lyle gestured again. "Fellas."

Gathering their gear, band members filed out.

The last to leave, Mavis was delayed further by Tim. "Nikki, a word?"

Returning to the stage, Jack spoke to Steve. "What a nerd!"

"As if women liked that nowadays!"

Susie waited for Steve to move to his keyboards so that she could access her drums. "I don't know about Nikki, but the *look* between them made my heart skip a beat. Even now, I feel a little fluttery at the thought of it."

Jack strapped on his bass. "I never took you for that sort of woman, Susie. Anyway, Nikki didn't like him from the get-go. Couldn't you feel the tension?"

"I did, and you know what that means …"

Jack and Steve looked befuddled.

"Nikki was attracted to Doyle. His farewell gesture signalled he definitely *didn't* see her as a commodity." At her kit, Susie called over to Steve, "I don't think you could ever pull it off so don't try it."

With her back to the audience and during the opening riff, Mavis stepped into her stage persona before turning around. She felt high on the adrenaline of the night. Without meaning to look for Doyle, she scanned the crowd, seeing him as he left the area. To her surprise, she saw Sarah, Gary's one-time girlfriend pass Doyle, another woman with her.

At the start of the next break, Tony disappeared into the crowd as the band exited to their haven. Ten minutes later, he returned with Sarah and her girlfriend. After introductions, and in an aside to Mavis, Tony said, "I didn't think you'd mind, seein' as how you and Sarah are friends."

Friends is stretching our connection, Mavis thought. "What brings you here, Sarah?"

"Tony."

"Obviously. I meant why are you in Sydney?"

"I've been seeing Tony on and off this year, and he suggested we have a Sunday date in the city. I'm staying at Monica's. We met when boarding at the Women's College in Sydney University. She's a music teacher and a fine singer although she's not ..."

Her smile fixed, Mavis tuned out from Sarah's talk and observed the wider scene. Periodically, Mavis made little noises such as, "Uh huh," and, "mmm."

Behind Sarah, Monica shared her attention between Jack and Steve. Her body language signalled deep interest in what each man said. Both men leant forward as they listened to her. While she sounded enthusiastic about their performance, she did not fawn over them.

Jack, catching Mavis' eye, held her gaze for a moment before winking at her.

Monica, realising she'd lost part of her audience, turned and followed Jack's gaze. Her smile at Mavis had a subtle but nonetheless challenging quality to it. With a touch on Jack's arm, Monica reclaimed his attention. Later, when Lyle offered her a drink, she seemed genuine in her appreciation. She even had something good to say to Tim about the sound levels. *A nice girl*, Mavis thought and then dismissed her.

In maestro mode, Tony stood next to Susie talking. She was polite but steered Tony toward Sarah. After making eye contact with Susie, Mavis stifled a laugh.

Tuning back into Sarah, who had progressed to tales of her London adventure, Mavis focused. "So interesting. I'd love to do that one day. Well, I'd better let you get back to Tony."

Relieved that Tony had reclaimed Sarah, Mavis returned to where she'd been sitting.

Flopping down on the chair next to Mavis, Susie tilted toward her. "Well, I hope these two don't become regulars."

"I doubt they will. Sarah has to be the sun in her man's universe, and we know Tony doesn't have the time needed for such an orbit."

* * *

Sitting in the waiting room of Julius Morrow's company, Entertainment Inc, situated in Pitt Street, Sydney, south of the mall, Mavis and

Tony maintained a façade of indifference about the length of time they'd been kept waiting.

Either this is part of a power play, Mavis thought, or *an example of really poor time management by Morrow.* She suspected a power play, designed to position them into accepting less than they had requested.

Aware of the receptionist's clean enunciation and crisp professional dress, Mavis felt inferior to her. Briefly glancing at Tony, she noted his business-like appearance and dress. He had never looked less like a musician. She wished now they had pre-planned their act and that she had dressed according to the part to be played that day.

For a while now, she had been conscious that her speech needed to be more polished. That she felt at a disadvantage in their business dealings because of it. Did she need vocal training though to break her speech habits? Could she do it by herself? *Only one way to know,* she thought, *give it a go.*

Another ten minutes passed before they were called into Morrow's office.

"Sorry about the wait," he said. After the ritual offer of coffee and opening small talk, Morrow said, "My goal is to be fair and reasonable in negotiations with our talent, and put in place a win-win situation for everyone. I've considered what you wanted. This is what I can offer you." He passed them each a copy of the next agreement.

Sitting back, Morrow scrutinised them as they read. Tony's head nodded occasionally. Mavis kept a poker face and her body still, despite being excited that the negotiations had played out for the most part in their favour.

Looking at Mavis, Morrow added, "You're not booked for the dates you indicated."

Mavis regretted Tony's question, "That was okay?" because she thought it ceded power to Morrow.

"Clubs care about bums on seats, customers enjoying the facilities, and the overall cash turnover. Entertainment is only of value to them because it draws business to their primary money spinners. From our perspective, this is a business. We've given you a break in taking you on. If you knock back work, there's always other talent willing to take your spot. Now," passing the agreement to them, "if this is okay, I'd like signatures here and here." He passed the agreement to Nikki.

"Can I have a few minutes in private with Tony?"

"Of course." Morrow vacated his office.

"What do you think, Tony?"

Husbanding his thoughts after reading the document, Tony said, "Financially, we're a lot better off. The guys will be disappointed about having to share rooms."

"Should we hold off now that we've agreed to try the big pub scene?"

"No, that'll take time to get in place. Havin' a contact doesn't mean we'll get work. Anyway, we can always insert pub gigs where we'd planned to do festivals. They're not a certainty either."

Chapter 12

J ack walked abreast of the other band members. "It's Saturday and the winter solstice has arrived to lighten our days." He winked saucily at a middle-aged woman as they entered the club. "Here we are happy to have yet another groundhog's day performance experience. Same stale smell of beer."

Steve said, "Check."

"Same tobacco-tainted atmosphere."

Tony said, "Check."

"Minor variations in colour scheme, laminated tables, style of chairs, tiles."

Susie said, "Check."

"Dimmed lighting, the exciting sounds and sight of poker machines."

The entourage in unison said, "Check."

Mavis took over the lead from Jack, "Performers grateful for the steady work and their growing public profile."

The band replied, "Check mate!"

That night, looking at the world through a club lens as she performed, Mavis realised she enjoyed her audiences and, for the most part, liked that world. Most people listening were there for a good time and appreciative of the entertainment. Some of the younger women on the dance floor were a form of performance art: playing out a presentation ritual to their male audience, clearly intoxicated, and without inhibition. She mostly found those women, a fixture in the club scene, amusing.

That night there were also a number of girls in the room packaged to look like the alluring images of women promoted in glossy women's magazines. Beneath the gilt of makeup, their faces reminded Mavis of Zoey. Using friends, obviously made on the night, to buy them liquor, they sloshed their drinks over the tables where they sat, and sometimes each other. Wobbling precariously on high heels, they preened themselves on the dance floor. At times, they drifted off to darker places, unaware they were seen, no thought to the potential consequences of the passions in which they indulged.

Mavis made a mental note *not* to venture into the ladies' toilets that night. She disliked the drug scene and hated the smell associated with the aftermath of binge-drinking. The blue lighting provided by management in restrooms had been a vain attempt to curb drug use.

Switching her focus to the gamblers in the background, Mavis could see the difference between the poker machine addicts and other punters. The signs of repetitive strain injury were evident as was the gamblers' fear that if a machine was left it would pay out a jackpot to an undeserving new punter in the seat.

Mid-song, Mavis realised that she had slipped into autopilot. Lyrics, her animated gestures, the onstage action, and the interactions with Tony and Steve that punctuated the lyrics had become a reflex response. The sort of reflex response people experience when driving long distances or like when breathing, which did not require conscious thought. *What song am I singing?* Tuning back into the performance, she felt lost for a moment.

Tony looked at her questioningly as he sang.

Recognising the song and passage in it, Mavis relaxed and picked up the vocals. *This*, she thought, *is something I'll have to be on guard against.*

With that song ended, Mavis said to her band, "I've had enough of other people's music. Let's rock this set to a close with two of our songs. We'll do 'Moving On' followed by 'Red Rover'. The vocals led into the first number with the keyboard following. Then the rhythm instruments joined in, picking up the beat, intensifying it, and driving the vocals.

In the mood for dancing, Mavis acted on impulse, stepping down from the stage onto the floor. She felt a sudden change in energy from the audience who responded to her descent. Playing to her audience, she interacted with them through song and dance.

On a natural high and during the musical interlude, Mavis returned to the stage. The drum and bass guitar riff that led into the final song quickened the tempo of the music. The other instruments added their voices to the rhythm before the vocals began. The already crowded dance floor swelled. No one was immune to the music, not even the punters on the distant poker machines who bopped along. A variation in rhythm led into solo vocals with the band clapping in time. Soon the open space area echoed with the clapping. Mavis then surrendered audience focus to Susie who re-entered the music with a drum solo. Mavis rejoined in song with the rest of the band at the end of that drum break. The music built to fever pitch. The dancers and the other audience caught up in the passion of the music responded enthusiastically. The applause at the end of the set was thunderous.

"Thank you. Thank you."

The applause continued.

"Okay, fellas, let's do 'Moonlight'." Her song lowered the emotional heat of the audience so that the band was able to leave the stage without another encore being demanded. "We'll be back in twenty." She followed the retreating band to a bland backroom.

Lyle had the room readied with hard drinks for the guys, coffee for Mavis and Susie, fast food snacks for the men, and a salad selection for the women. Discerning in his selections, he catered carefully for each woman's specific tastes without broadcasting his effort. His sense of chivalry signalled by the way he held out chairs for them.

Looking at that night's fare, Mavis rested a hand lightly on his arm. "Thank you for this. I really do appreciate ..."

The door opened and Tim entered. "Look who dropped in, guys."

Tony crossed to Sarah and Monica. "I didn't know you were comin'." He pulled Sarah aside, exchanging a series of tender kisses, reflecting a rapport that went beyond a dating couple.

Watching them, Lyle called out, "Get a room," before returning his attention to the group.

Meanwhile, Monica had crossed to the table and pulled up a chair close to Jack. She beamed at him before engaging Mavis. "Great end, Nikki, but what happened before that?"

"I went blank for a moment. Was it *that* noticeable?" Mavis looked to the rest of her band for feedback.

Monica answered without missing a beat. "I knew because Tony picked up your vocals. I've heard you all so many times now, I guess I know your routines."

Mavis raised an eyebrow. "Really?"

"Did you know we sing in the same key?"

"No."

Noting the change in Mavis' mood, Tim said, "Well, *I* didn't notice it. Tony's pickup was seamless."

Tony and Sarah crossed to the group but remained standing, Sarah stood to Tony's left, in close contact, leaning back against him.

With a warm smile, Mavis said, "Thanks, Tony, for the onstage save."

"You okay?" Tony asked.

"Yes, I was watching the audience and lost track."

"Lapses can happen when you're tired too," Susie said.

"Well, I am that. I'm not sleeping much at night. I don't think it was tiredness tonight, but boredom with that material. I slipped into autopilot."

Having passed a diet coke to Sarah, Tony picked up a bottle of beer. "Sleepin' pills are the answer. You'll be less likely to switch off when you're rested."

"Dr Tim won't prescribe me anymore. His advice, cut back on the stimulants and stick to a sleep routine."

"Don't see your family doctor!" Tony continued. "Dr Keyman's your man. He understands performers don't have the lifestyle or time needed to achieve sleep routines."

"I'm with Tony on that," Susie said.

Jack positioned himself opposite Mavis after standing and moving away from her. While he enjoyed sexually provocative women, he disliked needy women who latched onto him as Monica had done. "Intense physical exertion, Nikki, is better than pills. I've a few things in mind that might relax you."

"I'm not running through the streets with you lot."

"Stumbling is a better description," Susie added.

In a side comment to Lyle, Tim said, "Doubt that's what he had in mind."

Standing like a sentinel, Lyle's eyes narrowed as he considered Jack. At the end of the break, Lyle tried to manoeuvre a private moment with him, but Monica had attached herself to Jack again, foiling Lyle's plan.

As an observer of the scene, Susie read Lyle's purpose correctly. In a quiet word to him, she said, "Let Tony and me handle it, Lyle."

"As long as you do."

As they returned to the stage, Tony held Jack back. "Don't hit on Nikki if you want to stay in this band."

"Not your call, mate."

"She's a risin' star. Earthbound men like us, mate, won't be where she looks for her man if she decides she wants one. Do you see her givin' the time of day to the flash guys who've been followin' her? No. She's not interested. We're a family. I don't want you wreckin' that healthy dynamic."

"You speak to him?" Susie asked Tony at the edge of the stage.

Tony nodded.

Susie paused onstage next to Jack as he strapped on his bass. "Listen to Tony, Jack! Nikki has come to rely on you as a trusted *friend* and her creative partner. Sex may be on your mind but keep it out of your mouth. Neither Nikki or I like to be treated as objects. Find your entertainment with the groupies; they don't seem to care."

Having taken a pit stop, Steve returned late to the stage. He stopped for a word with Jack as they came together. "Could you have sounded any more like a jerk? I think not!"

While Jack tuned up, Mavis crossed to him. In undertones, she said, "I care for you, Jack, a lot, but—"

"You like my playin' but don't want to play yet."

With a graceful incline of her head, Mavis smiled at him before reclaiming the presence she needed on stage. After her signal to the band, a gutsy opening riff and strong drum beat led into the next bracket. Focused on her performance, Mavis contemplated the words she sang, looking for the nuances in the lyrics. She wanted to maintain a sense of spontaneity in her performance. *The mark of a true professional,* she thought. It was a matter of showing respect for the music and giving the audience what they were due.

In the audience, Monica sat with Tim following the set closely while Sarah sat nearby at a table, occasionally warding off unwanted male attention. Lyle, seeing the pressure Sarah was under, crossed to her table and sat with her.

* * *

Monday evening, a week later. Winter gales swept across the Keimera landscape. Rain, heavily angled and driving from a southerly direction, battered the township. The iron sheet roofing on Mavis' cottage amplified the sound of the beating rain but held its place despite the strong winds.

Inside, Mavis, Kate, and Gary sat in cozy comfort, enjoying *Friends* while Dan readied himself for bed. The thump-thump-thump, thump-thump-thump of small padded feet heading toward the living area lead Mavis to say, "I'm sorry. We'll have to turn it off until Dan's in bed. I can't have him …"

"Done." Gary switched the television off. "We'll catch it in reruns."

"Mummy, I feel sick." Dan crossed to where she sat in a well-cushioned cane armchair. "Can I have a cuddle?" and climbed into her lap without waiting for a response.

"You're very wheezy, Dan. I think I should rub your chest with Vicks again …"

"I don't like it, Mummy. It's gooey."

"It'll help keep your nose clear so you can sleep. How about we run the humidifier again tonight?"

"Okay."

"He's had a terrible cold and cough, followed by a bout of bronchitis," Mavis said, "but hasn't complained about it till now. Mum's been on top of it though."

"She's been up to the surgery twice a week, Mavis, the last few weeks."

"At *my* insistence."

"Yes, she told me."

"Did Mum tell you that she thought the locum was too complacent for her liking?"

"Dr Wallace is very experienced."

"When is Dr Tim back?"

"Tomorrow."

"Dan, how about we do another check of your peak flow? Hop down for me."

While Mavis crossed to her medicine cabinet, Dan sat on her chair.

"Do we have to, Mummy?"

"Yes."

"You're a stoic little man, aren't you, Dan?" Kate said, curled up on the lounge and leaning back against Gary.

"If you say so. What's stoic?"

"You're brave about being sick when you are and put up with it."

"Okay, thank you."

With a peak flow monitor and Dan's record chart in hand, Mavis returned. "Okay, little man, you know how this goes. Breathe deep and blow."

With a crease between her brows that wasn't quite a frown, Mavis recorded the latest measurement.

"Want a story, Dan?" Gary asked.

"Not really. I just want Mummy to rub my back til I go to sleep."

"Give everyone a kiss goodnight, Dan."

"I'll put the kettle on for a cuppa, shall I, Mavis?" Kate said.

"That'd be great. Want to get some supper to go with it?"

"Sure."

The kettle came to the boil and cooled to cold, and still Mavis had not returned to the living room.

From Dan's room, though their voices were muffled at times, Mavis could hear Kate and Gary's conversation.

"That's a big claim, Kate."

"Think about it, Gary. Film and television increasingly deal with the objectification of people in a non-critical way."

"I think you're going a bit far with your feminist views."

"It's not a matter of being feminist. It's a matter of questioning how life is *sold* to us in the media. While I appreciate you're a man of action, Gary, it'd be good if you became a man of thought as well."

"Ouch! I didn't see that knife thrust comin'."

"Don't stop, Mummy."

"Just checking to see if you were asleep, Dan."

"I'm not, Mummy."

"Sort've guessed that." Mavis stroked his forehead gently. His head, like his back, felt hot. "I think I'll give you some Panadol, Dan, in case you have a temperature."

"Okay."

On her return to the kitchen, Mavis found Kate sitting in one of the armchairs and Gary standing at the window, looking outside.

Recognising Mavis' footfall, Gary turned around as she entered.

"Everything okay, Mavis?" Kate and Gary asked in disunion.

"I didn't say anything earlier because I didn't want to frighten Dan, but his peak flow has dropped, and I think he's spiked a temperature. I don't get it. He usually responds to the medicine. Maybe I should take him up to the hospital tonight just to be safe?"

Gary said, "On a night like this? It's safer indoors. The doctor saw him two days ago, didn't he?"

"Uh huh."

"Then how bad can he really be?"

Kate frowned at Gary but spoke to Mavis. "Has Dan had all his asthma medication?"

"Yes, he has." Mavis crossed to her medicine cabinet that she had located above her refrigerator. Outside, gale force winds battered the landscape. "Geez, I hope the roof holds. I guess you're right about not taking Dan out in that, Gary." With a packet of paracetamol in hand and a thermometer, Mavis filled a glass with water from the kitchen tap. "Kate, could you get me one of those appointments tomorrow that Dr Tim holds for walk-ins?"

"Bring Dan down at eight, and I'll make sure he's seen first. That Panadol should hold his temperature down."

"I hope so …" Mavis disappeared back into the darkened part of her cottage, responding to Dan's, "Mummy!" Her concern about Dan deafened her to everything outside his bedroom. Eventually, his wheezing seemed to quieten. *Thank God for humidifiers and euca-lyptus,* Mavis thought.

Sitting on the edge of Dan's bed, she tuned into the noises from beyond Dan's room. The storm was building in its ferocity. Mavis was glad she'd opted to wait til morning before seeking medical help.

Gary's, "Rubbish, Kate!" carried clearly to Dan's room.

"The sexual freedom the feminist movement worked for has been hijacked …"

Concerned that Gary was in turbulent, potentially dangerous waters, Mavis wondered how she could rescue him.

"Give it a rest, Ken. I don't want to hear it!"

"I like to talk about this stuff."

"And I don't, so stop. Mind if I put the TV back on? I guess you'll want to watch something on the ABC?"

"What do you mean by that?"

There was a harsh edge to Gary's use of his nickname for Kate. "Let's not do this, Ken!" After a lengthy, awkward silence, he said, "Here, have the remote and surf the channels to see what we can … share."

Aware of Dan's slower breathing pattern, signalling deep sleep, Mavis removed her hand from his back.

Returning to the living area, she found Kate and Gary in, what seemed to her, tense silence. They sat oppositionally in the armchairs.

"Dan okay, Mavis?" Gary asked.

"Sleeping peacefully, but his body still seems hot. I've removed some of his bed clothing. It's so hard to know when I'm overheating him and when I'm not, especially on nights like this."

"Let me know how he goes at the doctor's, mate. I'm pushin' off. I'm off, Kate."

"I *know*. See you."

Gary left. The opened door as he departed showed how brutal the storm really was.

"What happened, Kate?"

"Gary and I are just so different. He absorbs stuff, without questioning it. I like to discuss the values and messages in the things we're exposed to. I'm so aware of the changes in life. He's not!"

"Like what?"

"Well, consider the representation of so-called 'normal life' and what is valued on film and television. It's not just a matter of art imitating life. Art is definitely shaping our reference point for what's regarded as normal. Compare the image and values of footballers from my dad's youth to now. You could drive a truck through the differences. Today's image is a tainted view of success for sure. Then there's the whole sexualisation of girls and women which is so different from the feminist view of sexual freedom. You see it everywhere: in magazines, in fashion, on streets, and especially in the music industry."

"I can see that. It's part of living in a democracy though, isn't it: the good, the bad, and all the stuff in between?"

"Well, yes, it is, but what worries me is the shift in what is seen as acceptable, and that people like Gary don't think about it and so their reference points change. At times, I think …"

"What?"

"That when the world says I'm odd, maybe I am."

"And maybe there are a lot of unthinking people out there. I, for one, appreciate your perspective on life. I wouldn't want you any different. You're wrong about Gary though. He thinks about things deeply although he may not voice it."

"I think …"

"What?"

"That it's not going to work with Gary."

"Oh."

"As my dad says, 'Time will tell.' Dad has a whole bunch of clichés to deal with relationship issues. He isn't very deep at times either."

"But you love him anyway."

"I do."

"And Gary?"

"It's not going to work. Down the track, I'll want to counter media influences if we have kids, and he'll see me as overreacting, and wall me out like he did tonight. The kids will side with him, and I'll be on the outer."

"Talk about crossing bridges before you get to them! Geez, I didn't realise you were on *that* path."

"You don't see it in Gary's behaviour?"

"To be honest I haven't been looking. I wonder what else I've missed." Noting Kate's dejection, Mavis added, "Why so upset if you've ruled him out?"

"I'm contrary, aren't I?"

Mavis threw a cushion at her. "You nong! You truly love him, and his warts don't matter! Besides, it wouldn't work out that way you say. Gary listens and learns!"

Throwing the cushion back, Kate said, "You're changing, Mavis."

"You think?"

"In the obvious ways like your speech. In subtle ways like your growth in confidence and openness to ideas. You're … *buoyant* nowadays."

"Yeah, that's how I feel. Y' know, I've been careless with my speech for a long time now. When I was a teen, I didn't want to be a stand-out. Lazy speech isn't good if you're a singer though. It puts you at a disadvantage in business as well which I'm sure you already know. I'm working hard to speak well naturally. As for ideas, as a songwriter, I'm interested in them. I think a lot about life now, its meaning, and how that can be communicated to an audience. It's both a satisfying and frustrating process. Want a cuppa? I'm having one."

"No, thanks, it's time I went too. I'll help you wash up first though."

"Don't worry about that."

"You sure?"

"Yes."

"Well then, I'm off … Be at the surgery tomorrow at seven fifty so I can get Dan in first."

"Thanks. We will be."

"Bye." Kate was glad now that she had opted to drive to Mavis' place after work rather than go home first and have Gary pick her up. As she tried to make dry, safe passage to her car, she had difficulty stopping her umbrella from inverting but succeeded somehow.

Back at her house, Kate regretted for the umpteenth time her rented two bedroom house only had a carport. The driving rain and wind at her place were far worse than what she had experienced at Mavis'. Her umbrella inverted, and she was drenched by the time she made it inside. Despondent and shivering, she headed for the shower.

*   *   *

Towelling herself dry, Kate attributed the sound of knocking to a loose sheet of roof iron and hoped it would hold in place until the morning. In her bedroom, she opted for comfort nightwear, zebra patterned pyjamas, before heading to the kitchen, her hair still wrapped into a turban-styled towel. She hoped a mug of warm milk would soothe her troubled spirits. It was her father's remedy in times of stress.

As Kate entered the small living area, she realised that someone was actually knocking on the front door. Crossing to it, she opened the door tentatively.

Gary fell into the house, having sheltered under the narrow porch as close to the door as he could. He was drenched. "About time, Ken. It's bloody miserable out there."

Kate closed the door but not before rain spattered the floor. "What are you doing here?"

"I wanted to set things straight between us." Gary moved toward the gas fire, a burning log simulation of the real thing.

"Can you hold up a sec? You're dripping everywhere." Kate unwrapped her hair and passed him the towel. "Stand on that." She raked her fingers through her hair, tidying it as best she could.

With both feet on the towel, Gary manoeuvred his way across the polished wooden floor to the fire. "I used to love scootin' along the floor like this when I was a kid. Would you mind gettin' me a change of clothes? I don't want to catch my death."

Back in her room, Kate took the opportunity to comb and plait her hair. She pulled out a pair of jeans, boxers, and a little-worn shirt from drawers where Gary kept clothes for when he stayed over. Before leaving her bedroom, she checked her reflection. *That look will not do!*

Swiftly, she unbuttoned her pyjama top, pulled off her long pyjama pants, threw them onto the bed, and searched her top drawer for a more tempting garment. She decided on black chiffon lingerie with a silk underskirt and shoestring straps. Back to the mirror she went. After considering her reflection, she decided against such an obvious look and message.

What followed was a stream of clothing with Kate alternating between looking-good but casual versus alluring and sexy. The pile of discards grew.

Getting a grip on herself, Kate resigned herself to the zebra pyjamas. As she finished rebuttoning her pyjama top, she paused. *Who knew where the night would lead?* Stripping off again, she opted for a new set of black lace underwear under her pyjamas. Catching a final glimpse of herself in the mirror, she thought, *At least I'm not an open book.*

On her return, Kate found Gary stripped down with the towel

around his lower torso. His skin had a subtle sheen in the firelight of the room. *Will I ever get past that thrill of seeing him naked?* She dropped his clothes on the sofa, aware of how much she wanted him. "I was on the way to making a cuppa before. Want one?"

"Sure. You did mean tea, didn't you?"

Kate laughed. "Yes."

Later, standing at the kitchen counter looking out at the raging storm, Kate felt strong hands unexpectedly at her waist and warm lips caress the nape of her neck. She leant back into Gary, content to be in his arms again, glad he wanted to remove what had become crooked between them.

"I'm sorry, Ken, for lettin' the fact that we see the world different get in the way of what we have. I got what you were sayin' at the time but felt dumb that I couldn't contribute and so got defensive."

Kate turned around to face him, resting her hands on his bare chest. His skin was warm to the touch. She looked at him questioningly.

"I've outgrown that shirt. Must be one from when I lost weight after that failed rescue. Jeans are fine though."

"Do you want me to—"

"No."

"I've never thought of you as dumb, Gary."

"I feel like it though … sometimes, not all the time."

"I'm sorry too, but the way women are treated really gets to me. I worry the world is backsliding and that ground hard won is being surrendered unthinkingly, and what gets me the most is that lots of women are buying what's being sold them." Misreading Gary's face, Kate added, "Look at me. I know I should shut up, but I keep banging on."

"No, you shouldn't shut up. It matters to you so it's goin' to matter to me too. It's what I expect of you, and what you already give me." Gary kissed her then, a series of open mouthed, gentle kisses that built into passion.

What happened next was not the wham bam, thank you, ma'm sex so commonly portrayed in the movies. It was not a matter of clothes being ripped off or of buttons popping when lovers were lost to lust. No one fell over furniture on the route to consummation. It was not a wrestling match.

"Bedroom or the rug in front of the fire, Kate?"

Kate remembered the chaos of her bedroom. "The rug."

"Good, I like looking at your body in the firelight."

Kate arched an eyebrow at him before replying. "As I do yours."

With a bottle of red wine in hand and glasses, Gary led the way to the living room. It was bathed in soft firelight augmented by light from a corner table lamp. After uncorking the wine bottle, he left it to stand. Grabbing a few cushions from the lounge and armchairs, he positioned them on the floor.

Kate felt a sudden surge of shyness. Surprised, she remained standing.

With a smile that radiated from his eyes, Gary patted the spot next to him.

Her pulse pounding, Kate returned his smile but remained where she was. Having considered putting on some sultry music, she decided against it. She had the power to turn Gary's passion into all-consuming fire. She just had to relax and release the temptress within.

In a slow, playful striptease, Kate slowly undid one button and then another on her shirt. Each movement had a hypnotic quality. She lingered on the last button before removing her hands. The shirt parted, revealing the line of her full breasts. "You think my heart's here, don't you?"

Gary nodded, savouring the moment.

"But really it's been with you for a long time."

With her fingers on the shirt's edge, she ran her hand down the material, conscious of its softness. Her hands came to rest on her hips, fingers splaying inward and down.

Considering Gary, she switched to her pyjama pants. With a show manufactured out of undoing the cord tie at her waist, she loosened the cord, pulled her pants outward from her waist, and let the pants fall to the floor. With a delicate foot movement, she stepped out of them. She had beautifully proportioned legs.

Maintaining eye contact, Kate sauntered toward Gary, and then around him, tousling his hair. She laughed when he reached for her, escaped his grasp, and stayed at a tantalising distance from him. After pouring them both a glass of wine, she handed Gary a glass, their fingers brushing. Their touch felt electric.

Back at where she'd been standing earlier, Kate tasted the wine, considering her next move. After emptying her glass, she placed it on a nearby coffee table. Next, she turned her back on Gary but looked over her shoulder into his eyes. With a subtle shoulder lift, she slowly let the shirt slide down to expose her shoulder. With a wink, she slipped the shirt off her arms as she turned to face him. It too fell to the floor, revealing her bra. Her skin was flawless; she had rejected the recent fashion trend for strategically placed tattoos.

Gary reclined on his arms, enjoying the show, at ease with his obvious arousal. His admiration for the beauty of her body, fit but still curvaceous, revealed by his slow upward-sliding, appreciative study of her body.

Arching her back, Kate undid her bra, and eased out of it. She tossed it to Gary who caught it in a deft move. As he did, Kate positioned herself so that Gary had a side view of her. Then, in a delicately assertive manner, Kate removed her black lace panties in a fluid movement and sank feline-like to the floor before moving to him.

Sitting up, Gary pulled Kate to him, rolled her onto her back, and then positioned a cushion under her head. He ran his hand languidly over her body, barely touching the bloom on her skin, the gentlest of caresses, intent on giving her as much pleasure as touching her gave him. Her skin in the firelight had a silken radiance. His hands came to rest finally on her full breasts, soft and supple to the touch.

"You are really beautiful, do you know that?"

Kate stroked his face. "I want us to be one, Gary."

With lips slightly parted, they tasted one another in a teasing series of kisses that transformed into passion. Their lovemaking was pleasure-charged and free of issues revolving around power and domination. It was a matter of enjoying each moment, of thrilling to the many ways a man and woman can touch one another, of building finely exquisite excitement to exultation. Their union was about revelling in the joining and luxuriating in the wellbeing and contentment that followed climax. They fell asleep that night in the firm belief that once again all was right with the world.

*   *   *

The morning had a post storm stillness to it although the sky retained a bruised quality.

By the time Dan was dressed and readied for the trip to the doctor's, Mavis noticed that he had a blueness to his features which were also pinched. He was breathing shallowly but without a wheeze. She hoped that was a good sign.

"You okay mate?"

Dan nodded. He lacked the breath to speak.

True to her word, Kate had organized for Dr Tim to see Dan first.

After a close examination, Dr Tim crossed to his desk, picked up his phone, and rang his receptionist. He waited. "Dan will have to be hospitalised, Mavis. Ah, Nadine, call for an ambulance. Tell them it's urgent … a severe asthmatic attack. Which nurse is on duty? … Ask her to come to my rooms."

With the arrival of the nurse and the resuscitation trolley, the doctor disappeared into the wider surgery. As the nurse placed the mask over Dan's face, she explained how the oxygen mixed with the nebuliser medication would help him breathe. Then she administered an intramuscular injection of adrenaline.

Meanwhile, Mavis overheard the doctor talking to Kate from where they stood in the corridor. "I don't want to alarm Mavis, but …" The doctor stopped talking, having realised the door to his room was open. He moved to close it before speaking further.

"Don't worry, Mavis," the nurse said, having known her since their school days.

Time felt like it had been suspended. Mavis dimly registered the doctor's returns between patients.

On hearing a siren, the nurse excused herself and left the room.

"It's okay, Dan. Mummy's here. I'll keep you safe."

The sequence of action following the ambulance's arrival was a blur for Mavis. She registered little beyond Dan's difficulty in breathing, his paleness, and the change over in oxygen and nebuliser equipment.

At the hospital, Dan was rushed into the emergency unit. At his bedside, Mavis held Dan's hand as medical staff acted with a strong sense of urgency.

Shocked by the turn of events, Mavis registered only key words said to her by treating doctors. "Critical condition ... Haven't heard a chest that bad in years ... Important to keep him calm because fear can make it worse."

Gary arrived at the hospital an hour after Dan had been admitted into intensive care. Gary was denied entry.

On receiving a message from him, Mavis asked a nurse, "Would you speak to him for me, and fill him in on the treatment here?"

The Mills arrived not long after Gary. They too had to wait.

In the waiting room nearby, the nurse explained, "I'm sorry, you can't see Dan today. We need to keep him as settled and calm as possible so that his breathing isn't impaired further. Extended family can unwittingly transmit their anxieties and tip the balance ..."

Time and the day passed with Mavis having little awareness of its passage. While Dan was awake, she told him stories, sang to him, and held onto his hand tightly. His breathing remained shallow even with the aid of oxygen. Her focus never wavered. She let go of his hand only when medical staff needed her to relinquish her place.

Throughout that day Mavis prayed silently to God, aware that she rarely gave Him notice. *Please, don't be an indifferent force at a distance. Dan and I need You to care. Please, please, don't take him from me.* Dan continued to struggle for life's breath.

In the early evening, something Kate had once said about sexist conditioning returned to Mavis, giving her pause. *Whatever you are, please forgive my assumption, and help my son.*

At ten that night, a nurse said to Mavis, "You should go home. Your man's waiting for you outside. He's been here all day with your parents. I've kept them updated."

"I won't leave Dan. Can you ask them to go home? Tell them … I'll call them if … when Dan is out of this stage."

The night slowly faded into dawn. Mavis stirred at his bedside at first light. On checking Dan's breathing, she thought it seemed deeper, his colour better.

The treating doctor arrived at six, consulted with the nursing staff, read the records, checked Dan out. Taking Mavis aside, he said, "The worst of it has passed."

"Dan's safe?"

"Yes."

"Thank you." *Thank you.*

"You should go home."

"He's all I have … No, I'll stay with him."

"He's going to need his mother healthy and strong when he's released from here. You've seen how vigilant we are with him. Go home. He's safe. Yes, nurse?"

"There's a man just arrived. He asked me to tell Mavis it's Gary."

"You need to go home," the doctor continued. "If your boy sees you so strung out, it could make him fearful and that …"

"I know; fear can result in his airways narrowing further. Okay, I'll go. Do *not* let anything happen to him, please."

Mavis fell into Gary's arms, the torrent of emotion pent up in her over the past days and nights released.

"It's okay, mate. Here, sit down and have a good cry."

After the peak of Mavis' distress had passed, she asked, "What sort of mother am I, Gary, to have let this happen?"

"Inexperienced, mate, just like I am. Now we know how fast things can change, we'll be more vigilant, and Dan won't ever be at risk again. C'mon, I'll take you home. Kate sends her love. I'll come back and stay with Dan while you sleep, but you need to tee it up with the doctor."

Mavis returned to the intensive care unit, explained Gary's role in Dan's life, gained permission for him to take her place at Dan's bedside, and then left.

At home, Mavis updated her parents on Dan's medical state, had her first meal since the crisis had begun, and then went to bed. She fell asleep easily but didn't sleep long. Midday, when she padded into her kitchen, she found Kate putting the finishing touches on Mavis' favourite comfort food: butterfly cupcakes decorated with strawberries, freshly whipped cream, and a dusting of icing sugar.

"I took the day off after Gary called and said you were coming home. Flex-time owed to me; Dr Tim understood. I know your mum wants to prepare all your meals, but I needed to do something to help too. She understood where I was coming from. Gary called an hour ago to let you know Dan is doing even better. I managed to grab the phone on the first ring. Did it disturb you?"

"Didn't hear a thing."

"I think Gary is right in that I should drive you back to the hospital given you're stressed and naturally distracted by it. Just a safety measure. We don't want any … I won't tempt fate by saying it."

On Mavis' return to the hospital that afternoon, she learnt that Dan would remain in hospital for at least a week, perhaps longer. Her heart lifted when she saw him. Though clearly ill, he was alert although shaky from the medicines he'd been administered.

With the lights in the intensive care unit dimmed, Dan nodded off to sleep while Mavis caressed his forehead. "I promise you, Dan, Mummy will make us a better life." She left him a few hours later knowing he was definitely on the mend. She rang Gary and waited within the hospital foyer until he pulled up in the drop-off area.

"Brrr, it's cold tonight, Gary!"

"No cloud cover." Gary grabbed a woollen throw-blanket from his back seat and passed it to her. "Kate thought you'd need this."

"I'm assuming everything is right with you two again."

"Better than all right. I've realised I love Kate."

"Oh, Gary, I'm so glad you *finally* see what I already knew!"

Gary didn't add that he had been racking his mind in the waiting hours at the hospital for an ultra romantic way to propose.

As Gary angle parked in front of the Mills house, Marg came out to greet them. "Supper's ready." She tightly hugged Mavis who was wrapped inside the blanket, feeling like she was a parcel and her mother the string. The extended family was a convivial group as they shared supper in the Mills' lounge room. Mavis opted to sleep in her parents' house that night.

Wednesday lunchtime, Susie and Zoey visited the hospital to see how Dan was progressing. Zoey had bought Dan a handheld computer game.

"It's something Dan told me he really, really, really wanted, Nikki, when we were at Parkes, but he said you said he had to save for it."

Susie added, "I hope you don't mind …"

"Of course I don't. Visitors are still restricted, but you can wave at him through the window. I'll take the gift into him so you can see his reaction when he opens it."

Delight summed up Dan's reaction best.

On her return, Susie said, "So … the guys want to know what we'll be doing about the pub gig tonight and the Sydney gigs this weekend."

"What? Oh. You'll have to do them without me of course."

"Dan's out of the woods though, isn't he?"

"But still in intensive care as you can well see."

Silence. The women avoided eye contact by deflecting from each other.

Mavis moved closer to the viewing window and watched Dan.

Zoey, uncomfortable with the tension, drifted away to the chairs where she sat flicking through magazines. She glanced at her mother who had walked back down the corridor a way and come to a weight-shifting standstill.

Susie steadied herself with measured breathing before she approached Mavis. "Won't your no-show null-and-void the agreement, Nikki?"

"I don't think so, not if the band shows up."

"But you don't know for sure."

The women held each other's gaze for what Zoey thought was minutes. Susie dropped hers first.

"I don't think it'll be an issue, Susie. The entertainment management doesn't usually catch our shows. The guys can ditch the Elvis numbers for the time being. They'll be happy about that at least. If they add the new material to the mix, and Tony does my vocals – he knows them – it'll work. We're not scheduled for the auditorium gigs this weekend so it really doesn't matter. You'll be right … and, yes, I'll call Tony."

"Not anywhere near as good though. The guys won't understand."

"That's not my problem. As you said when you auditioned for our band, a musician with a kid has its own complications. It's just a fact. If I have to *choose* …"

"No. They're big boys and can suck it up and get through the gigs. We're all in it to play as *your* band."

"Okay … Good and all as it is to see you and Zoey here, isn't she supposed to be at boarding school in Mittagong?"

"Yes … She's been suspended."

Mavis glanced at Zoey who was unsettled by the glance. "What? She's only been there a term. Why?"

"From my perspective, for nothing heinously wrong although the school management has her choices listed up there with the crimes of the century. Zoey had a breakout of non-conformity and breached their rigid dress code. The school was appalled by that act of rebellion and even more by my complacence. We agreed though that her follow-up offence was serious. She skipped sport training on the Games Field Friday afternoon, with some girlfriends, and left the school grounds early. Each girl had two exeats to cover her absence from school on

Friday and Saturday nights under the pretext that they were staying at one of the girl's homes in Moss Vale. Her parents, thinking the other girls had parental approval, allowed them to take the train to Sydney so they could go to a rock concert. They stayed at the Swissotel in Market Street courtesy of the Moss Vale parents. Zoey had read that RedSun had a gig at the Enmore Theatre that weekend and wanted to hear them. I think it was a status thing with her friends as well."

"I don't get it. Why didn't she ask you instead? It doesn't make sense."

"She knew I wouldn't take her anywhere near that particular band. As for trying to make contact after the show ... I've been loud and clear about my feelings on that since Parkes when I told her the background to her birth."

Mavis looked at Susie puzzled.

"The biological link is the lead guitarist in RedSun."

"Oh."

"Zoey has some father fantasy ..." Susie rolled her eyes. "I just can't get through to her on that score. So I told her I'll take her to meet the biological link in 1998 if she continues to get good grades and stays out of trouble. She knows she shouldn't expect anything from him but does anyway. Kids! Why do we have them?"

"So how did they get sprung?"

"There was a falling out between the girls because Zoey had implied she'd be able to get them backstage and couldn't. It ended up with them carpeted in the principal's office for the second time that week, the first being the Monday morning. The school heavies had been waiting for them when the girls tried to sneak back in."

Mavis returned to Dan's bedside, disturbed by Susie's unfolding family drama. Mavis did not want Terry, her ex-boyfriend, figuring as Dan's father in any version of their lives. It was a comfort to her now that Dan's birth certificate had a blank against the father's name. *When the time comes,* Mavis thought, *I'll tell Dan I don't know who his biological link is.* She did not think about the implications.

* * *

"Well here I am!" Monica said, brighter than her red lip-gloss, as she stepped onto the stage. Her look was urban upscale.

Tony crossed to her. "Thanks for comin' on such *short* notice."

Susie noticed something pass between them. *Was Tony cheating on Sarah?*

Turning to face his band members, now standing aligned with arms folded, Tony added, "The show has to go on *and* with a full band *or* the agreement is null and void!"

Jack acted as spokesperson. "You talked to Nikki about this?"

"I did."

"She didn't say anything when I called before the gig last night."

"Well, Jack, it's because we're not on her mind. Now, I've talked through the set lists with Monica. This will be our running order for the night." He passed out the list, a small C6 sized card. "Any comments?"

Susie smiled at Monica, "Thanks for helping us out." Then she stepped into Tony's space. "This has a clandestine feel to it. I'm not happy!"

With his back turned to Tony and Monica, Jack mouthed to Susie, "This seem right to you?"

Susie responded with a slow negative headshake.

In command, Tony ran through the sound checks. "Okay then, let's rock and roll!"

Performance-wise the night went well. True to her earlier claims, Monica *did* know all the vocals. Added to that she was a good mimic and had obviously studied Mavis' style. With the exception of Tony, the band felt like Monica was an ill-fitting garment; the cut was not quite right, and there was a problem with the tolerances. That Monica knew the vocals to recently developed, original material heightened their uneasiness.

That night the audience were responsive but not enthusiastic. The band was background to the social setting of the club.

"See you next week," Monica said after bar drinks which had

followed their final set. She left as brightly as she had arrived, unaware of the internal tensions within the band.

Sitting on a stool, leaning back with his elbows on the bar, Jack said, "Next week?"

"I've booked her for all the gigs."

Jack shook his head and let Susie take up the verbal baton. "Even if Nikki was on board with this, you should've discussed it with us first."

"I formed this band. I don't have to consult anyone."

Steve spoke up for the first time. "Things have changed considerably since then, mate. If I remember rightly, Mason Andrews formed Velum not you. We voted him out because of his addiction. The same thing happened with Matt Peronas. It wasn't just your call then, and it hasn't been for some time now."

"When Nikki continues to be a no-show, you'll see I'm right. I'm out of here!"

Susie sat up at that. "What! And not help with the gear?"

"It's why we pay the roadie." Tony knocked back his drink and left.

Disgruntled, the rest of the band bumped out. Before getting into the car with Lyle and Tim, who waited with their windows down, Steve said, "I feel like we've cheated on Nikki somehow. How come Monica knew the new material?"

Jack turned the key in his car's ignition. "I don't like this, not one bit. How are we goin' to tell Nikki?"

Steve looked to Susie for the answer. "Not while she's in crisis that's for sure."

In chorus, the men asked, "Then when?"

* * *

Monday two weeks later, with her legs pulled up against her body, Mavis sat within Gary's brotherly embrace while Kate made them supper. Dan was out of hospital and sleeping in his room. The wind ululated across the cottage's iron roof.

In response to a knock, Kate said, "I'll get it."

"Hi, fellas, Susie. Of course, come in."

The band, minus Tony, entered with a sense of purpose. Mavis crossed to greet them.

"So cold tonight!" Susie said, taking off her sheepskin jacket and passing it to Kate. With heavy coats piled high, Kate considered where to put them. Her indecision translated into dithering movement. In the end, she dumped them on the small dining table.

After an affectionate exchange with Mavis, Jack and Susie sat on the armchairs and Steve pulled up a stool. Mavis' face was white and reflected the strain she'd been under. She had returned to the sofa and sat next to Gary.

"So how's it been *without* me, fellas?"

Susie and Steve looked to Jack. "Like a car in need of a desperate tune. Nikki, we've a problem, and there's no way to tell you but straight."

Kate crossed to the lounge area, concerned, standing behind Gary and Mavis.

"You know Tony booked Monica for the gigs but what—"

"He did what?"

Band members glanced uneasily at one another, their suspicions confirmed.

"Who, Jack?"

"Monica."

Mavis digested that news. "What was he thinking? There's no way she'd pull it off. Have we lost the work?"

"No to that. She knew our material off pat. It's pretty clear Tony's been preppin' her to take your spot. In fact, he's offered it to her."

Jolted and suddenly feeling sick, Mavis stared at them, her thoughts frozen.

Jack moved to the sofa and sat next to Mavis on the unoccupied side before placing a comforting hand on hers. "We've told him it's not on but want to know how *you* want to deal with the issue now. Do we tell him he's out or do you?"

Stuck in the moment, Mavis had difficulty thinking. Swamped

by a rush of dark feelings she had thought left in the past, she closed her eyes. Her face was stripped of its colour.

Aware of Mavis' trembling, Gary said, "Get her a whiskey from her dad's, Kate." He put a protective arm around Mavis.

Kate returned moments later with a bottle of Jameson's in hand. Susie, in the process of making tea for everyone, had a glass ready for her.

Concerned, Kate sat down beside Mavis after bumping Jack aside.

Grimacing, but with a sense of flowing warmth and returning clarity, Mavis said, "I hate that stuff."

When everyone was seated in the lounge area, Mavis withdrew from the shelter of Gary's arm and grounded her feet. "You're *my* band. I'll have to deal with it tonight otherwise I won't be able to sleep. Jack, will you call Tony and ask him to come over?" Sitting there with an appearance of calm, Mavis felt the dark eddies of emotion swirling around her. "Gary, a word?" She stood and moved off to the doorway leading into the darkened corridor.

Feeling like ants were crawling over him, Jack crossed to Kate who was now washing up. With an eye on Gary and Mavis, he asked, "You're Gary's girlfriend, right?"

"I am."

"You comfortable with what's between them?"

"Yes."

"Is this some sort of ménage-a-trois then?"

"Goodness no! Gary has been her rock for God knows how long. His love for me is *very* different from his love for her. If you're interested in her, it's a fact that you'll have to come to terms with."

Jack looked across the room at Mavis. *This was band business!* He resented Mavis involving Gary and wished he could overhear what was being said.

Mavis' eyes reflected her concern. "See my dilemma, Gary?"

"I do but that doesn't stop me hatin' his guts! He needs to be given his walkin' orders."

"That was my first reaction too, but if I do that, as a band, we lose *big* time."

"I can't see how you can keep him though."

"Is letting my emotions lead me wise? In the past, I've reacted to things that have happened, not thought ahead to the consequences."

"So do that now. Take a break in your room and get some quiet before you deal with this."

The band waited uneasily for Tony to arrive, small talk filling the void.

Knocking at the door caused Gary to call Mavis who returned as Jack opened the door.

Tony entered with Sarah as his support. He carried himself with a cocky, defensive air.

'Pleasantries' over, Tony and Sarah sat on the stools offered to them.

Holding herself so tight that she'd thought she'd shatter, Mavis felt the latent anger rise within her.

Feeling like a cheating husband, Tony met her gaze. His hold on Sarah's hand tightened.

Sarah thought to ease the heat on him, realising their self-serving objectives had blinkered them. "Nikki, it's partly—"

With a raised hand, Mavis stopped Sarah. "I have no idea why you're here. *This* is a band meeting. Kate, Gary, if you don't mind, could you take Sarah over to my parents' until I've had this meeting? I'll call when I want you back." She waited until the door closed behind them. "Tony, I value you for three reasons. You're a really good guitarist and know all our material. You keep our accounts in order, and you've been important in getting us business. You've clearly overlooked one important fact. The Nikki Mills Band is *my* band. How you could do this is *beyond* me! That said, I will *not* put up with disloyalty. A big part of me feels like giving you the boot, *good and hard*, but having thought about this, I'm choosing to see your behaviour as a *massive* brain fart during a crisis. So, I'm giving you the choice of staying or not. *I've* decided it's time we set our sights *a lot* higher. If you choose to stay with *my* band, you need to know your place." She leant back against her lounge and waited.

Humiliation comes in many different sized packages. Tony felt the weight of what had been passed to him. His colour steadily heightened as he considered his options. Only one was attractive. *So this is how Pete Best felt?* Pete Best being the ousted fifth Beatle.

In charged silence, Mavis and the band waited.

"Looks like I owe you an apology, Nikki. You're right; I had a brain fart. It's your band, I get it loud and clear. Thanks for not askin' me to fall on my sword. If this was medieval times, I'd pledge my fealty to you but—"

"It's not, but I accept it anyway. One other thing, *everyone* helps with the bump in and out. If you could pick up Sarah on the way out, Tony, I'd appreciate it. I'll leave it to you to tell Monica."

Tension eased out of the room after Tony closed the door. Band members stood and shook off their stress.

A tsunami of tiredness engulfed Mavis. "If you don't mind, can we call it a night? Susie, would you let Kate and Gary know I'll see them tomorrow? Thanks, fellas." She rose to see them off, Jack being the last to leave.

"Nikki, I'm not happy about you involvin' Gary. You should've turned to me. I'm the closest thing you have to a partner in this."

Mavis held back a knee-jerk retort and took a measured breath before replying. "Fair enough. I'll consider that. Good night, Jack." She was aware she had to maintain harmony in her band and avoid overreacting. She disliked Jack's statement of claim over her. She had been there. Done that before. She would not make that mistake again. She saw him now without the glaze from his sexual glamour veiling her sight.

After sauntering part of the way down the driveway to his car in the street, Jack stopped. He sensed his relationship with Mavis had changed somehow. Confident that whatever ground lost could be regained, he resumed his walk to the car.

With the door closed behind her, Mavis returned to the lounge.

Years of pent-up emotions engulfed her. She cried, mostly because she felt the relief of a butterfly finally escaping its cocoon.

Later when she had calmed, Mavis went to bed, eventually falling to sleep with dreams of spiralling CD sales and no-standing-room gigs at the major live music pubs in Sydney and Melbourne.

When she woke the next morning, she thought, *Now, to make it so.*

Chapter 13

The Nikki Mills Band, with Gary and Kate in tow, entered the recording studio built on a rural block west of Sydney. The anteroom, also known as the control room, was a deep turquoise colour with contrasting, white vertical stripes covering the joins in the wall panels. On one side of the room, a luxurious black leather lounge, modular in style, was positioned between two black contemporary styled armchairs. A pine coffee table littered with *Rolling Stone, Blender, Music Business*, and other industry magazines was positioned in front of the lounge.

The professional audio equipment for digital recording, routing and manipulating the sound was on the other side of the room. Beyond that were smaller rooms: microphoned isolation booths for instruments, the vocalist, and backup singers.

"Wow!" Kate voiced what her companions felt as they absorbed the details of the space. Their simmering excitement came closer to the boil.

"We've sunk a bundle into this place! My name's Waz Kirby," said the owner, producer, and audio editor.

"So who are you now?" Jack quipped.

"Oh, that's humour? Keep it up and one day you might even be funny." Kirby looked at him with disdain. Kirby wore a black T-shirt that declared his loyalty to Cold Chisel, blue washed jeans, and black sneakers. He said, "Gary, mate, good to see you."

In the background, Mavis had quiet words with Jack about their playlist. Susie watched them, heard it was all business, and then wandered around the studio looking at the collection of photographs, cars and bands, displayed on the wall.

"Back at you," Gary said as they exchanged an emotional hand-shake. "How's Samantha? The kids?"

"Sam's well, but fed up with the starving artist scene. She's training to be an Art teacher. My boy is a ball of energy and into soccer like I was. Our little girl is distilled sunlight. And you?"

"As before. You know Kate, and this is …" Gary had intended introducing Mavis who had crossed to them.

"G'day, I'm Tony O'Brien. I'm the one who organized these sessions."

"Waz Kirby. As a matter of curiosity, how did you find us? Reputation? Referral?"

"Yellow pages."

"Oh."

"And a comparative call around to see who had the most expertise and the best deal. The clincher was that Gary knew you and of your client base. You've done work for some pretty big bands."

"I have indeed. Mavis or Nikki? What should I call you?"

"Nikki's my stage name. People who truly know me call me Mavis."

"I guess it's Nikki then. Have a seat."

Kirby's partner, responsible for audio-mastering, and their sound recordist pulled up black-seated chrome stools. Mavis, professional mask in place, sat between Gary and Kate with Tony positioned beside Kate. The band, with the exception of Susie, had crossed to their booth and were setting up.

"Gary speaks highly of you, Nikki," Kirby said. "You're Dan's mum, right?"

"No one else."

Kirby assessed Mavis. He thought she looked more Gary's type than Kate. Kate had to be a special kind of woman to accept Gary's obvious love for Mavis, unconsummated though Gary insisted it was, and his commitment to her kid. Kirby understood the intensity of emotion that a man felt when he fathered a child. "Dan's a good kid." Noting Tony's attempts to interrupt and redirect the conversation,

Kirby added, "We caught your band at the local Leagues club recently. Nikki's got an unbelievably inviting tone."

"Great vocal colour," his partner added.

Mavis beamed, enjoying the compliments.

"Nikki has a great ear and sense of rhythm as well," Tony said, taking the focus, "and the band is tight." He resented Gary assuming any role in their business.

"She has, and they are!" Kirby continued. "We were struck by the way you guys clearly listen and use your aesthetic sense when playing. So many bands don't! We've had a lot of local bands record their CDs. You're the first one from further afield."

"Well, feel like warming up before we begin the first session?" his partner asked.

"Sure," Mavis said, finding her voice. She crossed to the vocalist's booth and donned the headset. "Mind if I run through some scales?"

"Go for it," Kirby said from the mixing desk.

Susie stood before a striking, informal shot of Cold Chisel backstage somewhere. "Who took all of these photos? It's an interesting mix of subjects."

Kirby replied, "They're mine. I used to work for News Limited till 1995 and then moved into PR. That shot of the Lexus on The Nurburgring was taken earlier this year when the company flew me to Germany. The west wall is a mix of local bands and other commercial work. The east walls are festival shots, and as you can see from the southern wall, I've graduated to bigger name groups."

"I like the behind-the-scenes shots best; an intimate look at the lives of individuals within a band. What sort of camera do you use?"

"A Cannon EOS IN. I don't think digital cameras are really up to scratch as yet for quality photos. Maybe down the track."

Susie replied, "I'm currently using a Canon EOS 5QD. It's part auto and part manual."

"Yeah, and it has some pretty good breakthrough technology to boot."

Susie added, "I tossed up between that and the Nikon F90 and F801 but opted in the end for Canon."

"A Holden versus Ford choice, eh?"

"No, it wasn't really about brand preference. More the quality of what I could take."

"Susie, are you goin' to do this or what?" Tony called.

"Coming."

"Thanks for doing this at a cost rate, Warren," Gary said standing next to him, watching Mavis.

"I owe you, mate, more than I can hope to repay. Besides, the guys and I think Nikki has that special something needed to make it big in the industry. The band is good, real good. Her music is great! She knows the road is going be tough though, doesn't she? The Australian music industry is like a funnel, wide at the intake and narrow in output. With so much talent out there, it's important to have a strategy for getting heard. Of course, the CD is an important step, but marketing and a decent budget for it are the keys to sales. You could mention to Nikki that the Internet has potential as a future marketplace. I'm adding that branch to my media tree as well."

"I'm sure the band have the marketin' side in hand," Gary said. "I'll pass on your advice about the Internet."

"We're free for dinner at my place tonight and tomorrow. What works best for you?"

Gary hesitated. He had planned to propose to Kate that night and had organised a romantic dinner for two. While Gary considered a tactful way out of the invitation, Kate answered.

"Tonight'd be great. Gary and I are goin' back in the morning."

Gary's smile turned upside down, but no one seemed to notice.

"Here's my address. Seven-thirty for eight then? Nikki, are you ready to get down to business?"

The rest of the band responded with check calls.

When the initial recording session ended, the sound recordist asked, "How many voice tracks will you have?"

Mavis looked at him questioningly. "Wasn't that obvious when the guys did backup?"

"Yes, that was, but what I mean is that for recording you can double track your own vocals on key sections of the song and do your own harmony. It'll give you a much fuller sound, and it'll complement what the guys are doing."

"It's not reproducible live though," Mavis said.

"Just as the spell of seeing and hearing a performer live isn't reproducible on a CD. To compensate for that we add to the vocals. Added vocal tracking is an audio attempt to mirror the presence you project in performance. Even here in the studio, that is considerable."

Kirby said, "You've got a good keyboardist. Why is he only using piano sounds?"

Steve replied for Mavis, "That's all my keyboard can do."

"You can use the studio keyboard if you want. It's a fully synthesised Roland. For the Bluesy numbers, you need a great brass sound. The Roland can give you that."

Steve looked at Mavis. "Nikki?"

Mavis replied, "The problem is that when people buy this CD it needs to be true to our live performance sound. We have to live up to the expectations of our audience."

"I'd love to upgrade to a Roland, Nikki, and of course, if it gives us a better sound, I'd happily take on that debt."

Jack stood next to Mavis, his shoulder brushing hers."CD sales should pay that off pretty quick."

Kirby shook his head. "Never count your chickens before they're hatched in the music and media industry. Go second-hand, you can save money."

Steve crossed to the Roland and ran his hands over the instrument in a sensuous way, tickling the keyboard. "Oh, I'm in love. Nikki, we'll have to score some brass accompaniment tonight before tomorrow's session."

Mavis crossed to Steve. "Oh! It *does* sound good. Let's do it. We can meet in my room back at the motel. I can scat the brass section, and we can take it from there."

"Why not come back to my studio later, say after six? Business is slow in the lead up to Christmas. It's free then. You can use the Roland to explore where and how you want to introduce a brass section as well as any other additions you want to make to the sound and score. May I suggest you consider adding fiddles to some of the country rock numbers? It's a hole I could hear today."

After a quick conference, Mavis said, "That's *really* generous of you. Yes, we'll take up that offer."

Four days later the business of recording ended with a quality product that Mavis was proud to say was their music. In the euphoria of the experience and with dreams of quickly hitting the charts, the band, after private consultation, committed to production of twenty-five thousand copies.

Tony, caught up in money-making fever, concluded, "We can do it. It's a huge savings per copy, and in the long run, it's a much better return for us."

Kirby frowned, torn between his drive to do business and the obligation he felt toward Gary. "Much as I enjoy making money, I feel I should sound a warning bell here."

Jack lounged back on the sofa he shared with the other male musicians. Physically, he claimed a lot of space. "How many do record companies aim to sell for an artist to go gold?"

"About five thousand units per week over a seven week period. Given this is your *first* CD, you should be more focused on getting a ranking. Don't fool yourselves. It'll be hard."

Tony whistled. "Thirty-five thousand!"

The band could 'hear' the ring of dollar signs as they lit up Tony's eyes.

Aware she had caffeine jitters, Mavis put her coffee mug back on the table. "It's time you came back to earth, Tony. You're in danger of oxygen deprivation. We'll stick to what we've ordered and can afford, thanks."

"I think that's wise. In the next week or so, I'll notify ARIA that you want to have your CD sales tracked and provide them with the necessary information for inclusion on its chart database. I'll have the CDs barcoded to facilitate cataloguing. It'll be easier this year, as ARIA have been collecting sales data electronically from music retailers. You'll be set then for the not-so-easy step of getting your CDs into stores and organizing airplay. All that's left now is for us to crack open a bottle of bubbly and christen this CD and toast to your future success."

*   *   *

In the last week of August as that month's winds blew through Sydney, stage two of CD sale or bust went into full swing. By day while they were in Sydney, the band hit the pavement and road, targeting chain store music retailers such as HMV and Sanity as well as the big independent retailers across the greater Sydney region. Starting in the city and working in pairs, taking a compass rose point for their directional attack, they gradually worked outwards to the limits of suburban Sydney, returning to their accommodation before each night's gig on the club circuit.

From short-lived meetings with harried management of the inner city stores to the extremities of the city's north, Steve and Tony learnt there was a widespread resistance to the stocking of independently produced and released CDs. Retailers were vocal about their preference for dealing with the big record producers.

"We're a business, man," a manager from the Pitt Street HMV store had said, "you've got the cart before the horse. Musicians make us money, not the other way around. It'd just be a waste of our space if you don't have a marketing machine behind you."

Undeterred, Steve and Tony pushed further north to Gosford and then Newcastle. By their Saturday night gig, they knew defeat.

From Burwood to Penrith and beyond to the Blue Mountains city of Katoomba, all of the store managers told Susie and Tim the same thing, "Not interested!" Only one manager showed empathy for their situation, a pimply, twenty-something manager with lank hair and a preference for torn denim. "Lady, it's a plus your CD is eligible for the ARIA charts, but you'll never make the sales that'd justify us stocking you unless you get airplay. Without that you're pissing in the wind."

"Susie, this is sounding more and more like the chicken and the egg conundrum. Might as well hit the local radio stations while we're out this way."

Having finger-walked through the Yellow Pages for addresses, Susie and Tim assumed a no-retreat no-surrender attack on radio stations in the western suburbs as they worked their way back to their accommodation on Friday. Immoveable, they waited in narrow, seat-less foyers for the opportunity to talk to program managers. When waved off like an annoying fly, they doubled the enthusiasm of their pitch. It was a rare moment when a manager accepted a CD with a commitment to listen to it later. By Saturday night, Susie and Tim saw only a faint flicker of hope amidst the ash of their aspirations.

Meanwhile, Mavis and Jack zigzagged across the southern regions of Sydney from centre to centre, store to store. They began the first day in good spirits, excited about the prospect of placing CDs in music outlets and the cash return from sales. At every store, they were waved off with, "Not interested."

Over the next day as they travelled between stores, there was an increasingly awkward silence between them. When they did talk, their exchange was stilted and limited.

At the end of the second day, taking a leaf from the ingenuity tree discovered by Susie and Tim, Mavis and Jack decided to hit the southern radio stations. Like Susie and Tim, they found commercial radio producers were not interested. Even the receptionists at the respective commercial stations refused their offer of a free CD.

Community funded stations were a somewhat different story. Occasionally, a producer would accept a CD when the pitch to them became passionate although no one made a commitment to air it. Mavis saw a glimmer of hope but not the light needed to guide their way.

Late Saturday afternoon, Mavis and Jack arrived back at their accommodation in the inner city. With the engine turned off, they sat in glum, silent disappointment.

"Well, this is a fine mess we've got ourselves into, Jack."

"I'll say!"

At the close of Saturday night, the band chilled in the break room. Depression, the elephant in the room, took up a lot of the emotional space.

Wired by numerous amounts of coffee consumed that day and determined to deny defeat victory, Mavis rallied them. "We need to think innovatively and review what we take for granted so that we can identify what marketing opportunities are *really* out there for us."

Constipated thought followed.

Lyle finished off the cold remains of a pizza. "I'm not above floggin' them at gigs. That's a start at least."

Jack felt obliged to say, "I'm sorry, fellas. Who'd have thought it?"

"Not me for one!" Tony said. "I'm sorry too, fellas. I guess I was drunk on the experience and threw business sense to the winds. This proves though that we're better off bein' content with what we are and the money we make from that. A bird in the hand is—"

Susie hit Tony over the head with an unopened bag of crisps. "And with that philosophy, English sailors in the sixteenth century on their seaward explorations toward the new world would have said, 'Hey, let's rediscover Spain. It's too scary to go beyond the known world. As for the cost outlay, there isn't any money to be made in the unknown to justify the expenditure.' So we've had a setback. So what! At least we've got a quality CD to send off with our applications for festivals. That's got to be a positive."

After grabbing for the crisps bag, Steve popped it open. "Continuing in Susie's nautical vein, we need to up anchor and venture forth boldly into new musical worlds."

In reaction, the other men around him scrunched up their food wrappings and threw them at him.

Crisp in hand and poised before his mouth, Steve said, "We haven't tested those introductions to the iconic, live-music pubs that Sean

Doyle gave you as yet. It's time we did. A groundswell in our fan base will move those CDs faster than … than Lyle can scull a beer." Steve shoved Lyle. "No one's in your class with that, mate."

Susie nodded approvingly at Steve. "He's right."

Emptying his wallet onto the table, Tony sifted through his accumulation of business cards. "And we've held off on this intro to TSUAF Media as well. I reckon we need big management behind us rather than faffing around."

Pregnant silence filled the break room as they waited for Mavis' reaction.

Mavis fingered Doyle's card. "We'll hold off on *this* and see what TSUAF Media have to offer. It'd be good to have someone else do the legwork and set up the gigs."

Taking a crisp from Steve's packet, Tony said, "I'm ready to give away a percentage cut. It'd be worth it." Taking in the open-mouthed reaction of the group, he added, "Well, it would!"

Pocketing Doyle's card safely, Mavis stood. "Okay, we have a way forward. Lyle will flog the CDs, and Tony can set up the meeting."

"You'll *let* me do that? I thought, after you transferred bookkeepin' to Kate, you no longer trusted me."

"There are degrees of trust, Tony. Besides, it made sense to reduce your responsibilities, and Kate's the sort of woman to read the fine print. She won't ever let me down."

Understanding her subtext, Tony covered his embarrassment by stacking his collection of business cards into a neat, ordered pile. He tapped the cards on the table before returning them to his wallet. "We also need to make the most of any contacts we have. Susie, you need to exploit your connection to RedSun."

"There isn't any connection. None at all, Tony."

"Not what a little birdie told me."

Susie's eyes narrowed. "And what birdie is that?"

Having crunched the empty pizza box into a bin sized portion, Lyle canned it. "Me. A few gigs back, some of the guys in RedSun came into the bar for a meal after their gig. Our band were really on fire that night, and the place was packed! Max Ryan, their lead guitarist, came up to Tim and asked about *you* although he knows you by some other name. I was sittin' with Tim at the time. Max Ryan wanted to know how long you'd been playin' with Nikki."

Tim deposited the empty bottles and cans he'd been collecting into the bin. "Their roadie came by later and asked who you were on the town with, Susie."

"And?"

Tim and Lyle answered in unison. "We knew *nothing*."

"Good!"

Tony said, "That's a contact, Susie, that we need you to use. Maybe it could get us a supportin' gig, some CD sales, and airplay."

"It's not happening!"

"Think about it."

Susie stood. "I have! Subject closed. Lyle, can you pack my gear first?"

"Sure thing."

Jack returned chairs to under the table where they'd been sitting. "Nikki, we still on Sunday night?"

Movement within the room froze.

"Nikki and I are *workin'* on a new song!"

A wise, 'Oh!' was the reaction.

"Tim and me will stow the gear in my garage since no one needs it before the next gig. Which club is it anyway?"

"Who knows?" Tony looked around at them.

Jack said, "Does it matter to any of us now? We all have the schedule. What on earth are you doin', Steve? It looks like you're channelling a scene from Play School."

For this generational group, Play School, an ABC television production, had been part of the essential childhood viewing experience.

"I am. Whoo, whoo! The band train to success is departing soon. All aboard! First stop: benefit from known contacts. Second stop: get management. Third stop: the sweet taste of success. Fourth stop: the adulation of fans! Last stop: the power of money." Steve chooffed off with an occasional train whistle, followed by the other men following his lead.

"Nikki, men never truly grow up, do they? You ready?"

"As I ever will be."

The women walked back to their car.

"It was good of your parents to include Zoey this weekend. I felt bad being away when it was her weekend home."

"The sleepover last night was not a big deal. As for today, Gary took them to Jamberoo for the afternoon."

"That was good of him."

"He loves doing that sort of thing with Dan. It was something he missed out on as a kid. He says fathering Dan makes him feel good." As an afterthought, Mavis added, "Kate went with them since Zoey was going. I guess we should've cleared it all with you first."

"I don't have any concerns about that. So, has Gary popped the question to Kate yet?"

Laughing, Mavis closed the passenger car door. "No. He's been trying to but he can't *create* the right moment. Something always goes wrong. He has his heart on it being extra-special and memorable."

"You've a unique relationship with him, them."

"I count my blessings about that when other things are getting me down."

"Have you thought about how their marriage will affect Dan? If they had a kid, Gary would have less time for Dan."

"You're wrong there. I might have feared that once, but not now."

"Talking about fears … RedSun are the headline act in the Evans Theatre the same weekend that we're booked into the Penrith Leagues Sports Club."

"When's that again?"

"A way off. I bought Zoey a ticket for each of their shows. Much as I hated it, I made contact with Max, and we're meeting up after the Saturday show. I don't want to ask him for business favours. That would just contaminate things. You okay with me *not* approaching Max Ryan?"

"Course I am. You sure about her meeting *him* though?"

"I don't have a choice. She's determined to one way or another. I don't want to think about that any more. These are exciting times, Nikki. I've a really good feeling about TSUAF Media."

"Me too."

"Just as well I've help to get off to sleep tonight. You want one?"

"No, I've got my own, Susie."

"Medicinal, not human I hope."

"Whatever do you mean?"

"Jack."

"I'm not so stupid. The tension between us works lyrically and musically. I won't put that at risk."

"It is though. Men like Jack have huge egos. If you don't cue him somehow that you're out of his reach, the string holding us all together will snap and that'll be it musically. It's happened with heaps of big bands."

Wired and fired by her will to succeed and disturbed by Susie's warning, Mavis found it difficult to sleep despite the help of the 'aid.' She finally did so with two tablets in the late hours of the lightening dawn.

* * *

Having slept in on Sunday, Mavis and Susie did not re-engage with the wider world until they turned on the radio during their drive back to Keimera. The afternoon news broadcast began with, "The world mourns today the death of Diana, Princess of Wales. She was involved in a fatal car crash in a tunnel at Pont d'Alma, Paris, in the early hours of this morning, Sunday 31st August, at approximately 10.30 a.m. Australian eastern standard time. The princess' companion, Dodi Fayed, and their driver were also killed. At this stage, the accident is attributed to pursuit by paparazzi whose obsession with the princess appears to have brought her to this tragic and untimely end."

Stunned, Mavis turned the radio off. Incredulous, both women experienced a flood of intense sadness. The rest of the trip home was a sombre one.

Taking the left turn off the highway into Keimera, Mavis said, "No *happily ever after* in this world's stories."

"Is that what you're looking for, Nikki?"

"I'm not looking."

"If you were?"

"No." After a pause, Mavis said, "*Happily ever after* would be like having endless groundhog days. That's not to say I want the highs and lows of the romance days either. If love is in my story, I want to be safe in the knowledge of it in the bad days – everyone has them, even George and Minna. I want my man to love me even when I least deserve it."

"Because that's when you need it the most?"

"Exactly! That way it'll survive. I want a satisfying love life, one that is free of domination and aggression."

Susie frowned, surprised by the insight into Mavis' past.

"What about you, Susie?"

"I'm happy with my life and not desperate for a relationship. Been there. Done that. I thought I had found the love of my life, when I believed in such things, but … ," Susie paused.

Aware of the sudden emotion that had come into Susie's voice, Mavis waited for her friend to close her personal Pandora's box. As driver, Mavis' eyes remained fixed on the road ahead. She too had ghosts she thought long term rested that, at times, unexpectedly brought the trauma of her past back into her present.

"I hope there isn't such a thing as the love of my life, otherwise …" A period of silent reflection followed. Then more upbeat, Susie said, "I've got Zoey to consider nowadays too. I have to be careful about the sort of man I bring into our lives. I'm content to live my life as it is at this stage. Besides, it would take a very special kind of man to cope with our lifestyle, and then, there is always the issue of male ego to contend with."

"As the lives of stars and celebrities repeatedly show us."

Mavis parked on the street in front of the block of flats where Susie lived. "Have you read that biography on Diana? I did."

"I don't have much time for reading anymore. When I do, it's magazines. I'm interested in real life stuff now. If you can believe them, Diana was a captive of her circumstances."

"Aren't we all? I understood her mask of self-assurance as well as her underlying feelings of inadequacy and her need for public affirmation because she doubted her worth."

"So many of the stars seem to confuse adulation with love, don't you think? It's something I've talked to Zoey a lot about. She's prone to thinking the stars are people to copy."

"I was like that at her age."

"And now?"

"Evolving."

Chapter 14

Friday 19th September 1997, five in the afternoon. Travelling with her mother and Mavis, Zoey read aloud from a pamphlet included in the package sent to them by their agency. "Penrith Leagues Club, situated west of Sydney and about an hour's drive when travelling on the M4 motorway, is located in the foothills of the Blue Mountains. With a diversified entertainment outreach, the club offers a range of onsite activities to cater for people from all walks of life and interests." She silently read through the list of entertainment options. "There's heaps for me to do tomorrow while you're all sleeping in."

"Thank God, we've made it, Nikki," Susie said as they turned off on Mulgoa Road and into the Leagues Club's extensive parking areas. "That traffic was awful."

"The western glare was worse! What would we have done without sunglasses?"

"Wow!" Zoey said. "Will you look at that!"

"Impressive," Mavis replied, taking in the club's huge expanse of glass exterior walls and the acreage of parking lot.

Susie, referring to directions provided by the agency, navigated their way through the maze of parked cars to the area allocated for bands' parking. Their convoy pulled up next to them. Doors opened and closed.

"Massive!" Jack said as he and the rest of the band unloaded their gear. His hand came in contact with Mavis' when they reached for her suitcase. For a moment they were both still.

"Thanks, Jack, but I can manage it myself."

"Mum, look what's written on that big black bus pulling in over there. RedSun! Wish the windows weren't mirrored. Can't we go say hello now?"

"Play it cool, Zoey. Don't be such a fan! You're embarrassing me." Susie kept her back to the bus and hurried with the unpacking of their luggage from Mavis' car. "Zoey, here's your bag. Follow our guys, please."

Still staring at RedSun's arrival, Zoey said, "Why do they have a little bus as well?"

"The first one is the crew bus, Zoey. It would have arrived a lot earlier for the crew to setup."

"Mum, look! The guys are getting off. Let's say hello now!"

Susie grabbed Zoey and pulled her back. "And look like fans, or worse, be classed with those groupies over there? No, we most definitely can't! We're sticking to arrangements; tomorrow night after their gig." Susie retained hold of Zoey's arm and steered her toward the club and away from the possibility of a sighting by Max Ryan.

Mavis walked abreast of them.

"Wish you only had a ninety minute show to do, Mum, like Red-Sun. We could spend more time together then, like a real family."

"Well, we don't. Besides, you and I are a real family, and Max is—"

"Only the biological link, so *you* say, but he *might* want to be more than that when he sees me."

"That way lies heartache, Zoey. I knew this was a mistake. C'mon!"

* * *

Later that night at ten and amidst the crowd spill from the Evans Theatre, Zoey arrived at the Sports Bar; RedSun's concert for that evening over. The night was a first for Zoey in many ways. She had only seen The Nikki Mills Band in rehearsal before and so was amazed to see their transformation in front of an audience and in performance mode.

"Hang on little lady," one of the bar security men said. "ID please."

Zoey held up a band ID. "My mum's the drummer in this band. There's Tim, their soundie. My instructions are to go sit with him."

"I'll escort you, if you don't mind. The only drink for you tonight is soft."

"You don't have to worry. My mum has the eyes of a hawk and would swoop down on me like I was a field mouse if she thought I was drinking anything else. She's pretty scary when I'm a meal for her in that mode. This weekend is real important to me; I'm meeting my dad for the first time. I want to keep Mum sweet."

On Zoey's approach, Tim said, "I was wonderin' where you were. What did you think of RedSun? I hear you're meetin' their lead guitarist tomorrow night."

"He's totally cute. They're all hot! Don't tell Mum I said that though."

"I won't. Here, I've kept a chair for you. You know, Zoey, Nikki decided tonight to change the material in tomorrow night's last two sets so that Susie is released for your meet with Max Ryan. It's hard to do a set without a drummer, let alone two."

"I didn't know."

"I don't get why this is such a big deal?" He looked at Zoey.

"I'm a fan, and Mum is so protective of me. She didn't want anyone to think I was just a groupie."

"That makes sense. Musicians like that have preconceptions about young girls chasing them."

"It does, doesn't it?

"You should thank Nikki when you get the chance. What she has done is a very big deal!"

"I will! Wow! Nikki's amazing! They're all just so musically fantastic!" A little later Zoey added, "I'm sure it'll be alright if I get up and dance. Those girls over there aren't much older than me. No one is bothered by them on the floor."

"No, you stick it here as per Susie's directions to us both. Those girls are over eighteen, can legally be served alcohol, and are free to knock back drinks like that. Besides, it's got real crowded in here."

"Thank you," Mavis said from the stage. "We'll be back in twenty."

The band joined Tim and Zoey and crossed to a backstage room for their break.

Lyle had set up the break room with their usual libations in anticipation of their ritual thirst. He also provided a variety of snacks as was his habit. CD marketeer extraordinaire that he had become, Lyle sported a cotton flat cap that he wore on a jaunty tilt and rimless glasses in the style of John Lennon. His black T-shirt had the band name in white emblazoned across the front. "You won't believe how many CDs I've sold tonight."

Jack pulled out the chair for Mavis. "A record breakin' one hundred and fifty?" He received an appreciative smile in response from her and a quizzical glance from Susie.

"Nuh, three hundred! And there are even more people ready to cough up the cash."

A round of whistles, "Bloody fantastic," "You're kiddin'me!" and "Finally!" followed.

"I'm off to the van to get more. I always knew it was worth carryin' extra stock."

Jack passed Zoey a can of lemonade, recognising it was out of her reach. "So how was RedSun, Zoey? You can do the fan gush with us; we can handle it."

"Cutting edge and on fire! Even better than when I saw them at The Enmore. It all went so fast! The audience didn't want them to finish. That part was so exciting: foot stamping, cheering. RedSun even got a standing ovation. They didn't give an encore though. The support band were okay but nothing special. Definitely inferior to you guys; no way in your class. You're as good as RedSun."

Tony puffed up. "But sadly not paid anywhere near as much."

Steve mentally debated lighting up a cigarette from the packet he kept in his duffle bag. He was finding it a hard habit to kick. "We're hopin' to be a support band sooner rather than later."

"The audience came and went during the support band, mostly because they weren't so good although I did see people return with glasses of wine."

Having popped a nicotine lozenge, Steve snapped the tin closed and then pocketed it. "Cigarettes and alcohol both demand feedin'. Some people just can't hang out for breaks. I've known musicians with that cravin' who need to kick it."

"In the interval, people around me were whinging about how slow bar service was."

Susie frowned. "And what were you doing at the bar, Zoey?"

"Geez, Mum, chill, will you? I was nowhere near the bar. I overheard people around me talking after they came back from the bar. I don't know what they were on about though because the bar was crowded with staff."

Susie stood, her frustration obvious. "If you'll excuse me, I need a break and a walk. Zoey, ..."

"I know, stay put."

"Wait for me, Susie." Mavis grabbed a drink and followed.

Back in the bar, Susie said, "I'm so het up about tomorrow night. You've heard her. How am I going to console her when her fantasy is shattered?"

"It's my experience that things are never as bad as we imagine them. The worst it can be is civil and short-lived."

"I haven't spoken to Max in just over sixteen years. I'm a bit freaked out about that as well."

"I feel for you. I don't want Dan or me to ever see Dan's biological link!"

"What? Isn't Gary his father?"

"Godfather."

"Zoey has godparents. She never hears from them nowadays. Our lives diverged and ... they were never like Gary though, even when they were on the scene. He really fathers Dan. Zoey thinks Gary is just the best ... I think she's hoping Max will be like him. God, I need a stiff drink!"

With her drink in hand, Susie returned across the tiled floor to Mavis who waited on the carpeted area. Susie waited for her to finish the autograph and fan interaction process.

"Sanna! Sanna!"

Susie froze.

Mavis noted Susie's shocked expression and then the good-looking man approaching Susie. He dressed the part of a rock musician. Susie turned to face him.

"G'day." Max Ryan ran a calculated eye over Susie. "Beautiful as ever. Your band is great!" Then recognising Mavis, he put out his hand to her in greeting. "Nikki Mills, I take it."

Accepting the offer of his hand, Mavis said, "Yes, and you are?"

"Max Ryan. Sanna's *long* forgotten ex." He turned back to Susie. "I was surprised to hear from you. A problem with the maintenance payments?"

"Not a money problem."

A gush of fans at his elbow interrupted the conversation. They clustered around him, buzzing their enthusiasm.

Accepting being put aside, Susie said, "C'mon, let's get back to the band." She led the way.

Mavis asked, "So how come you're Sanna to him and Susie to us?"

"When I was with Max, we were pretention without cause. I'm grounded now and Susie's part of being that."

"Sanna!"

Susie continued walking.

"Susie, you can't just ignore him, especially given what's planned."

Susie stopped and turned around. With a winning smile, she looked at Max but noted the deficit of groupies. "You losing your appeal with the younger female set?"

"No … I told them I was with friends and needed some privacy. I arranged to give them time later."

Susie thought, *I bet you did.*

"C'mon," Max said, "sit over here with me where we can talk."

"I guess I should leave you two alone."

Reaching out for Mavis and taking hold of her hand, Susie said, "No, stay. Please!"

Max said, "Versed as I am with the nuances of female signals, I take it the tryst tomorrow is not what I took it to be."

A romantic at heart, Mavis' interest in the pair heightened.

"*My* daughter wants to meet you." With nothing else to say, she just looked at him.

"*So,* that's what tomorrow night is about! I thought … Your message didn't say anything about the kid. It never occurred to me …"

"The meeting is important to Zoey."

"That's what you called her?"

Suddenly emotional but covering that surge well, Susie nodded.

Max said, "My mum's name."

"I always loved your mum. I was sorry to hear …"

"Yeah, that's long ago now. I don't know that I want to meet *your* Zoey."

"That's what I thought which is why I arranged for us to get together. I was surprised you agreed to even that. I intended bringing Zoey along and hoped your practiced charm would switch into play when you saw she was a fan. I *promise* it'll be the only time you have to deal with her."

A period of tense silence followed.

"You didn't give me a say in the past either, or a choice, Sanna. I had a right to one then like I do now."

"I don't want to do this, Max, not again."

Mavis spoke up, "Well, Zoey's here this weekend and *stoked* about meeting you, Max. She's such a fan! Zoey had tickets for tonight's gig and for tomorrow's show as well. It'll break her heart if you don't meet her. Worse, Susie's heart!"

Max assessed Susie. He scratched his close cropped auburn beard in thought.

Susie's face was expressionless, her demeanour measured. She looked passed Max.

"What does Zoey know about me, Sanna?"

Without looking at Max, Susie said, "You didn't want to be a father. You *supported* my right to have an abortion. You're only a biological link in the parenting chain. Not a parent though. No intention of ever being one. I held off telling her anything until after her fifteenth birthday. She asked, insisted. I thought it was time."

"December last year, right? And the maintenance payments?"

"As I agreed back when … She knows nothing about them. You were right, if she knew, she'd have invented a fantasy about you. I have not sugar-coated our careless conception of her."

After another silence, he said, "Fair enough. We'll meet as agreed tomorrow night."

Looking at him then, Susie said, "Thank you for that. If you'll both excuse me." She stood and headed for the privacy of outdoors.

Max and Mavis sat in uncomfortable silence for a while, each with their own thoughts. *There's no way I'm ever going through this,* Mavis thought. *How can I avoid it though?*

"Who's your management?" Max asked for want of something to say.

"You mean the agency that books us into clubs?"

"No, I mean who controls your product and your career direction?"

"We do at the moment, but it's a blind process. Who do you recommend?"

"We're with YME. They're not interested in rising talent though; just names. We've been lucky in that they are prepared to give us some say in our product and its direction. A lot don't and won't."

"Thanks. Do you know anything about TSUAF Media?"

"They're a powerful player in the industry. Not *our* preferred style of management though."

"You know, Zoey is a really good kid. Gets great grades at her ultra expensive private school in the Southern Highlands."

"Which school?" Then in response to Mavis' answer, he said, "My mother's old school. Figures." He exhaled. "Okay, I know the sort of woman that school produces. No problem. I've time to get my head around this." He stood. "If you'll excuse me."

"Sure." Mavis was left alone at the table. Having noted Susie's earlier exit path, she went in search of her. She found her outside, an emotional mess.

"Max hated his father, Nikki. He never wanted to be like him, not in any way. Even the idea of being seen as a father in absentia was just too much for him. He never understood that the issue between us was not that he didn't support my right to abortion, he did, but not my right to choose. We got bogged down in what his rights were and then that drifted somehow to his inability to resist the allure of groupie adulation. Having had a choice has made such a difference to my ability to cope, especially when it has been hard. I've never seen myself as a victim of circumstance. This is so much worse than I ever imagined. How am I going to get through the next twenty-four hours? And then after that?"

"I don't know, but you're not alone in this. I'm here. We'll get through it somehow. I'm sorry to say we have two more sets left. Are you up to it?"

"I have to be. I'll go straight to the stage if you get the guys. Run interference for me with Zoey before the set starts, will you? I'll be fine and up to dealing with her afterwards." And she was. That night in the privacy of their shared room, Susie said, "Zoey, you have to play it real cool tomorrow night. Max Ryan is only the biological link in the parent chain. I know you want him to be more than that, but he's not and doesn't want to be. Our paths crossed earlier tonight."

"So that's why you and Nikki didn't come back to the break room?"

"That's right. I've assured Max you get it."

"I've heard you, Mum, *every time.*"

"Good, then tomorrow night will work out fine."

*   *   *

Max Ryan's meeting with Susie and her daughter was arranged as a late dinner event Saturday night in the most up-market of the restaurant options at the Penrith Leagues Club. It was a ritzy, glitzy venue.

Zoey had dressed with great care. She wore a variation of the Kogal fashion popular in Japan and the rage in some sections of Australian teenagedom at that time: sweet Alice black shoes, distinctive loosened socks that suggested leg warmers, a pleated emerald green mini-skirt, a beige bodice, a short fitted matching jacket, and a soft green patterned scarf woven into her dyed hair. The crimson in her hair had been reduced and black was now the dominant colour.

By contrast, Susie wore a brown, fitted, thigh length, knit dress that featured thin white horizontal lines that ran in tight concentric rings from her navel to just below her backside. She wore dark black stockings, ten denier, that accentuated the curve of her legs. Her feet were shod in deep brown ankle leather boots.

Mother and daughter had taken great care with their makeup that evening before they separated for their respective gigs.

"Looking good, Sanna," Max said as he followed her and Zoey to their table. "Front *and* back."

After being seated, Zoey said, "So, Max, you're the missing link!"

"Zoey!"

"I guess I am. It's how I wanted it … Zoey, you're not what I expected, not at all. You remind me of your mum when she was your age. She didn't have dyed hair though."

"I haven't seen any pictures from those years. I think Mum got rid of them all."

Max looked at Susie.

Susie said, "We've always lived in small places, and I just didn't have storage space. I dislike my life being cluttered with stuff."

"Yeah, I feel the same about baggage, Sanna. Given the hovering waiter, I think we need to consider our order."

It was a beautiful meal and the conversation remained small talk until dessert was served.

"So Max," Zoey said, "why didn't you want me?"

"Zoey!"

"This is between Max and me, Mum. I have to know."

Considering Zoey over his glass of red wine, Max took his time before replying. "It was never about you. This 'you' and any other version of you just did not exist as far as I was concerned. It was really about me and how I felt about fatherhood. Conventional life just isn't my thing."

"But I exist here and now. By other people's standards, you are my father."

"Zoey! I'm sorry Max. I went over this with you, young lady, last night."

"You did, but no one asked me what I wanted or how I've felt all this time. How come you get to choose, and I don't get a say?"

"I asked Sanna the *same* thing when she went all pro-life on me. We were having sex; life was sweet. Then she made it complicated. Surely in our day and age, a man has a right to choose just as much as a woman does?"

"Those issues are yours and Mum's. I'm talking about me. I missed out on having a father, and I want one! I know I'm being a problem now, but I promise you, I won't be a problem daughter. I won't! You'll like having me around once you get used to the idea of me. I'll make you proud; I will!"

Gutted, he said, "Well, Zoey, Sanna will need to find a man who wants to take on that role. I'm not that man. If you'll excuse me, ladies." He stood and without another word, crossed to the register, paid, and then left.

Crying, Zoey said, "I thought if I put my case, he'd want to be my dad."

"I know you did. Max has always had such issues with the whole idea of fatherhood … Sometimes people can't be what we want them to be. We have to accept that, otherwise the road ahead is nothing but grief. C'mon, let's get back to our room. Can you hold it together til then? I wish now we were going home to Keimera tomorrow, but the band has that management meeting on Monday."

"It's okay, Mum, let's stick to the original plan. I'll catch the bus back to school tomorrow evening. There's a pickup for returning students from Central station. I'll be fine." Back in their shared room, Zoey crawled onto her mother's bed and cried herself to sleep. Susie, distraught herself, covered Zoey with blankets, and then lay in contact with her daughter, feeling helpless.

* * *

Monday 22nd February, 1998. Situated in an Elizabeth Street, Sydney, skyscraper, TSUAF Media Group had offices close to the top floor. Tony swore he felt the building moving when they stepped out of the lift and into the plush reception area. A complex range of emotions surged through each band member.

Looking around him, Jack said, "This is more excitin' than being able to afford accommodation with a mini-bar."

Laughter eased their collective tension.

Antique brown leather lounges were grouped for conversation around a coffee table to the right and left of a huge reception desk. TSUAF was inscribed in stainless steel lettering on the wall, light coloured, wood panelling to the rear of the reception desk. Set within that wall and indiscernible at first and even second glance was a door. The other walls had frame-to-frame pictures of the company's stable of artists and talent, including headline-making football stars.

Behind the reception desk sat a sleek, highly groomed, coiffured young woman who checked off the band's name on her computer screen before buzzing an interior office.

"Please take a seat. Mr Winston-Baker won't be long." In reality that translated into a forty five minute wait in an increasingly crowded waiting room of hopefuls.

Leo Winston-Baker 's appearance, when he finally emerged from his office, was striking to say the least. He had tight curly red hair shaped into a poodle cut that was reminiscent of Lucille Ball's 1950s hairstyle. He wore a leather jacket, an open-necked plain shirt, jeans, and boots. Like the receptionist, he appeared highly groomed. As he shook hands with each band member, they noticed the man's preference for expensive rings.

"Sorry to keep you waiting. I was talking to one of our talent in L.A. Please come in." He led the way into his office.

The room was massive in proportion. To the left stood a ten-seater conference table. His desk was positioned to take advantage of spectacular, unobstructed views of Sydney Harbour provided through a floor-to-ceiling glass wall.

Having directed the band to the conference table, he took a seat at its head. "I see here that you've already been through our vetting process and have demonstrated a sincere interest to avail yourselves of our considerable power in the marketplace. You will be aware that our team is a group of industry savvy individuals who represent a stable of some of Australia's top talent as well as many of its rising stars. We know how to build an image for an artist that will effectively sell our client to any desired audience. In today's tightening music industry, record companies want to know their investment will be returned and not put at risk. Their decisions are based on statistics about what products are selling and what is not. Perception is all important in the world of music if you want to make it big, and I'm talking big in capital letters the size of that wall."

Leo Winston-Baker referred to a leather bound, gilt initialled A4 folder, the first in a pile. "Our field representatives report that you've already twigged to the fact that raw sexuality sells on stage although it says here that needs to be developed a lot more. We here at TSUAF are committed to remoulding your band's image so that it titillates your audience's desire, sells you as the band to be heard, makes money for all concerned, and satisfies that appetite artists and talent have for genuine marketplace recognition. Your struggle to make it to the top is over when you sign with us." He paused and poured himself a glass of water from a jug to his right. "Ready to proceed?"

The band nodded.

Leo Winston-Baker passed a leather folder to each band member. "You have been provided with a copy of the proposed contract and after that, an outline of our plan of attack for each of you. Please read through the contract now." He waited for them to do so.

"Sixty-five percent of any income we generate goes to TSUAF?" Mavis said. "That seems ..." She searched for a tactful way to say it.

"Unreasonably high," Tony concluded.

"If you were making five hundred a night divided between you, perhaps it is, but not when you're making the astronomical figures quoted on page eight of the outline."

The band flicked to page eight. The men whistled. The women were impressed.

"Also consider that we expend a considerable outlay up front, long before you earn us a return. We carry the cost of your image transformation – a considerable expense when there are five of you to remould and coordinate to fit the message we sell through your band. Then there are the marketing and publicity costs, the costs associated with your entrée to the makers-and-shakers in the music industry, the greasing of access to television shows and other promotional events that will project you into the public's psyche. Everything costs money in this business, even getting accepted into festivals and work as a support band for the stars in the industry. Of course, there is always the financial risk and potential loss if you fail to play the parts we prescribe for you in both the constructed version of your personal lives as well as in the public arena."

"Constructed version of our personal lives?" Mavis asked.

"We construct that personal reality based on what the marketplace says is selling. Ordinary people love to know the dirt on stars and when there isn't any, we invent it for the media. For that reason, don't read your own press. We use the salacious clues to your life to tease your audience and to keep them interested in you as a product, to want to hear you and see you."

In Mavis' silence, Susie said, "That's a pretty cynical view of people."

"It's an informed and well-researched view. Everything we do in the marketplace is based on statistics. Those statistics give stakeholders, such as record companies and the big entrepreneurial enterprises, comfort that their money is secure when it is invested in you. There is a cost to every success in this life. If you have any problem with what I've said so far, there is the door."

Mavis and Susie made eye-contact that spoke volumes. Neither woman wanted the details of her past or present life featured in magazines sold at supermarket outlets or in news agencies. Uneasy, they looked at the men who seemed unperturbed with what had been said.

"Good," Leo Winston-Baker said. "Nikki, as you represent the brand, I'll begin with you. Market statistics show this vision will catapult you to stardom. Imagine if you will the stage …

Nikki Mills is a blonde siren who projects a hint of vulnerability. Her designer clothing is artfully cut to feature her assets: full breasts and an hourglass figure. The air sizzles around her. Her scent, the essence of enticement, draws men to her, awakens their primal hunt impulse, activates the alpha instinct within the male psyche. Women recognize her as a symbol of power. Magazines laud her beauty, charm, and intense sexual allure.

On stage, The Nikki Mills Show is a highly theatrical, magical extravaganza that generates surprise and wonderment in the audience. The show is a feat in production and effects. The iconography is carefully planned and staged. Each performance, Nikki enters the stage on a pedestal elevated well above the masses. The songs are developed through research and tested extensively with focus groups. Her dancers are the best in the business. Our choreographer is adept at revealing the messages within each song, heightening the titillation, and exciting the audience.

Nikki's public life features her search for true love and the passing parade of candidates who audition for the role of her hero: strapping football stars, rising stars in the tennis world, smouldering rock idols, movie stars, high-profile businessmen who control industry, and overseas' trendsetters. Ordinary people see their own desire for acceptance and love played out in her life. They empathically connect to the brief glimpses of her private pain, her vulnerability, revealed through paparazzi-captured candid moments.

Nikki Mills is rich in all the ways that count in this world. In her private life …"

Mavis stood, having 'seen' enough. "That is not the life I want to live, not the songs I want to sing, not the show I want to perform." Without waiting for her band, she left.

Slow to react, Susie followed her.

The men registered the sudden static and loss in transmission and then realised that the plug had been pulled on that footage of their success.

Having missed the lift that Nikki and Susie took down to street level, the men were forced to wait. Gobsmacked, they stood in silence. When the lift returned, they entered it. During their descent to street level, the spell slowly faded.

Looking around for Nikki and Susie, the men were worried when the women were not obviously in sight.

A shrill, two-note whistle followed by, "Oi, fellas," from Susie on the footpath in front of a cafe across the street dispelled their general concern.

The men crossed to the cafe, reorganized the round tables, sat down, and ordered. Immersed in the calming business of orders, their thoughts and emotions continued to be in tumult.

Returning from the men's room, Steve asked, "What spooked you, Nikki?"

Unable to explain how she'd felt as she'd listened to Winston-Baker, Mavis remained silent.

Susie spoke instead. "You get, fellas, that sooner or later one hundred and one variations of chocolate becomes tasteless, don't you?"

With an eye on Mavis, Jack said, "I've always liked chocolate, Susie."

"You might, Jack, but what about audiences? You think there's longevity in being what is essentially one flavour in the shop?"

Steve asked, "Did anyone order for me? I'm with Jack on this, Susie. I would've liked the opportunity to find out."

Jack fiddled with the sticks of sugar on the table. "We did, mate, and I didn't say that, Steve."

"Well," Tony said, "I liked the cards dealt to us on the table."

Mavis stared into the street. "There's Monica."

"Where?" The men turned, this way and then that.

"I meant Monica would go along with you if you want to be that kind of band."

Jack voiced the band's reaction. "No one said that, Nikki."

Drinks and a liberal serving of cakes were served.

Depressed silence followed.

"We're back where we were then," Steve said.

Mavis replied, "I'd rather stay in the small arena than stand on *that* pinnacle of success."

Jack said, "Pity, I was enjoyin' the view. Did anyone else see the air steam when 'transformed Nikki' passed?"

The men nodded.

Steve scratched his five o'clock shadow. "Just as well you left, Nikki, I would've needed oxygen if he'd gone on much longer."

Having savoured his coffee much as a smoker does a cigarette, Jack said, "Seriously, I think I speak for everyone when I say we're happy travellin' the road you choose."

It was the first time Mavis felt like smiling since leaving TSUAF.

Having misunderstood Mavis, Steve said, "It's hard to believe Elvis is back in the buildin'."

On the same wavelength as Steve, Jack added, "Not so lucky!"

Susie's thoughts drifted to events earlier that weekend. She remembered the heartbreak she'd felt when she'd been just a little older than Zoey was now. She knew her daughter's pain. For the first time, she wondered how Max Ryan was coping with it all. The pain in his face as he'd listened to Zoey, sharp as a knife, had cut Susie. She wondered if he saw that he had become what he had sought to avoid. Did he see in Zoey's pain what he had felt as a boy and later a man?

With reviving spirits, Mavis said, "No, you've got that wrong. I've had enough of performing in a straight jacket. Elvis has *definitely* left the building. Shaun Doyle is right; we need to build our fan base. I'll stay in Sydney overnight and make contact with those pub booking agents I can't speak to this arvo. Who's going to make phone contact with the Melbourne pubs Doyle recommended?"

"I'll take the Tote," Susie said. "Jack, you do the Esplanade, and Tony the Palais."

Mavis stood. "Today was a good thing, fellas."

They looked up at her.

"This way we stay true to ourselves, control our image, and I have the freedom to score life's song."

After splitting their bill at the cash register, the band went their separate ways after a round of hugs. When Mavis came to Jack, the rhythm of farewell broke. There was a self-conscious pause followed by a distant, lifeless hug.

The last to leave, Jack glanced at an attractive woman sitting at a table for two in the window bay. Her eyes were on his face. She licked her lips as she parted them in a smile.

Diverted, Jack dropped into the vacant chair at her table.

The woman beckoned the waiter. As they placed their orders, Mavis returned, having discovered her mobile phone was missing. She did not see Jack at first or he her.

Disappointed that her phone was not at the table they had vacated, Mavis crossed to the café counter. Waiting there for service, she saw Jack and smiled to herself. Some things never changed. She found comfort in that. Jack's world was as she thought it to be.

"Can I help you, madam?"

"Has anyone handed in a mobile phone?"

Hearing Mavis' voice, Jack turned and looked across the room.

Mavis arched an eyebrow at him and inclined her head in acknowledgement. She held his gaze for a moment and laughed when he winked at her. It was the first time her heart had not missed a beat in response to his wink.

The waiter held up her phone. "Is this what you're looking for?"

"Yes." Relieved in more ways than one, Mavis left after placing her hand briefly on Jack's shoulder as she passed. "See you."

As the café door swung closed, Mavis heard Jack telling the woman about their band. Mavis thought she knew where that revelation would lead. Her step was lighter as she walked toward Pitt Street Mall where she had arranged to rendezvous with Susie.

Chapter 15

"And that," Mavis said to Gary and Kate who sat nestled together on Mavis' cane furniture, "is all I know of Susie's story. Can you see how Zoey's situation applies to Dan and me in the future?"

"Poor Zoey," Kate said.

"How am I going to avoid that?"

"Can you avoid it?" Kate asked.

"She has to. The alternative doesn't bear thinkin' about."

"You know I left the place for the father's name on Dan's birth certificate blank. I've thought I'd say I don't know who the father is."

Incensed, Gary said, "So in the difficult teenage years ahead of you, Dan will think you were a slut! Another sort of pain for you both to bear. Been there. Felt that. Bad news for you! Doesn't matter if it is true or not, and it gives sting to the mud-slingers when the word, bastard, is levelled at you!"

"Gary is right, Mavis. Better for Dan to know the truth about his biological link than think that of you."

"From what Susie told me, part of the issue with Max Ryan is he doesn't want to be anything like his father, even if it is in role only. What if Dan reacts to the truth like Zoey did? What if Dan reacts like Max Ryan and decides never to have children?"

"That's a lame excuse for any man," Kate said.

"I understand where he's comin' from," Gary said. "I might have felt like that if I hadn't been dropped unexpectedly into the miracle of birth with Mavis."

"Mavis, Dan won't feel like that. He has Gary as his chief role model and then there is his grandfather and my dad. Dan's spent a lot of time with all three men. All different, but they share one thing in common; they are caring, non-violent, really good men."

"That's a really good point, but I still need to know what to tell Dan. I could invent a father figure who died before Dan was born and before we had time to marry. I'd say we had planned to. That would take the cut out of bastard if that were ever an issue."

Kate adjusted her position on the lounge. "Seriously, has it been an issue these past thirty years? C'mon, that's one of the benefits of the women's movement,"

"If you're male and it is literally true, it hurts. It hurts me still! Only people with the luxury of legitimacy think it doesn't matter. As for adults who say it won't matter to their children, that's their cover story to justify their own actions and choices. Life is tough enough without givin' someone who wants to hurt you that sort of ammunition. Who knows in the future where the values pendulum will swing? We don't know what career path Dan will choose and whether it will matter then or not. Mavis is right; there has to be a story that protects him."

Kate moved to the kitchen for a glass of water. "Either of you want anything while I'm up? Tea? Coffee? Water?"

Mavis shook her head while Gary replied, "No, thanks."

"This just goes round and round in my head at night, Kate, and I can't sleep."

Sipping water as she returned to the lounge area, Kate asked, "Nightmares from the past?"

Mavis nodded.

Gary straightened, grounding his feet. "It's obvious, mate, isn't it? We'll say I'm his dad."

Kate choked, the water having gone down the wrong way. Neither Mavis or Gary noticed.

"I've always been in the picture, Mavis, as far back as the photographic evidence of his life goes. We'll come up with some story that explains why I didn't marry you and why we decided to leave my name off his birth certificate. I could legally adopt him to make amends now."

Gobsmacked, both women looked at him.

Mavis crossed to hug him and did. "So generous of you, Gary." Coming out of the hug, she said, "But no, I could *not* do that to you. I don't want Dan to ever think that you have been anything other than the *really* good man you are."

Kate finally found her voice. "But, Gary, there are lots of people in the wider community who would know that for a lie. Dr Tim for instance knows about Terry. Remember, he was the treating doctor at the hospital the night you took her in after she'd been bashed."

"Stop! Don't take me back there, Kate," Mavis said.

"Then there's your parents, Mavis. Besides, I wouldn't like it, especially if ..."

Mavis answered, "That's understandable. I wouldn't either, Kate, if our positions were reversed. Back to Dan. What can I tell him?"

After lengthy, silent consideration, Gary said, "A sanitised version of the truth *won't* set up a false picture of Terry. That or find a man you love enough to marry and who'll want to adopt Dan ... Dan might never ask, you know. It might not be an issue in his life like it was in Zoey's."

"Gary, Mavis needs peace of mind now. Have you forgotten Mavis that, as Dan's sole parent, you have control over *when* that happens?"

"Oh, yeah!" Relief spread across Mavis' face. "I'll tell him the truth when he's eighteen. I guess honesty is the best policy. I don't want him seeking out Terry."

"Speaking of which," Gary said. "What did you leave unsaid earlier, Kate?"

"Nothing."

"And I thought Theresa was the only master of subterfuge and diversion."

"Gary, how can you link us in the same breath? Theresa is only interested in her image ..."

"She's the cutting edge of the modern woman, Kate."

Kate grinned at him. "She's the very model of a modern matron general."

"She quotes the facts cosmetical, from surgical to chemical."

"She's very well acquainted with matters transformational."

"And understands that women, both liberated and traditional, succumb to pressures patriarchal."

"While thinking she is the very model of a modern woman general."

"That's really clever, fellas."

Kate replied, "It's a game Gary started back when he was under the influence of Gilbert and Sullivan. Since then, he's done it to lighten the mood when Theresa comes up. He has *heaps* of verses, Mavis. Do you want to hear the whole thing?"

"No, she doesn't, but I'd like to *hear* the answer to my question. C'mon, out with it."

Kate looked at him for a time before saying, "Okay. I wouldn't like people thinking you were Dan's father, especially if we get married down the track."

"If, Ken? We are."

Mavis stood. "Gary, hold on. Not like this. Just give me a moment." She moved around the room, switching off lights and flicking on the lamp. "Let me get the atmosphere right at least."

Kate followed her, reversing what Mavis had done. "Now you've put Gary on the spot, Mavis. I don't think he meant ..."

What the heck! Gary thought. "Kate Patricia Denford. Come over here!"

Taking advantage of Kate's return to Gary, Mavis hurriedly dimmed the lighting. "Gary, what about the you know what?"

"Forget it, Mavis."

Determined the proposal would be private, Mavis retreated to the hallway. As she passed her stereo system, positioned on a buffet, she slipped a discarded CD into the player, thinking the first song was 'I Finally Found Someone' by Bryan Adams and Barbra Streisand. Mavis grabbed her CD player remote control and headed into the darkened region of the cottage. Dan was asleep and corridor light disturbed him.

"Sit here please, Kate."

Mavis flicked the player on without confirming it was still set to background music. Instead, a track from Dan's 'Bionicles' CD blasted them. Jolted, Mavis turned the player off. "Sorry, miscalculation!"

Laughing, Gary called, "I can do this without your help, mate." He knelt before Kate. "I've been tryin' to propose to you for ages, but every time something got in the way. There isn't any other woman I would want to spend the rest of my life with. I want to grow old with you, Kate. Will you marry me?"

"Oh, Gary! Yes, I will."

After allowing them time for a kiss, Mavis returned. The couple separated as she re-entered. "I'm *so* sorry for that stuff up. You *did* it, Gary, *finally*! Kate, you have no idea how many times his plans backfired. He had some absolutely fantastic romantic scenarios set up and each one fell through."

"Well, I wouldn't have had it any other way than this, Gary."

Gary struck his nonchalant Mickey Mouse pose and beamed.

* * *

Spring blossomed from its budding glory. Longer, warmer afternoons meant that coastal life moved outdoors once again.

Sitting on a stool at his grandparents' kitchen bench Wednesday night, Dan could hear the sound of neighbourhood children. "Can I go play, Gran?"

Marg rinsed her hands at the sink. She'd been preparing baking goods for the small business enterprise she'd begun at the start of winter. "You finished that homework?"

"Can I finish it later?"

"*No*, the deal is you do it *before* play. You can't have much more to do, surely? You've been at it an hour." Marg crossed to him. "You haven't even made a start, Dan! What's all this doodle?"

"Can't I go and play?"

"No, we tried that before, and it didn't work. You have to finish this first!"

Dejected, Dan leant his head against his hand.

"Don't drag this work out until night, again! It's not a lot to do. Just get it done!"

"I don't want to."

"When I come back from talkin' to Pop, I want to see this done." Marg picked up a tray with a teapot, two cups, and a serving of cake and headed to the front verandah.

Dan sat there in glum silence. After a while, he slipped off the stool and crossed to where his grandmother had left dough scraps. He returned to his sitting place, pushed his schoolwork aside and created little creatures.

When his grandmother returned, Dan had a collection of zoo animals.

"You had better have finished that work, Dan."

Marg looked again at his bookwork. In silent disgust, she bundled Dan's animals back into a pile of dough, Dan fighting her as she did.

Mutinous, Dan slid off his chair, ran into the room he stayed in while Mavis was away, and threw himself onto his bed, howling. Marg followed, remonstrating with him.

The slam of the front screen door signalled Trevor's entry into the fray.

"Not again, Marg!"

"He's as stubborn as a mule. I've decided to let it go this time."

"And let him win? What sort of life lesson is that?"

"It's Mavis and the green peas all over again! I'm *not* goin' down *that* track. We'll have to leave this to Mavis to sort out when she comes home. In the meantime, Dan can wear the consequences of no homework when his teacher asks for it."

* * *

Monday, late afternoon of the following week, Dan stood at one of two bins in Mavis' small kitchen. In an accusatory voice, Dan asked, "What's this, Mummy?"

Mavis looked up, pausing in the process of sorting and folding her washing. She was in her lounge room, her washing basket resting on one of the armchairs.

"You know what it is, Dan."

"You said we'd recycle, and you've broken your promise! Miss Andrew says every little bit of recycled waste *matters*."

Very aware of their role reversal, Mavis said, "I plead insanity to the court."

"Not funny, Mummy! Pop is right. You don't follow through on your responsibilities."

"He said that to you?"

"No, he was talking to Gran. I don't know about what. He stopped when he saw me."

"Put that can in the *correct* bin, and come over here." She waited for him to sit and pulled the chair across so she faced Dan. "I'm sorry about the can, matey. As for being responsible, I'm doing my best. I know I've been away heaps, and we haven't seen as much of each other as we used to. You know travelling to Melbourne is longer than to Sydney. We looked at the map together and talked about it. Remember?"

"But you're hardly ever home, Mummy, and then Jack is here a lot when you are!"

"Not a lot, Dan, sometimes. That's because I'm trying to break into the big music scene to make more money so that I can be home lots more. You know Jack and I write music together."

"Can't you do it while you're away? Not in my time?"

"Not really. Look, I'll make sure you get *more* time with me alone when I'm home. Now, what's going on with you and schoolwork?"

"Nothing."

"Yes I know that. Why aren't you doing it?"

"I don't know."

Mavis scrutinised him. "In the scheme of things, a few days of missed homework is no biggy. Promise me you'll do your part and get the work done with Gran while I'm away."

Dan's reply was drawn out, "Okay."

"Now, am I forgiven? Come here little man, give Mummy a hug." Mavis squeezed him ever so tight. "I love you *so* much!"

* * *

For the next two weeks, Dan refused to do homework. Concerned *and* after discussion with Kate and Mavis, Marg organized for Dan to see Emma Stone, the psychologist at the family practice they attended.

After a few sessions of play with puppets and talk over drawings with Dan, Emma Stone spoke to Marg privately in her office. "As you thought, Dan resents his mother's absence. He withholds what you want because he thinks she's withholding what he values. Not a conscious act, but it is the underlying logic to his actions. My advice: don't make it such an issue. He's in second grade. Homework shouldn't even matter. Reading sure, but not other stuff. Let Dan learn the consequences of his actions. He's a competitive little boy; he won't like other kids getting ahead of him or getting rewards at school when he doesn't."

Much as it went against their grain, Trevor and Marg did not push Dan about his homework. They maintained the ritual but let him go after the hour assigned for it had past. Unexpectedly, it was Zoey who helped Dan. Back in Keimera for a short suspension over a breach of conformity, she stayed at the Mills'.

In the afternoons when Dan came home, she too set up her homework at the kitchen bench. They chatted and talked schoolwork in that time. Later they adjourned to the living room and read in companionable silence.

* * *

October 1997. Mavis sat outside her cottage, hours after she had put Dan to bed that Friday night. *A whole weekend free from musical commitments! A long weekend at that!* She had been initially disappointed when the band had not been accepted for a major Sydney festival that weekend but now felt liberated instead.

The evening's chorus of insects was in full-throated song. Exhausted though she was, she was unable to sleep. She inhaled deeply. The air had a sweet freshness to it so different from that in the pub scene. The balmy night heralded the approach of summer. The sky was studded with stars. As she listened to the night, she heard rhythm in nature's orchestra. Each instrument had its sound, scale, and part. A song came to mind. She returned indoors to score it on manuscript.

That done, she decided to warm some milk, her mother's cure for sleeplessness. Regretting the lack of Milo to disguise the taste (pantry stocks were low), she grimaced as she drank. Her thoughts drifted to the life she had lived as a receptionist and the life she now lived. In so many ways, life was better. *It's a long way to the top though.* Just the thought of that road made her weary.

Returning outside, she thought about Jack. The danger point with him had passed. They had become 'just friends'. Their musical partnership seemed strengthened somehow.

In the hush of the evening as she relaxed in the squatter's chair, she was aware of the infinite movement around her. Nature's orchestra, attuned and responsive, led by an invisible conductor played its symphony.

Aware that she was going through post-performance adrenaline crash after the hectic schedule of the past weeks, Mavis decided it was time to reduce her dependency on medicinal sleeping aids. Surely, now was the time for her to sleep naturally.

Weary, she returned indoors. Rinsing her mug and putting it onto the draining rack, she wondered, *Will I ever be able give myself to someone completely?*

Luxuriating in the heat of the shower, she lost time.

Towelling dry, a rush of thoughts returned. So many trips back and forth between Sydney and Melbourne. Always so much to organize.

In bed, Sleep shunned her.

Wired, Mavis thought about the possibility of having a man in her life. She wanted more than sexual gratification though. She needed a stayer, not a player, and someone *not* in her band. Rolling over, she ached for the intimacy of a relationship. It had been *so long* since she'd been held in that way, since she'd experienced love through touch, delighted in loving caresses, felt the exploding joy of union.

Throwing off her sheet and getting up, Mavis felt her way up the darkened corridor. In the doorway leading into the open plan living area, she fumbled for the light switch before finding it and flicking on the light. Then she made her way to the kitchen. With the freezer door thrown wide open and a cold pack on the back of her neck, she cooled down.

Later, resigned to sleeping pills, she took one and went back to bed.

An hour later, she took another.

Time ticked by noisily in her bedroom. In a partial doze, she felt for the bottle of tablets.

At two o'clock, her memory was foggy. *How many tablets have I taken?* She lay stuck between wakefulness and dozing.

Desperate to sink into Sleep's enthralling embrace, she downed pills with the aid of water from the bottle she kept on the floor beside her bed.

Finally, Sleep swept her off her feet, lowered her into its currents. She surrendered to its watery embrace, completely. Sank into its ocean depths, deeper and deeper.

Daylight expelled the last vestiges of darkness from Mavis' room. She did not hear Dan exit to his grandparents for breakfast even though he had unwittingly left the screen door to sigh and then loudly click shut – a sound that usually woke her. She remained unaware of the increasing noise of traffic as the weekend tourist trade kicked into full swing. She failed to hear Dan's return an hour later, noisy though it was. She did not register her bedroom door opening with its characteristic creak as her mother looked in on her before heading off to the beach with Dan and her husband.

Sleep was wonderful. Cold, dark, thoughtless. Its strong currents pulled in one direction only, downward. Further and further into them, she sank.

In the early afternoon, Dan's voice, muffled and distant, called to Mavis. She waved it off and sank toward the ocean's floor. The voice, insistent and demanding, called to her again and again. *Go away,* she thought.

No! was the answer. *I need you! Mummy, Mummy, Mummy! Don't go!*

Pinioned and immobile, Mavis tried to return. That frightened her. She struggled to break free of Sleep's vicelike hold.

Give yourself to me! Sleep demanded.

No, Dan needs me! She struggled against the dark dominion. Could not find the way up out of its depths.

I need you! Mummy, Mummy, Mummy! Don't go!

She struggled now, determinedly. Searched for a way up through the lightless currents.

Mummy, Mummy, Mummy!

I'm coming! I'm coming!

Wakefulness fought with Sleep.

"Dan?" Mavis called weakly.

No reply.

Struggling to throw off Sleep's formless body, Mavis called out, "Dan!" but there wasn't any strength in her voice.

The house was silent.

Fear added its strength to Mavis'. Together they pushed Sleep away from her.

Crying, Mavis called out, "Dan!"

Groggy and barely able to rise, Mavis dragged herself to Dan's room and then to the living area. "Dan!" she tried to yell but her voice was weak. Too heavy to go further, she slumped to the ground, crying.

Meanwhile, Kate, walking down the narrow path past the Mills' house toward Mavis' cottage, heard her distress. Rushing in through the front door, unthinkingly left unlocked earlier that day, she found Mavis on the floor, sobbing.

Speech was difficult. Mavis' mouth and tongue refused to work for her.

"Mavis! What's wrong?"

"Dan … Something's happened to Dan … I heard him callin' … I'm so heavy! I can't … Get me to him … Please!"

"Calm down, Mavis. I just left him over at the beach with your parents and Gary. Gary's teaching him to surf."

"Wh … Whaat?"

"Dan's fine. I called over to see if you were awake yet and if you wanted to have a late afternoon tea with us up at The Argyle this arvo. Here, let me help you up."

"Dan's okay?"

"Yes."

"But he was here, callin' and callin'." In the distress of the moment, Mavis' speech had reverted to old patterns long established.

"No, he's been over at the beach since around eleven. I know because I've been on surf patrol today."

"Eleven?"

"It's three now."

"Dan hasn't been here?"

"No."

With her legs curled beneath her, Mavis sat on the sofa trying to decipher what had happened. Kate sat next to her, worried.

"Are *you* all right? Your speech is *really* slurred."

"I don't … Make me a coffee, Kate. The real kind. I … I need to wake."

After making a fresh six-cup pot of coffee and concerned by Mavis' state, Kate took the liberty of going into Mavis' room. She returned with the bottle of sleeping tablets. "Did you take any of these last night?"

"Some."

"Know how many?"

"A few."

Kate read the detail on the bottle. "Dr Keyman! That quack!" Crossing to Mavis, she said, "I should give Dr Tim a call. Have you checked over."

"No, I'm comin' out of it now. I feel terrible though. That coffee ready yet?"

"There should be at least one cup if not the whole pot."

Sitting silently next to Mavis, Kate wanted to deliver a cautionary tale about dependency on drugs, medicinal or otherwise. She did not.

"What was that then?" Mavis asked.

"I don't know."

Mavis savoured the dark bite of the hot black coffee. "It's bizarre."

Silence wedged between them.

After her fifth cup, Mavis said, "Can you flush the tablets down the loo? The prescription is in my top bedside table drawer. Tear it up, please."

"It'll be my pleasure." Kate did as she was asked. In fact, she took satisfaction in the shredding and flushing of it. On her return, she said, "Mission accomplished. How are you feeling now?"

"Really heavy, but it's not as frightenin' as it was."

"I don't like this. We should see Dr Tim."

"No! Haven't I had enough shame to overcome? I don't want anyone else to know about this. Not ever! I'm awake; that's what counts! Promise me!"

Troubled, Kate remained silent.

"Kate?"

"Can you stand and walk unaided?"

"Sure." Like a newborn deer, Mavis' stand was wobbly and momentary.

"C'mon, I'll help you. Maybe a cold shower would help?"

Mavis sat on the toilet, head in her hands, as Kate organised the shower. "It's ready."

Trusting Kate to have the water temperature right, Mavis stepped into the water. "Oh, oh, oh!" She stepped out of the water. "It's freezing! Why the-?"

"It shocked you to alert though. Maybe I was a bit over zealous."

Mavis fiddled with the tap, adjusting the temperature to temperate. "A bit?"

"Will you be okay if I wait in the hallway?"

"I think so."

Kate sat on the corridor floor near the open bathroom door as Mavis, shaking badly, dried herself off. Mavis emerged, her wet hair wrapped in a towel, wearing a long T-shirt, and slumped onto the floor next to Kate. "Don't tell anyone, *please*, and that includes Gary."

"I've been struggling with this, Mavis. It's too—"

"I'll do whatever you want."

Kate played with her fingernails as she thought the situation through. "You'll agree to get help with whatever it was that led you to this?"

"Okay."

"And you have to let me come with you when you do."

Silence.

"It's no deal otherwise, Mavis." Kate put an arm around her shoulders. "I've got a higher authority to answer to if anything happened to you because I kept quiet about this."

"God?"

Kate shook her head. "Dan."

Mavis smiled. "It's a deal then."

"Now, about The Argyle …?"

"What time is it now?

"Four-thirty. I'll go back and tell them you didn't feel like it."

"No. Can you tell them we'll meet them up there? Would you drive me though? I'm still too heavy to walk."

* * *

The interior of The Argyle was Federation pink, the walls decorated in images from 'the happy days' of the 1950s.

Afternoon tea was in full swing when Mavis and Kate arrived. Dan was full of his kneeboard surfing adventure whereas the Mills had news of the town gleaned from passing acquaintances met down at the beach. Their conversations interlaced throughout the late afternoon. Only Gary noticed Kate and Mavis' subdued state as they sat at the glass topped, chrome tables, listening. He sensed Kate's concern.

"Give your mother a hug, Dan," Mavis said which he dutifully did."I *missed* you." A wave of emotion engulfed her, but she did her best to keep it hidden. She wanted to hold onto him tightly but made herself release him.

"When I'm older, Mum, Gary says he'll teach me how to ride the waves like the boardies do."

"I'm fine with him doin' it Hawaiian style."

"Your mum means strikin' a pose as you ride the wave in," Gary said.

"No radical turns and manoeuvres, Gary."

"It's a lot safer than the skate parks, Mavis. Dan was tellin' me about one of the kids in his class who broke his arm …"

"Gary, this isn't up for discussion."

"Fair enough. Kate, you missed your dad. He dropped in at the surf club to catch up on …"

Mavis tuned out of the conversation. She had realised for some time now that there was danger for her in the lifestyle she'd been following. She considered her options. *Which path is the better one for me to travel?*

As Gary talked, Kate kept a discrete eye on Mavis. She seemed frozen and conflicted.

The Mills joined in the conversation, commenting on Kate's father's work in the local Rotary club. They were impressed by her father's support of George Madison, a significant figure in the Keimera community, in lobbying government to improve aged care facilities in the region. Kate's comments were more polite and non-committal than indicative of genuine engagement with what was being said. The Mills didn't seem to notice.

Gary did though.

"We like your father's lady friend," Marg ended.

"Theresa?" Kate asked, knowing the answer before it was given.

"They seemed very much a couple. We had a really good chat when we met up down at the beach."

"Theresa was with Dad?" Kate asked Gary.

"She was. Did you know she used to surf?"

"*Sure* she did. That's just a bid to connect more to Dad."

"She had some good tips for Dan."

Still don't like her, Kate thought. "Garnered from listening to Dad no doubt when he gave nippers tips." Standing, it was Kate who initiated the closure of the afternoon tea. "Well, this has been lovely."

Farewells completed, Mavis' parents expressed interest in a return wander to their home via the harbour walkway.

"Can I go with them, Mummy?"

"No, Dan, I want you to come home with me. We could stop at the playground near the fisherman's co-operative first though if you want."

Kate asked, "You up to that, Mavis?"

"For Dan, yes."

Watching the Mills family separate and walk away in different directions, Gary put an arm around Kate's waist, "Something is up. What?"

"Nothing."

"C'mon, I thought we didn't keep secrets from each other."

"I share everything about *my* life with you, Gary. Things are fine. I was just trying to get my head around the Mills' view of Dad and Theresa." Kate had given Mavis her word and she intended to keep it. "I just don't know what Dad sees in her. Mum was such a natural beauty. She embraced her age at every stage."

"Whereas Theresa is very well acquainted with matters transformational."

Kate grinned. "I thought you were giving Gilbert and Sullivan a rest."

"For the most part I am, but sometimes the lines just come to me. You know with Theresa in the picture, you don't have to worry so much about your dad bein' lonely or check in on him every day to make sure he is okay."

"And if that hasn't been an issue for me?"

Gary considered Kate's reply. "Much and all as I like your dad, what if it is an issue for me then? I don't like that we compete for your time, attention, and affection."

Kate looked at him, her head askance. "That's how I feel about Dad and Theresa. I feel so much more pressure with her in the picture."

"Why for God's sake?"

Kate shrugged. After an extended pause she said, "Maybe, because as you said, the focus of Dad's life has changed. I'm not the centre of it, and I'm used to being it. I feel …" Another lengthy pause. "I feel like I've lost value somehow."

"Well that's something I never thought I'd hear you say. You've always seemed so centred in who you are as a person. Look at all the guff you took years back when you forced your way into the surf club's male clique."

"This is different, Gary. It's something I'll have to sort out."

*   *   *

Later that night, once Dan had settled down to sleep, Mavis curled up on her cane lounge in sombre reflection. Anguished, she fought to control her distress. Woman and mother though she was, had she *really* left behind the girl she had been, that girl's insecurities, and the way she had lived her life in reaction to the circumstances around her?

Dialling her parents', she said, "Dad, can you come over awhile?"

Recognising the suppressed distress in his daughter's voice, Trevor said, "Your mum and I were just sitting down to a movie, but I'll come if you need me to."

"Thanks, Dad."

Trevor entered the cottage. "How can I help, love?"

"Just be here for Dan in case he wakes up. I need to talk to Mum." With that, Mavis left.

Sitting in her lounge room and resigned to the family dynamic, Marg leafed through *The Women's Weekly*. She was surprised when she heard the rear screen door close and even more surprised at the sound of the footfall approaching where she sat. Standing on the threshold of the room, Mavis said, "Can I have a cuddle, Mum?"

"Course you can. What on *earth* is wrong?"

Nestled within her mother's embrace, Mavis just cried. Not the heart wrenching sounds of despair but more the emotion associated with feeling lost, rudderless and out of sight of land.

Understanding that there are times in life when tears are necessary, Marg said, "It's okay, Mavis, you're not alone in whatever it is that has upset you. I'll listen when you're ready to talk."

Time passed in silent comfort.

Eventually, Mavis found her voice. "I'm really worried about the choices I'm making. At the time they seemed the better path, but then once I'm well down it I see it's more a track. It's then that I make mistakes, big mistakes, because I react to stuff without really seeing beyond it to the risks."

"I think I understand, but can you give me an example?"

A period of silence followed in which Mavis worked out what she could say. Eventually, she said, "Performing. It wasn't something I planned to return to. It just happened. At Christmas you said, I don't value who I am and what I have. At the time, I thought you had it all wrong, but now I think you might have been right. I love singing in front of an audience and creating music. There isn't any doubt Dan's life and mine are better. The audience feed me in so many ways: energy, affirmation, admiration, love, but it isn't real love, is it? There's more to a successful and complete life, and it can't be measured like I thought."

"And that makes you unhappy?"

Mavis nodded, emotion again welling up within her.

"You know what the problem is, so work to overcome it."

"I thought you'd tell me it's best to stop performing. Isn't that what you and Dad want?"

"We're talkin' about *your* life, Mavis. You need to live it on *your* terms, not ours. All your father and I want is for you to be content and financially well off. We had thought our property would give that to you eventually, but there is merit in you earnin' it yourself."

"But what if in all the frenzy of trying to make it in the music industry that I miss what really matters?"

"You only miss seein' things when you're not truly *looking*. It doesn't sound like that'll be the case with you. Sounds like you've done a stocktake of where you're goin' and that you've recognised the pitfalls whatever they are."

Mavis nodded again.

"We can only live life with good intent, Mavis. It's the same as bein' a mother. We do what we think is right at the time even if, in the heat of the moment, it turns out we were wrong. Hopefully, our children will forgive us for any mistakes we make, big or small. Even if they don't, all we can do is learn from it and move on, and try to find some personal peace. Hopefully, forgiveness comes later rather than not at all." Marg paused. "In those stormy teenager years, we said some really cruel things to one another. It was a terrible time for us both. You've never let me talk about it until now. I am *so* sorry that I didn't show you the patience you needed from me... I hope you can forgive me for my flaws." Marg waited. In the ensuing silence, she resigned herself to accept that the forgiveness she craved would not be spoken. "Do you want to tell me what has gone wrong and scared you so?"

Mavis shook her head.

"You know, we haven't cuddled like this since you were sixteen. I used to love those Sunday morning cuddles when you came into our room in the mornings. I miss that contact ... a lot."

"Mum, can Dan and I sleep over tonight, maybe the next couple of nights?"

"Course you can. You know wherever we are there is always a room for you and one for Dan."

Mavis nodded.

"Dan's asleep though, isn't he?"

"Dad can carry him over. I'll get him now. I love you, Mum."

"And I you."

Mavis left.

Troubled, Marg moved to ready Dan's room and then Mavis'. While she supported Mavis' right to choose her life's path, Marg did not view work in the music industry as a real job. It was unknown territory, and neither parent could help Mavis map her course through it.

Chapter 16

S urveying her cottage in the two weeks before Christmas, Mavis felt once again her inability to keep her life ordered. She earned enough money now to have a housekeeper and decided she would get one. *God knows I need one*, she thought. She knew why her mother did not pitch in but wished it was otherwise.

Where to begin? she wondered on that Monday morning. The laundry was chaos. The house was strewn with life's discards. Both her room and Dan's were a mess. *It doesn't matter*, she thought, *a start is a start.*

With the remaining dirty laundry sorted into piles, the clothes line full, the clothes dryer in spin, and the washing machine churning away, she attacked her room. Midway to order, she uncovered a score that she'd been working on a week ago and had taken to bed because the music would not be quietened until it had been scored.

Sitting on the floor now, she heard the symphony of the life around her. Attuned and her mind full of notes, she scored the music. Then she moved to her piano to see if what had been notated when played was in accord with the life heard around her.

Outside, her mother, hanging out her washing, smiled at the piano music. There was joy in it as there was in the light-flooded day.

That afternoon with her house reclaimed, Mavis headed off to yoga which she did with at-home mums in the afternoon. Yoga had been Kate's idea, and was not something that Mavis enjoyed. It was the trade-off that Kate had insisted on if she was to keep Mavis' secret.

"Pills," Kate had said, "are not only a negative pathway to sleep but deadening as well. I'm surprised you have the energy to perform, let alone write music. Yours is the only secret I'm ever keeping from

Gary. Give me your word, Mavis, that you'll keep up the sessions when you're home and make it part of your sleep routine here and when on the road."

"You don't have to worry, Kate. I know how important this is."

That afternoon at yoga, Mavis realised that being off balance, out of control, feeling awkward, and dependent on others were not states she liked. Wobbling on one leg in a pose she particularly disliked, she steadied herself against the wall near her. *Those times are done,* she thought.

"Quieten your minds," the yoga teacher said. "Focus on your breathing. Centre yourself."

* * *

Sunday 22nd February 1998. Despite the weather forecasters' predicted thirty-eight degrees Celsius for that day, onshore breezes made the afternoon feel cooler. In an effort to avoid the compounding heat of their homes, families from the local region and further afield sought relief from the afternoon heat on the grassy parkland slopes between the harbour and the main road that ran through Keimera.

The parkland was abuzz with families, tourists, and the weekend harbour markets: art displays, craft stalls, and produce vendors. Here and there, medieval styled tents with little pennants on the guy ropes added to the festive feel.

Having enjoyed the luxury of a free weekend with only an afternoon practice on the Saturday, Mavis and Susie now walked along the pathway that followed the curve of the retaining wall that separated the harbour and parkland. As was her custom, Susie carried her camera with her. Ahead of them, Dan and Zoey, both wearing trendy sunglasses and clothing that reflected their idea of 'fashion cool', walked toward the marina laughing and chatting.

"The school principal called me and asked for my approval before giving Zoey a parcel they'd received during the post Monday. The principal voiced her reservations about any of her girls receiving gifts from rock musicians."

"How did she know that?"

"The sender details on the parcel. She read it to me over the phone: Max Ryan, RedSun, YME and then the business' address details. I explained the relationship."

"What? You said Max was her biological link in the parenting chain? I'd like to have heard her reaction to that."

"No, I used the father in absentia phrase. Neither Max or Zoey need know."

"So what happened?"

"I asked for their receptionist to call me back when Zoey came to collect the parcel. I wanted to know what he'd sent and hear her reaction."

"And?"

"I got the call. While I was holding on, I could hear Zoey amidst a chatter of schoolgirls. You know, I could imagine her standing there in the front office foyer. It's elegantly furnished and has lots of school memorabilia on display. The school showcases all of its successes for prospective parents and their daughters."

"Go on."

"Zoey sounded puzzled as she took the parcel. Then there was a moment of silence followed by an attempt at nonchalance when she showed the sender details to her friends. "*See*,' she said, 'I told you Max Ryan was my father.' Some girl said, 'Getting a parcel doesn't *prove* he is your dad.' I would've liked to have been able to reach down that phone line and deliver a smart slap to that girl."

"Lucky for her, you couldn't then."

"I may still if I hit that attitude when I'm up there for parents' day. Anyway, Zoey turned to her and said, 'I don't *care* what you think. I *know* he is.' Then I heard another girl call out, 'Hey, Zoey, where are you going?" to which she answered, 'Somewhere private.' I have no idea where she thought that was. It wasn't to her room though as that is dorm accommodation. Anyway, the receptionist, who is an institution in the place because she's been there that long, called Zoey back and told her I was on the phone. She then put Zoey in one of the conference rooms and transferred my call through to her. It was an emotional moment for us both. I grew really impatient with Zoey. It took forever for her to unwrap the package, and there I was hanging on at the other end of the phone. After what seemed ages, I heard a sudden intake of breath, and then she came back on the phone. I told her she should've ripped the paper off and not kept me waiting."

"And?"

"It's sort of sad. She said, 'I want to save everything, Mum'." Susie paused, overcome by emotion. "The whole thing still chokes me up."

"*And*?"

"Max sent her an album of pictures from our teen years and our time together. With the album was a card … It read, 'To Zoey, from your missing link'."

"*Oh.*"

"I know. Give me a minute."

Mavis, seeing the children were getting too far ahead, called out to them. "Hey, you two. Wait there."

"I told Zoey not to read too much into the gesture and, for once, I think she's taking my advice."

"It means something though, right?"

"Maybe. Zoey and I'll play it cool and see what comes. No expectations means no future pain."

"Well, I find it all *very* interesting."

Fifty metres from them, Mavis saw Dan with a hotdog, bought from a vendor positioned in the marina parking area. Zoey had fish and chips. Near them stood two teenage boys.

Just beyond them, a flock of pelicans staked ownership of the boat ramp with some of them perched on mooring posts.

"Why do teenagers *never* listen? I told Zoey to lay off the chips. She knows I've a slow cooker roast on and didn't want her appetite ruined. My parents are back in town for a week, and I wanted everything to be just *right* tonight."

"Fish is a healthier option than hot dogs. Dan gets hyper on the nitrates. I'll have to have *another* talk to him about *doing* what he's told."

One of the older boys said something to Zoey that didn't carry back to Mavis and Susie. They did see Zoey look coyly over her shoulder at the boy before replying. Then with a perfect take on 'I'm too cool to waste my time on you' manner, she strolled off.

Dan, oblivious to the teenage interaction, followed, waving his bun in the air as he called out to Zoey. When she didn't slow down, he broke into a run.

A minute or so later, Zoey turned around as Dan reached her, bumping into him. As they recovered from the contact, a few of the pelicans from the roosting flock tracked Dan in that distinctive, lumbersome way that pelicans move when on land. Their attention focused on the hot dog and bun flapping around his hand.

Zoey looked in rapid succession from one side of Dan to the other. There were pelicans to the right and left, zeroing in. One pelican scoping the food in Zoey's hand veered toward her. Seeing the widening pelican's beak, she abandoned her dignity to the wind. She fled with a squeal. The sophistication she'd previously cultivated left behind along with her sunglasses.

Taken aback, Dan laughed at Zoey's spooked departure. He did not notice a pelican, marginally behind him, opening its cavernous beak to grab the food in his hand. When he felt the wrap of the pelican's beak around his hand, Dan too fled with a squeal. The teenage boys, who had been watching them, laughed so much they overbalanced on the hitching posts they were sitting on and fell backward onto the grass unhurt.

"And life," Susie said, "is much like that."

The beeping of a car horn and calls of, "Nikki Mills!" made them look around.

"Susie, is that Shaun Doyle? What on *earth* is he doing here?"

"Talk about coincidence. This is the most unlikely of things to happen."

"And yet, here he is." Mavis walked across to Doyle's car, calming herself as she did

"Can you point me in the direction of a petrol station? My tank is seriously low. When I pulled off the bypass, I thought one would be easy to find."

"Your second mistake. There's only one. Just follow the road north through the town."

"You holidaying down here, Nikki?"

"No."

Having turned off the engine, Doyle opened his car door and stepped onto the grassed area where the women stood. "G'day. You're Nikki's drummer, aren't you?" He offered her a hand.

"Susie Blake."

They shook hands.

"Nikki, you visiting Susie?"

"No."

"Work with me, Nikki, it's called having a conversation."

Mavis maintained eye contact with him, noting the green flecks of colour in what were very grey eyes. "I want to keep my *personal* life private, Mr Doyle."

"Shaun."

Aware she was background scenery, Susie crossed to Zoey and held Dan back from going to his mother.

"I should thank you, Shaun, for calling the booking agents to grease our way."

"What, you thought the business card was it?"

Mavis nodded. "Without your help we wouldn't have got gigs with them."

"My gestures are never empty promises."

Looking into Doyle's eyes, when they were so close to one another, unsettled Mavis as it did Doyle. Suddenly self-conscious, she changed her stance so that she was no longer looking directly at him.

Doyle mirrored her action.

"So where have you come from, Shaun?"

Doyle leant back against his car. "Bateman's Bay. I hear your band is doing *really* well in Melbourne and Sydney. I was at The Annandale a few weeks back. You slayed them that night."

"We did that. It was such a buzz seeing my name on the black-board above the awning, especially knowing Midnight Oil and Jimmy Barnes had been up there before me."

"Nikki, why don't you show me where the petrol station is and then we can have a chat over coffee?"

Mavis considered his offer and, to her own surprise, accepted it. She crossed to Susie and the children.

"A management offer in the wind, do you think, Nikki?"

"Possibly. Why else would he want to chat?"

"Why indeed? The kids and I'll take the lighthouse route back to your place. We'll see you there later."

Mavis knelt so that she could make eye contact with Dan. "I won't be long. Listen to Susie and do what she says."

Returning to Doyle, she found him in the car.

"Whose kids?"

"Dan is my son. Zoey is Susie's daughter."

His car engine revved into life.

"Take a U-turn and head north."

*   *   *

After solving Doyle's petrol crisis, Mavis took him to a restaurant that overlooked the harbour, just north of the town. It was a relatively new addition to the local scene – an architectural dream of vast expanses of glass and sails. Mavis and Doyle sheltered from the fierce after-noon sun under the sails.

With his emotions well-in-hand, Doyle, interested in Mavis as a person, tried to get a handle on her circumstance. He did so, not by asking her questions, but by sharing details of his own life.

It was not what Doyle said about himself but more the developing rapport between them that aroused Mavis' interest in him as a man.

Once again she felt the charged atmosphere between them. *Was he a player or a stayer?* Distracted, she missed his question. "Pardon?"

"What do you want from a relationship?"

"*Pardon?*"

"A *business* relationship."

"*Oh.* I don't want to be marketed as a sex object. If our music is sold that way, and I'm pitched to fulfil some sort of male fantasy, I won't be able to have any sort of personal relationship. I'd lose my market appeal if I did. *Our* image has to be built around the music."

"Sex sells."

"Been there. Heard that. Not interested. I've learnt to read the fine print nowadays. We've made enough mistakes. I don't want to be exploited. I want quality representation."

"To get Gudinski from Melbourne or my agency, you'll need to convince us that you're head and shoulders above the rest, worth the investment, and deserving of that sort of creative freedom."

"Oh, *we're* worth it. Just you wait and see. Well, I'd better get back to my family and friends." Irritated, Mavis stood. "Interesting chat, Shaun." She shook hands with him, taken aback by the static discharge as they touched.

"Did you apply for the Southern Bays Festival, Nikki?"

"We did."

"You'll have some fierce competition to get a slot there."

"I'm not worried about that." But she was. Mavis left, insisting on paying for her coffee on the way out.

*   *   *

Singing 'On the Road Again', The Nikki Mills Band headed south to Melbourne through the autumnal landscape. For the second verse, Mavis changed the lyrics to 'When We're Home Again' while the men continued to sing backup vocals. They travelled in a hired mini bus with a trailer carrying their gear hitched to it.

Melbourne claimed to be Australia's cultural and music capital. If you measured that by the proportion of live-music venues to the size of the city and amount of supportive infrastructure, it was.

The band made faltering progress that afternoon through Melbourne as Susie had the bus stop and start so that she could capture their experience in a series of photographic shots. Having scoped the city in their previous visits, she now knew what pictures she wanted: wide boulevards of Plane trees lining the city streets; clattering trams, reminiscent of San Francisco but without the hills, networking the inner city; the impressive Edwardian Baroque architecture of Flinders Street Station and its expansive dominance over a city block; the extensive parklands, and the Yarra River running through the city.

Later when the band were on foot, Susie recorded the cosmopolitan environment ranging from chic restaurants to cafes wallpapered with band posters: Australian Crawl, AC/DC, Cold Chisel, The Birthday Party, The Living End, Midnight Oil, Nick Cave and the Bad Seeds and so on.

As with the Sydney pub scene, volume had to go up. In conflict with the obsession with loudness, Mavis found a compromise by intensifying the rhythm, creating a big *fat* beat. She did not sacrifice the clarity of vocals though or the balance within the band.

Alternating between weekends in Sydney and Melbourne for months and months on end, the band made the most of their weekends in Melbourne. Their motto, success or bust. They did matinees, afternoons, late spots, and all three in a day given the opportunity.

Their subsequent rise in popularity was attributable to their unique sound and original music not heard before in Melbourne. Mavis' lyrics conveyed an intimate picture of life that resonated with audiences. The diversity of their material had wide appeal, making the band broadly popular. CD sales escalated. Lyle, sporting a pencil thin moustache and chin-tickler goatee, was swamped with customers.

Coming off stage for a break during a late night spot in August, band members literally stepped into Lyle. He was breathless and excited. "Molly Meldrum is in the crowd. I offered him a CD, *and* he took it!"

Ian 'Molly' Meldrum was an iconic music critic, journalist, record producer and entrepreneur. Mavis believed Meldrum to be one of the most influential people in the Australian music industry. During his stint as host on *Countdown* in the eighties, his show gave national exposure to select musicians, often rocketing them to stardom. Later in the nineties, his 'Molly's Melodrama' segments on *Hey, Hey, It's Saturday* extended his already significant reputation. With his backing, bands rose from anonymity to fame. His promotional support could *not* be bought which was one reason it was so valuable.

Steve scratched his recently grown beard. "You know what that means?"

"He's interested!" was the unison reply.

Returning to the stage, full of dreams, their performance was sharpened by a rush of adrenaline. That session ended with Mavis' sensual delivery of 'Heat' which left the audience pumped and wanting more.

Lyle again met them as they came off stage. His lower lip dragged on his boots. "Molly's left."

The air went out of the evening, leaving them all deflated.

Walking back to their rooms at two in the morning through the cold and drizzle of that Melbourne night, Mavis sang 'On the Road Again' slowly, dispiritedly. The rest of the band joined in, the discordant sound reflecting their mood.

Gradually, Mavis' spirit lifted. *We're a success by many a band's measure.* She increased her walking tempo and her song became upbeat, energised. The supporting vocals followed suit.

Glad that a driver came with their bus hire, the band and support crew slept for most of the return trip to Keimera.

On their arrival at Mavis' home, their first stop, and as her gear was being unloaded, Marg Mills met them at the gate. She waved an envelope excitedly at them. "Look at the sender! It says Southern Bays Music Festival."

After ripping the envelope open, as her band clustered around, Mavis yelled, "We're in!"

Chapter 17

Thursday before the October long weekend, 1998. From the comfort of their living room, the Mills watched the six o'clock Nine news break with its coverage of the music festival.

An establishing shot of the region showed the scene for the television audience as the reporter began. "Revellers continue to roll into the Bays Music Festival in southern New South Wales for this music extravaganza. We've been told the crowd currently stands at fifty thousand with more people expected to arrive over the next day. A sell-out at seventy thousand, people have already set up camp days in advance of the event, transforming this picturesque farmland into a massive tent city."

The television view cut to a medium shot of the reporter in front of a mammoth stage shielded from the elements by a truly impressive marquee which extended far back behind the stage. "This reporter was struck by the military-like organization of the event for what will be a truly memorable and eclectic music festival.

All the big names in the Australian music industry are scheduled here. The bulk of the show though will be featured bands, hopeful of making an impression on audiences and accelerating their rise to fame and fortune. The line up in this four day festival, beginning midday tomorrow, includes the juggernaut bands Cold Chisel, Midnight Oil, and Powderfinger to name but a few."

Trevor said, "Even though I'm really excited for Mavis, I worry about the values of that world and how it might affect her."

"Don't worry, love. I'm confident now she knows the hardships and heartache that can come from misguided choices."

"You sure of that?"

"More than sure."

"Grandma!" Dan entered through the back door which slammed after him. "I think *that* is Zoey arrivin'. I'm hungry. When's dinner?"

"Ready now that Zoey has arrived. Wash up first." To her husband, Trevor, she said, "I'm glad Mavis changed her mind and decided to let Dan stay with us. *That* place looks as if it would be easy to get lost in." She stood and crossed to their front door, opening it. "Zoey, so good to see you. Any problem gettin' away?"

"None." *Once I got over the fence, it was easy.* She smiled as she imagined being a fugitive, the ringing alarm bells and flashing lights warning of her escape. Few people understood the bars to being released a day early from school. She had volunteered to help the next school year's intake of Year Sevens to sweeten her principal. "Thank you so much for having me."

"Couldn't have you stayin' home alone especially over a long weekend. Where are your grandparents travellin' this time?"

"Italy and then Greece."

"I've put you in Mavis' room like last time. Trevor and I've played with the idea of travellin' overseas but so many of those places are filled with foreigners. I don't know how all those people get on not speakin' English."

"I don't think they would notice it because there would be lots of people who were born there who all speak the native language."

"Still ..."

"My grandparents don't seem to mind." With her small suitcase placed on a chair, Zoey unzipped it. "I *really* like staying here. Until I met Nikki and all of you, I never really knew what being in a family was like."

"Oh, love." Marg hugged her. "I've cooked all of Dan and your favourites for dinner. I've even made that cheese sauce you like for over your cauliflower. Wash up and come out when you're ready."

* * *

Earlier that same day at the Southern Bays Festival site, Mavis' band drove at a snail's pace through the festival complex, following the signs to the bands' registration area. At their destination, they disembarked in the car park.

Looking at the signage, Susie said, "This is like following the yellow brick road."

With Lyle, Tim, Tony, Jack *and* Steve carrying two sealed boxes of CDs each, Mavis finally made the festival's makeshift office at the back of the huge stage marquee. Festival staff inspected the boxes, noted the information label from producers certifying the number of CDs per box and the CD cover still intact across the top of each carton. After a careful check, the staff person said, "That's ten thousand to be exact."

With their CD supply receipted and having completed the rest of the registration, the band retreated a little way from the office so that they could look at the bundle of information they'd been given.

"Hey, those chairs over there are vacant now." Tony pointed to a round of white plastic chairs. After sitting, they scrutinized the performance schedule.

"I've found us," Mavis said. "We're listed for three performances: eleven Friday night and … oh my God! We're listed at seven before Natalie Imbruglia on Saturday evening!"

"No way!" Jack said.

"You're kiddin'!" Steve said.

"Show me!" Tony said.

Mavis passed the brochure to Tony, and the others crowded around him. Amazed, he passed it to Jack.

"Wow!" Jack leant back in his chair.

The group just sat there in silence, gobsmacked. Mavis, finding her voice first said, "We have a third gig midday Sunday as well."

Tony said, "And look who else is on the bill! Cold Chisel, Midnight Oil, Powderfinger, Silverchair, *and* RedSun!" He wished Sarah had been able to come with them, but Mavis continued to be adamant that he keep Sarah away from the band.

Steve spoke up. "I'm so glad I have all of next week off. I'm not leavin' until after I've seen *and* rubbed shoulders with those guys. I intend to party *big* time."

"Well, fellas, this woman is sticking with Nikki and leaving as planned after our last gig. No way do I want to get caught in the traffic leaving this place at the end. Good luck getting near the head-line acts and getting past their gatekeepers. Besides, apart from their vanguards being here early, those bands themselves will be in and out the same day if they have only one performance here. Didn't you notice the route marked VIP on our way in? Ease of entry and speed in exit are the key words for them in this event." Susie stood. "Let's find our accommodation, people."

"Everything is marked clearly on this map," Mavis said. "Susie and I will lead the way."

Back in their respective cars again, they followed the makeshift 'street' signs to rows of Thai huts, like the sort miners use, that had been trucked in by event organizers for performers.

"What's our hut number, Susie."

"Forty-five, Nikki."

Susie read out the hut numbers as they passed. "How easy is this!"

"There it is!"

After parking their two cars and van in the designated area near their hut, the band regrouped.

Steve, a plumber by trade, said, "Wow! Just look at the amount of PVC pipin' around here!"

"What is that enormous thing between the huts?" Susie asked.

"A water bladder," Steve continued. "That means each hut must have its own bathroom."

"Really?"

"For sure, Nikki."

"That's a relief. I wasn't looking forward to sharing with a host of others. So good we don't have to!"

Susie said, "It's good we're cordoned off from the general public.

No need to worry about the press of groupies here! Listen up, guys, do *not* bring anyone back here!"

"That's disappointin'," Jack said. "I've come to appreciate that perk."

Looking at him, Susie asked, "And what happened to the muso who wasn't interested in picking up chicks?"

"At the time, I made it clear it wasn't my *motive* in joinin' Nikki's band. I didn't say I'd knock back any women who were interested in me."

Steve said, "I think the same rule should apply to you two as well!"

Susie put her hands on her hips. "When have we ever shown an interest in that?"

"We have standards!" said Mavis.

Susie added, "Neither of us wants to be left carrying a baby."

"Haven't you learnt yet? Those girls are strictly interested in image and status! They're not interested in any of you as a person."

"Nikki, bein' a trophy is fine with me," Jack said. "That street goes two ways."

"And I could have done without that insight into you, Jack. So sad!" Mavis opened the door to the hut and led the way in, stopping at a communal space at the front of the hut.

Jack followed her in. "When music takes over your life, and you're workin' hard to make it like we are, it can be lonely in the offstage hours. How else are any of us goin' to meet a woman that might be more than an overnight lay? Am I right, fellas, or what?"

"Right," was the unanimous response.

Mavis turned and considered Jack as Susie passed her, walking down the long corridor on one side of the hut to the door at the other end.

Aware of his other listeners, Jack added, "Besides, booze and exercise of one sort or another are the best ways I know to come down after a gig."

"Right again," most of his male listeners said from the ease of the communal area chairs.

"Sleepin' pills are safer than sex nowadays," Tony said.

"But nowhere near as much fun," Steve added.

Jack spoke under his breath as he passed Mavis on his way to investigating their quarters. "Don't judge me, Nikki. What other sort of women do I have time to meet? You're not interested in me, and Susie is sure as hell not."

Susie called out, "Hey, there's a kitchen with a fridge and a microwave. Pity we didn't bring real food. It would've been a relief to escape a weekend of fast food." She continued to explore the hut. "All the rooms have double bunks. Yay! Looks like we have *all* this space to ourselves." Returning to the communal area, Susie said, "This is better than anything we've stayed at so far."

Jack returned just after Susie. "So, Nikki," Jack asked, "who is bunkin' in your room?"

"No wolves that's for sure," Susie answered for her. "I am of course."

Steve said, "I'm *not* bunkin' with Tony. He gets stinky when he is nervous."

Tony looked at him sharply. "Something the women could've done *without* knowin', mate!"

Jack said, "We should draw names from a cap for roomies. Both Tim and Lyle snore! I don't want to bunk with either of them again if that can be helped!"

Steve said, "A name draw is the only fair way. I'll organise it."

"How amazing is the organization here?" Mavis said.

"Stands to reason," Tony replied, "especially when you consider it's been going a few years now."

"Here." Mavis handed Lyle the relevant parts from the handout. "This is all the stuff on setup and sound checks. There's a map there too."

Anxious about their roles, Tim spoke for himself and Lyle. "We're goin' to find where to store the gear, when I can do the sound checks, and the timin' for when to set up." When they returned an hour and a half later, they found everyone had unpacked and settled into rooms.

Tim found Mavis lounging in the front room, studying some of the registration paperwork. "If you thought this was organized, Nikki, wait til you see the sound setup! More gear than I ever imagined, and I've got a really good imagination. I'm in heaven!"

Tony's head popped through his room's doorway. "Let's get the lay of the land. Find where we warm up and check *everything* out."

Susie called out from her bedroom. "Best to eat when we can. Queues are going to be long over the weekend, and we don't know what is available."

"Hey," Jack walked into the front room, some paperwork in hand. "It says here, there are mess tents and food vendors scattered throughout the camp, and the performers' one is open ... wait for it ... twenty-four-seven! Nikki, can you see it marked on the map?"

"No ... Yes, I can."

The men said, "Let's eat!"

*   *   *

The group found the mess tent adjacent to the stage and its related marquee. Within it, clearly sectioned off was an area for bands and another area for festival staff. Holding up their IDs, which hung on lanyards around their necks for scrutiny by the security guards, they entered the mess tent. It was cafeteria in style with hot food, cold food, a self-serve salad bar, and even an ice cream machine. There were also microwaveable meals available for anyone who wanted to eat in the privacy of their huts.

Susie hesitated over the pre-packed meals. "Do we want to take any of these meals back to our hut for later?"

"Good idea, Susie." Lyle opened a refrigerator door. "Tim, you do the desserts." With thought, they selectively collected an assortment of packs.

"It would mean washing up," Mavis said. "Fellas, Susie and I are *not* cleaning up after you this weekend. Anything you use in the hut, *you* clean up when you're done."

Tim and Lyle looked at one another and then down at the

collection in their arms. On the same wavelength, they returned the packs to the refrigerator shelving.

By the time Lyle and Tim had worked their way through the cafeteria queue, the rest of the band were well into their respective meals.

After putting his tray down next to Jack's, Lyle moved to Mavis and bent down for a word in her ear. "Would it be uncool to get some autographs? Some of my favourite bands are sitting around us."

"You know the answer, Lyle."

The big man looked like a kid without money in a lolly shop as he surveyed the scene. "Lyle?" Mavis looked up at him.

"I'm going back to have my meal."

"And yet you're still standing here."

"Oh, yeah, I am." Lyle looked down at his feet. "Get walkin'."

Susie, her camera resting on the table, unobtrusively lifted it periodically and recorded the scene. She had learnt long ago that the art of candid photography involved not drawing attention to herself and being part of the background.

Meal over, they explored the surrounding area while Susie looked for potential scenes that she could photograph and that captured the essence of the experience. Standing in the audience area and looking toward the stage, they were impressed by its size.

"Huge!" Tony articulated what everyone else thought when they looked at the stage. Turning back to look from the stage view at audience level, they were astounded by the scale of the lighting stands surrounding the festival acreage and encompassing tent city. The lights were the sort usually found in the biggest football stadiums, except here they were mounted on trucks and flatbed trailers. Each truck had a generator. Likewise, the speaker columns were situated on trucks and at a distance from the audience to enhance the sound.

"Wow!" was the collective response.

Susie said, "I never thought I'd be taking photos of something like this. I'd love to get a shot of that from a higher level." She clicked away happily.

After that, they retreated to their hut, torn between excitement and being overwhelmed.

The rest of the afternoon passed back at their hut with individuals dealing with their mounting nerves in their own way.

Well before their scheduled slot for stage checks, the band returned to the performance space with their instruments for sound checks as other bands around them had. Lyle and Tim helped Susie with her drums.

"I should've listened to my mum years ago. Drums are bulky, awkward, and need to be handled with care. She wanted me to play a piccolo. Be careful with that bass. Sorry, fellas, just my nerves showing."

Tim carried the snare drum while Lyle carried the bass. "I don't want you around when we have to bring the whole kit down here and back."

"Just make sure you are *both* sober when you take my gear back. Wish now I'd had our name printed across the drum face!"

Tim continued, "And this bloody camera of yours, Susie, just adds to the awkwardness of the whole thing as well as getting to sound checks."

As they approached the staging area, the lights came on, more to warm them up than to provide illumination. The festival people also needed to see that everything worked.

"Tim, hand over my camera. I'll never forget this, but just in case I do." She captured the scene in a series of carefully framed shots.

"How surreal is it!" Tony stood on the stage apron.

Everything was bathed in an unnatural yellow light.

"Wow! A light show as well!"

Tim went back to the sound booth in front of the stage and sat in with the festival people operating the booth.

"Next!" called one of the stage managers.

"That's us," Mavis said.

The band plugged into the sound system and ran through one of their songs to get the sound levels right.

At the end of their run through, Jack said, "How good was that? We could actually hear ourselves. I've never played with monitors before."

"I've never had my drum kit set up on a mobile stage for ease of bumping in on a stage before."

Lyle crossed to the band from the wings. "Ten minutes, fellas, is all we have for setup. The stage manager has a stop watch runnin'!"

Meanwhile, back at the sound booth, Tim recorded the settings needed on the mixer.

On the way back to their hut, gear in hand, Mavis said, "I'm so excited."

Tony added, "I just can't hide it!"

The rest of the entourage said in unison, "I know! I know! I know!"

*   *   *

Nine that Friday night. Backstage, Mavis and her group stood as other bands did, apart from one another. Ahead of them in the line-up, most musicians followed a ritual of warm-up and focusing, designed to keep them calm, flexible and centred before their performance. Each group had its own idiosyncratic ritual. A few had none.

Ten-forty. Waiting in the wings, Nikki and the band saw what could only be described as a universe of people. A sea was just too small to describe the scene.

Standing in silent awe, dazzled by the blazing lights, overwhelmed by the enthusiasm of the crowd, and impressed by the musicianship of the band on stage now finishing off their set, Mavis felt her nerves increase. She looked at her band.

Susie was limbering up her wrists, drumsticks in hand. She wore a bold, geometric patterned, figure hugging, thigh length, knit dress over black leggings, and ankle high sneakers. A half a dozen or more sticks protruded from her belt.

Jack was playing air bass guitar. He had opted for a leather waist-coat over a muscle T-shirt, dark jeans, and sneakers.

Tony stood stoically. A statue came to mind. He wore a white T-shirt, blue jeans, and sneakers.

Steve, dressed in low-key denim, leant into Tony and said, "We're not in Kansas anymore, Toto."

Having failed to get a reaction from Tony, Steve added, "Relax, mate."

Tony just nodded at him.

After adjusting her headset microphone, Mavis looked at Tony. "You okay?"

"Yeah, I'm good, or at least I will be once we get started. I never thought this would be so loud! All that practice bumpin' in and out over the last few years will kick in soon. I never thought of it as rehearsal for something like this. Never imagined I'd play at something like this."

"You okay with the headset?"

Tony nodded at Mavis.

As the explosion of applause faded, the previous band left the stage via the left-hand side.

The stage manager signalled Mavis' crew who waited in the right-hand wings. Lyle coordinated everything that moved onto the stage while the stage lights were dimmed. With the exception of Mavis, they all helped position the gear. She waited in the wings, imagining herself as Nikki Mills. She checked her appearance. Her choice of clothing for Nikki was always made from soft fabric that had a romance feel and look about it. The material flowed gently around her, like pale blue water over rock, revealing her figure and yet concealing it at the same time. Her hem line was angled to showed off her bare, tanned legs and strappy high heeled shoes. She knew that the intended ambiguity in her clothing worked. Men clearly responded to her allure and yet treated her with respect. Men did not behave as if she or Susie were slutty. Stepping into her Nikki persona, she moved onto the stage in the faded light as her band assumed their places.

A spotlight focused on the MC. He said, "For the next hour, you'll be entertained by Nikki Mills and her band from Keimera. Put your hands together for a warm welcome."

The lighting changed. Spotlights accentuated the position of each performer amidst the wash of general lighting.

Mavis stood with her back to the audience mid-stage. She had never performed before a crowd that was already cheering. She wondered, *Can we get them to listen to us? God, I hope so!*

The set opened with a keyboard interlude, single notes at first that built into a fuller sound.

Listening, Mavis thought she heard the crowd settling. She waited for Susie to enter on cue.

A single resounding beat on the amplified snare drum from Susie signalled Tony's fuzz guitar entry coordinated with Jack's bass. The distinctive sound of the bass pedal thump accentuated the first beat of each bar in the gutsy riff. The music built to a crescendo with the synthesised brass from Steve's keyboard adding backing. Then there was a sudden rest, a four beat pause. You could hear a pin drop. The crowd was silent.

The keyboard led the way into the song while Susie tapped the high hats in a blues staccato rhythm. Mavis knew her cue was two bars away and followed a complex drum round by Susie. Mavis turned and walked forward, owning the space. Once in her new position, her voice rang out clearly. She was alive! She was her music!

Focused on the story embedded in her song, the nuances of its emotion, she captured the imagination of the audience. Having a good time, she interacted playfully with Tony and then Jack. The audience ate up her interplay with the men, the staged relationship.

Years of working together had made them tight and confident. It was very different to playing in a club. This was true concert performance.

Mavis felt the return of energy from the crowd. It was amplified by the size of the audience and bigger than any cathartic reaction she had previously experienced. It was tsunami in its proportions. Instead of drowning her, it lifted her powerfully, carried her effortlessly, gracefully into the next song and through that to the songs that led the band to the end of the set.

Over the crowds' outpouring of appreciation, the MC said, "Wow! How about that! The Nikki Mills Band! You can purchase their CDs at the sales stalls; check your programs for details. They are on again tomorrow night at seven before the amazing Natalie Imbruglia and again on Sunday at midday!"

Exiting the stage via the left wings, Mavis and her band paused on the steps descending into the backstage area. Security staff in their black caps, day-glow yellow shirts, black trousers and shoes were everywhere. They were committed to crowd control and restricting entry.

A good part of the area had been sectioned off by various media outlets: magazine, newspaper, and television. That part of the scene reminded Mavis of the televised red carpet scenes of the annual Academy Awards. There were at least two open bars functioning. The rest of the space was filled with the glitterati, glamouratti, festival sponsors, representatives from record companies, PR people, entertainment management, and local VIPs. Gatekeepers hovered near the bigger name bands, checking and controlling access to them.

"Hey, Susie," Steve said, "there's your mate from RedSun."

Susie ignored Steve and looked in the other direction.

Tony added, "As well as the who's who in the entertainment business. Oh my God, there's Molly Meldrum."

"Where's Tim and my camera?" Susie said to no one in particular.

At the bottom of the stairs, a media guy snaffled the band and escorted them to a media tent adjacent to the backstage area. They were directed to a trestle table with microphones on it and white plastic chairs behind it.

Unprepared for the interest and the barrage of questions that came with it, the band deferred to Mavis as their spokesperson. Handling the questions as best she could, Mavis kept her replies to talking points developed for other promotional activities. Her unprepared answers included, "Thrilled to be selected to be on the festival CD

… Didn't know a video was being produced of the event but excited that we'll get to be the audience to our own performance when it's released."

Returning to the backstage marquee, the band separated as Susie said to Mavis, "Temptation Circuit here they come."

Much later that night Tim found Susie and Mavis. His voice reflected his relief. "Here, take this monstrosity of a camera. Why can't you settle for *a point and shoot* one like the rest of us? It's been so hard to find you. I wish now that you'd listened to your mum as well. Lyle and I had a hell of a time gettin' the drum kit and the rest of the gear back. Yes, yes, we did it safely."

"Because I'm interested in the art of photography and not just happy snapshots. I do appreciate you carrying it around for me though. Well, I'm off to chronicle all of this."

Mavis said, "Tim, great work coordinating the lights with the sound! You're not just a sound guru. You are an artist!"

"Gee, thanks, Nikki. Look, it's real wild out there. Let me know when you want me to walk you back to our hut. I'm just goin' to hang with the other crews out back."

"I don't need an escort, Tim. I'm heading back now."

"Yeah, you do."

From behind her, a man said, "Nikki Mills; good to see you and your band here."

Turning, Mavis replied, "Max Ryan as I live and breathe. Congratulations on the European tour next month. Wish we were so lucky."

"Thanks. You and your band rise to new heights every time I hear you perform."

"RedSun really rocked the world tonight!"

"Like you, we fed off the audience adulation."

"We haven't reached the adulation stage yet. I know what you mean about the energy though. There is us, the crowd, and then that added thing that comes alive when performers and audience connect."

"Sanna around?"

"Yes, she is doing what she loves, second to music."

"Photography."

"In one. Now who said that relationship was forgotten?"

"I believe I said I was Sanna's *forgotten* ex when we last spoke."

"A bit hard when she has Zoey to look at every day. She has your eyes." Mavis smiled at him. "That was a nice thing you did for Zoey. It meant a lot to her although it didn't put the *sceptics* at her school in their place. She'd been a bit silly and told them of the relationship before they all skipped school and went to see RedSun at the Enmore last year."

Max frowned. He knew all too well the sharpness of teenage tongues when at boarding school. His father had set him up for a similar pain more than once. He did not like being the cause of it. *Was that impossible to escape?*

"Well, if I'm not mistaken, here's Susie!"

"Max!"

"Sanna."

Mavis stood aside, enjoying their meeting until Susie looked pointedly at her.

"Okay, I know, two is company and three is a spare wheel the car doesn't need. I'm off." *Pity,* Mavis thought as she left them, *I love romance even if it is ultimately impossible.* Getting to the exit took longer than Mavis had expected. Her progress was regularly slowed by well-wishers and interrupted by representatives from record companies and entertainment management. With her fist full of cards and arrangements for some preliminary discussions after the Sunday performance, she neared the exit. As she did, Tim materialised.Outside, a press of high-pitched fans, eager to make contact in whatever way they could with the bands or people associated with them, blocked the pathway back to the huts. The last time Mavis had experienced this level of frenzied activity blocking her path had been when she'd sought advice at a women's clinic in Marrickville over eight years ago. The noise and the press was as nightmarish in proportion. It wasn't Mavis' idea of a dream experience, and she doubted it would be anyone else's. In the end that night, she needed the support of four security people and Tim to get her safely back to her hut.

"Way too much effort to get back," Tim said after they had arrived back at their hut. "That was exhaustin'. I think I'll drop in at some of the hut parties goin' on around here. You sure you're okay now?"

"So sorry, Tim, you're missing out on the backstage fun. Tomorrow, I'll have security people as my escort. I'm fine here. Go ahead and enjoy yourself."

Secure in the knowledge that doors were locked, Mavis lingered in the shower, enjoying her solitude after the high of performance. After she towelled off and changed into her shorts and knit green top, she walked down the corridor into the communal area, her meditation CD in hand. With the lights dimmed, she assumed a cross-legged, straight body pose and imagined herself as a hill, grounded in the terrain around her. The pose signified, *I am here. I cannot be moved.*

Using a remote to activate the CD, she focused on her breathing, and on increasing the oxygen levels in her system. After a timed interval, her CD recording of a resonating sound began. Using diaphragmatic breathing, Mavis harmonised with the note in a controlled outward breath, taking care not to fade out while the recorded voice took a breath. She continued thus, slowing her breathing, changing the pitch of her harmony and focused on being one with the sound. After forty minutes, music faded in, taking over from the recorded voice, signalling the last stage of the meditation process. In a relaxed state, Mavis refocused on her breathing, consciously took control, returning it to a natural depth.

Weary and ready for bed, she retired, locking her room door for security. Outside and around her hut, the party continued.

Some hours later, the unexpected click of a key and the subsequent opening of the external door disturbed Mavis. She heard at least three of her band return. Their deep male whispered voices carried to her even though it was clear they were attempting to enter the hut noiselessly. Muffled noises sounded for in the hut followed finally by silence.

Falling back into sleep, Mavis wondered about Susie's whereabouts. In a restful doze, Mavis was brought back to her surroundings with the turn of another key in the external door lock and the arrival of the remaining band members, Susie included.

Listening, she heard Susie's tread to the bathroom and the men head for their respective rooms. The sound of the shower reminded Mavis of the fall of rain. She fell asleep comforted that the house was full and that they all had time to sober up if that was needed.

*   *   *

The next day, Mavis was first to rise; by her wrist watch, it was nine. She felt energised and thought a solitary walk to the mess tent was in order.

Outside, the world around her slumbered. The push and shove of the fans had given way to peace. The distinctive smell of wood smoke from campfires pervaded the air. Further afield, tent city was returning to life slowly.

At midday, as the band shared a meal in the mess tent, Tony said, "Last night was a great beginning. So glad all we have to do today is chill and then perform tonight."

Mavis said, "Now that you raised that, I want to vary the material."

"What? Why?" Tony asked.

"Tonight's time slot and the fact that we're in a support role for Natalie. I see this as a type of audition. A chance to show any management out there we recognize the need to have the crowd emotionally loaded for the big name performer. I want work as a support band as we move forward in the industry."

"So what's the playlist?" Susie asked.

Mavis pulled six sheets of paper from her jeans' pocket, one of which she gave to Tim.

"Not one of my songs, Nikki." Steve blanched. "Not in front of a crowd this size!"

"Get your head around it, Steve. Anyway, I thought you'd come to enjoy it."

"After I've done it, but I hate the anticipation and the foretaste. It's like my relationship with tarty lemon in meringue pie."

Mavis looked at him, confused. "Okay."

Jack said, "I get it. Whiskey has a hot foretaste that makes a man grimace but the aftertaste … ah!"

Tony spoke to Steve. "Haven't seen you refusin' any whiskey, man."

"This isn't negotiable, Steve." Mavis pocketed her copy of the set list.

The journey to the stage that Saturday evening seemed to move faster than the night before. Detached that evening from the scene around her, Mavis had time to observe the hustle and bustle of the backstage post-production show. Bands who had performed earlier that day were in full party mode enjoying the open bar and their audience. Hangers-on seemed to have made it into what had been a secure area. *By invitation?* she wondered. Media were everywhere, engrossed in the promotion business of the festival. Security seemed thicker than ever.

Waiting now at the steps that led into the stage wings, one of the stage managers said, "You're in a support band time slot. Added to what you want to achieve here tonight, you need to load this audience so that they are cocked and ready to fire when Natalie comes on stage."

Mavis nodded. "Knew that already. I've sequenced my material accordingly."

"Thanks for the pressure, man," Steve said. "We know this is make or break time."

In the wings, Mavis felt calm. The pre-show edge that she had come to expect and rely on had deserted her. She looked at her band. Susie and Jack were immersed in their warm-up ritual. Tony still looked like a stunned rabbit caught in the headlights. Steve was doing his best to distract him with humour that Mavis knew was Steve's personal stress release valve.

The full stage lights dimmed as the spotlight picked out the MC who farewelled the onstage band and ran through his shtick. Her band moved into action. Still in the wings, Mavis closed her eyes and thought about her Nikki persona. She stepped into her, leaving Mavis and all of her concerns behind. Mentally, she ran through her performance: heard the notes, saw her moves, watched her playful, sometimes teasing, interaction with the men.

The stage manager pointed to her. "You're on."

Mavis moved into position and waited for the drum and bass riff. The audience sounded wild, caught up in the excitement of the festival and involved in their own show. Her performance edge returned. She felt her pulse responding to the energy of the opening riff. She loved this particular bass line and drum sequence, complex in timing and yet elegantly simple. She fed off the crowd's reaction, growing in her performance dimension.

The set began with four strong contemporary bluesy rock numbers, alternated with hip hop with Steve, and then progressed into their best songs. Every song had been crafted and polished. Each song featured variety in rhythm, interesting bass lines, and showcased the musicianship and talent of her band. The music built to a crescendo that led into the last song of the bracket.

The outpouring from the audience lifted Mavis. She soared on their emotion. Improvising, she dialogued with her three men through movement, suggesting a story about the band's relationships. Jack and Steve clearly enjoyed the ad-lib from the get-go, playing to Mavis and the crowd. Tony took a bit longer to free up. When he did, he vied with Jack and Steve in music and action. As her last notes rang out, Mavis felt the reluctance of a lover in farewell.

The stage lights dimmed amid riotous applause as the spotlight picked out the MC. Disoriented, Mavis just stood there. Steve, noting her inaction, took her by the elbow and said, "C'mon. Time to go." He led her offstage in the dimmed light. "My God, listen to that reception for Natalie!"

Backstage, football stadium sized television screens transmitted the onstage show. On the descending backstage steps, Mavis paused and took in the televised onstage scene. *Wow! Will I ever want to be that big?* Standing there, she knew it was no longer an impossible task. *One day, I will be.*

One of the media gatekeepers met the band as they reached the floor. "Molly would like to meet you, Nikki. Bring the band along too."

With the anticipation of children on Christmas morning, the band followed Mavis onto Meldrum's television set. They did their best to appear cool but did not quite pull it off.Seated on a sofa and wearing his trademark Stetson and dressed in black, Meldrum stood when Mavis entered the spotlight of his media area. He was smaller than the band had imagined him, their perception based on his television appearances on *Countdown* and *Hey Hey It's Saturday.*

"An impressive performance tonight, Nikki. Your band not only did *not* disappoint, I think you'll find it has fed the passion that produces fans."

"That's kind of you, Molly, even if it is an overstatement of our impact. There are so many great emerging bands here, it'd be hard to be a standout."

"And yet you *are*! I predict you'll go far in this business."

Meldrum exchanged some banter with the guys and then fare-welled the group.

Giving up their seats to other talent, the group moved off to a nearby bar.

"I'm walking a dream." Susie expressed what the rest of the band felt. "Where is Tim? I want to capture Molly and other 'names' in candid moments."

A bevy of glamour gilt beauties clustered around Jack. Steve and Tony both held smaller courts.

"Tim! Finally!" Susie crossed to him and then disappeared.

Lyle and Tim stood as bookends to Mavis, filling her in on *their* perspective of the world they had entered.

"Nikki Mills!" Shaun Doyle, sleek and highly groomed, approached her. His coal black hair had wavy blonde tips through it. He wore an open-necked, solid colour sports shirt, a cutaway unbuttoned vest, jeans, and dark shoes that were neither sneakers or business footwear.

"Shaun Doyle."

Having stepped inside Mavis' personal space, Doyle grinned at her. "Holding your own I see."

Mavis held his gaze. "Actually, we're trying to do more than that. Good to see you."

"Is it?"

"Of course. You've flagged your interest to your competition." Mavis brushed her voluminous hair off her face. "So helpful of you."

"I'd like to put a deal to you tomorrow afternoon after your last gig. Interested?"

"Possibly."

"I'll have one of my people bring you and the band to me when you're done."

"One of your people?"

Doyle clicked his fingers. A dark haired twenty-something man in torn jeans and a muscle shirt stepped forward named Morgan Smithers.

Mavis glanced at the young man and then considered Doyle, not too sure what she thought in the face of such behaviour. She raised an eyebrow at him.

Doyle smiled at her. "Too much flexing of power muscle for your liking?"

"I'm not into pretension. We'll see you tomorrow. C'mon, fellas, we've places to be and other people to meet." She walked off confidently. Determined not to lose power in her exit, she scanned the crowd for known faces and saw Susie talking to Max Ryan. She walked up to them. "Max. Susie. Hope I'm disturbing something."

"What can we do you for?" Max asked.

Mavis passed him the card. "You know anything about this agency. Susie and I have met the man and—"

"Like him."

Max frowned, considering Susie. "You do?"

"Absolutely."

"Hm. Harbourside Agency are top notch. Not as big as Paul Dainty, Michael Edgely, or Mike Welch but getting there."

"Why the interest now, Nikki?"

"We have a *business* meeting with Doyle tomorrow, Susie."

"Take a page from our lesson book, and don't commit on the spot. A musician's biggest enemy is his desperation to make it big. We've learnt that the hard way. If you've got someone who'll protect your back and has business acumen, take him. Be careful what percentage you give away and the length of the contract."

A giggle of glamouratti descended on the group, their focus on Max Ryan. "If you'll excuse me, ladies."

"Old dogs, old tricks." Susie watched him depart. "If there's one thing men in our industry share, it's a hunger for attention."

"Just the men?"

"Point taken. We all want the validation of our talent, but ..."

"Jury in on Max then?"

"Still out. The verdict is under serious consideration and some debate. I'll see how he plays out the groupie attention and what he's like in the weeks and maybe months that follow."

"I'm out of here, Susie. And you?"

"No, I'm hanging around a bit longer. I want to capture those rare unguarded moments where musicians reveal themselves and not how they're packaged for the fans."

Outside, fans lobbied exiting performers for attention. Mavis thought they did this indiscriminately. It came as a surprise therefore to hear. "Nikki! Nikki! Over here!" as fans clamoured for her attention.

A word from the security guard escort prompted Mavis to cross to the crowd. They were controlled and not the frightening press of the previous night. She was amazed to see copies of her CD thrust at her with requests for her signature. Those that didn't have CDs asked her to sign their shirts, their arms, and anything else available to them. She was overwhelmed by the pleas for a happy snap with her and uncomfortable with their need for physical contact.

The tenor of her meeting with her fans changed when she decided to move on. The people at the rear, anxious to make contact with her, pressed forward, crushing people in their way. The security people, obviously experienced at their job, swung the barriers forward to a ninety degree angle making contact with the other side of the cordoned walkway, relieving the crush, and literally fencing out the crowd.

Back in her hut, Mavis followed her coming-down-from-performance routine that guaranteed her natural sleep. As with the previous night, her sleep was disturbed but not disrupted by the staggering returns of her band.

*　*　*

The next day, Sunday, Mavis', "Rise and shine," met resistance.

On their staggered entry into the kitchen, the men responded grumpily when she refused them access to the hair of the dog that had bitten them.

"Where has this out-of-character overindulgence come from, fellas?"

"We were on such a high, Nikki." Jack and Steve were in best mate mode. "The liquid supply was one endless top up."

Tony wore sunglasses. "What they said."

"From the start, you *all* said you were serious about the music and less interested in the lifestyle. What happened?"

"Glitter and glamour," Jack said.

Suffering from a thumping headache, Tony poured himself a mug of black coffee and then looked for sugar. While he opened and closed cupboards, Jack picked up the mug and passed it to Steve. Jack then poured himself a coffee. Tony returned, looked at the empty place where the mug had been, shook his head, and looked around him, confused. *I had a mug. I know I did. Where did I put it?*

Mavis shook her head in disbelief. She poured Tony another and passed it to him. "Thanks. You know, I thought I did that already. I'm worse off than I thought."

"Unbelievable!" Mavis walked down the corridor to the sitting area, her voice getting louder as she left them. "I thought you guys were *so* much cooler."

The men followed her.

Jack flopped onto the modular lounge. "Never experienced *anything* like it before, and that's sayin' something!"

Steve sat next to him. "We were like goldfish ... ooh, something new ... ooh, this is new."

Tony chose the floor. "What must it be like to be famous?"

"A road to overindulgence *and* self-destruction if we're not careful. C'mon, let's get dressed and then head off for some food. You all need a good meal tucked into you before our midday show."

"Don't mention food, Nikki," the men said as one. Reading Mavis' expression correctly, they tried to morph their groans into expressions of enthusiasm.

"Last night's overindulgence had better *not* affect our last performance!"

"It won't," was the unison reply.

"I want everyone's head clear when we meet up with the various management groups this afternoon. Understood?"

"No issue," was the collective response.

Tim leant against the doorjamb. "Nikki, I'll hang back here for the next few hours *if* you don't mind. I'll grab somethin' from the mess tent later before the show. I *seriously* need some quiet."

"Not you too, Tim?"

"Afraid so. I just need an hour or so more sleep, and I'll be fine."

"Anyone know where Susie is? Her bed was slept in but ..."

Lyle walked into the area. He was upbeat and none the worse from the night before. "You lookin' for Susie? I saw her with Max Ryan, having breakfast about half an hour ago. Mighty cosy they were too."

"Good to see at least one man had sense last night. I'll give the rest of you an hour and then we're *all* out of here."

Over brunch, the men discovered the restorative effect of good food. Susie joined them for coffee.

Mavis looked at Susie quizzically. "How are things?"

"Good."

"Good meaning?"

"Max and I had a frank and honest talk. I'm not sure where we're going, but we've begun the journey."

Mavis beamed at her.

Susie stood and took Mavis aside. "You're such a romantic! It won't be a happily ever after thing. That's impossible given the business we're in."

"I know that. Still, the road to understanding has to be a good thing. It's hopeful at least, and hope is what gets us out of bed every morning."

In better spirits, the men shared their experiences of the night before ending on reflections about memorabilia and speculation about their CD sales.

Tony still wore dark glasses although his headache was subsiding. "Fans want memorabilia as well, not just our CDs. I wish I'd known; we could've cashed in. Nikki, Jack lost his waistcoat during his encounter with the fan kind."

Steve chuckled. "The fan kind … love it! He was lucky to get away with his pants still on."

"I never thought being groped by so many women at once would be anything other than pleasurable. I was *so* wrong."

Steve aligned his knife and fork on his plate, dumping his scrunched napkin on top. "I was caught up in the fan grab for souvenirs too. I was afraid I'd go down the pipe and panicked. I offered up my plumbin' business cards as tokens. When there were none left to autograph, I signed off on shirts and bodies but lost a T-shirt in the process." Steve paused. "I'm expectin' a surge in business."

They all laughed.

"For real?" Susie asked.

"Yeah! Musos in this scene live a flush life."

"Enough with the plumbin' jokes, man!" Jack said.

Tony said, "Based on the number of CDs I autographed last night, they're sellin' pretty well."

"Anyone else see them?" Mavis asked.

"Heaps," was the general response.

"A few fans with CDs collecting all our signatures?" Mavis asked.

"The ones I signed were clean," Susie said. "I was amazed fans actually recognized me."

"I signed heaps of clean CDs too!" Steve echoed Jack a split second after him.

Tony said, "Well, let's hope the sales ratio is as good as one CD per two hundred people. That'd be three hundred in twenty-four hours. Maybe we'll sell more by close of the festival."

As the rest of the band finished their meals, two festival staff approached Lyle, standing as gatekeeper to the band.

"This the Nikki Mills band?"

"What's it to you?"

Although wearing festival attire, the spokesman pulled his festival ID from his wallet. "Your man back at the hut said we'd find you here. We have a business problem."

"Nikki, for you."

Concerned, Mavis stood in front of the men but was dwarfed by them in height and size.

"What's the problem?"

"We've had a huge run on your CDs and wanted to know if you had any more with you in case of this happening?"

"You've *sold* out of our CDs?" Nikki asked.

"But there were ten thousand!" Tony said from behind her.

Consulting his paperwork, the festival spokesman said, "That's right, and there's still a huge demand back at the sales stalls. We were hoping you had more here in anticipation of this eventuality."

The band reacted with whistles and excited exchanges.

A side look from Mavis cooled their outward displays of exuberance. "Lyle, you bring any more CDs?"

Lyle gestured broadly. "Does the desert have sand? Of course I did! Follow me, fellas."

After Lyle had left with the men, Mavis looked at her band. "Wow! How unbelievable is that!"

Steve recovered from the shock of it first. "How much do we clear for one CD?"

Tony looked up from his calculations. "After we've deducted production costs, the festival application fee, the costs associated with being in the festival, and the festival's percentage cut, we've made one hundred thousand dollars!"

Jack whistled. "And it looks like we're goin' to sell even more!"

Bug-eyed, Steve said, "Geez, I could *upgrade* my Roland *and* pay off my debt!"

Susie said, "And we didn't have to sell our music soul to do it."

Elation best described the mood of the band as they waited for their last show.

*　*　*

The journey of that Sunday midday performance had been designed to emotionally load the audience for The Nikki Mills Band farewell. So it came as a surprise to them when, before the start of the set and after noting that the audience were hyped super high, Mavis said while they were still in the wings, "We'll start with a show stopper and then reverse order the material, fellas."

"What?" Tony said.

"Listen to the crowd, Tony. They'll be hard to settle. Susie, I'm thinking we should do 'As the Crow Flies'. That opening drum flourish is spectacular! If that doesn't capture the audience, nothing will."

Susie nodded. "Okay. I'll need some time to get into that headspace before we go on though."

"And you're stayin' with the pick for the final song?" Tony asked.

"I know I said this weekend was all original material, but my gut feeling is we need to farewell the crowd with 'I Will Always Love You'.

To do that, we need to change the playlist so that the musical journey prepares the audience for our finale."

Susie said, "It's my *favourite* song."

Tony added, "I still say it's a risk doin' any Whitney Houston number. It's your call though."

"Where's your faith in Nikki, man?" Jack asked.

Mavis' call on the set was proven correct. Her instinct for shaping the audience's emotional journey held true.

While enjoying the crowd's enthusiastic response to the second to last song of the set, the band, with the exception of Steve on keyboards, put down their instruments and stood in a neutral position, relinquishing all focus to Mavis. Steve relinquished focus too but remained poised at the keyboards ready to join her on cue, his being the first instrument to back her in the song.

It was a daring and dramatic move, unexpected by the audience and the other performers in the surrounding arena. 'I Will Always Love You' began colla voce with Mavis' voice, clean and unembellished, the only musical sound. The crowd stilled. The first refrain cued Steve's entry with piano and strings. At the start of the second verse, bass entered followed by the distinctive sound of the drummer's stick hitting the rim of the snare drum. Rhythm guitar entered, with Tony picking out the chords. The music and its emotion swelled. Steve switched to the sax synthesizer and performed his solo.

As long as she lived, Mavis thought, she would always remember this day, this moment, this feeling, that sense of completion and connection. An almighty thump of the bass drum, kettle, and snare signalled the final refrain and key change. Her thoughts switched now to Dan, her parents, and her friends as her voice soared, stretching two octaves and then quietening in the closing words of the song.

There was a period of silence after the song ended that allowed Mavis to return to earth. Amidst the roar of the crowd, the band stood in acknowledgment of the applause. On a count from Mavis, they bowed with a simple lowering of the head as the noise washed over them.

On the other side of the stage, one of the band members there said to the MC, "Geez, how are we supposed to follow that? Give them an encore so that the audience can be returned to us."

The MC replied, "Cold Chisel is scheduled tonight, mate. I have to save as much time as I can for them. You're on!"

The backstage scene as The Nikki Mills Band descended the rear stage stairs, despite the time of day, was the same as the night before. It was as if the party had never ended.

A press of agency representatives clamoured for Mavis' attention.

The Harbourside Agency assistant waited for an opportunity to get close to them. "If you're ready, I'll escort you to Mr Doyle."

The group exited to a nearby tent which was sectioned off into partitioned areas with spacious aisles between.

Doyle rose as they neared his area.

Each band member felt the warmth in Doyle's handshake and the personal quality to it. They sat down on comfortable sofa lounges positioned into a conversational square. Beyond them, the media lights and whir of interviews elsewhere was background to their meeting.

Mavis left the initiative to Doyle, thinking he needed to win them. She did not want to seem eager to sell herself or her band. After the preliminary small talk and schmoozing was over, Doyle offered the band champagne – not the cheap kind but Moët & Chandon. Mavis' slow turn of head and arched eyebrow in reaction to the men's warm acceptance of the alcohol resulted in a collective response of, "No, coffee would be fine."

"Mineral water for me," Mavis said, followed by a similar request from Susie.

After drinks were served with a plate of appetisers to boot, Doyle settled down to business. He sketched the history of The Harbourside Agency and identified its major talent. "You've developed into an original sound and have a terrific product that we can make work better for you."

"What do you mean *better*?" Mavis asked.

"Provide you with high profile, high paying gigs and first class marketing. We'll work to ensure your percentage cut from any record deals work to your advantage."

Mavis nodded slowly. "Interesting. I'd like to talk it over with my group *after* the festival when everyone is back in Keimera. I assume you'll table the whole offer and its fine print at a later meeting?"

"Shall I arrange an appointment with you at my Sydney office, say Friday of this week?"

Mavis shook her head. "No, that won't work. My son has a school concert that I *don't* want to miss. If you *are* serious about representing us then I can fit you in at four that afternoon in Keimera. If not, that's fine. We're in no hurry to be signed up."

The men in her band schooled their faces at her boldness.

Doyle clicked his fingers. His assistant materialised with his appointment book. He considered it for a moment. To his assistant, Doyle said "Reschedule my other appointments so I can travel to Keimera on Friday." He looked back to Mavis. "At four it is then."

Standing, Mavis said, "Done. See you later. If you'll excuse us, we have other meetings and offers to consider."

"What other meetings?" Tony asked when they had returned to the backstage tent.

"At least four, and I'm testing them all. I want to see the degree they are willing to put themselves out to represent us. I don't want to sign with anyone who sees the arrangement as one way with us working to make *them* money."

Susie added, "We're not interested in a variation of TSUAF."

"Exactly!"

No sooner had Mavis replied then they were set upon by a mixture of record company representatives and other entertainment management groups. It was an exciting afternoon. In parting from the men and before she and Susie headed back to the hut to pack, Mavis said, "Make sure you're all sober before you drive. Don't screw this chance up for us now with an accident or worse." To Susie she said, "I get now why the big name groups travel in buses."

Chapter 18

Back at Keimera and the Mills household, the people who mattered to Mavis: Dan, her parents, Kate and Gary sat with Zoey watching a media highlight of the festival on the Sunday night news at six-thirty.

Dan said, "Was the whole world there?"

Zoey kicked her shoes off and curled up on the lounge. "The world is so much bigger than that, Dan. Bigger than the size of the Pacific Ocean to the horizon on a clear day from Showground Peninsula. That's like a pond compared to the world population."

Dan sat in stupefaction, trying to conceive of anything that big.

Zoey suddenly sat upright. "There's Nikki and the band!" The television showed the camera panning to a shot of the band on stage that Sunday. "And there's Mum!"

Kate said, "Mavis is glowing!"

Gary added, "And sounds *amazing*! I wish they hadn't cut the scene off there!"

The tooting of a car horn in the Mills' driveway brought the inhabitants out to see Mavis and Susie who had just arrived.

After kisses and hugs all round, they returned to the lounge room. Mavis and Susie recounted the band's adventure excitedly in tag team style. Then everyone adjourned to the kitchen for dinner. The evening passed in high spirits.

Zoey and Susie were effusive in their thanks to the Mills for their care of Zoey when they departed that night.

The following Tuesday, Dan and Zoey returned to their respective schools. Mavis and Susie enjoyed the free day in their own unique ways.

On Wednesday afternoon, the band regrouped in Mavis' cottage.

Laid-back, Susie enjoyed the cushioned comfort of the armchair as the men strolled in. "Good to see you're all in one piece and not the worse for wear."

The men were full of stories about schmoozing with celebrities and the end-of-festival traffic jam.

"We decided not to leave until this mornin'," Steve said. "It was either that or sit in the traffic for who knew how long Tuesday. Traffic was still a beast when we left today."

Tony added, "I've never seen anythin' like the cleanup crew that descended on the place after the festival."

The distinctive sound of released gas accompanied Lyle's popping of a can of coke. "Like an army of ants!"

"Let's get down to business," Mavis said. "I've asked Kate to sit in on my meeting with Doyle as well. His is the last in the week."

Tony nodded, his demotion from business manager long forgotten. "And she has the intellect to see beyond the glitter and glamour of it all."

After some general murmurings in which different perspectives were stated, discussed, and ruffled feathers smoothed, Jack voiced what the others felt. "Agreed."

* * *

Thursday at eleven in the morning, Susie received another phone call from the principal of Zoey's school. "Really, Ms Blake, I am getting tired of the need to make these calls. A big black tour bus has parked in the school's driveway and is causing a squealing disruption to our morning tea break. It arrived before the break so I had time to call Zoey to the front office. If this is to continue, then you will need to add this man to the access list for Zoey. Does Zoey have permission to speak to a Mr Max Ryan today?"

"Yes, she does." Susie said, wishing she had a crystal ball to see what was going on at the school.

Having hung up, the principal left her plushly furnished office and went to the elegant small waiting room nearby. "Zoey, come with me, please." She led Zoey down a corridor lined with photographs of past principals to a large conference room. She opened the door to reveal a seated Max Ryan. "Fifteen minutes, Mr Ryan, and then Zoey has to be back in class."

"G'day, kid."

"Mr Ryan." Zoey moved to sit in a seat adjacent to him. "What are you doing here?"

"Nikki Mills told me some girls at your school have been giving you a hard time over your parentage. It's exactly what I wanted to avoid, especially since I'd suffered similar stuff myself. I thought, since we were passing through the area and visiting our singer's mother, that we'd all drop in to clear up that issue for you. Take the sting out of anything that can be said to you in the future. Prove you're not a liar."

"Oh." Zoey said, followed by silence.

"C'mon, kid. You need to give me something here. I know you've been hurt. I'm giving you the choice you asked for. At the festival, Sanna said you and I both have a choice in this matter. Your mother is right. Look, this is all new to me. If you want me as a father – the sort of father I'm capable of being – then I'm here. I won't ever be a live-in dad though, more a father on the fringe. I'm not perfect so there'll be stuff ups. It's not because I mean to hurt you though, but because I'm flawed, very human, and have no idea of what it means to be a good father or any type of father for that matter."

"That's what Mum says when we hurt each other: flawed and human. Parents do it blind, she says."

"Sanna says you don't forgive easily. Is that the case?"

"I don't know. I haven't thought about it."

"Well, I'm like that. Once hurt, even though I might love someone, I won't let them get close to me again. It was that way with Sanna. Time is running out, Zoey, if that clock up there is right. How do you want the rest of your life to be?"

Silence.

"Would you like to see our tour bus? Our singer hates flying so it's pretty well decked out for interstate travel. God knows how he'll cope with the European tour and getting there next month. C'mon, I'll introduce you before we shove off."

A squeeze of excited girls clustered around the tour bus when Zoey and Max emerged from the building. A cluck of teachers were doing their best to control them and maintain some decorum. On the paved, curved, outdoor entrance to the office, the band, dressed in jeans and T-shirts, signed autographs for the line-up of girls and for some younger teachers. The principal stood apart from the scene.

Outdoors, Max added to Zoey, "There are lots of biological links out there who, when given a chance to be a father, prefer not to be and remain happy with that." He walked ahead to his band members. Zoey followed in his wake, school girls gawking at her.

"Zoey, this is our singer, Jimmy Bevan. His mother lives in Bowral which is why I've been able to drop in today. And these…" He introduced the rest of the band.

The school bell, signalling the end of the break, rang out loudly.

Teachers shepherded the girls back to their classes. "Zoey," the principal said. "Time to go."

"Well, kid, I'll send you postcards from Europe then." Max stood uncomfortably in the scene.

"Okay." Zoey said. "I'd like that." She turned her back on him, took a few steps, and then stopped. She struggled visibly with her emotions. Turning, she crossed to Max and looked up at him. "Fringe father it is then." She hugged him and that was when her emotional control broke.

Totally disquieted by the events, the principal said, "Zoey, you must go to class now."

Moved also but containing it, Max Ryan said, "It's a pact then, and you'll forgive me when I stuff up badly, and especially when you don't think you can?"

"I'll try."

"I have to go, Zoey. I'll make sure I see you and Sanna in Keimera before we fly out."

"Okay."

Crying, Zoey returned to the building as the tour bus drove off.

The principal said, "The best thing for you young lady is a talk to your mother. I'll call her."

*   *   *

Friday afternoon, Keimera. The mellow tones of Etta James' song 'Push Over' rang out from the Mills household. Inside, members of The Nikki Mills Band sat in the lounge room enjoying a sumptuous afternoon tea.

Tony fingered through Trevor's extensive vinyl record collection. "My dad loved Etta's music too. Her vocal quality and presence on stage marked her as a star."

"Sure did," Trevor replied.

Tony coveted the records. "This is a *remarkable* collection, worth a bundle!"

Susie asked, "Did you see the televised 1993 Grammy's when she was inducted into the Hall of Fame?"

"With Mavis in the house, would we be allowed to miss those awards? For once, I was glad we watched them."

Outside, Shaun Doyle parked his car in the angle parking at the front of the Mills' house. Standing beside his car, he absorbed the beauty of the harbour scene through the silhouette of the towering Norfolk pines that lined the main street. There were a few outstanding towns on the Sapphire Coast, and this was one of them. He looked at his watch. Ten minutes to four. He strolled over the road to the harbour parkland.

At exactly four o'clock, Doyle knocked on the Mills' front door.

"Yes?" Marg feigned ignorance of the identity of the man before her and worked hard to contain her excitement.

"Mrs Mills, I take it. My name is Shaun Doyle. I'm from The Harbourside Agency. I have an appointment with Nikki. I assume she is your daughter."

"Oh, yes, Mr Doyle. We've been expectin' you."

"Call me Shaun, please."

"Come in. Mavis won't be long."

"Mavis? I'm here to see Nikki Mills."

"That's my daughter's *stage* name."

Marg led Doyle into the lounge room, where the band sat listening to Etta James' rendition of 'Trust in Me'. They stood on Doyle's entry. Marg reintroduced them. Some inconsequential small talk about music followed before Marg guided Doyle to Mavis. She was in the kitchen.

As Doyle walked down the corridor that ran through the centre of the house, he noted the simplicity of lifestyle and the gallery of pictures that chronicled a girl's growth into womanhood and then the incomplete journey of a boy.

"Mavis, Shaun Doyle is here." Mavis sat with Gary at the kitchen workbench helping Dan with a third grade research project, the sort of project that parents usually hate because it requires skill sets children that age don't have.

Standing, Mavis shook hands with Doyle. Her eyes twinkled and a smile lit her face. "Good to see you actually made it, Mr Doyle."

"What I say I do, Nikki."

Once again, Mavis noted the warmth in the man's grasp. She liked what he projected.

Doyle looked at Gary, extending his hand; he had taken control of the scene. "Mr Mills I take it?"

During what can only be described as a firm handshake, Gary replied, "No, I'm Gary Putnam. Dan here is my godson."

"And this is my son, Dan," Mavis continued.

Following Gary's lead, Dan hopped down from his stool at the kitchen bench and extended his hand. "Nice to meet you, Mr Doyle."

"I thought we'd have the meeting in my cottage."

Smalltalk occupied the pair as they left the house and crossed the back yard.

As Mavis opened the screen door, she called, "Kate?"

"Coming." Kate appeared, having been in the bathroom.

"Shaun Doyle, this is Kate Denford, a close friend and the band's business advisor. I've asked her to sit in on the meeting."

"Good to meet you, Mr Doyle."

They shook hands.

"I'm not used to such formality. Call me Shaun."

Mavis gestured to her lounge room. "I've taken the liberty of preparing afternoon tea. It's more a meal really than a tea. I thought it'd stave off your hunger on the return trip to Sydney."

"That's considerate of you."

"Will you make it back in time?" Kate looked at the wall clock.

"Sure. I don't need to rock up until after eleven-thirty. Your parents Etta James' fans?"

"Yes."

"See what higher education does for you?"

Both women looked blank. It was a *what the ...?* moment.

Mavis recovered first. "It's made you an expert in stating the obvious?"

"Exactly. James was an exception to the rule. She stayed on top even though she had a diverse singing style. "

"Shall I serve, Mavis?"

"If you don't mind. I'd say that Etta like Tina Turner had career longevity because of her diverse style."

Doyle sipped the cup of tea Kate had handed him a moment earlier. "Few artists can get away with crossing genres though. A performer has to establish her creds with the audience before she can diversify."

"I disagree. I don't like the preoccupation with labels and pigeonholes. Our gigs at Southern Bays, in Melbourne and Sydney show the truth of that quite clearly. The challenge and the interest for me in performance is setting up the journey so that I take the audience with me. It's about subtle manipulation to achieve acceptance. "

"As are so many things," Doyle replied. "I hear you played the front room at the Espy." The Esplanade was widely known as one of Melbourne's top live music venues.

"We did. Such a buzz!"

Over afternoon tea, Mavis listened as Kate discussed Doyle's contractual options and the breakdown in income. Periodically, Kate deferred to Mavis who asked a question to clarify her understanding. Mavis took over the conversation in matters that she most cared about. "No, sorry, not that." She apologised out of habit rather than with sincere intent. "I want control over all aspects of the music: lyrics, sound, image. In any negotiations for a record deal, you need to know I want the final call on the end product. No way do I want to sound overproduced like so many female headliners today."

"Nikki, you need to understand that part of our job is to manage your image in its entirety. That means ..."

"I am no one's puppet, Mr Doyle. I certainly don't want my band's image remolded to fit someone else's frustrated musical desires or intent. Your company, from what you've been saying, is interested in The Nikki Mills Band as a product because we are original and have demonstrated audience appeal. That appeal is because we aren't clones of anyone else."

"True, but in our marketing of you and in our search for investors we need to be able to quote statistics. Those statistics come from historical data on what is selling. Of course, you can write the lyrics and melody. You'll have a lot of input into the form the music takes and a significant amount of say in production. Final say resides with the producer though. The form has to be shaped by him on advice from the marketing team. We can't sell you if you don't take our market advice. You need to be flexible in this, and ..."

"Our music is about the song in life, in my heart, and the world around us. I take the style from those varied sources. That's what gives me power in performance. That's how I connect to audiences. The bottom line, Mr Doyle: I'd rather stay in the small arena than concede to what you ask."

Silence. Doyle helped himself to a sponge cake filled with jam and fresh, double-whipped cream.

Kate raised an eyebrow at Mavis, unobserved by Doyle.

"Good cake, ladies." Doyle made them wait for his answer. "Obviously you've been caught out or burnt by a management company before. Do you have any existing contracts that I need to know about?"

"We've had a pretty flexible *agreement* with Entertainment Inc which provided us with some work in the Sydney club circuit. It gave us room to do the pub scene so I don't think there's an issue. Would you like to see it?"

"Yes, actually, I would."

Mavis left them to chat while she went to her bedroom for a copy of the agreement.

"Did you have a good trip down here, Shaun?"

"Yes, Kate. The new highway makes it quite fast. So much better than that single lane, two-way road my family used to travel on to Bateman's Bay when I was a boy. A blind man could've run that trip faster than we did in that traffic."

Kate laughed. "Yes, it was horrendous in those years. So, how many children do you have?"

"I'm not married."

"A better half?"

"Not yet. You?"

"Oh, I'm engaged to Gary."

"The man in the kitchen with Nikki's boy?"

"That's right. We're Dan's godparents."

Doyle nodded, digesting those facts.

Mavis returned. "Here it is." She passed the paperwork to Doyle who read it carefully.

"A standard agency agreement. There isn't any bar in this to me signing you."

"That's *if* I like what you put on the table. We have had other offers – very attractive ones too."

"But left mine to last?"

"That's right."

"Well, I'd better sum up what's on the table then. We have agreement on the following. We work for the best cut available for every gig and any other deals we make on your behalf. Prospective deals are to be cleared and confirmed by you before final commitment is made. Our fee is forty-five percent of your gross income for any work organised through us. You pay your band whatever you've negotiated with them. It's you we're signing up, not the individuals in your band. We control the direction of your career in consultation with you. You control all aspects of the music and your image. You continue to own copy and performance rights to all of your music. Any directions we may wish to take can only be done with your consent."

Mavis looked at Kate who nodded at her. Doyle remained focused on Mavis.

"Do we have a deal then?" Doyle asked as Kate unobtrusively cleared the coffee table.

"You have the authority to make that commitment?" Mavis asked.

"I do. If you're in agreement, I'll have contracts drawn up and express posted down for your perusal. If all is in order, you sign on the post-it, flagged pages and then return them to us."

"And my appearance? We haven't discussed that as yet."

"Nothing wrong from where I am sitting or with anything I've seen so far. You have taste and a distinctive style."

A returning Kate looked expressively at Mavis again, her approval of the man's words obvious.

"Now that business is over, would you consider showing me around your town, Nikki?"

"Happy to, but the wind seems to have picked up. Do you have a coat?"

"Oh, I don't think that's necessary."

"Okay, but I'll need one."

As Mavis donned a finely patterned, woollen coat taken from a cane coat rack near the front door, she spoke in undertones to Kate. "Will you stop looking at me like that when he says things you appreciate? Seriously, it's hard not to laugh, and that could be misunderstood."

"Sorry, I like him. When you mentioned him before, you *never* said how cute he is. He has such a strong, positive aura."

Raising her volume for Doyle's benefit, Mavis said, "Kate, would you let everyone else know how things went. I'll give Mr Doyle a tour of the town, the highlights anyway."

"Good to meet you, Kate."

"And you."

Doyle went outside.

Kate leant backwards with an eye on Doyle, making sure he was out of earshot." I think he likes you. It's hard not to like him."

"And you don't think that's part of his skill as a negotiator, Kate?"

"You're not attracted to him?"

"Course I am. I'm a woman. He's a practiced charmer. There are so many of them in this industry. Anyway, our relationship is *business*, not romance. I'm *not* ready for anything like that yet."

"You do know the really *big things* in our lives don't come on a timetable, don't you?"

"Stop! Kate, you're making me self-conscious."

"Well, I for one am looking forward to the next stage in your story."

"Aren't we all?"

Outside, Doyle had realised his mistake. "Brrr! You're right, but it was such a beautiful day. What happened? I expected crisp, not freezing."

"Onshore winds can add a chill factor. The forecast is for a seriously cold night, and I heard there were fresh snowfalls at the Snowy. Still want that tour?"

"After I get my overcoat from the car. I always carry one at this time of year just in case."

"And while you're doing that, I'll just pop inside for a word with my band."

Doyle walked up the narrow driveway at the side of the house while Mavis walked inside. In the kitchen, she embraced Gary before lifting Dan off his feet and whirling him around. Returning Dan to the floor, Mavis knelt at his eye level.

"Did you get the deal you wanted, Mummy?"

"I did indeed, little man, and who am I doing this for?"

"Us."

"We all have our parts to play while Mummy's away touring, right? No more hassle over homework or being angry because I'm not here."

"Cause when you're home we want to make the most of it."

"Exactly, and not waste time on things that should've been done when I was away." Mavis hugged Dan tightly. "No one could love a son more than I love you. Remember that. Now, I'm off to show Shaun Doyle the town. Want to come?"

"No, thanks, Mummy. Gary and I are goin' up to the Madisons' to play with Uncle Michael's train set. It's the biggest, the best I ever saw. Uncle George promised he'd get his old train set out too."

"So you said when I came home after your last stay with them."

After she stood up, Mavis and Gary hugged.

"I'm on the way to being the person I was meant to be, Gary."

"You already are that person, mate. Don't forget that, not ever, no matter where fame and fortune takes you."

"I won't." Mavis paused. "Gary, I've never said before how much I value our friendship. You keep me—"

Marg rushed into the kitchen. "Kate told us the good news! You're going to be a star."

Trevor followed close on his wife's heels. "We're so proud of you."

"Doyle's not promising that, Mum. Besides, I don't *have* to be a star, I just want to be the best I can be, and make heaps of money doing it."

Mavis hugged both parents before walking east through the house. On the threshold of the lounge room, she paused and absorbed the joyful outburst before her. Lyle's cap was midair. Jack and Steve shared a chest bump. Tim and Tony had arms linked with Susie as they danced in a circle.

Jack saw Mavis first. "We did it, Nikki!" He swung Mavis off her feet while the others crowded around them. Grounded again, she hugged Susie and then each of the men.

Susie looked at Mavis. "This must be how the astronauts felt when they took their first step on the moon."

Tony added, "Our first step on the stairway to fortune and fame."

Although Tony had expressed Mavis' thought, she said, "Let's not get ahead of ourselves. It's a long road to the top, and when we get there, we want to stay there." Then, unable to contain herself, she said, "I'm so excited!"

"I know!" Susie hugged Mavis.

The rest of the band followed her lead in a spontaneous group hug, the emotion they shared too great to express in words alone. They were one in that moment.

As the band came out of the group hug, Marg, Trevor, and Gary with Dan entered the room with wine glasses. The adults carried three bottles of champagne that Kate had purchased in anticipation of the event.

Marg passed Mavis a wine glass as Trevor poured drinks for the others. "It's a pity Mr Doyle didn't stay, Mavis. You should've invited him to dinner."

"Doyle! Dear God, I forgot about him! I've got to go. See you all later." Mavis passed her mother the wine glass and hurried out the front door.

Doyle stood on the footpath in front of his parked car. "I was beginning to think you'd forgotten about me, Nikki."

"As if I could ever do that." Mavis linked arms with him, companion like, accepting the intimacy between them, her joy overflowing. She loved life and everyone in it.

Surprised, Doyle steadied himself. "Keimera reminds me a lot of Kiama. It was one of my family's preferred Sunday drive destinations when I was a kid. We never made it down here though."

"Keimera is tucked away on the coast, easily missed, especially now the bypass has been built. The peninsulas here are quite different from those in Kiama as is the hinterland, Mr Doyle."

"Shaun. I thought we'd settled that. So what should I call you? You seem to go by two names here."

"My given name is Mavis, but my professional name is Nikki. The use reflects the basis of my relationships. Nikki is fine. That's how the band think of me. The only people who ever call me Mavis are those who I'm *truly* close to and trust."

"Mavis it is then … So what did your parents think they were gifting you when they named you?"

"Musicality and the ability to make the day brighter through song. A mavis is a song thrush – an ordinary brown speckled bird – that is associated with the coming of Spring. It knows its true purpose and lives life accordingly."

"You're anything but ordinary."

"Thank you, Shaun, but I'm content to be that bird."

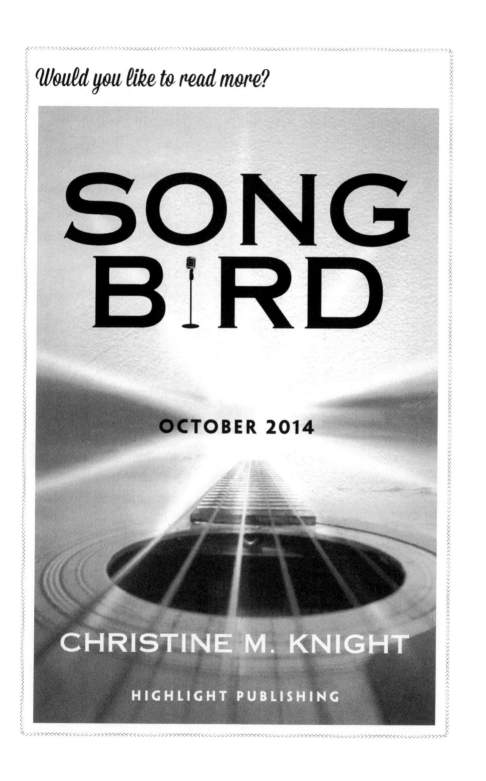

Would you like to read more?

SONG
BIRD

OCTOBER 2014

CHRISTINE M. KNIGHT

HIGHLIGHT PUBLISHING

IN AND OUT OF STEP – the first novel in the Keimera series

'Think about the woman you're becoming!' Leonie said, trying to prevent Cassie's flight from home and the problems there. 'You could find yourself out of the frying pan and into the fire.'

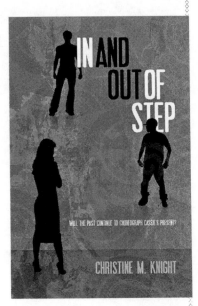

Her past denied and dance championship dreams discarded, Cassie Sleight leaves home. In the seemingly idyllic coastal town of Keimera, she starts a career on the English staff of the local high school. Exposure to Mark Talbut, a man struggling to be modern yet threatened by power shifts in the workplace and in society, causes Cassie to assess her reactions as a teacher and a woman. As she does so, the secrets of her past surface. Will that past continue to choreograph Cassie's present steps? What sort of woman does she become?

In and Out of Step looks at how the world a person lives in shapes that person for good and for bad. It is a story about friendship and family, belonging, alienation, discovery, sexual harassment, and change. The title alludes to the way Cassie Sleight uses dance as a way to interpret life and process her reactions to it.

Printed in Australia
AUOC02n0636060614
261526AU00004B/5/P

9 780987 434852